ALAN HAMILTON finds th ... there is
a mystery or something une
imagination they give the wr
up. At heart he's a conspira
him accident is usually more

As an antidote to the
a publisher's editor for non-fic
articles. He lives by the sea in the South West of the UK. His hobbies are cooking and cryptic crosswords in the national newspapers, winning first prize twice in ten years.

stalemate

Alan Hamilton

SilverWood

Published in 2014 by SilverWood Books

SilverWood Books Ltd
30 Queen Charlotte Street, Bristol, BS1 4HJ
www.silverwoodbooks.co.uk

ISBN 978-1-78132-204-8 (paperback)
ISBN 978-1-78132-205-5 (ebook)

British Library Cataloguing in Publication Data
A CIP catalogue record for this book is available from the British Library

Set in Sabon by SilverWood Books
Printed on responsibly sourced paper

Stalemate

***Chess** – the state in which the player to move is not in check but cannot move to any other square.*

A Scene of Crime

It's chilly in here and there's a sickly-sweet smell together with a whiff of singed fabric. The gas lamp to the right of the mantelpiece is lit but turned low, giving everything a yellowish tinge. Heavy curtains cover the bay window so no one outside can tell if there are any lights on.

This tiny room is crammed with furniture and bric-a-brac. An old-fashioned dark wooden dresser dominates, the top and open shelves overflowing with ornaments and papers. In one corner there's a two-seat open-backed sofa with a violin case balanced on one arm. Above the mantelpiece hangs a large mirror, partly obscured by half a dozen framed photographs and a glass urn. In the window bay a table has a plant on it, then across the window a chaise longue with two cushions and, in front, another table with yet another plant. An upright piano, a music stand and two formal, upholstered dining chairs are in here as well. Almost every available inch of the walls is covered with framed pictures and ornamental plates, and photographs occupy every surface. The effect is to make the room seem even smaller than it is.

There's someone in here too, lying on her right side diagonally across the hearthrug, her feet close to the fender in front of the unlit gas fire, her right arm beneath her body, her left draped over her chest with the hand almost touching the floor. Around her head and soaking into the rug is a halo of congealing blood, brain tissue and bone. Just above and in front of her left ear her head has been smashed open and with a little more light it would be possible to see clearly the part of her brain that has not been dashed out. The violence of the attack has splattered blood all over the walls in the back right corner, yet not one of the many objects that fill the room has been disturbed.

Time is suspended. For a short while yet no one, except whoever did this to her, knows of her fate, not even the neighbours on the other side of the thin party wall that divides these terrace houses. The silent room waits for the next act, the discovery, the throwing of light on an appalling deed. When that happens it will change everything, not only for those finding the dead woman but also for all affected by the discovery who will struggle to keep their heads above the flood of consequences.

The wait is nearly over. Someone outside the house is trying to unlock the front door. Unsuccessfully, it seems, since whoever's there knocks to attract attention. A few minutes pass. Someone tries the back door, followed by more knocking. After a short silence the same thing again at the front door.

A little while later the door into the room is pushed open. There's a sharp intake of breath, then the gas is turned up full and what has been done is revealed.

The shadow of a tall, thin man, grotesquely elongated by the lamp, is thrown against the walls. The man and the shadow stoop to take the left wrist of the woman. There's no pulse. It's about a quarter to nine in the evening of Tuesday, January 20th 1931. The place is 29 Swindon Street, Anfield, Liverpool. The man's name is Walter Henry Bruce. The dead woman is his wife, Janet.

Part 1

Preparation

1

A Sentence of Death

Monday, July 13th 1930

Around the middle of the afternoon, Walter Bruce walked slowly and reluctantly towards his doctor's surgery. Slowly, because the weather was oppressive, the kind that drains energy. So hot he was uncomfortably aware of the stink of horse dung and of drains not flushed for a couple of weeks. Even at this pace he felt generally gritty and grimy – the texture of the streets of small terraced houses baking in the tired heat. Not far off to his left he knew the Liverpool Football Club ground was sleeping in its summer torpor. On still winter Saturday afternoons he could hear its roars quite clearly at home. He'd never been there, though, nor had any wish to. He could always find something better to do with a Saturday afternoon than stand bellowing at men paid good money just to kick a piece of leather about.

He walked reluctantly because only seventy-two hours before he had been discharged from hospital after a month as an in-patient. He knew from his own assessment of his condition and from things heard and said during his stay that there would be no good news for him in the report Dr Clarke would have on his desk.

The doctor's was one of the few imposing houses on Priory Road, double-fronted with a gabled canopy over the front door. The surgery was at the back, furthest away from the noise of traffic. The heat of the day was softened by blinds drawn over the windows, a blessing to a man sweating in a long outdated Edwardian white wing collar above a black tie, the tail of which disappeared into the black waistcoat of his equally black suit.

Dr Clarke shuffled the papers in front of him and looked up at the thin, gangly man with sparse grey hair, yellowish complexion and lugubrious expression, made the more doleful by a straggly moustache through which a little of the original ginger contended with the salt-and-pepper of age.

'You came to me in late May complaining of pain in your lower back and groin and of sharp pain when you had to postpone relieving yourself. You had chronic thirst and headaches that at times made it impossible to concentrate on anything at all.' He looked up at his patient as though this statement was a question. The patient nodded.

'I referred you to the hospital. You were admitted, let's see, on June 9th and you remained there until Friday last.' He looked up again as though for confirmation. Bruce mumbled, 'Yes'.

'I have their report here, Mr Bruce. Would you like me to read it to you?'

'Only the important bits.' He was resigned to its likely message.

'Mm. Well, they confirm your left kidney is missing...'

'That's not much of a discovery. It was taken out at Guys in oh-seven, when I came back from the East. You knew that.'

The doctor went on as though he had heard nothing. '...and the right one is diseased and no longer working properly. They say surgery is impracticable. Any treatment can only be medicinal. Palliative. Do you understand what that means?'

He nodded again. 'They said the medicine would help with the pain and the headaches. Nothing more.'

It was the doctor's turn to nod. 'You're going to have to take things a lot easier from now on. And always make sure you've a supply of the medicine. Never miss a dose.' He tapped his teeth with the cap of his fountain pen. 'I don't suppose this is what you wanted to hear.' He observed his patient's mouth form the shape of an 'O', as if he were whistling, though no sound came out. Clarke had seen him do this in the past – a sure sign of agitation. As clear a one as this undemonstrative patient had ever given, and then only because he'd had plenty of occasions to see him stressed.

Bruce spoke. 'What if I do not take it easy? I cannot afford to retire. I have a wife to keep.'

The reedy voice with its careful enunciation and no discernible accent was of a man who had worked hard at sounding like an educated professional.

He watched the doctor closely. He could read the strain on the man's face, knowing the part of the doctor-patient relationship practitioners dreaded most – giving bad news.

'If you go on as you have been, I give you a year, not much more.'

Behind his circular spectacles, Bruce blinked. The 'O' grew more pronounced. 'I appreciate your honesty.'

The doctor shrugged and briefly extended the fingers of both hands upwards. 'You have a right to the truth, though it gives me almost as much pain to tell it as it must give you to hear it.'

'And if I were able to "take it easy", as you put it?'

'Well, if you weren't out walking the streets in all weathers six and a half days a week, being obliged to have a cup of tea at every house you call on *and* if you had proper, regular, nourishing meals with competent nursing whenever you were too poorly to work – which you will be quite often...'

'And the prognosis then?' Poorly disguised impatience.

'You could stretch it out to five or six.'

Bruce sat back in his seat and folded his arms across his chest.

'What you're telling me is that at best, provided I change my life, I've five or six years more to live and that would be punctuated by spells of being quite ill. At worst, if I don't change my life, I'll probably be dead by the end of next summer.'

The doctor nodded, almost imperceptibly.

'But earning my living means walking round Clubmoor, calling on twenty-five clients a day, whatever the weather. There's no other way to do it.'

'Couldn't your employer find you a clerical job at head office?'

'They probably could. But it wouldn't bring in anything like what I earn now – and I don't exactly get fat on that. Anyway, my wife would have a fit if I took a big drop in salary.'

'Well she must accept it if she wants you to have any chance at all of seeing out these next few years. Does she realise she'll have to look after you properly, assuming you can't afford professional nursing?'

'We haven't discussed it. You know her well enough. She's not healthy herself. Always seems to have something wrong. Usually pretty soon after I'm off colour. If anything, I think she'd expect me to look after her as she gets older.'

'I had noticed. But you're the one who is really ill. She's going to have to change.' He paused and Bruce detected his doctor's lack of confidence in the power of pity to alter Janet's attitude to life. 'Do you want me to talk to her?'

Bruce sighed. 'I don't think so, but thank you. At her age people don't change. She was never cut out to nurse anyone.' He managed a wan smile. 'No Florence Nightingale there, I'm afraid. No Florence Tyler, either', he added.

'Florence Tyler?'

'A nurse at the hospital. She really took her profession seriously. One reason I feel a lot better in myself today than when I went in.'

'I'm glad you were well cared for in there.'

Bruce began to unfold his long frame and rise from the seat. The appointment was over. 'I hear what you say, Doctor, but I'll just have to grit my teeth and carry on regardless.'

Clarke rose to see him out. He made a shrugging gesture that signified hopelessness. To Bruce he might as well have ritually washed his hands. 'I have warned you. I can't be responsible if you don't follow my advice.'

Bruce walked the mile home in the stale and sticky heat. The sky to the west was bruised greyish purple and thunder rumbled in the distance. It seemed an appropriate backdrop to the news he had just been given – as though life was indeed a conspiracy against him.

In parallel with a life-long history of bodily malfunction was another of personal frustration and disappointment, only partly a consequence of his physical condition. Whatever he'd tried to do seemed to have been dogged by bad luck. He'd taught himself sufficient science to be appointed a part-time lecturer in chemistry at the Technical College, yet they wouldn't make it permanent and he'd not taught for a number of years now. He'd read widely enough to appreciate and be able to initiate philosophical discussion but the kind of people he'd had to live and work among were so decidedly un-intellectual that he'd had to make do with arguing things out in his own diaries. He'd taught himself to play chess although his skill had never risen above the intermediate level, and in the chess club he'd helped start he was rarely a winner. Even learning to play the violin so as to perform some of the classical sonatas with Janet had made him feel he was a talentless and clumsy beginner.

He'd tried so hard to rise above his origins. He'd travelled as a young man to India and the Far East in a series of clerical jobs. All that had achieved was to make him more aware of his petty bourgeois status in the eyes of most expatriates, and added to the damage to his health. Back in Britain in 1910 he'd been appointed a party political agent and, finally, his life seemed going in its true direction. He'd loved politics. It met his deepest desires to do work of some importance, it put him into a different social milieu and seemed at last to have justified his efforts to broaden his intellect. That chance to lift his career onto a higher plane had coincided with meeting and marrying Janet, whose good looks, education and social talents made her the perfect wife for the future he had in mind.

And then that War had put paid to all of it. Domestic politics were suddenly irrelevant and the local party, most unfairly he'd felt, told him it did not need, nor want to go on paying an Agent. And what had he, with all his potential and arduously self-taught education, ended up as? A footslogger, that's what: collecting insurance premiums door-to-door in a down-at-heel suburb of Liverpool, earning a steady, modest salary. He'd taken this job as 'The Man from Farsight' during the War and was still in exactly the same place sixteen years later. They had slipped down the social scale, which he had accommodated with customary outward indifference. Janet, however, had never stopped letting him know how much she resented it, pushing him to apply for a more senior post and constantly recalling something better than the grey dullness of their lives. He'd felt unable to explain that his family background and limited formal education ruled him out from consideration for a supervisory post; that he came from the wrong class; that if he went on doing his collection job steadily, honestly, and efficiently he was secure for life, but if he tried to climb higher up the ladder his fingers would be stamped on hard by those ahead of him; that he'd be seen as one with ambitions above his station and might find himself with no job at all.

He reached home just before it started to pour – a rented two-and-a-tiny-third-bed terraced house in a dead-end street, the front door almost but not quite opening on to the pavement. At the back, a yard between the scullery and the outdoor privy, bounded on each side by the high walls of neighbouring houses, was pierced by a wooden door leading out into an alley at the back. Still, he consoled himself, the house was only fifteen years old, soundly built, and it had an inside bathroom and toilet upstairs.

He went through the scullery into the kitchen. This was where they spent nearly all their housebound hours. The front room, the parlour, with Janet's piano and formal furnishings, was only used when visitors called or when they played music together.

The kitchen table took up most of the room. Janet had the *Evening Echo* spread out on it. She looked up as he came in. 'Well, what did he say?'

'That I have to ease off a bit at work. Perhaps not do as many calls a day. For a while, until things settle down.' He was perfectly aware he was doing what he always did when life conspired to deal him a blow: push it to the back of his mind and make the best of the bad job. It was a kind of safety valve or perhaps more like taking an aspirin for debilitating pain. It let him carry on as normal which was, he had always found, the simplest and least contentious way to deal with problems.

Janet had the last word. 'You should've listened to me years ago, Walter, when I told you to apply for a supervisor's job. But you wouldn't, would you? Now look where your lack of initiative has got us. How are we going to manage if you earn even less than you do now?'

2

The Idea

Thursday, 18th – Tuesday, 23rd December 1930

For nearly half an hour he sat, chin propped on left hand, staring out at the rain-sodden sky and the glistening backs of the houses of Richmond Park. Even if Janet wondered why he'd stayed upstairs when he should have been getting back to work, he knew one thing – this tiny eight-by-three-foot room with the microscope, the scales and the bottles of chemicals on the bench in front of him was his science lab, his sanctuary, and she'd never walk in on him there. But nothing else was clear cut anymore. He had never imagined anything like what he'd just found out. Although, he admitted, his imagination never stretched very far and had long since shrivelled up. As long as he could remember he'd stuck to facts and logic, which he appreciated was why he'd never been more than a third-rank chess player.

What he had held between the fingers of his right hand for most of the past twenty-five minutes was a fact. A certified copy of a birth certificate. His wife's. It told him she was nearly seventy, not fifty-three, as she'd led him to believe. That her father had been a smallholder farmer in north Yorkshire, not the veterinary surgeon from Sussex she'd always said he was. That her real mother had the very prosaic names of Martha Ann, formerly Brown. All that stuff about her being a French lady called Veronique was a lie too, a figment of the imagination Janet had in spades. Everything he thought he'd known about her had been built on thin air, created by deception.

There it was: eighteen years older than him. She'd lied

about it sixteen years ago on the marriage certificate, stating she was thirty-seven when she'd been fifty-three, and had kept up the pretence ever since. On their wedding day she'd been old enough to be his mother, older, in fact, than he was now. Whether she looked it or not, she was an old woman and now he came to think about it, some of her frailty and declining health was certainly an indication of her real age.

That wasn't all. The certificate had come with a letter that morning. The writer claimed – and the words had the ring of truth – to be the illegitimate son of the woman moving about in the kitchen below him. No address, but dated the previous Tuesday. Typewritten, formal – and unsigned.

Tuesday, December 16th 1930

Dear Mr Bruce,

Your wife, my mother, gave birth to me in 1893 when she worked as a governess in a private school in Leeds. My father was probably her employers' eldest son. I was placed in an orphanage as a new-born infant.

I managed to trace her through a private investigator and came to Liverpool on a Tuesday towards the back end of last month to reassure myself where she lived. I had written, asking her to meet me, to be reunited with the mother I had always wanted and to whom I have been a credit.

When we did meet earlier this week in Southport she told me she did not want to be reminded of her past and would not see me again. She made it clear she takes pride in the fact that she has always been able to present herself as much younger than she really is. Perhaps she has deceived you, too, so I am giving you evidence of her real age. When I observed her last month she was showing two young men out of the door at the back of the yard. I asked her about them and she was clearly embarrassed and refused to talk

```
about it. You may wish to satisfy yourself that
there is nothing improper in her meetings with
them in the afternoon while you are at work.
I am, sir, your servant.
```

Reaching down to the floor, he picked up the envelope this had all come in: his name and address typewritten, postmark illegible.

He scratched his head as though that might help him better understand the information that flooded him.

He knew now why she'd slipped off to Southport last Monday afternoon. He'd only discovered she'd been because her journey back to Liverpool was delayed until the early hours of Tuesday morning by a railway accident. Arriving home from work at six, he was surprised not to find her there. Finally, after midnight, he'd gone down to the police station to see if she'd been in some sort of accident in the winter fog. But the whole time he knew he was less concerned with the possibility that she had been killed or seriously injured, than with having the orderly and predictable pattern of his life upset. And when he'd got back and found her at home he consciously hid these feelings behind a mask of concern. 'Where've you been?' he'd asked, 'I thought something terrible must've happened to you.'

She'd given no indication of understanding or of being touched by his anxiety and he'd certainly got no credit for it. Rather, she seemed irritated he hadn't taken it in his stride. 'I went up to Southport to meet an old friend I haven't seen for years, Walter. All the trains back to Liverpool were delayed by an accident.'

'You didn't tell me you were going.'

'Why should I have? I don't have to tell you everything I do.'

'Yes, I know,' he said, trying to be reasonable, 'but I don't think you've ever made a trip like that on your own since we've been married. Who was it you went to see? Do I know of her?'

'How do you know it was a 'her', Walter? I'm not going to stand here and talk about it. I'm extremely tired and I just want to get to bed.' Their relationship was such he asked no more questions nor raised the matter again the following day. Now he knew she'd been taunting him.

He took out his pocket watch, accurate to the minute, calibrated daily to the signals on the wireless. He stood up. Time to be about his business, to go down, put on the mackintosh, pick up the bag and try to separate the work from a personal crisis enfolding him in emotions he distrusted and felt to be beneath his dignity. He picked up the letter, the copy of the birth certificate and the envelope, tore them into tiny pieces and dropped them into his wastepaper basket.

Downstairs, collecting his hat and raincoat from the stand jammed in the little space just inside the front door, he went on through the kitchen where Janet sat at the table with the newspaper.

'I'm off now.'

She didn't raise her head. 'Aren't you a bit late?'

'There was something I needed to do before I went back.' Now was the moment to tell her what he'd just found out.

But he couldn't. She still didn't look up. 'Oh. What time will you be back?'

'The usual. About six.' Glad to escape with that minimal communication he hurried through the scullery and out of the door, across the yard and into the narrow alley that ran between the backs of the houses in Swindon Street and of those facing Richmond Park. The same route he took every working day – through another alley into Richmond Park, turn right, and walk to the end to the tram stop. Familiarity and predictability the key to all his activities – even to the area a ten-minute tram ride away, the 'patch' he'd covered for nearly sixteen years. He could probably have found his way round it blindfolded. Streets of small terraced houses, made drearier by the Liverpudlian chill, mist and rain, up and down which he trudged, collecting premiums, making payments, occasionally writing new policies. He'd once described his own tall, gangling figure in motion as 'two yards of animated bone'. Those who saw him noticed the odd gait and the impression of an elderly but well-maintained scarecrow, in his wing collar, formal suit and bowler hat. For them he had become part of the scenery.

Between making calls that afternoon he ran over in his mind what he had learned. Janet was seventy. And he'd be lucky if he ever got to fifty-seven. He was going to end up looking after her, not the other way round. He'd told the doctor last summer she would never take care of him, and he hadn't even known then she was so much older. Why hadn't he recognized the signs? For years she'd claimed to be delicate. She haunted the doctor's. She'd let the house go even though they'd a cleaner coming in once a week. He had to tidy up after her. Every time he had a bad turn she had one too, a kind of tit-for-tat. When he went down with something she told him he was malingering. Some nurse she'd be. There'd be no chance of easing off at work; she'd be constantly taking to her bed and he'd be coming home to deal with whatever she needed or wanted. She'd have him shortening his life to make hers last longer.

He knew what he wanted to happen.

If he could ease up and be looked after in a professional way it would do him more good than any amount of medicine, and if he could stretch things out to five or maybe six years, who knew..? They might have come up with a cure by then. In any case, even if they didn't he'd have a dignified and comfortable last few years. But he'd need a nurse like Florence from the hospital to have any chance.

He had a sense of needing to do something but for the life of him he couldn't see what or how. Blocking his path to a dignified end was the slight but immovable figure of an elderly, hypochondriac, parasitic and deceitful. The more clearly he saw the nature of his problem the further away its resolution seemed to be.

He stopped in mid-stride. A man, hurrying behind him almost cannoned into him and swept past with a curt and grudging apology.

It had come as a shock how little he'd known about Janet. She'd had a child out of wedlock which she'd abandoned. Might there have been more than just the one? What kind of life had she been living before he met her? Did he accept the implications in the letter that, even at her age, she might be entertaining – if that was the correct word – younger men behind his back? No, it wasn't that far-fetched. When first married he, an inexperienced virgin, had been surprised by her skill and evident pleasure in lovemaking, introducing him to acts and feelings he'd never enjoyed before, and never would again after everything fell apart at the beginning of the War, when they'd both toppled off the plinth they'd built for themselves.

He had to accept it had been easy to deceive him.

Nobody would believe she was as old as that. No, they'd say, she's middle aged. She'd still kept some of the prettiness; her face clear and unlined, plenty of hair and teeth still her own. She dressed dowdily but said she couldn't afford better because he didn't earn enough. Perhaps it helped her feel younger, allowing men to take liberties with her. Though surely they wouldn't know she was as old as she really was.

He reached the door of his next client. As he was about to lift the knocker, a thought came into his head so sharp and clear he allowed the metal to remain in his hand.

He knew who they might be. Maybe she'd been doing this regularly on a Tuesday afternoon and her son just happened to be there on one of them. Next Tuesday he'd check if he was right. He could rearrange work to make time to watch the house. If he was around at about four and anything was going on, he'd likely see them. It'd be almost dark, too, so he'd be nearly invisible. And if he saw nothing then he'd do the same each Tuesday until he was satisfied either it wasn't happening or... it was.

He let the knocker fall and waited for the response. He'd worked out his next move. Now he could concentrate on being the man from Farsight.

Around ten to four on the Tuesday afternoon he stood strategically at the corner of Letchworth Street, just where Richmond Park made a left-hand dogleg, giving him a clear view of all exits from Swindon Street. His position was beside the blank wall of the corner house. He'd altered his appearance as best he could, exchanging his conspicuous bowler hat for a soft trilby. Janet had noticed that. 'Not wearing your round hat, Walter? How on earth will your customers know who you are?'

'They're not customers. They're clients', he'd said.

'That's a very fancy name for them', she'd countered,

'grubby little people with grubby little lives paying their few grubby pennies a week so one day they can be buried properly.'

'It pays the bills.'

She'd sniffed. 'What time will you be home?'

'About six as usual,' he'd told her.

So there he was in shadows thrown by the low light of the street lamps, with his raincoat collar pulled up. No one came near; he may as well have been the only person out of doors on that dank late afternoon.

He didn't have long to wait. He'd picked the right Tuesday. A few minutes after four he heard men's voices and laughter and two came out into Richmond Park from the narrow passage leading to the back of his house. One a burly, well-built, fellow in a dark coat and a cap, with a purposeful walk. The other thinner, in a trilby hat, almost trotting to keep up with his companion. They turned away from him and went up the street towards the church and the main road.

He knew who they were all right. One of them he had not seen for nearly two years but the other he'd come across regularly, and as recently as a month ago.

Whatever the letter writer's motive had been in passing on his suspicions, Bruce now knew he was being cuckolded. The two he'd just seen cheerfully making their way from his house, having been let out of his own back door by his own wife, had no doubt been having a good laugh at his inability to perform the marital duties they were doing for him.

Although he had now seen it with his own eyes he found the situation bizarre.

They surely couldn't be paying her for the privilege? Even if she were the age they probably thought she was they'd only be doing it if there was something in it for them. They were ne'er-do-wells the two of them, the only things they thought about were drink, girls, natty clothes and showing-off. And he knew that to pay for that they were both quite willing to borrow, wheedle, cheat or just steal from others. It occurred to him then that she might be paying them. But if she were, what with? Perhaps she'd always had a bit tucked away somewhere. He remembered back when they'd first met she seemed to have money of her own. If there was any left she'd kept it closely to herself; not a penny had ever found its way towards their living expenses.

Chilled but feeling unable to go straight home and give an explanation of why he was back early, he decided he may as well complete this utterly atypical afternoon by taking the tram into the city centre.

Twenty minutes later he sat warming his hands on a cup of strong tea, a cigarette between his lips, the fug in the teashop beginning to thaw him out, the windows blearily reflecting the cheap Christmas decorations and their corrupted message of goodwill to all men. On his mental chessboard he began to set out thoughts that contained no goodwill to anyone.

If this was a game of chess it was one he had to win. Winning meant another five or six years to wind down his life in peace and quiet. But there were some serious threats to see off before he could be sure of winning. There was no point beating about the bush, something had to be done about Janet. It wasn't just that she'd never look after him as the doctor had said she'd need to, there was the other thing. If what she was doing with those two got out, if the neighbours had the slightest suspicions, it'd run like wildfire. He told himself he didn't care who did what to or with her, he was long past being jealous. But he wasn't having them all laughing at him because he was too out of touch to notice that she was playing him up. Or worse, thinking he did know about it and was complacent.

He pictured the prize as he sipped his tea: a final few years peacefully pursuing his interests while being professionally cared for. He realised how much he had wanted this ever since his hospitalisation, but he hadn't let himself think it possible until Janet's true age and moral failings had been thrust under his nose.

But there was Janet standing like the opponent queen on a chessboard – between him and victory. He'd never get any peace; she'd make a huge fuss if he said he was going to work less or be a clerk in the office. And even if he could afford both to keep her and engage professional care she'd very quickly have the nurse looking after her. Given how old she was, and her hypochondria, it wouldn't be long before it'd be a full-time job. It wouldn't work. If they went on as they were it was all up with him.

He noticed the waitress hovering close to his table, took the opportunity to order a second cup, and reflected.

He'd shared a home and a sort of life with her for over sixteen years. When he came to think of it, that'd been a bit like a game of chess too. He'd gone from the enthusiastic opening – through a midgame of jogging along – to the endgame of barbed neutrality, a sort of emotional desert where no win was possible, a kind of stalemate. That had been the pattern for the last five years.

The further the happy, early days of their marriage receded in time the more he treasured what he remembered of them and substituted it in his mind for what he had now. The Janet of those memories had long since gone but her essence remained like a perfume, the hint of which brings into some unexpected situation a sharp reminder of a once-loved one. In her place was someone who irritated and depressed him, and who, as she often made him aware, despised him for his humdrum calling and precise, finicky habits. They exchanged increasingly fewer words, preferring silence. When dislike or anger broke through this shell in the form of her carping, hurtful asides and disparagement, or his condescension, it was never in the presence of anyone else. Others might think them a contentedly married couple. He knew the truth was well concealed behind a curtain of civilised indifference and of keeping themselves to themselves.

The second cup arrived. He lit another cigarette, finding the café uncomfortably warm, took off his raincoat, hung it on the back of his chair.

What to do went round and round in his head.

Perhaps he had grounds for divorce. She was committing adultery with those young men. But he couldn't afford it. Divorce was for the well-heeled. What he'd got saved up would soon be spent on solicitors and then there'd be nothing left to pay for the care. He wouldn't have achieved anything. Perhaps he could tell her he knew what she was up to and threaten her with exposure unless she left home. She'd deny it. His word against hers. And he'd destroyed the only bit of evidence he had. She'd see him off; she was certainly not going to leave their home willingly. And if life was difficult now it would be impossible after he'd done that.

Thoughts of removing her permanently from his life rose like snakes in the pit he'd seen in India: insidious yet compelling; a writhing, slithering mass of evil mesmerising him. As much as he'd known he ought to, he'd not been able to look away. And here he sat now, staring fascinated into the snake pit of his mind.

He finished the tea, put on his coat and went out into the wet and chilly air to go home.

As he sat on the tram, among a smell of damp clothing and infrequently washed bodies, he asked how he, in his own estimation such a law-abiding man who'd always had a sense of right and wrong, could have sat there, teacup warming his hands, thinking of getting rid of his wife?

The ability to plan and deliberately kill someone was not an accomplishment you could learn, like chess or the violin. When the intended victim was close to you, someone you lived with, it called for hardness of heart, insensitivity to pity, indifference to suffering and denial of the sanctity of human life. You might have the idea but if you didn't have these qualities you'd never progress beyond that. The point was though, he knew he did have them; had always had them. He'd made himself indifferent to his own suffering. He'd always been impatient with the sentimental nonsense talked and written about how precious life was. In his view a lot of people didn't actually deserve to live and simply fouled the nest for everyone else. India and the Far East had impressed on him how cheap and transitory life was. He needed to remember what he was thinking of was merely removing the opponent's piece, so that his pawn could reach the back row of the board and become whatever he wanted it to be.

After tea he went up to his lab, ostensibly to bring his books up to date before paying in his collections. But the thoughts nursed in the café kept intruding. He got up, and silently, so as not to alert Janet downstairs, moved about on the landing. First he looked back into the lab.

Poison? But it had to be slow and look like illness. She mustn't think anything had changed. How long would it take to kill her? Would it leave him time to enjoy those five or six years? And his knowledge of chemistry might well attract suspicion when she finally died. Their doctor might cotton-on. Too many imponderables and time not on his side.

A half turn and he faced the bathroom.

Drown her in an overfilled bath? Quick, but needed fast, strong and co-ordinated action. In his enfeebled state he'd probably make a mess of it.

A complete turn and he was looking at the bannister along the landing.

Could he give her a push? There were bound to be questions even if it looked like an accident. And he'd be the sole suspect. What if the fall wasn't fatal and she was able to point the finger at him? If he were to have any chance at all of surviving even a few years in comfort and dignity he must come up with some way that eliminated Janet from his life, yet left no likelihood of his being suspected responsible. And soon.

These strategies in his mental game came up seriously short but he was unable to think of any others. It seemed like everything else so far in his life – yet another game he'd lose, another failure to make things go the way he wanted, another instance of putting up with whatever life or his opponent handed out to him.

3

The Opportunity

Wednesday, December 24th 1930

In the early afternoon, as Bruce left a house in Missouri Road and walked along the street toward his next call, he was accosted with 'Merry Christmas Mr Bruce' from a car that had just pulled up to the kerb ahead. The smartly-dressed and somewhat louche figure of Glyn Davies appeared, with his carefully waved hair and toothbrush moustache, and his hand extended.

Bruce, who thought Christmas a waste of working time and an excuse for drunkenness and idleness in the name of a defunct religion, kept silent, taking the hand to return the greeting, and getting a strong waft of brilliantine in the process.

'What brings you to these parts?' Bruce asked him.

Davies oozed affability and his hail-fellow-well-met tone irritated Bruce, although he gave no sign of it. 'My girlfriend Iris – Iris Thomas – lives in this street. At Number 7. She gives piano lessons you know.'

Bruce hadn't known but found it very interesting. Davies, one of the two he saw coming from his own home yesterday, had got a regular girlfriend.

'What are you doing these days Glyn?'

'I'm with Standard Life now, Mr Bruce. Tell you what, let me give you a little Christmas present.' And he went back to the car, leant into the back then hurried round to thrust a company calendar into Bruce's hand.

'Thank you, Glyn. Can't have too many calendars.' Then, as though it were an afterthought, 'Do you ever hear anything of Phillip Jordan. I haven't seen him for ages.'

Davies grinned broadly. 'Oh, Phillip's fallen right on his feet. He's been working for a big bookies over the water and he's just got engaged to the boss's wife's sister. Lucky so-and-so, eh!'

Bruce thought that relationship sounded rather complex and had the ring of one of those prohibited in the Old Testament. But then, as a lightning flash illuminates the night, he realised this was news indeed and very interesting. He could bet the girl knew nothing about her fiancé's visits to Janet.

'Well, when you see him, give him my regards and congratulate him for me on his good fortune.'

With a wave of his hand Davies walked off towards Number 7. Bruce watched his progress then resumed his walk, evaluating what he'd just heard.

Glyn Davies and Phillip Jordan had both worked for Farsight as agents. Jordan had left them well over two years ago under some kind of cloud Bruce had not been able to learn more about. Davies had started with the Company as a sort of trainee and had frequently called on Bruce with messages from Bruce's supervisor for whom Davies was acting as a dogsbody. But after a period as an agent with his own round, he had also left under a cloud about a year before. Bruce knew rather more about that particular cloud since his supervisor had confided to him that Davies had misappropriated sums collected and had been stupid enough to think the Company, with its sophisticated accounting systems, wouldn't find out. Davies's father had made up the shortfall so although he had not been dismissed it was very likely that the young man had been encouraged to move on.

Almost exactly two years earlier, Bruce had had a bad go of bronchitis and stayed in bed nearly three weeks. As soon as he was too poorly to go out to work Janet had said to him, 'Why don't you get that nice Mr Davies to help out with your round. He's much younger and healthier than you. He'll do it in no time.'

He'd countered that Davies was inexperienced. He'd only just started his own round. 'Pooh,' Janet had said, 'what experience do you need to do what you do?' He'd said, 'well if it were that easy everybody'd be doing it.' And she'd responded drily, 'everybody wouldn't do it, Walter. It's not much of a job is it?' At the time he'd seen nothing suspicious in any of this. Now he saw more clearly. To make it easier for himself Davies had brought along Jordan, an experienced insurance agent who said he was temporarily out of work, and Bruce had agreed to Davies sharing the load. Both men had visited him at home regularly to drop off the collections from clients. Janet had been particularly taken with Davies who, besides a charm irresistible to women, had pretensions to being an actor and singer. From his sickbed he'd heard the young man sing ballads from the musicals, Janet accompanying on the piano. He'd also quickly discovered that Davies was up to the tricks that were to make him a marked man at Farsight. The canny Bruce was too old a dog to be taken in and had pulled Davies sharply up over bookkeeping errors and short payments. Davies, seeing the light, had quickly set matters straight and no more had been said. Only later had Bruce heard that Davies had acquired a 'reputation' with his employers.

Finishing his round of calls and going slowly home, Bruce could see a faint but positive solution to the problem of what to do about Janet. The seed of a plan had begun to germinate that just might see him home and dry.

4

The Plan

December 25th 1930 – January 18th 1931

The Christmas break was short enough for Bruce to live with his dislike of it and all it stood for. On Christmas Day morning Janet went off to the red brick monstrosity of Holy Trinity. He spent most of that time in his back-bedroom laboratory mulling over what he had learned the previous day, and how it might help him achieve what had now become his clear objective – to give himself five years of peace and comfort before the inevitable end.

Cookery was not one of Janet's accomplishments; their Christmas dinner lacked a great deal of the festivity associated with the date. Cold meats bought the day before and kept out of the way of the cat was what it came down to. As it had been last year, and the ones before that.

They ate to an accompaniment of Janet's sighs which increased in frequency and volume. She ate the last, wiped her lips and propped her chin on her hand. He knew what was coming.

'Oh, when I think of what Christmas used to be like in Harrogate.'

He did not respond. 'In Harrogate' meant, 'Before I met you.'

'I'd so many friends. We'd go to each other's houses, have parties. We dressed up. I'd play and people would gather round the piano and sing. And we always gave each other such beautiful presents. Everywhere was decorated...'

A brief pause. Janet gazed into a vision of Christmas Past.

' ... and The Stray was covered with snow. And at night the houses with their windows all lit up so prettily. A sky full of stars.

Oh, those were real Christmases! Not the kind I've come to now.'

Every year it was the same, although he had the feeling that with age the memories became more and more of an illusion.

She hadn't finished.

'I never wanted to come here. Why, oh why didn't we stay in Harrogate? Such a beautiful place. You could've got another job there but you didn't even try ... no, you just let yourself be persuaded to come here. To Liverpool! Of all places ... to peddle insurance.'

She looked up and across at him.

'You said it would only be temporary. I remember that quite clearly. You'd move up to something better, soon. Soon! It's been sixteen years.'

He did not respond. He'd heard this in one form or another many times over the past six or seven years. Best to let it pass over his head.

After tea they went into the front room and practised a couple of piano and violin sonatas. Janet was a good pianist. She played with emotion and a delicate touch which suggested more than just the conventional facility acquired as a young woman. He had only begun to play the violin a few years earlier and was still taking lessons. His playing was like his chess: plodding, logical and unimaginative. Although he made no obvious mistakes he tended to lower the quality of their duo. Still, it was one of the very few activities they undertook together. And so the day passed.

On Boxing Day afternoon they had a visit from sister-in-law Violet and her son Alfred. Bruce's younger brother, James, had a post with the government printer in the Malay States but his wife and son had come back on their own so that Alfred could study medicine at Liverpool University. Bruce liked his nephew and got along with his sister-in-law so the time made a pleasant break in the day and gave relief from brooding over his still unformed plan.

But the following Sunday morning, while Janet was again at church, he developed the idea that had been forming as a potentially workable way of settling the future. He sat in the kitchen rather than up in his lab. It was warmer and gave him room to move about as he struggled to give a logical shape to an scheme that had yet to become a plan.

The first thing he must do was tell Davies and Jordan he knew about their visits to Janet and what went on. He'd need to make much of his anger and disgust. Then he had to make them believe he was contemplating divorce proceedings against his wife, naming the two of them as co-respondents. Of course they wouldn't know he'd rejected it as unaffordable. And finally, he had to bring home to them what would follow from the scandal they'd be dragged into.

Taking his diary, he opened a blank page and wrote out these steps. Seeing them in black and white confirmed they were a foundation. Exposure would be a threat neither Davies nor Jordan could ignore. He could hear himself building the picture for them and see, even smell, their fear. He'd say to them, 'This won't be just any old divorce. The papers will find the story irresistible. Think how they'll write about it – the insatiable middle-aged wife with not just one but two young men, perhaps both together providing what she craves. And of course it wouldn't be possible to keep your names out of it so it would certainly mean your girlfriends and fiancées – and their families and relatives – would want nothing more to do with either of you. In your case, Phillip, it could very well mean the loss of your job too.'

They'd see that their greed and stupidity had given him the power to ruin them.

The more he thought about this, the more he believed it offered the best, possibly the only, way to remove Janet while keeping himself at arm's length from the actions involved. He had neither the physical nor the mental strength to kill his wife. But if he could persuade Davies and Jordan to do it in their own interests, he could tell himself he'd never been a murderer.

For a long time he'd rejected the possibility of any kind of afterlife. It did not stand up to the searching light of reason. But recently, with the probability of his own imminent death, he'd read a good deal on the subject; enough to entertain the possibility that he might after all meet Janet 'on the other side'. If his idea led to a practical outcome and there was, in spite of his scepticism, an 'other side', there would be no blood on his hands; the last person Janet had seen would not have been him. It was rather like taking out insurance. Very apt, the simile seemed to him.

On the same diary page he wrote.

'When I think about it my hands tremble and I feel my heartbeat picking up as though I had a fever. After all these years of law-abiding probity I'm proposing to have my wife killed. Anyone who knows me would think I'd taken leave of my senses. But I don't feel mad. It actually seems quite logical. I'm not thinking of doing this because I hate her. Indifference towards her, yes, but not hate. Even after the way she's treated me over the years. Even now when I know she's deceived me about her age. That she's never told me she's got a bastard son. And even after she's doing things that'll expose me to ridicule and ignominy in our community when, not if, it gets out. It doesn't take much to set tongues a-clacking round here. None of it makes me hate her, though. All things being equal I'd probably put up with it, as I've done with everything else these last ten years. But all things aren't equal. If I don't do this what's the alternative? A miserable end to a life that's so far been long on frustration, disappointment, and drudgery and short on peace, pleasure, and satisfaction. There's got to be a twilight of comfort and content for me before the night falls. I owe it to myself.'

He read and reread this passage, the blue-black ink drying out on the white of the page. It was his confession and justification rolled into one. Setting out in a logical and clear paragraph the problem and its solution. The final sentences seemed almost poetic to him.

But he would leave no hostage to fortune. The entry had served its cathartic purpose. He carefully removed the page, folded it into a spill and put a match to it. Watching it burn down in the ashtray, the words had left the paper and were now etched on his brain.

He got up from the table and made himself a cup of tea. His thoughts moved on from the plan to the men he would use to carry it out and the likelihood of their cooperating with him.

He saw Davies as a liability. A blabbermouth with a propensity to show off. But involvement in murder wouldn't be something he'd boast about and he certainly wouldn't want his parents to discover he'd been committing adultery and was a party to killing the woman involved.

It boiled down to whether he was reliable enough to carry out his part on time and as instructed.

Jordan had the most to lose from exposure. That bookmaker he was working for really was a biggish business. Married to the owner's sister-in-law he was going to be very much 'family'. His future would be made, at work and socially. So he'd be the one who'd have to do the actual killing. From what he'd seen of him two years before he seemed harder material than Glyn. He'd be physically capable of it and mentally focused enough to follow his part of the plan to the letter, especially when he understood he had no choice.

He conceded it was possible that one or both of them would refuse to kill someone in cold blood. But, like himself, they had no other options. He had to make them aware of the danger to their reputations and futures while convincing them he had a plan that would work, that allowed for contingencies and put all three of them beyond suspicion of any involvement in Janet's death.

The cup was empty. Janet would be home in a few minutes. The morning had been fruitful. He could move forward now.

He managed to 'bump into' Davies on the Tuesday, the next to last day of the old year. The younger man seemed, as he was intended to be, surprised to see him.

'You're off your patch, aren't you, Mr Bruce?'

'Well, yes, Glyn, but I wanted to see you and I thought I might find you around here.'

'What about, Mr Bruce? What d'you want to see me about?'

Bruce thought he detected some nervousness. Part of the plan was to create apprehension and alarm and that seemed to be working. Davies must know this was no accidental meeting. 'I don't want to stand here talking, Glyn, but it's important you and I have a chat. How about next Friday, half-past two at The

Copper Kettle in Lime Street – just over from the station? I have to be down in the city then. Would that be all right with you?'

'Can't you tell me what it's about?'

'I thought I might offer you a bit of advice, Glyn. Seeing how it's a new year and you with a new company and that.'

'Oh, I see.' Davies looked away, his brow furrowed and his eyes anywhere but directly on the other man. 'I'll be there then, Mr Bruce.'

'Yes, please, Glyn.' Bruce made it sound less of a request than an order and turning away, said, 'I'll see you there. Friday. Two-thirty.'

He walked off with an almost jaunty step. He'd put the wind up Davies and no mistake. Usually so cocky, the fellow's manner betrayed he had some idea, probably a very good one, of what the conversation would be about. Then he came to an abrupt halt. What if he'd so frightened Davies that he didn't turn up on Friday? He walked on, slowly now. He'd have to repeat this afternoon's intervention but spell out the threat to Davies' future right there in front of him. There were risks in doing that, not least being seen in earnest and possibly animated discussion with Davies quite close to home. Nothing was ever easy. He'd see what happened on Friday. Unusually for him, Walter Bruce slept very badly that night. Lying awake next to Janet he could not stop thinking that here they were, still sharing a bed, going through the ordinary routine of their lives as though he'd never had the idea that troubled him equally with the thought of carrying it out and of failing to do so. And now he'd gone beyond just thinking about it. When he met Davies the day after next he would be more than half way to setting in motion the killing of the woman whose sleepy snuffling next to him implied an unruffled ignorance of any such possibility.

He got up in the semi-darkness and, as he'd done ever since they'd been married, went down and made her a cup of tea. Again, as he ever did, he urinated, shaved, dressed, combed what was left of the sparse covering of the top of his head and went down for porridge and a cup of tea. He and Janet, she in her dressing-gown, on either side of the kitchen table.

The Wednesday and Thursday passed. He went off to his round at about ten, came home for his dinner at one, went back to work at two-thirty and then finally home for his tea at six. The milestones of his day did not change but what he found strange – so much so that he was concerned she would notice it as unusual – was that he went out of his way to be nice to her. Almost as if, having decided what to do with her and being on the edge of setting a plan in motion, he was making it up to her over the little time she had left.

On the Friday he finished work earlier than usual and then had a shortened dinner break, having told Janet at breakfast he had to see someone on his round at two o'clock.

When he got to the café at two-thirty he was relieved to see Davies already there, at a table for two, tea cup in front of him, eyes following the pert bottom of a waitress from table to table. He started as Bruce appeared in his line of sight. Bruce took the other seat and slowly and purposefully wiped his glasses on a clean handkerchief. The deliberate silence was his opening gambit and he waited for Davies' response. After a few minutes of breathing on and polishing the lenses, during which Bruce could see from the working of his face the other struggling with curiosity and apprehension, Davies was forced to make his move – to break the silence which he clearly found unbearable.

'What was it you wanted to talk to me about, Mr Bruce?'

He told himself not to disclose his next move too soon. Keep his opponent on edge, curious yet fearful.

'I think you know very well, Glyn. If you didn't, I don't suppose you'd have actually come all the way down here just to humour an old codger like me. And you were even early. That's not like you.'

'What is it I already know, then?' Davies looked sulky; probably now wishing he hadn't kept the appointment.

He struck, scattering Davies' poorly constructed defence. 'How often have you been to my house in the afternoons this past six months?'

'I don't know what you're talking about.' Davies looked down at the table. Fidgeted.

Before Bruce could take up this challenge, the waitress arrived.

Young and pretty, her black and white uniform emphasising olive skin and dark hair crowned with a tiara-like cap, her stance said she was aware that Davies had been eyeing her up before and after he'd ordered. Bruce asked for a cup of tea, adding, 'do you want another, Glyn?' Davies was silent, not even looking at the girl; that told him all he needed to know about the other man's confusion. 'Just the one then, please Miss.'

He sat back in his seat and looked at Davies. It was warm in the café and he noticed the sheen of moisture on the other's brow. 'Come on, Glyn. I saw you leaving my house last Tuesday afternoon. Someone else saw you coming out of there at the end of November and took the trouble to write to me about it. Wasn't just you he and I saw, was it?' He introduced a new line of attack, a thrust down Davies' unprotected flank. 'By the way, I saw your girlfriend – Iris, isn't it – the other day. She really is a beautiful girl. Any young man would be proud to have her on his arm. She could have any fellow she pleased, that one. So why on earth are you making the beast with two backs with someone old enough to be your mother?' He just stopped short of saying 'grandmother'. With his pretensions to being an actor, Davies might get the Shakespearean reference. Even if he didn't, Bruce rather liked the metaphor.

Davies' face was pale, there was the smell of nervous sweat. But he still did not speak – his gaze was riveted on his now empty cup.

'Look, I've every right to be angry. I've been deceived by my wife and by someone I looked on as a friend.' He'd try to shame Davies, though he doubted how effective it would be. 'You owe me some answers. How long's this been going on?' Davies' voice was hard to hear, soft and hesitant. 'It started after we did that work for you.' He looked up to deliver his excuse. 'She paid us, you know. We needed the money. I wasn't earning much, Phillip was out of a job.'

'Oh, I see.' He made the expression drip with disgust. 'And has this payment for services rendered continued from then to now?'

'No. It only went on for a few months. Three or four. Then last summer, while you were in hospital, I called round to see how you were and she invited me in to sing with her playing the piano. I went round once or twice and then Phillip started coming too.'

'Did you, or Phillip, suggest it went beyond a sing-song?' He thought he knew the answer.

Silence again. Davies would not meet his eyes.

'Come on, did you or didn't you? This is my wife we're talking about.'

Davies swallowed. 'She offered to pay again for us to be nice to her.' He fell quiet.

'Yes?' It was less of a job getting it out of him than he had feared. On the other hand, an easy facility for confession might not be what he'd want in a co-conspirator to murder. Then came a revelation.

'A couple of months ago we told her we were going to stop. She said if we did she would tell you. It must have slipped out before about Phillip's going out with Brophy's sister-in-law. She threatened to write to Brophy, telling him about us and her.' His shoulders slumped, he looked down again. 'Oh, God, what a mess.'

Mate. Black's defences in disarray and the king, Mr Phillip Jordan, pinned in a corner with nowhere to go. Walter Bruce could not help a thin smile of satisfaction. Probably one of the best games he'd ever played.

'Well, I do know about it, but not from her. She wouldn't have told me either. But you must take her threat to expose Phillip seriously. She's capable of doing that out of spite. You told me he's engaged now, so Brophy's going to be his brother-in-law. I imagine any scandal reaching the Brophys would be disastrous for him.'

'You're not kidding! They'd drop him so fast if the story ever got out.'

'Has he come up with any ideas for what to do about it?'

'He said if she carried out her threat an' wrote to Brophy, he'd brazen it out, like. Say she was a woman who'd had a grudge against him from back when he sold insurance. Just out to do him damage. But we haven't stopped, as you know.'

Bruce drained his tea. Sounding as aggrieved as he could he

countered, 'Yes, well he might've been able to talk his way out of it if I didn't know anything. But, of course, I'm of a mind to bring an action for divorce against my wife on the grounds of her adultery with you two and that will put the kibosh on your chum's plans to secure a good marriage and an advantageous position with the family business, won't it? Oh, and what will Iris think? Your father for that matter?'

Davies appeared close to tears. In fewer than twenty minutes his world had turned to ashes around him and he was at Bruce's mercy.

'Please don't do that Mr Bruce.'

'Why not, Glyn? You see there are a couple of things you don't know. I only found out about them just before Christmas. My dear wife has a son. Not mine. One born forty years ago and brought up in an orphanage. He traced her and has been in touch with her. She must have felt he was a real bad penny turning up out of nowhere like that. It was him who wrote telling me he'd seen two young men being shown out of my house one afternoon – he'd been watching it evidently – and when they met he'd asked her who you were. She'd been embarrassed and clammed up, which made him suspicious. Oh, and he also sent me her birth certificate. She's eighteen years older than she said she was when I married her. She's not my age at all. She's seventy!'

Davies raised his head and blinked. He looked as though he were going to be sick. Bruce provided a verbal emetic. 'So you can imagine how this story's going to sound once the papers get hold of it. They'll be like dogs with a particularly disgusting bone.' He drained his tea, got up and adjusted his raincoat. 'I must be off now, Glyn. I suggest you get hold of Phillip just as soon as you can and tell him all three of us need to have a talk. I may be able to help you both get round this mess you've landed yourselves in. Let me know where and when in the next few days. Perhaps over the water, somewhere we won't be recognised.' He took the slips for the teas to the cash till and paid. As he left, he turned once and saw Davies still sitting, deflated, at the table, his face pale, chewing his bottom lip.

One down, one to go.

5

Between Saturday afternoon and Sunday evening Bruce applied himself to the plan he must have ready for Davies and Jordan. He caught himself being irritable with Janet and irritability was not an emotion he ever let her see, preferring to cloak it in behaviour sometimes long-suffering, occasionally condescending. Up in his laboratory he expressed some of this strain in his diary, something he did not keep on a daily basis but to record feelings and events he thought important, or often, as if compelled to write them down in cryptic phrases, his struggles to make sense of the people and the world that surrounded him. On that Sunday he betrayed, for anyone who looked beyond the actual words, the difficulties and frustrations that kept company with his planning. He wrote, 'must work out some definite scheme properly planned and rigorously adhered to, each particular difficulty tackled and overcome.' This entry he did not erase.

But by the Sunday night he had a plan. One that would give him an alibi for the actual time of Janet's death, provide evidence of a motive for someone to have killed her and make it highly unlikely that whoever investigated her murder would consider complex solutions. A plan he would have no reservations about putting to his co-conspirators when he met them and which ought to help him overcome the biggest problem he faced; that no matter how much they knew it was in their interests to achieve the end, they would baulk at the means.

When Bruce went to work on the Wednesday there had been a night of freezing fog. Even with his preoccupations, he was entranced by the effect on the trees, shrubs and plants in the built-up district in which he lived and worked. He decided not to return to his round that afternoon and persuaded his wife to walk with him to nearby Stanley Park where the magic produced by these phenomena were more concentrated. Afterwards he could not explain satisfactorily to himself why he had done this, other than that now he had made up his mind to secure his freedom and had a clear plan for how to do so he in some way found it easier to be with her.

The shared experience in the Park ran against the grain of the direction he was following. He told himself, 'In this place I am her husband, reaching back into the past when I loved her; in another I am her nemesis, planning her removal.' The situation no longer seemed to him to be dichotomous but of a piece.

Once again he captured the strangeness of his two lives in that month with an entry in his diary: 'A night of keen frost. The fog gives an enchanted appearance to the plants and trees. Every twig and leaf bordered with a white rim of frost... I cannot recollect an occasion on which the hoar had produced such beautiful effects. After dinner I persuaded Janet to go with me to the park. She was equally charmed.'

The next day events moved a stage further.

Towards the end of the afternoon, with dusk gathering, he left a client's house in Lisburn Lane and saw Davies cross over the road in his direction. The two fell into step.

He asked the question. 'Well, have you and Phillip decided whether to meet me?'

'We don't have a lot of choice do we? You said you had a plan. We'll meet you and see what it is. But Phillip said to tell you, don't think he'll be easily persuaded.'

'It has to be next Monday evening, after seven-thirty. I shall tell her I'm going to the chess club to play a tournament game. I suggest you meet me at Breck Road station at seven and we go together on the train over to Birkenhead. We could meet Phillip in the refreshment room at the Woodside station. In all the coming and going we'll be pretty anonymous there.'

During the weekend he went carefully over his plan, looking for parts that might fail; where he might have underestimated the risk of suspicion falling on himself; where his co-conspirators might not understand or be able to perform their roles properly. He viewed the whole project as an exercise. It had its internal logic and the parts seemed to him to resemble the workings of a precision-made clock or watch. Or a well-constructed chess problem with its solution.

By Sunday evening he was confident of putting the plan to Jordan and Davies and that neither would be able to pick holes in it.

On the Monday morning, the 12th, he told Janet he would go to the chess club that evening to play a tournament match he'd had hanging over him for a while and that he would be home somewhere around eleven.

At twenty to seven he left the house and took trams to the station at Breck Road.

After a few minutes he was joined on the platform by Davies and they travelled together to Lime Street station. A short walk to another station and from there through the tunnel under the river to the Cheshire side, from where they walked to Woodside station, the terminus for the Great Western trains that ran down to Chester, Birmingham and all the way to London. During the journey neither man said much. Bruce was rehearsing what he was going to say. Davies was subdued – not his normal garrulous self. As they entered the refreshment room at half-past seven there was no sign of Jordan. They took a table in a corner. It had been a good choice. The place was full and the population shifted and surged with the movement of trains, the occupants of any table swiftly replaced by a new set. Waiters in smart jackets with white apron fronts over their trousers moved about carrying drinks and food. It would be hard to remember any particular person in such an atmosphere.

After ten minutes he began to feel anxious. He knew far less about Jordan than about Davies. Had he decided not to play? Davies, too, kept looking towards the door, then back at Bruce, frowning and biting his lower lip.

'Did you tell him where we were to meet? He couldn't have gone somewhere else, to another station, and be waiting for us there?'

'No, it was definitely here. For the reasons you said. It's a big refreshment room. Lots of other people.'

'You made it clear to him what's at stake. For him especially?'

'I did, Mr Bruce. I couldn't have made it clearer.'

He reflected, saying to himself, *Yes, knowing you, you're so unused to telling the truth you probably toned the message down.* He leant forward and spoke into Davies's face.

'I've been very patient considering the damage you two have done me. If he doesn't come tonight, he doesn't get a second chance. He's ruined.

Davies looked away, then pulled Bruce's arm. 'He's here. Thank God.' He raised his arm.

A thickset, powerful looking man crossed the room, weaving between the tables. He was wearing the same cap and bulky overcoat Bruce remembered seeing that afternoon before Christmas. He nodded to Davies but did not offer to shake hands with Bruce.

'Good evening Phillip', Bruce intended to keep the atmosphere friendly yet purposeful. 'I'm glad you've come. Thank you.'

Jordan did not reciprocate. 'Glyn says you've got something to propose to us, Mr Bruce. Let's have it then!' He had a strong Liverpool accent and a surprisingly high voice for such a big man.

'I expect Glyn told you my position as far as all this goes, Phillip. My wife has been committing adultery with you two and that puts me in an intolerable position. I certainly have grounds for divorcing her and your names would be joined in the petition as co-respondents. But I understand from Glyn that my wife has threatened to blackmail you by revealing your adulteries to your future brother-in-law. It seems to me that it would be better for all of us if my wife ...' He hesitated. He still could not say the words. Only a euphemism came to his lips, '...were out of the way.'

Jordan looked straight at him from under bushy brows. 'What do you mean by that?'

He blinked and went on, avoiding the direct answer to the question. 'I've come up with a plan. It'll work and I'll tell you how.'

Jordan leaned forward, his head thrust toward him across the table. 'When you say, "out of the way", exactly what have you got in mind? Go on, let's hear it.'

Just then the waiter arrived to ask them what they wanted. Bruce said tea, Jordan followed suit, and Davies went for a fizzy lemonade. While they waited for their order, Bruce decided that rather than let Jordan dominate the meeting he should expose his plan to them.

'What I have in mind is this. Next Monday evening I shall go to the chess club at the café because I have another match to play. Like this evening, I shall tell my wife I'm going, but unlike tonight, I really shall go. I'll get there at a quarter to eight prompt. At a quarter past seven you, Glyn, will telephone the café. You know the number? Well, of course you do, you have your drama rehearsals there.' Davies nodded. 'Good. The time is important, no one will be there then who knows my address. You will ask if I'm there. I won't be. You'll ask for someone in the chess club to pass a message to me when I arrive. It'll almost certainly be the chess club captain, he's always there early. You'll tell him you're anxious to see me the next evening at seven-thirty because you have some business for me. Now this is the essence of the whole plan and it's vital you get it right, Glyn. Give him an address in Mossley Hill, Number 25 Menlove Gardens East; East mind, get that in your head. There is no Menlove Gardens East. There's a North, South and West but no East. I know that for a fact. It's all new houses round there but your old boss lives not far away, Glyn, as you'll recall, so I've made sure the address doesn't exist. Because it's all new, nobody at the club's likely to know there is no Menlove Gardens East. Stick to the simple message, Glyn – you want to see me tomorrow night at that address about possible business and will they please pass the message on to me. Tell them it's important I get it because you haven't time to call back. Oh, and make sure if one of the café waitresses answers your call first that she doesn't recognise your voice. From when you're speaking your lines, or whatever it is you do.'

He stopped and looked at each of them. They did not move, their eyes fixed on him.

Bruce continued to unfold his plan. 'Now that message means I shall be out of the house, miles away, on the Tuesday evening from a quarter to seven to half-past eight. Next Tuesday. A week tomorrow. I shall be looking for a client I've never called on before at an address I've been given and making sure plenty of people know I'm trying, or have been, to find it.' He paused. 'Understood so far?' The other two nodded, he could feel their concentration, the physical pressure of it upon him.

The waiter came with their refreshments. It provided a useful break, giving Bruce time to go over the next step in his head.

'We need a name for this caller. One that whoever takes the message will write down carefully – and remember afterwards. Any ideas?'

Jordan took an old envelope out of his jacket and wrote on it, then pushed it in front of Davies.

'S N McQuillian', Davies read out. 'Where d'you get that from?'

Jordan pulled a face. 'Oh, an insurance customer of mine from way back. I borrowed his premiums when I was short and the Company made a fuss about it. He's not a name I'd forget in a hurry.'

Bruce was shocked at the way Jordan gave them this news. He seemed to think nothing of it.

Well, now he knew what got Jordan thrown out of the Company. What a fine pair the two of them were. Not an honest bone in either of their bodies. But then, that's why he was trying to recruit them.

'Very good, Phillip. Certainly a name I'd remember if I heard it once. McQuillian. Like MacWilliam, only odder. That'll do perfectly!' He smiled at them both. Neither of them returned his familiarity.

Bruce moved on to the next stage. 'When I get home from the chess club I'll tell my wife about the message and the possibility of a decent commission. She'll egg me on to go and I'll say I will. So on the Tuesday morning she'll know I'll be out of the house and quite a long way away for a large part of the evening. Now we have an outstanding bill at the doctor's which I'll tell Janet to go and pay, and to make sure she does I'll get her to leave the house at the same time as me, around ten o'clock. I'll walk with her down to Cabbage Hall where I'll take a tram to work and she'll walk along Priory Road to the doctor's. I want you, Glyn, to catch up with her and tell her you two want to visit. It's Tuesday, so that'll be no surprise. You'll need to keep an eye open for her – the best place to wait is by that telephone kiosk on the triangle near the Picture House. You know it?' Davies nodded.

'You'll have to start work a bit later than usual that morning, won't you? I'll have mentioned to her at breakfast that her sister-in-law wants to drop in during Tuesday afternoon – she often does, anyway, so she'll suggest you both take advantage of my being out until after nine. To have a nice, relaxed time.' He smiled again at the other two. They remained tense, their faces betraying the strains that had taken hold of them. What they were being told was no joke. Bruce went on. 'You tell her she can expect you just before half-past seven. You can't get there any earlier because Phillip has to come after work.'

Bruce leant forward, his face closer to the others, his voice quieter. 'Now the scene is set. I've gone out about six forty-five. She's on her own, expecting you. She's left the yard door unbolted after I left so that's your signal all's clear. But only you, Phillip, knock at the kitchen window.'

At that, Jordan lifted his head, licked his lips and shifted on his seat. 'You never answered my question directly did you? I know what all this is about. You want her dead and me to do the job for you, don't you?' His voice was pitched even higher than normal, the emphasis on the word 'me' reflecting a mix of disbelief and resistance.

'Keep your voice down, Phillip. Yes, you. Only one person can do this job.'

'Why not Glyn?'

'Because he'd fail. He doesn't have the guts. And he doesn't need to silence her as much as you do.'

Jordan clutched the sides of the table; knuckles white. Whiter even than his face. 'No, I won't do it. You can't ask me to. I'm not perfect but I'm not a murderer. Bloody well do it yourself.'

Bruce began to get up from his seat. 'Very well, then. I'll start the divorce proceedings in the morning.'

Before Bruce reached his full height, Jordan let out a moan of despair. 'No, wait.'

Bruce saw a dog he'd forced into a corner. It would like

to attack him because he threatened it but it wouldn't dare. He had a memory from long before in India where once he'd seen natives being forced to do something degrading. He'd felt their hatred for their oppressor but saw they understood if they refused they'd be thrashed within an inch of their lives. Jordan looked just like them and Bruce knew intuitively he needed to watch out. He had to get Jordan to accept he'd put himself in the corner and that Bruce was there to show him how to get out of it and have a clear run at his marriage; to help him manage what he'd got to do.

'Look, Phillip. You want a clean break from this mess you're in. Freedom from any chance my wife might get in touch with your brother-in-law to be. Freedom from the fear that rumours might reach your fiancée. The only way we can ensure it is the way I'm proposing. Doing it can be easy, quick and painless. Get her to take you into the parlour. Ask her to light the fire. Take a few steps back into the passage and grab my mac off the hook. Go back in and while she's bending down throw it over her head, grab the iron bar from the hearth and give her a quick bang on the head with it. That'll stun her – she's an old woman, remember. Then turn her on her back, get one of the cushions from the sofa and hold it over her face so she can't breathe. She'll be gone in a matter of minutes.'

'If you're so bloody clear about how to do it, why don't you do her in yourself, then?'

'Because, Phillip, if I do it, the police'll be on to me straightaway. I shan't have an alibi and when I'm questioned and in court later, the whole story'll come out and you'll still be the centre of attention. Mr Brophy won't be pleased and I'm sure his sister-in-law will be disgusted. If I go down, you go with me. My way, the police will have no idea who could have done it. They can't suspect me because at the time she died I was miles away and they'll have no other possibility. Obviously I'm not going to give them any idea I know who did it, am I?'

'He's right', Davies said, 'he's got it all worked out.'

'All right for you', Jordan turned sharply on his friend. 'You aren't going to have to finish someone off with your bare hands are you?'

For the first time since he had formulated his plan, Bruce had serious doubts. Perhaps he'd overestimated the strength of his power over Jordan, and the man's willingness to accept that his future depended on following the plan. He'd expected Davies to be the one to have cold feet, to try to wriggle out of his part. But then, it wasn't Davies who'd have to smother Janet, was it? He watched Jordan and wondered whether he'd already lost this game.

This isn't how I meant to play him. Reading his face, hearing his voice, seeing the way he's sitting, he knows he's trapped. But he's angry because Davies and I will benefit from a crime only he has to commit. And not just any crime. Premeditated murder. Have I put too much reliance on his ability to carry out Janet's execution calmly, efficiently and without remorse? It's a bit late now if I have. I'm trapped too. If I carried out the threat I just bluffed them with I'd gain nothing. I'd still be stuck with Janet and suing for divorce would merely hasten my own end, even if by doing it I destroyed Jordan's chances. No doubt he'll create others. But I'll never again have a chance like this. I have to convince them my plan is fool proof. That if we just follow it to the letter the police won't look at us. That it's certain the crime will end up in a pile of unsolved cases in some detective's office.

'Phillip. We're going to make this look like a common enough crime. A housebreaking gone wrong. There've been a number of burglaries in the area in recent times. This'll look like another, but one where the burglar was surprised by someone coming downstairs and finding him. Before you leave you take the cash box down from the shelf in the kitchen where it always is, where I keep the collections before I pay them in, and you take what's in it. Throw the box on the floor. Then out the back door. You're leaving in a hurry – you've just been interrupted and had to silence the woman who's seen you. When you're outside you use the iron bar again to jemmy open the window into the scullery – where the sink is. Make sure you're wearing gloves the whole time. Down the yard, into the alley, then into Richmond Park where I'll be waiting. Tell me everything's gone according to plan and then Glyn will take you to his car and get you wherever you need to go. I'll give you plenty of time to get out of the area before I discover what's happened, get witnesses and call the police. You get rid of the iron bar somewhere well away from Swindon Street and you're out of the story. For ever. And so's Glyn.'

He paused. Davies nodded. Jordan's hands still gripped the edge of the table, his knuckles white. He did not nod. Bruce went on to the final result of his plan.

'The police'll assume it was our friend The Anfield Housebreaker. Who they haven't caught in more than two years. We couldn't have a better set of accomplices than the Liverpool Police. They couldn't catch a cold. Our local housebreaker may well be one of them anyway. Most people wouldn't be surprised.'

He sat back in his seat. 'Well, what do you think?' For all the world as if he'd outlined a plan for a relative's surprise birthday party.

Davies said. 'It's a good plan. Sounds like a perfect murder. And if they ever do catch your housebreaker they won't have enough evidence to charge him with it. They'll think there must be more than one of them.'

That was music to Bruce's ears. He rather liked it. 'The perfect murder.' He'd feel content going to his grave knowing he'd accomplished that; it'd be like bequeathing a chess problem only a grandmaster might solve, and even then not for many years. During what was left of his life no one would recognise it for what it was; he'd leave a clue among his papers. Yes, he liked that.

But Jordan remained silent, his fingertips drumming on the table top. After almost half a minute he turned to look at Davies, his voice far from friendly. 'That's what I thought you'd say, Glyn. You're a scally. Do it first, ask questions afterwards, that's your way. I know a lot more about our police than either of you. If they find this Anfield Housebreaker and pull him in for murdering Mrs Bruce while committing burglary they won't be that particular about the whys and wherefores of it, they'll make the charge stick. He'll be topped. And he'll have been innocent. I don't know about you but that'll be on my conscience as well as the other thing for the rest of my life; I'd have to make a hell of a lot of money to make that go away.'

Bruce eyed him carefully. 'I hope you don't mean by that you've had a brush with the police?'

'No, never. And it doesn't matter how I know the way they work. I just do.'

'Well, beggars can't be choosers', Bruce said, 'in any case, once the housebreaker sees the attention he's getting – though he knows it wasn't him – he'll probably either stop for a good while or more likely turn his attention to somewhere else.'

Jordan shrugged. 'All right, I'll do it.' To Bruce he had, on the surface at least, accepted that taking the role of a murderer was the lesser of two evils.

Bruce's attention was now concentrated on schooling the two in the commission of that 'perfect murder'. He needed to hear them each recite back to him the details of their part and know they'd marked, learnt and inwardly digested. The preparation, the timings, the action.

'Let's leave and walk slowly back to the station. Each of you go over for me what you have to do and when. When we get to the station we split up. After tonight we don't meet again until I see you, Phillip, at half-past eight next Tuesday in Richmond Park near the alley to my house. Oh, and both of you make sure you have a story to cover your whereabouts next Tuesday evening, one that other people can support.'

When he got back home he gave Janet a spirited account of his victory at the chess club and appeared not to notice her complete indifference as she busied herself with the various end of day tasks. He climbed into their bed exhausted and tense. It had been hard work and now the released adrenalin flooded him. The endgame was in progress. If he kept his nerve and his pawn did what he had to, the opposing queen was soon to leave the board.

Two days later he committed to his diary a coded sentence that encapsulated the agreed outcome of that evening. 'Wednesday January 14th. Reading very interesting book by J Lays published in 1889', he wrote. As he did so he prided himself on his ingenuity. He had put down on paper the cryptic notation of the execution of his plan. Slay J at 7.29 pm. That execution was now fewer than five days away.

For the final three days of the week Bruce had an attack of 'flu, picked up no doubt from the densely crowded, germ-filled winter atmosphere of a busy railway station refreshment room, if not from his fellow train passengers on the previous Monday. In his bed he sweated and shivered alternately, aching and miserable, adding to his fever the fear that his best-laid plans would be white-anted by whatever minute bacillus had entered his system. His dreams were of a much younger Janet and her lover, Jordan, tying him to a chair and forcing him to swallow poison. In another, the decomposing body of his wife in a threadbare shroud followed him down the street while all the neighbours stood at their doors and pointed at him. The main subject of these hallucinations had taken up her bed on the sofa in the kitchen and behaved as though he were putting it all on, something he was used to. But by the Sunday midday he came back to life, played duets with Janet for his sister-in-law and nephew and awoke a morning later to the week when all his planning would come to completion, and a new life could begin.

Part 2

Execution

6

The Telephone Call

Monday, January 19th 1931
Bruce awoke to weather that seemed designed to provide a perfect backdrop to the events due to take place within the next forty-eight hours. Not that he would for a moment have accepted the concept of a celestial scene-setter, but the windy, cold morning with its pulses of sleet did suggest funeral weather and mourners chilled to the bone, praying, if for anything, for the rite to be over and to be back in the warm.

Over breakfast he told Janet he had another tournament game to play; he had been asked the previous Monday evening and had agreed. He felt he ought to go down and get it out of the way, though given the weather he'd rather not have to. Janet said she supposed he'd better go if he must but not to stand around outside gossiping. 'After all', she reminded him, 'you've been hanging around the house having your bout of 'flu.' He interpreted that as 'and now it's my turn' – as if in response she told him she too had a sniffle and a tickle at the back of her throat.

Every other Monday Bruce took the afternoon off work so he was back home for dinner by two-thirty and afterwards could escape up to his room to catch up on bookkeeping and, more to the point, contemplate the evening's developments. He and Janet had tea together about six. Her incipient cold seemed to be coming along nicely.

Leaving his house by the back yard gate just before twenty past seven, he walked slightly less than half a mile to a stop where a tram then took him within spitting distance of the city centre café. Here the chess club met on the lower ground floor.

Just before twenty to eight he came down the steps into the café, the warmth welcoming even though he had had at most two to three minutes' exposure to the raw evening between getting off the tram and the café doorway.

He looked around at the familiar area given over to chess club activity. Dark wood panels, cream walls, tables set out with chess sets, some members, heads down, already concentrating on the early phase of a game. Over there was the notice board that had details of tournament games decided and those still to be played, and nearby the cubicle containing the telephone with the café number etched into the glass door.

Bruce was nervous but also aware he must not show it. He knew what was supposed to happen. That there would be a message but he would have to be patient and wait for it to come to him. But what if for some reason it did not? That Davies had welshed on their deal. Or that a waitress took the call and somehow didn't give it to a club member. Or Davies had made the call later than he had been told to and had been given the Swindon Street address by Michael Collinson whom he spotted as soon as he arrived. Collinson lived just yards away from him and was the only club member who knew his address. If Davies had rung at the time he should have Collinson would not yet have arrived. That was the whole point of the timing – that and, of course, Bruce not having arrived either.

Bruce looked round for but did not see the opponent he was supposed to play. Collinson drifted over to him and confirmed the other player was not there. Collinson and Bruce had been friends for many years and had been the founders of this club nearly ten years ago. Collinson suggested a friendly game but Bruce excused himself saying he had spotted McCorquodale with whom he also had an outstanding tournament game. The two settled down to play. Collinson, without an opponent, wandered round the room, stopping at the board where Knight, the club captain, was playing. Bruce had been covertly watching Knight and saw the captain get up from his game. As he approached, Bruce appeared to be totally immersed in developing his opening.

'I've got a telephone message for you, Mr Bruce.'

Bruce did not look up. In fact his concentration was far from on his next move. He now knew the project was off and running; the first element had happened at the right time and in the way he had ordained. 'Oh, who from?'

'A man named McQuillian!'

'McQuillian...' Bruce looked up now. He appeared confused. 'McQuillian?'

Knight nodded.

'But I don't know anyone called McQuillian.' Again the name was launched into the air for all around to hear. 'Who is he?'

There was a slight edge of asperity to Knight's voice. After all, he was the club captain and of a social standing significantly higher than Bruce to whom he had been placed in the position of a messenger. 'Well, if you don't know who he is, I certainly don't. However, I told him I'd pass the message on to you. He wants you to call at his house tomorrow evening at half-past seven. He lives at...' Knight consulted a manila envelope in his hand, '...25 Menlove Gardens East, Mossley Hill. He wanted you to know it's something in the nature of your business. He said he couldn't call you again because he's busy with his girl's twenty-first.'

Inwardly, Bruce was amused. Glyn had really set his stall out. But he'd done exactly as he'd been asked.

He shook his head as though this was all too much for him. 'I don't know the chap. Where is Menlove Gardens East? Is it Menlove Avenue?'

Knight now played his unintentional part in broadcasting this address. 'No, it's Menlove Gardens *East*.' And he put the crumpled envelope down in front of Bruce who made a production of pulling out a propelling pencil and a small pocket diary, then copying the name and address into it, emphasising the word 'East'. He handed Knight back his envelope. 'Well, I've no idea where it is but I suppose I'll find it.'

Knight and one or two other members lived in Mossley Hill but after some discussion it turned out none of them knew exactly where Menlove Gardens was and their suggestions as to how Bruce might get there were varied and vague.

In spite of, or perhaps because of, his inner delight at the success of the first part of his plan he managed a win over McCorquodale. At the end of the evening, just before ten-thirty, he and Collinson went home on the tram. Bruce was in high spirits and repeatedly went over his strategy and tactics in beating a player most people thought was better than him. It was not until they were walking the short distance from the tram stop alongside the high brick wall of the old Union Infirmary towards their homes that Bruce said, 'It's a funny name. I've never heard it before, have you?'

'I think I've only ever heard of one person called McQuillian', Collinson told him. Bruce mused that he wasn't sure he'd bother to keep the appointment, it all seemed rather strange. They parted and each went to his own house.

At bedtime Janet made a performance of blowing her nose and said her cold was getting worse.

'You ought to go to the doctor in the morning and get something for it. There's an account of his needs paying too. Perhaps you could kill two birds with one stone. When I go to work tomorrow we'll walk down to Cabbage Hall and I'll get the tram from there. You go on to the doctor's.'

Janet sniffed. 'But I've got a cold. You shouldn't ask me to go out.'

'You can wrap up warm. You'll only be out half an hour. The bill's overdue; it ought to have been paid two weeks ago.'

Then, almost as though his memory had been jogged, 'Someone left a message for me at the chess club. An address in Mossley Hill. Said he wanted me to call tomorrow evening; he'd put some business my way. Something to do with his daughter's twenty-first. Could be an endowment. Nice bit of extra money if it is. Don't know how he came to have my name, though, so I'm not sure if I'll go.'

'You go', she said, 'goodness knows we could do with the money. So you'll be out tomorrow night as well? What time would you be back?'

'Depends on how long it takes to do the business. Nine, half-past. I'll sleep on it.'

'Hmmm' and she lay down and turned away from him.

7

The Alibi

Tuesday, January 20th 1931

As soon as she was awake, Bruce told Janet he'd decided to keep his appointment in Mossley Hill that evening. Breakfast was slightly earlier than normal because of her visit to the doctor. Then the two set off through the damp streets to walk along Lower Breck Road to where it met Townsend Lane. As they approached the triangle of grass at the junction, Bruce thought he saw Davies's car parked over to his left. He didn't show that he'd seen it nor did he see Davies himself. The couple parted there, Bruce going right towards the tram stop, his wife crossing over the road and walking on up Priory Road towards the doctor's. It was just after ten past ten.

Even on this day of all days he didn't depart from the routine he'd followed for so many years. He worked his morning round and came home for dinner around two-fifteen. The rain had stopped; a cold front with some sunshine and a fresh breeze had taken its place so he hung his mackintosh on a peg in the passageway, put on a warmer topcoat and left again for work.

At about three-thirty, as he was walking along Maiden Lane between calls, a speck of grit blew into his eye and he rubbed it with his sleeve. This made it worse and finally he was only able to clear it with the old-fashioned trick of pulling his eyelid over the lens and flooding it with tears.

He completed his list of calls shortly before six, boarded one of the buses that now supplemented some of the tram routes, and was home for his tea at the usual time of about ten past six.

Janet had bought scones on her way back from the doctor and they sat down to eat. Unless something went unaccountably wrong this would be the last meal they would ever eat together. He was surprised at how unmoved he was. Somehow it didn't seem to affect him as it would have done even as late as the previous week. All he could think of now was what life was going to be like once tonight was over and done with. His needs being attended to; proper meals decently cooked; the sympathy and understanding of neighbours over his loss; the house clean and uncluttered – and he'd start with the table in this kitchen. An absolute muddle. That was how it had been for so many years and even at the very end it was no different. That was all going to change. He looked at her as she chewed. She had absolutely no idea he knew exactly what was going on in her head. Nor that he had engineered the evening activity she was looking forward to so that by tomorrow the fun and games would be over for good.

He called to her that he'd go up and change his collar and wash. Then he'd be off. 'And you'll be back between nine and half-past?' He noted her keenness to be reassured as to the time. He knew why.

'That's what I'd expect if it's an endowment policy he's after.'

Just after a quarter to seven he walked briskly to his tram stop. All his life he had suppressed his emotions and learned not to display either facially, bodily, or vocally whatever excitement or turmoil might be within him but this evening he felt almost jaunty. The pools of light from the streetlamps, the shadows between them, the shining steel of the tram tracks, everything seemed to be sharper and more in focus than it normally was for one who walked around with his head down. It felt good to be in the final stages of a plan that would establish that by any rational calculation he could not have killed his wife and therefore it must have been done by person or persons unknown as the phrase went. There'd be witnesses she'd been alive when he left the house; while he'd been getting ready he'd heard the *Echo* land on the floor inside the front door and Janet take it into the kitchen and then her speak to the milk boy as she handed him back the can. Almost immediately afterwards he'd gone out into the back yard telling Janet to bolt the gate to the entry as on his return he would, as he usually did when out in the evening, come in through the front door. And he'd told himself that was the last time he would ever see her alive. By the time he returned, the unfortunate, though necessary deed would have been done and he could start easing himself into what remained of the new life, observing, of course, a decent period of grief and adjustment to his loss.

He was on his way to the tram stop by St Margaret's Church at the corner of Belmont and West Derby Roads. Here the Number 26 would take him to where he could change to one going south-east towards Menlove Avenue. Although at the chess club he'd expressed general ignorance of the tram routes to Mossley Hill and had canvassed opinions on how to get there, he knew perfectly well. Every time he, with or without Janet, had been to visit his sister-in-law he had come this way. The flat she rented was in a house a short step from the route he would change to, the Number 4, when he joined it at the start of Smithdown Lane.

When the Number 4 arrived at six minutes past seven his first objective was to advertise his unfamiliarity with the tramway system and draw attention to being a stranger to the area. Having ensured he was the last passenger in the queue, as he put his foot on the platform he called to the conductor, 'Is this car all right for Menlove Gardens... East?'

'No', the conductor called back, 'you need a 5, a 5a, a 5w, or a 7.' Bruce made to step back off the tram. 'No, get on. I'll give you a penny transfer ticket. You can change to the right one at Penny Lane.'

Bruce stepped on to the platform and then dropped himself into the corner seat just inside. 'I'm a complete stranger to this area', he told the conductor, 'and I've got an important call to make in Menlove Gardens East.' As the tram rattled its way in the dark along Smithdown Road, Bruce seized yet another chance to flag up his intended destination and his need for help in finding it. As the conductor passed him to collect from the upstairs passengers, he said, 'You won't forget, will you, it's Menlove Gardens East, I want?' A little further along a ticket inspector stopped the tram and he, too, was drawn into the exchanges. He came down to where Bruce sat. Above the rattling of the car he called, 'The conductor says you don't know how to get to the Menlove Gardens area. You need to get on a 5a at the Penny Lane interchange.' Bruce thanked him. Now there was no question but that the conductor, the inspector and every other passenger on the lower deck, would remember his nervousness, unfamiliarity with the tram routes that served the area and the name of the suburban road he was so anxious to reach.

When the tram arrived at the interchange the conductor was insistent Bruce take the Number 7 car which was waiting. This degree of help was actually problematic because Bruce knew perfectly well which car to change to. He had travelled the route several times in the past either to visit Calderstones Park or Woolton Woods with Janet. He didn't want the 7 but the 5a, to which he hurried in spite of the shouted warning from the conductor of the car he'd just alighted from to take the Number 7.

He was only on the 5a for a stop or two but even in that short time he'd made it clear to the new conductor, and anyone else within earshot, that he needed to be put off the tram at Menlove Gardens East. A short way along Menlove Avenue, the conductor called him on to the platform and pointed out a road running away to the left. 'That's Menlove Gardens West. You'll probably find where you're looking for over in that direction.'

Bruce repeated the formula he'd been uttering all evening. 'Thank you. I'm a complete stranger around here.' And stepped off the tram. It was twenty past seven.

Crossing over the left hand carriageway from the tram tracks that ran along the centre of Menlove Avenue, he was now in a residential area several degrees more salubrious than both where he lived and worked. The houses along the Avenue were probably not much more than ten years old, mostly detached with garages for the car and substantial front gardens. The edge of the Avenue was lined with trees, the street lighting good and a steady flow of motor traffic as well as the passage of trams in either direction. A nice place to live and the right kind of area for Mr McQuillian and the twenty-one year old daughter for whom he was considering an endowment policy.

Bruce walked up Menlove Gardens West. Here the houses were perhaps slightly smaller than those along the main road but were even newer, three to four years at the oldest. There was a sizeable triangle of open grass and Bruce, holding to the right of the road, reached Menlove Gardens North which led eastwards. A little way along here he spotted a woman, silhouetted against the indoor lights, coming out of a house on the other side of the road. He crossed into the middle, raised his hat and called to her. 'Excuse me. I'm looking for Menlove Gardens East. Do you know where it is?'

'Not really', she called back. 'But it's perhaps an extension of Menlove Gardens West, which is just up there'. She pointed. 'It's all so new round here it's hard to keep up with where anything is.'

Bruce thanked her and, as though following her suggestion, retraced his steps, turning to the right along the part of Menlove Gardens West he had not already walked. Here, new-built and partly finished houses were interspersed with those already occupied; the further into the Gardens area he went the more it became a building site and the more likely that people he asked would not be sure that there wasn't a fourth Menlove Gardens.

Here he ran into a young man and repeated the question he had asked the woman he had seen a few minutes earlier. 'I don't think there is a Gardens East,' was the response and the young fellow, seemingly in a hurry, went on his way but not before Bruce had voiced his intention to call at 25 Menlove Gardens West in case he'd been given the address incorrectly.

He was as good as his word. At Number 25, but in Menlove Gardens West, he asked the woman who answered his knock if a Mr McQuillian lived there. The answer was 'No'.

'I was told he lived at 25 Menlove Gardens East. This isn't it, is it?'

'No, this is 25 Menlove Gardens West. And no one with that name lives here. In fact, I've never heard that name before. Mind you, we've only lived here a few months and it's all new round here. Seems to be growing all the time. Who told you there was an East?'

'Well, I had this phone message yesterday asking me to call at 25 Menlove Gardens East to meet a Mr McQuillian because he had some business for me. It's funny isn't it, there's no East.' And with that he lifted his hat again and walked off back to the street.

Now he walked up Menlove Gardens North, noting that the house numbers were all even, and then where it emerged onto Menlove Avenue he saw someone waiting at a tram stop – the next one up from where he had got off. He made a point of crossing over the road to the stop and asked the man if he knew where Menlove Gardens East was. He got a shake of the head. 'Can't help you, I'm afraid. Don't live around here.'

In spite of it being a chilly, wet winter evening Bruce had now managed to accost four different people in his search for the frustratingly elusive Menlove Gardens East and the occupant of Number 25, the unusually named Mr McQuillian.

He set off now to fulfil the most important element in the plan for the evening, the one support for his alibi that would carry the most weight.

Just past the tram stop, Green Lane crossed the Avenue. And Green Lane was far from foreign to him. His Farsight supervisor, Albert Willesden, lived at Number 34, a good-sized semi-detached between Menlove Avenue and Allerton Road.

Bruce crossed over the avenue and set off down Green Lane. His relationship with Willesden was comfortable. Bruce's age, experience, reliability and probity didn't call for much in the way of supervision and within his somewhat restricted notion of the nature of friendship, he regarded Willesden as a friend and the feeling was reciprocated. He'd made a number of visits to Green Lane two years earlier when Willesden had discovered Bruce's wish to learn the violin and had given him some initial lessons. The centrepiece of his alibi had always been to call on his friend – and chief – to tell him the story of the telephone message, the fruitless search and to ask whether he, Willesden, had any idea where Menlove Gardens East might be, since the other three Gardens were not much more than five minutes' walk from his front gate. The other people he had gone out of his way to ask information from were merely to prove, if it were ever to be necessary, that he had indeed been looking for Mr McQuillian in the right place and that this could be corroborated by the unimpeachable witness of his own chief on whose home he had stumbled as if by chance and to whom he had reported his failure and frustration.

As Bruce went through the gate into the front of Number 34 he was quietly yet deeply pleased with the way things had gone, both on that evening and on the one before. A few minutes later, as he opened the gate to step back on the footpath, he could barely take in that a central piece of his construction had gone missing. There was no one at the Willesden's. It hadn't occurred to him that the man and his wife might have gone out on a Tuesday evening. The silence surrounding the house seemed eloquently to confirm to him that the one person he'd relied on to testify to his full but fruitless search in the area wasn't available.

He might be no stranger to disappointment but this came as a shock. He'd been borne along by the smooth working of the plan so far and this was a nasty and disconcerting warning that plans are just that, concepts. He remembered reading somewhere about military plans and their not surviving intact the first brush with the enemy. For a few moments he stood on the footpath, his arms slack by his sides, his fingers clenching and releasing, breathing deeply. Then he began to walk slowly down to the junction with Allerton Road. On his previous visits he'd approached the house from the direction he was now going so he knew what he would find there. Shops and a large cinema where there would be any number of people he could add to those who had seen him and who would remember the time they had done so.

As he got to the end of the lane he spotted the very person he needed to make up for the loss of Willesden. A policeman. Bruce turned towards him. 'Constable, do you know of Menlove Gardens East?'

The reply was instant and straightforward. 'There isn't an East, sir. There's a North, a South and a West. Definitely no East.'

'I've been to Menlove Gardens West. The person I'm looking for doesn't live there. I'm an insurance agent, constable, and last night a Mr McQuillian left me a telephone message at my chess club asking me to call on business at Number 25 Menlove Gardens East. When I went along the Gardens North and South all the house numbers were even, so it couldn't have been one of them.'

'McQuillian. McQuillian. Well, I know this area well, sir. I've never heard of anyone called that. Try 25 Menlove Avenue. Maybe the message got taken down wrong.'

'Thank you, officer.' And then, as he was about to walk away, 'Is there anywhere I could see a directory?'

'I'd try the Post Office along there, sir. Or you might do as well at the police station,' he pointed in the opposite direction. 'Ask nicely and I'm sure they'll let you see the one they have there.'

Bruce began to pull out his watch. 'What time does the Post Office shut? It's not eight yet, is it? No, it's a quarter to.'

The policeman took out his own watch. 'That's right, sir, just on a quarter to,' and he proceeded at constabulary pace along Allerton Road.

'Thank you, again, officer.' Bruce watched him go with a good deal of satisfaction. He had just established on the most authoritative of evidence, a policeman's watch, that at a quarter to eight he was miles away from Swindon Street and couldn't possibly have been involved in whatever had happened there. All the same, he put the idea of going to the police station to look at a directory out of his head – it might just equate to putting it into the jaws of a lion, so he followed the policeman until he reached the Post Office. They didn't have a directory there. 'They might have one at Alldays over the road,' they told him, so Bruce crossed over.

At the newsagent, he asked for a local directory. One was found. Bruce laid it on the counter and started to leaf through it. The manageress came over. Bruce looked up. 'Do you know what I'm looking for?' Not surprisingly, she said she didn't. 'Well, I'm looking for Number 25 Menlove Gardens East.'

'There isn't an East. Just North, South and West.'

He repeated what he'd said to the police constable. It was the way to broadcast his fruitless search to as many ears as possible.

'I've been to Number 25 Menlove Gardens West but the person I was supposed to see didn't live there!'

The manageress pulled down her customer account book. 'Number 25 Menlove Gardens West isn't one of our customers. So I can't say who lives there. Sorry about that.'

'Do you have a McQuillian as a customer?'

She looked again through the book. 'No, no one of that name. Actually it's not a name I've come across. I think I'd know if we had a customer called that.'

Bruce acknowledged her help, riffled through the directory for a minute or two longer, then walked out of the shop and boarded a Number 8 tram to begin his journey back home and all he expected to find there. It was just after eight o'clock.

As the tram whirred and whined, grinding on the corners, swaying on the uneven tracks, its single eye and clanging bell bearing down on anything or anyone risking to cross its path in the darkness, Bruce settled in his seat and let the tensions of the evening drain out of him. His part of the business had gone well. He had travelled to an area far from where he lived, had established before several witnesses that he was a stranger to the place, only there because he'd been asked the previous evening to go to discuss business with someone he'd had no dealings with before. All right, he hadn't been able to add the call on his chief that was meant to have capped the arch of his alibi but the passage with the policeman pretty well made up for it. He turned his mind to the end of the return journey.

When he got home he was going to find his wife the victim of a strong and ruthless burglar who'd been surprised to find someone in the house and taken steps to avoid identification. He'd raise the alarm, the police would come. He'd explain he'd been out and tell them where and why. They'd look for clues but there'd be precious little for them to find and after a day or two things would quieten down. He'd pester the police for results of course; they'd get increasingly apologetic as the days passed and they were no nearer to finding the criminal. He'd give it a few weeks and then get in touch with Florence Tyler and arrange for her to come in and look after him. That would seem perfectly reasonable; he was in poor health, the person he'd been relying on to care for him had just been taken from him in tragic circumstances. The blow from his bereavement would make it the more essential he shouldn't try to struggle along on his own. So far things had gone very much as he'd planned them. He'd still got to deal with finding Janet dead in the house but what he'd find wasn't really so far removed from him than the living person who'd blighted the last five years or so of his life. Give it time and he'd be able to replace that dead relationship with strong and happy memories of an earlier one. The past few years would, as it were, be consigned to the attic of things he no longer wanted to be reminded of.

He noticed familiar landmarks from the other side of the glass mingling with the reflections from the interior lights. He'd have to get off at the next stop.

Just before eight-thirty Bruce stepped off the second tram at St Margaret's Church and retraced his earlier walk, which in three to four minutes brought him out through an entry or alley into Richmond Park. As he emerged a shadow moved out of the darkness of the entry opposite him, the one leading to his back door, the one he'd seen Davies and Jordan come from on the Tuesday before Christmas, just four weeks earlier. Bruce stopped and Jordan crossed the street to him. 'Well?' Bruce asked him. Under the low level street lamps he could see the other man's limbs seemed to be disarticulated and his teeth were chattering, but in spite of the cold Bruce could see from his face he was sweating heavily. 'Well?' said Bruce again.

'It's done.' Jordan blurted out. 'It's bloody well done and just see you keep your side of the bargain.' He seemed to be fumbling in his coat pocket for something but unable to pull whatever it was out. Just then someone passed them on the other side of the street. A young woman hurrying along on clicking heels who then crossed over to go into Letchworth Street.

'Did you do what I told you? Force the window at the back? Make it look as if someone broke in?' Bruce asked him in a loud whisper. He could see Jordan was shivering; he could not keep still. He simply shook his head, turned, and walked away quickly at first then breaking into a run along Richmond Park towards the main road and Holy Trinity Church.

Bruce crossed over and slipped into the anonymity of the dark entry. He used it to stop and try to pull his thoughts together before he went to his house.

All he had asked him to do was to meet him and give a quick run-down on what he'd find when he got in. He'd just seen a nervous wreck who couldn't put two or three words together, a madman with starting eyes and terror written all over his sweating face. He hadn't done the second most important thing in the plan. He hadn't left any signs of a forced entry and a robbery. Yes, Bruce had had some doubts but he had thought Jordan would show coolness and detachment, especially as he'd had time to prepare for it and his future depended on doing it efficiently. God knew what was waiting for him in there.

With growing apprehension and a feeling that things had slipped out of his control, he went up the entry and turned into another that emerged in Swindon Street between Numbers 19 and 21, then walked the four doors down to his own. As part of his plan he'd intended to draw his return to the attention of his neighbours either at 27 or 31 or both by knocking loudly at both his front and back doors in a way he thought would be bound to bring them to their own doors to find out what was going on. He would tell them his key did not seem to work in the lock as though it were deadlocked from the inside. But no one came to either of his neighbours' front doors so he retraced his steps to the entry that ran behind the houses and found, as he expected, that the door into his backyard was unbolted. He banged on his back door. Again no neighbour appeared. He went back to his front door and repeated what he'd already done, again with no result. Already disoriented by the state of Jordan and his unsatisfactory report he was returning in some desperation to his back door when, just before he reached the entrance to his own yard, his neighbours from Number 31 appeared in the entry in front of him. With hats and coats on they were clearly going out. Blessed relief allayed the panic that had begun to tear at him.

Thank goodness he'd run into them at exactly the right time. He was beginning to worry about how long he might have to knock on each door before he aroused enough curiosity from the neighbours on either side. His luck was in – if he'd come home ten or so minutes later the Springers would have gone out and he'd have been wholly reliant on the people at 27.

Even after living next door to them for ten years Bruce was not on familiar terms with his neighbours. Janet might have spoken to Sybil Springer from time to time and on the odd occasion invited her into the front room, although he wouldn't have been told about that anyway. Ted, the husband, had never to his knowledge been inside his house. He needed them now, though, to bear witness to the fact that Janet was dead. First he had to make sure they recognised his anxiety over being unable to get into his own house and his wife not answering his knocking to open either door. He also needed to engineer it so he went into the house before they did, discovered the murder of his wife and invited them in to see it.

Mrs Springer was polite. 'Good evening Mr Bruce'.

'Have you heard anything unusual, any noise, coming from my house in the past hour or so?'

Oh, damn it, that wasn't what I'd meant to say. I thought they were just going to walk off and I was desperate to get their attention. I should just have sounded anxious; surprised to find the yard door unlocked and not able to open the doors; my wife, who wouldn't have been out this evening, not answering my knocking. Why should I assume they'd have heard anything untoward? If they had, they'd have told me as soon as they saw me.

'Why, what's happened?' Mrs Springer asked him.

He recovered somewhat. 'I had to go out this evening on business. Now I seem to have been locked out.'

Mr Springer asked, 'Have you tried the back door into the kitchen?'

'Yes, but it won't open either.'

'Try it again. If you can't manage it, I'll see if my key will fit.'

Bruce walked away towards the back door then turned briefly toward the waiting couple.

'She won't be out; she has such a bad cold.'

He reached the door and gave the handle a twist and a push. It opened immediately.

'It's opened now', he called.

Just as he had hoped and expected, Mr Springer reassured him. 'We'll wait a minute. See if everything's all right.'

Inside his house Bruce quickly discovered that Jordan had indeed made no attempt to simulate a burglary. The scullery window remained closed and the cash box in its usual place high up on a shelf in the main kitchen. Moving quickly, he ran upstairs calling 'Janet', loudly enough to be heard by the waiting neighbours. He turned up the gas light in their bedroom and struck a match to see into his laboratory both of which would tell the watchers he had gone upstairs to look for her. Then he ran downstairs into the kitchen where he ripped the door off a cupboard he'd made for his photographic equipment and threw it with some coins from his pocket on the floor. Going along to the front door he set the snib on the lock so his failure to unlock his front door could easily be explained. Finally he pushed open the door into the front room where a single gas lamp on a low setting gave just sufficient light for him to come face to face with the outcome of his pact with his co-conspirators.

Any expectations that Jordan had followed his instructions on the way Janet was to be killed were blown violently away. Any suggestion that an old woman had been tapped on the head and then quickly smothered by a burglar caught in the act was rudely refuted. What he saw in front of him was not murder, it was slaughter and the violence with which it had been inflicted stupefied him. He could only gasp, then, as a modicum of self-possession returned, move to turn up the light. That revealed in stark reality the blood splashed on the walls and the battered, still profusely bleeding, remains of what had an hour earlier, probably less, been his wife. Instinctively he reached down to take hold of her wrist. There was no pulse. How could there have been? What lay in front of him on the hearthrug had been beaten to death in a paroxysm of fury and of hatred.

Despair in the form of questions flooded his brain.

What has he done? What has he done? Such a mess. He's turned the room into an abattoir. It wasn't necessary. So cruel. Now no one's going to believe a burglar did this because in any case there's no sign of anyone breaking in. I have to think fast and make the best of it. Why did I ever think Jordan was the right one for this work?

He had no time to stand and contemplate the wreckage of his plans. The Springers were still waiting outside his back door. He had to act now as one who had come home to find the entirely unexpected murder of his wife in his front room.

He hurried out into the back yard. He was shaking. The logical and theoretical assumptions he had entertained that the dead Janet would look normal, even peaceful, and that it would be obvious that some intruder was responsible, had been superseded by stark reality. Nevertheless, what he said bordered on the banal.

'Come and look; she's been killed.'

Without a word between them the Springers followed him into the house, through the scullery and the kitchen to the door of the front room. It was clear from their gasps that his neighbours were as shocked by what they saw as he had been. He turned and saw Ted Springer reach out to take hold of the door frame before stepping into the room. All three bent to look closer.

Bruce murmured, 'They've finished her! They've finished her!'

Mrs Springer took hold of Janet's left hand.

'Oh the poor darling.'

'Is she cold?' her husband asked her.

'No'.

All three stood up. As neither family had a telephone, Mr Springer offered to go to fetch the police. Bruce agreed.

'Yes, and for a doctor but I don't think it's much use; they've finished her.'

The three retreated from the front room to the relative normality of the kitchen. The Springers were shown just how relative even this normality was. Bruce pointed out to them that one of the doors of a cupboard filling the left hand recess next to the cast-iron range at the other end of the room had been torn from its hinges and lay on the floor together with a few coins.

'See, they've wrenched that off.' So there had been a robbery as well as the brutal murder in the next room.

Mr Springer asked, 'Is there anything missing?'

In response, Bruce drew himself to his full height, reached up to the top shelf above the cupboard, seven feet above the floor, and brought down a small metal cash box; it was not locked.

He peered into it, poked about in it with his long, bony fingers and then pronounced in his fussy voice, 'about four pounds. But I can't say for certain until I've checked my books.' However he put it, he could not make it seem more than a paltry sum to have killed someone for, an impression reinforced a moment or two later when, after he had been upstairs again to see if anything else had been taken, he told them, 'Everything's all right up there, there's five pounds in a dish they haven't taken.' The impression he intended to give was that this was a burglary disturbed by a householder. Having killed the witness the burglars fled with what they could grab on their way out which had been very little.

Mr Springer left by the back door to fetch the police. When he had gone, his wife and Bruce were drawn again to the front room where they both knelt on opposite sides of the body. This time when Mrs Springer took hold of Janet's hand she told Bruce it felt as if the flesh was distinctly cooler than it had been not many minutes before.

'They've finished her', Bruce repeated, 'look at the brains.'

Poor Sybil Springer, traumatised by the experience of seeing the devastation of another human being with so many injuries and those so raw, could think of nothing else to say but, 'I wonder what they've used?'

At that Bruce was struck by the possibility that Jordan had compounded his failure to do as he had been instructed by leaving the iron bar in the room with the body. He couldn't see it and surreptitiously patted round the edges of the rug to feel if it had been pushed underneath it. He was relieved to find nothing.

The pair stood up and then Bruce peered forward again, bending from the waist. He was looking over the body from the left side and had seen something tucked in under the right side bunched up around the shoulder and the neck.

'Why, whatever was she doing with her mackintosh – or my mackintosh?'

'Is it your mackintosh?' asked the distraught woman.

Bruce stooped again and this time touched the material. 'Yes, it's mine.'

Part 3

Investigation

8

Enter the Police

Tuesday, January 20th – Wednesday, January 21st

At ten past nine there was a rap at the front door of Number 29 Swindon Street and Mrs Springer went to let the caller in. She found she couldn't open the door and turned to Bruce for help, which allowed him to demonstrate why he hadn't been able to open it with his house key. He released the snib or catch, with which it had been deadlocked from the inside and then he was able to open it. Following up Ted Springer's report of the crime to the nearest police station, a local man, PC Evans, stood outside. Bruce greeted him with, 'Come inside Officer, something terrible has happened.'

Evans went straight into the front room. The first thing he did was to take hold of Janet's right wrist, which up to then had been under her body as she lay on her right side and in doing that he changed the position of her body. Bruce saw him feel for a pulse; knew he wouldn't find one. 'I felt her wrist when I found her. It seemed still warm to me, so it couldn't have happened a long time before.'

Evans straightened up. 'It's still a bit warm. How did this happen?'

'I don't know. I'd been out to see about some insurance business in Mossley Hill. I only found this', he gestured towards the body, 'when I got back home.'

'Let's have a look upstairs,' Evans said to Bruce and ushering Bruce in front of him they stopped on the landing. The constable peered, with Bruce looking over his shoulder, into the small laboratory and workshop. It was in darkness but Bruce, from the landing, told Evans that nothing had been disturbed or was missing. Evans turned away and gestured toward the gas light on in the bathroom.

'Why's the light on in here?'

'It's usually on in the evening. It gives a bit of light at the top of the stairs.'

Standing at the door of the middle bedroom the policeman asked Bruce, 'and why's the light on in here, too?'

'It's our bedroom. I changed in here before leaving to go out and probably left it on myself.'

Then Bruce drew Evans's attention to the pound notes sticking out of a jar on the mantelpiece and started to remove them.

'Here's some money they haven't taken.'

'Put it back, sir, immediately. That's potential evidence.'

Looking around the room, Bruce volunteered, 'No one seems to have been in here.'

Evans, however, took a further look and then they moved on to the larger front bedroom directly above the crime scene. This room was unlit but looking through the open door the disorder was obvious, the bedclothes only half on the bed and two pillows on the floor – although there weren't the obvious signs of the housebreaker's modus operandi; the ransacking of the room for valuables, open drawers and cupboard doors with the unwanted items thrown about. The two men came back downstairs and went into the kitchen. Mrs Springer knelt huddled next to the range where she had managed to get a proper fire going from the embers. Bruce told Evans about the money missing from the cash box. Then, rummaging around under the cloth covering the kitchen table, he produced Janet's handbag which had been lying on a chair only partially concealed. Bruce muttered, seemingly to himself, 'they didn't find that then. They must have left in a hurry.' He was now fully aware that since nothing seemed to have been taken from the bag and there were no signs of burglary upstairs, the police would conclude that if Mrs Bruce had been murdered in the course of someone or other's committing a robbery then the robbers were quite remarkably inept at what should have been their primary activity. From there, Bruce reckoned, they would go on to consider whether the woman's murder had been the main event and the signs of a robbery a crude attempt to divert attention from that. Such was the position that Jordan's incompetence had landed him in

Finally the two men returned to the front room where Bruce lit the left hand gas light on the chimney breast. Evans then closed the door on the scene and both men returned once more to the kitchen.

Around twenty minutes after Evans's arrival his immediate superior, Sgt Donoghue, arrived and the two began an examination of the front room. Bruce, standing in the doorway, saw how, in the better light, Evans bent forward to look at something tucked in behind the head and shoulders of the body. He stood up and said to nobody in particular, 'That looks like a mackintosh.'

Bruce turned to the coat rack in the passage leading from the front door.

'It's an old one of mine. It usually hangs here.'

Before either of the officers could follow up this revelation, there was another knock at the front door and a big man, taller even than Bruce, thrust his way into the narrow passageway.

This was The Honorary Advisor to the Liverpool and Birkenhead CIDs, a strongly-built, handsome man with an immediately obvious air of self-confidence, a professor, no less – Professor Ernest McLintock – occupier of the Chair of Forensic Medicine at Liverpool University and Examiner in Medical Jurisprudence at a number of others. He took charge immediately, ordering everyone out of and away from the crime scene and set about examining the body and the area surrounding it. He had come to establish three things. How death had occurred, when it had occurred and, if possible, any information that might help the police with their job of finding out who was responsible for its occurrence.

Bending down beside the body, he saw a large opening in the left side of the victim's skull some two inches wide by three long, through which bone and brain tissue bulged out and from which some of it had soaked into the hearthrug. When he examined the back of her skull, on the same side as the opening, he found a deep depression and the back of the skull had been deformed and forced upwards towards the crown. A hair pad the victim had used to make a bun had been wrenched off her head but was still attached by blood and brain-matted hair. While her hands had bloodstains on them they held nothing nor did he find any blood beneath her fingernails. There could be no doubt about the cause of death. Blows with something heavy delivered with great force to the victim's head, although it would have been impossible at that stage to say how many.

His next, and most vital, task was to establish when Janet Bruce died. McLintock had two ways open to him to do that which he ought to have used in combination. Although by no means a wholly reliable guide, he could have made observations of body temperature over a period, taken ideally with a rectal thermometer, which he could compare with a formula that plotted the rate of cooling and therefore indicated a window of time within which the victim could have died. The other means was observation of the progress of rigor mortis – the amount of time it takes for the body to become rigid – but without the cross-check of the body temperature decline it was notoriously open to inaccuracy, being dependent on the age of the victim, her state of health, build and weight as well as the air temperature round the body. But when he searched his bag for the rectal thermometer McLintock could not find it. He had to rely solely on measuring the progress of rigor mortis and to save himself from the embarrassment of admitting he had been careless, he had to make a virtue of relying on it.

McLintock was well aware that rigor mortis could start within two to six hours after death and his first impression was that in this case it was just starting. So death had probably occurred about two hours before he arrived which would have put it around ten to eight.

McLintock knew too, of course, that the rate of progress of rigor mortis was significantly related to the age of the dead person. The older, the quicker the progress. So he called Bruce into the room and asked, 'How old is Mrs Bruce?'

Bruce recognised the dilemma. He had enough basic

medical knowledge to know if he told McLintock Janet's real age, the Professor would reckon the progress of rigor mortis to be quicker than if he said she was the same age as he was. If he did that, however, and there was any public statement about her age it would cause great surprise to those who knew them and might well arouse suspicions that he had recently found out Janet's true age and that he was therefore not as well disposed towards her as he'd always made out he was. So he told McLintock fifty-two, the same age as himself. To McLintock, therefore, the victim was middle-aged rather than elderly. The temperature surrounding the body also has an effect on the progress of rigor mortis since the body cools more rapidly if the surrounding air is chilly. The outside temperature that evening had been no higher than forty-two degrees Fahrenheit, and even though the body had been on the draughty floor of an unheated room yet Mrs Springer had found her still warm to the touch at nine o'clock and Evans felt some residual warmth a quarter of an hour or so later. McLintock, who certainly was aware of this effect, did not ask either of them about it.

He examined the blood splashes on the walls. Most of them were in a line that took in the left hand far corner of the room opposite the door and extended in one direction along the back wall of the room and in the other along the chimney breast. Some were almost at the level of the picture rail, though the majority were about four feet from the ground.

The next arrival, at five past ten, was the head of Liverpool CID, Detective Superintendent Patrick Connor, accompanied by a sergeant. With a noticeable Irish accent, Connor was heavily-built with dark red hair brushed away from a centre parting and the bearer of a prominent and intimidating moustache. He stayed no longer than to do a quick appraisal of the crime scene. Bruce, who was hanging around the door into the kitchen, heard Connor ask McLintock if he had any thoughts on the time of the woman's death. 'I'd say from the progress of rigor mortis, around two hours ago,' was the response. Connor got a verbal report from Evans as the first policeman to arrive and a short account of what had happened since a quarter to nine from Bruce and the Springers. When he found that neither Bruce nor his neighbours had a telephone in their home, Connor and his sergeant returned to the local police station to contact his superiors and initiate a police search of doss houses, all night cafes, railway stations and anywhere else a man, probably blood-stained, might have tried to go to ground.

Between Connor's departure and his return at ten-thirty, three other senior policemen called, attracted like wasps to a jam pot, and made this small house decidedly crowded. And not just crowded; as well as McLintock, each began in his own individual, undirected and non-forensic way to examine the body and the house from top to bottom for clues, perversely contributing to the contamination and possibly the disappearance of the very evidence, if any there was, they were looking for. In those hours immediately after the crime they fully justified Bruce's comments to Jordan and Davies a few days earlier that the local police were likely to cover any tracks the murderer may have made. One of them, Det. Insp. Bright, who arrived with his sergeant, actually knew Bruce whom he acknowledged with a curt nod. He had had an insurance policy with Farsight for many years and Bruce collected the regular premiums.

Mrs Springer had sent her daughter to fetch Bruce's sister-in-law and his nephew from their flat a mile or two away and they added still further to the numbers now congregated in Number 29.

In the midst of all this coming, going and tramping over the tiny house, Bruce sat forlornly in the kitchen, only then, an hour and a half later, reacting to his discovery with tears, smoking one cigarette after another and mindlessly stroking the cat on his knee.

It was as though he'd frozen or turned to stone in that moment when he first saw Jordan's fearful handiwork for himself; the utter devastation of a woman he had once loved and, in spite of what he knew about her and his need to be rid of her, had never hated. How different the removal of Janet in theory and the awful reality of it. When he moved, when anyone, even his relations, spoke to him it was as though he had no feeling, was numb with all his senses suspended and his body disjointed. But behind the outward effects of shock he was beginning to recognise the position he was in. He had expected Jordan to carry out his task coolly and efficiently, mentally ticking off the things he had to do to achieve the objectives of a quick and relatively clean killing of Janet and leaving evidence from which the police could only assume this to be a murder committed in the course of another crime by someone unknown to the victim. Now he cast his mind back he had been concerned about Jordan's response when told of his allotted task but he had placed his faith in the man's doing, in a workmanlike way, what was needed to protect his future. And look what had happened. He hadn't allowed enough for the unexpected, for the imperfections of human nature. Jordan had snapped, had used excessive violence as a madman might, and had wreaked such havoc even the police seemed to be appalled.

It was this separation from the reality that surrounded him that led him to say to Mrs Springer, pointing at the people milling about in and out of the rooms and up and down the stairs, 'If Janet had seen all this she would've gone mad.'

Until he'd encountered Jordan in Richmond Park not much more than an hour and a half earlier, he'd been quietly confident he was going to achieve his objective with the minimum of fuss, and had already cast himself in the role of innocent co-victim of a terrible but random crime. The un-jemmied window meant, and he knew it, that the suggestion of a break-in by local burglars was so flimsy as to be laughable, and the damage inflicted on the murdered woman such that the police would strain every nerve to find the homicidal maniac who could have done this. And they would soon work out that whoever that person was had been let in rather than having broken into the house. He was now at some risk of being seen as implicated. Still, he thought, I have a good alibi. I certainly wasn't in the house when she was killed. I need to keep my wits about me, appear to be suffering from shock and be as helpful to the police enquiries as my role would lead them to expect me to be.

His impassivity might, however, be interpreted as an unnatural degree of control and possibly callous indifference to what had happened.

He'd acquired this carapace of detachment and resignation when faced with disappointment and frustration because he'd had a great deal of those two to put up with in his life. It served him again, now his plan to assure a peaceful, even enjoyable final few years of life had been marred by someone else's failure to carry it out; Janet messily and inhumanly battered to death in their front room; the touches not made that would have had the investigation off on a false scent right from the start. A final proof that he could expect nothing positive from life and that a stiff upper lip together with anaesthesia of the brain was the only way to make any of it bearable.

When Connor returned he set about looking for evidence of a forced entry. It was the natural thing to do considering the number of burglaries in the area over the past few years. But there was nothing at all that indicated a break-in at Number 29. He asked Bruce where he had been that evening. Bruce told him of his journey to Mossley Hill in pursuit of insurance business. He then showed Connor the broken cupboard door in the kitchen and lifted down the cash box from the shelf. 'They've taken four pounds from this', he told him. Connor saw the hinge was broken. He also saw the few coins scattered on the floor. 'Where did you find this box when you first went into this room?'

'Up there where it was just now.'

Connor rubbed his chin.

'I can't understand why a thief would go to all that trouble, putting the lid back on the box and then stretching up to put it back where he found it', he told Bruce.

Bruce shrugged, remembering that his instructions to Jordan had been to remove the contents and throw the box on the floor.

As the local constable had done earlier, he asked Bruce to follow him upstairs. Was there anything in Bruce's laboratory-cum-workshop that was missing, that might have been used as a weapon? Bruce assured him that everything was in order. In the middle bedroom Connor noticed the banknotes in the jar above the fireplace and, without touching them, peered closely at them. He looked into the front bedroom, 'Was this room in this state earlier today? Before you went out?'

'I can't say. I haven't been in this room for at least a fortnight as far as I know.'

Back downstairs, Connor went first to the front door and asked Bruce for the key. He went outside, shut the door and then opened it with the key. 'It seems all right to me but the lock is badly worn,' Bruce heard him say, but before he could explain that he had found the catch down on the lock, Connor had motioned for him to go back into the kitchen and had himself swept into the front room and started an examination of the body. After a minute or two he called Bruce from the kitchen. 'How were the blinds in this room when you got home?'

Bruce sensed the need to be careful what he said. The front room should have been in darkness. Janet had obviously lit one lamp to provide a background light to what she expected Jordan to do with her.

'They were drawn and there were no lights on', he told Connor. 'I lit a match'.

'Didn't you cry out or shout?'

'No, at first I thought she'd gone into the room and had some kind of fainting fit. My first thought was to see to her.'

Connor turned his attention to the mackintosh tucked in by the right side, none of it appearing to be beneath the body. 'Is this your mackintosh?'

Bruce stood there, his fingers digging into his cheeks, his voice and brain no longer working together. In his plan there had been none of this close, almost hostile, questioning. Connor repeated himself in a slightly different form.

Did Mrs Bruce have a mackintosh like this?'

Again, silence from Bruce. That he had already said it was his to Mrs Springer and to the two policemen who were earliest on the scene, Connor could not know. The Superintendent told his sergeant to pull it out from under the body; he did so and handed it to Connor who took the garment by the sleeve and shook it out.

'This is a man's mackintosh', he said holding it out towards Bruce.

Bruce stretched out his hand and took hold of the coat but still did not speak.

Now it became clear that the coat was heavily blood-stained inside and out, and also that the skirt of it had been burnt.

Bruce spoke.

'If there are two patches on the inside it's mine. It is mine. I wore it this morning but the day turned out fine; I wore my fawn coat this evening. Of course it wasn't burned like that when I wore it.'

'Where did you leave it then?'

'Hanging in the hall at half-past one'.

This would be a long, long day for Bruce. At twenty to midnight Connor invited him to go along with Bright and the sergeant to the local police station to make a statement. At the same time the powerful arc lights Connor had earlier arranged to borrow from the fire brigade arrived and were being set up to light the house from outside, front and back.

The police activity around the Bruce home had attracted the attention of a fair number of the population of that part of Liverpool in spite of the late hour and the winter chill. As he left the house with the two officers the crowd in the street shuffled and murmured. He was sure some of them would assume he'd 'confessed' and was being 'led away'. It wouldn't take much for one to tell others he'd seen the glint of handcuffs.

As soon as Bruce arrived at the Anfield Road police station it seemed ominous to him that although he'd made it clear his wife was already dead when he found her, he was first examined for any traces of blood on his hands or on his clothing. There were none, but it suggested to him that the CID already had a view about the solution of this case.

Then he made his formal statement to Bright, beginning by asserting that, 'My wife and I have been on the best of terms all our married life', and going on to give a detailed account of his whereabouts and doings during that day. From about half-past ten in the morning until just after two in the afternoon he said he had been on his insurance round. As usual he had returned home for his lunch, he called it 'dinner', which gave him an hour's rest before he returned to his round again, this time exchanging his raincoat, which he had worn in the morning, for an overcoat because the afternoon was cold but dry. Shortly after six he was home again and had tea with his wife.

He said he'd already decided to go later that evening to pursue some potential insurance business from which he expected there could be a substantial commission. He had an appointment for seven-thirty in a part of Liverpool a few miles from his house but well off his 'patch' and which he had been asked to keep through a message left for him on the previous evening. At that stage he said nothing about how, where or when he had received that message. He said he left his house at a quarter to seven and then described his journey by a series of trams to the address he'd been given. When he arrived in the area where he supposed the address to be he couldn't find it in spite of making enquiries at houses in the area, of a police officer and then at local shops; in every case the person he was asking either didn't know where it was or thought it didn't exist. A look in a local directory confirmed that there was no such street and at eight o'clock he had given up and gone home. He described the difficulties in getting into his own home and then how he had met his neighbours just as they were about to go out. Finally he came to the part where, having looked all over the house and seen the damage to the cupboard in the kitchen, he found his wife lying on the floor in the front room and, 'Concluded she was dead.' He also told the police he had first noticed the mackintosh at the back of her body as soon as he had discovered it, not the second time when he'd had Mrs Johnston with him. He ended the statement, 'I have no suspicion of anyone.'

Once he'd read and signed it, Bright asked him if his wife would have been likely to let any caller in while he was out.

'No, not unless she knew them personally; if she did, she would show them into the parlour.'

'Did she have any money on her?'

'I think she had some, but I don't know where she kept it.'

Then he told Bright about the message that had sent him to Mossley Hill that night.

'Do you know anyone called McQuillian?'

'No. I said at the time I didn't know anyone called that.'

'Do you have any idea who might have sent the message to the chess club?'

'No, I can't think of anyone.'

'Did anyone know you were going to the club?'

'No, I didn't tell anyone I was going and I can't think of

anyone who knew I was going.' Bright didn't follow that up by asking if he had not even told his wife.

After giving his statement Bruce was left to sit in weary, chain-smoking misery. About three in the morning Connor arrived back at the police station. Entering the interview room he talked in a low voice to Bright, then dropping a copy of the statement on the table he turned to the man who had made it.

'Is there nothing more you'd like to tell us, Mr Bruce?'

Bruce shook his head.

'You're sure?'

Bruce replied from the depths of exhaustion. He could hardly keep his eyes open. 'What about?'

Connor did not respond, stared hard at him, picked up the statement and left the room.

His day was even then not yet over. The police had made it clear he could not return to sleep in his own home and arrangements had been made for him to stay with his sister-in-law. He was driven there in a police car and Bright took statements from the two relatives, only leaving finally at five having told Bruce to be at the offices of the CID in the city at ten. They had further questions to ask him.

Bruce didn't sleep at all; his brain wouldn't allow him to.

Janet hadn't been dead even twelve hours and his plan was beginning to unravel. They hadn't actually said anything to confirm it but he couldn't help feeling the police were already looking at him as a suspect. He was sure he wasn't imagining it; Connor's attitude to him all evening and then finally at the police station and Bright's terse instruction to present himself at the CID Office in Dale Street certainly didn't give him the feeling they saw him as a victim deserving of their sympathy. Still, no matter, his alibi was rock-solid. At the time Janet was killed he could prove he was miles away and the police would never in a month of Sundays get the idea he was the puppet-master behind it. Three people, including him, conspirators in a murder to a carefully constructed plan; that would be far beyond their powers of imagination. He needed to keep reminding himself that the police were really a bunch of clodhoppers. He could easily keep several steps ahead of them. All he had to do was check himself when answering any questions they put to him, make sure he didn't say anything that gave the slightest hint he knew any more than they expected from a husband who returned from an evening looking for a business contact and found someone had murdered his wife in their home.

The police should be thinking that whoever made the call to him at the chess club wanted him out of the way so that his wife could be killed. The caller was probably the murderer himself. The call could have been made from anywhere in Liverpool, or even from somewhere else. Where would the police begin looking? Why would anyone want to kill Janet? Well, if that damned Jordan had done his work properly it would have been obvious. His house was next on the local housebreaker's list. They'd seen him go out. They might have thought Janet had gone with him so there'd be no one at home. They were caught in the act. They had to get rid of the witness. But the situation was very different now. The police must now have to work on the probability her killer was someone she let in, or who forced his way past her, who murdered her and then tried to make it look as if it had been done in the course of committing theft.

Should he tell the police about Janet's son? He might well have taken vengeance on his mother for the humiliation he had from her. But if he told them about that they'd ask him how he knew about the son and when he knew. And he'd destroyed the letter. If the police accepted there was an illegitimate son they might well assume he, the husband, had killed Janet because he'd found out about it. And if they didn't believe it, then he'd obviously made it up to put them off the scent. No, he decided, better not tell them anything – for the same reasons he'd told that professor Janet was only fifty-two.

9

Questions

Wednesday, January 21st

Before Bruce set off for his appointment at Dale Street, Violet told him, 'When we were all in the kitchen last night I had a quick look in Janet's handbag. There was an old letter in there from a sister called Frances with an address in Brighton. I wrote it down. We ought to let her know what's happened.'

'Yes, she mentioned Frances once or twice in the past. I didn't know they'd had anything to do with one another, though. You're right. I suppose she'll be the only living relative Janet had. I've never heard of any others.' He trailed off, 'She never said much about her family. None of them came to our wedding.'

Violet sounded her usual efficient self. 'Leave it to me. I'll find out how to reach her. I'll try the post office. She might be on the phone in Brighton but if not I'll send a telegram. Don't you worry about it ...'

'Thank you, Violet, you're very kind.'

'Not a bit of it. You've got enough on your plate you poor man. I think it's jolly unfeeling of those policemen to want you to go down there this morning. You need to get some rest.'

'I know, I know. But I'd better go. The sooner they've asked all their questions, the sooner I can start thinking about the funeral.'

When he got there no one seemed to know what to do with him. He was lodged in a series of offices, being moved to another when the one he was sitting in was needed by a detective, and mostly left to sit on his own, working his way through a pack of cigarettes. Around mid-morning Bright found him and asked him to go through his visit to Mossley Hill the previous evening. In his search for the elusive Mr S N McQuillian, who had he spoken to and where? Bright took copious notes. Then he was left alone again. Towards lunchtime Bright came back and this time escorted him to Connor's office.

'I understand you employ a maid,' the Superintendent said knowingly. 'Tell me about her.'

Bruce was puzzled. 'I don't know what you mean by a maid. We've never had a maid. Who told you we had?'

'We had a caller this morning who told us you do.'

'Look, my wife had someone come in for a morning once a week to help her with the cleaning. Someone one of her friends put her on to. I've no idea what her name is nor where she lives but I wouldn't describe her as a maid, would you?'

Connor grunted. Bruce felt he ought to squash that kind of rumour and make the police look stupid for even suggesting it.

'Anyone who thinks we are, or were, the kind who could afford a maid must have a pretty fertile imagination.'

'All right, all right.' Then Connor shouted to his secretary outside his office door, 'Get Inspector Bright in here. Go and wait in the interview room Mr Bruce.'

'There's some money I need to pay in to Farsight today. May I leave to do that?'

Connor waved him away. 'Yes, but get back here once you've finished.'

Bruce thought it a good example of just how the police were grasping at any straw that Connor should have been so keen to catch hold of the idea he and Janet had a maid. From the Superintendent's face and the way he'd thrust his body forward towards him, he'd thought he was on to something. Bruce ran his tongue over his lips. The police would be inundated with titbits of information, some real, others invented, about those involved in the case. Any murder brought them out like flies buzzing and clustering round fresh dung. Did the police think the maid had killed her mistress? It was more likely they'd jumped to the conclusion the maid had been *his* mistress and he'd done what any husband did in such a situation; got rid of his wife. A thin smile spread across his features. Keeping a mistress. With his disease? Fat chance.

As he was leaving, Bruce was told his nephew, Alfred, was in the building and asking to see him. They walked together towards the Farsight offices, also in Dale Street, and Alfred told him why he had come into the city centre to find him.

'Mother said to tell you Aunt Frances is arriving tonight at six-thirty. Lime Street. Mother and I'll be there to meet her off the train.'

Bruce was surprised and expressed it. 'What, coming all the way here? From Brighton?'

Alfred explained. 'She runs a boarding house in Brighton so they'd got a telephone. Mother managed to speak to her early this morning to tell her what had happened to Aunt Janet. She asked Mother to call her back and that's when she said she was leaving on her way up here and would be at Lime Street on a train from Leeds at half-past six. It's a terrible business isn't it, Uncle. How could such a thing have happened?'

'I don't know, Alfred. I'm at my wits' end trying to make some sense of it. Thank you for coming down to tell me. Let your mother know I'll be at the station too.' He left Alfred to make his way back home, went into the Farsight offices to do his paying-in and then back to Police Headquarters.

Back there he puzzled over why this sister, who'd never visited Janet in all of sixteen years, would make a very long and tiring train journey once she was dead? Maybe she knew, too, that Janet had misled everyone about her age. Maybe she had known long ago and always disapproved. He supposed it was possible she might even know Janet had had a child and disowned it. If that was the case it would make for a difficult meeting and very awkward if she brought it up. He'd have to pretend he didn't know. Where was she going to spend the night if she was getting there at half-past six?

Nevertheless later that afternoon he asked Bright if he could go to Lime Street for the rendezvous with his sister-in-law. Bright went off to see Connor and came back to say he could go but that he should return after her arrival as there were other questions to ask.

Bruce met up with Violet and Alfred just before the train bringing Frances was due. Bruce still felt uneasy about the meeting. 'How are we to recognise her?' he asked Violet.

'We won't, but she'll see us. I told her there'd be three of us together and more or less what we looked like. She'll find us, don't worry.'

She was right. As the carriage doors opened, only a few compartments up from where they stood a small, well-dressed, middle-aged woman came towards them accompanied by a man. As they reached the waiting three, the man set down the woman's bag on the platform, bowed from the waist in an old-fashioned way, touched the brim of his hat and then walked on past them towards the barrier.

Alfred stepped forward to do the honours and picked up her bag. 'Aunt Frances? May I introduce my mother, Mrs Violet Bruce and my Uncle Walter?'

'And you must be Alfred. Thank you all for meeting me. I've been on the go since early this morning. But it's always nice to find a fellow passenger who's a proper gentleman and interesting to talk to.' She extended a small gloved hand. Each of them took it formally. As they walked towards the barrier, Bruce heard Violet ask her if she had made any arrangements to stay in Liverpool. It seemed she hadn't. 'Well, we'll be more than happy to put you up,' Violet assured her.

This immediately presented a problem. Frances would obviously need to have Alfred's room and he would bed down on the sofa in the living room. Where did this leave Bruce? He thought straightaway of returning for the night to Swindon Street. Any reluctance he felt at having to do this, to go back and spend the night in a house still splashed with his wife's blood, was outweighed by his embarrassment at meeting Janet's sister this way. Not only because of what he knew and suspected she knew about Janet's past and misrepresentation of her age but because she looked like a better turned-out and slightly younger Janet and he could not face the prospect of a length of time in her company. In any case it would be completely impractical for him to add to the numbers at Ullet Road. So he told them he had to return to the police office and would make his own arrangements for the night. He saw them into a taxi and then walked wearily back to Dale Street.

He spent most of the next three hours there alone with his thoughts.

They were definitely treating him like a suspect. But what could they have to go on? As far as he could be sure there was nothing that could possibly incriminate him or link him to the person who did do it. The iron bar was definitely not in the house. Removing it was about the only thing Jordan had done as he was told. Probably it had been what he was trying to pull out of his coat pocket in those few minutes in Richmond Park. He, or Davies, would have disposed of it well away from Anfield where it would never be found. Simple self-preservation should have seen to that.

Around nine Bright came to speak to him. He looked down in the mouth. Bruce was secretly amused. He was willing to bet there had been another lead that hadn't gone anywhere.

'Do you remember the milk boy coming to the house yesterday evening?'

'I can't say I remember him calling. I was upstairs getting ready to go out. I thought I heard my wife say something to someone and shut the front door just before I came downstairs to leave. But I couldn't be certain of it.' He was about to ask Bright what the importance of the milk boy's call was but the Inspector was already half out of the door. Bruce called to him, 'I can't stay with my sister-in-law again tonight. My wife's sister's come up from the south coast so there's nowhere for me to sleep there. May I go back now to Swindon Street for as long as she stays?'

'I'll have to ask the Superintendent.' And Bright was gone.

A little later, just before ten, he came, together with a sergeant, and motioned to Bruce to go with them.

'Superintendent Connor says you may go back to Swindon Street tonight but only for tonight. Tomorrow night, no. By the way, I might as well warn you, we've taken away the toilet bowl – as evidence.'

Bruce was puzzled. Evidence of what? Why the lavatory? But thought better of asking.

'I'll manage, there's an outdoor one too in the yard.'

He was taken back to his home in a police car and left to his own devices.

At one point in his insomniac vigil he recalled lines from Macbeth he hadn't read or heard since boyhood, about sleep knitting up the ravelled sleeve of care and, perhaps even more appropriate, about having murdered sleep and therefore sleeping no more. He had had the option, if so it could be called, of either the bed shared until two days ago with his wife whose imprint on the pillow and faint smell on the sheets he could yet detect, or of that in the front bedroom directly above the space still spattered with the same woman's blood. He had gone for the front bedroom as the lesser of the two evils, straightened out the disordered coverings, put the pillows from the floor back onto the bed, undressed and stretched out on it. Outside the street was quiet, the house itself silent and, he felt, distinctly unwelcoming, although he thought that was probably as much due to the range having been out for a day as to any irrational fear or foreboding about what had happened yesterday. After a while, finding the dark oppressive, he got up and lit the lamp, turned it down low, then propped up on the pillows to contemplate his position.

Ever since seeing how Janet's death had been carried out in almost wilful disregard of his precise instructions, the idea had rooted itself and then spread outwards that he had had no direct involvement in it. It was not what he had intended, therefore he was innocent of any connection with its outcome. The murdered woman had somehow been translated in his mind from the self-centred, parasitical hypochondriac who had come between him and his need for a quiet and comfortable progress down the final mile of the vale of years, who had kept dark secrets from him, who had deceived him, to the Janet of fifteen years previously.

That Janet was the real one. The one he loved and would have cared for and who would have as lovingly cared for him. The one who was a friend as well as a wife. Whose interests and opinions chimed with his. Who respected and admired his erudition and his intellect. In her going, her image had sloughed off the things he had disliked, resented, found difficult to live with, and what had been left behind were those characteristics he'd originally fallen for. And *that* Janet he would miss and mourn. Seeing Frances had shown him how Janet should have been.

This feeling of innocence and of being a griever gave him strength. He could face and cope with whatever suspicions the police might have about him. Bruce knew almost exactly when Janet died and he'd overheard the professor fellow confirming it to Connor. If the police went by what their medical experts said then he was miles from the house at that time.

The way she was killed; I never wanted it done like that. It was supposed to be clean. No blood. I told the fellow how to do it. None of that blood is on my hands. Jordan failed me. The man got himself in a state and left without even seeing to the simple job of making it look as if there'd been a break-in. Well then, he ought to feel a bit of the pressure, and serve him right too. The police won't have any reason to pursue him and he'll surely have his alibi ready, but if they did drop in on him it would concentrate his mind wonderfully on how grateful he should be that the woman's husband is taking all their attention and not him.

Still, maybe it would actually take the pressure right off me if I pointed the police in his direction – and Davies's. After all, they've both got records of helping themselves to other people's money and it wouldn't take the police long to uncover what they were doing with Janet. Then they'd know they'd got the actual murderer and his accomplice; they wouldn't bother looking any further. And if those two claim I coerced them into it, well it'll be my word against theirs. Me, with a string of witnesses to say how reliable and trustworthy I am and how Janet and I were a loving couple; them with a bad record at their employers' and with every reason to want to silence a woman they'd been having a sordid affair with, a woman who was blackmailing them, saying she'd expose them if they tried to put an end to it.

He wriggled to get more comfortable. It really was chilly up there, so he pulled more of the covers over himself. As if reflecting the increased warmth of his feet, he followed a less vengeful line of thought.

Perhaps turning them in like that would be going a bit far. And risky too. He didn't want neighbours – and relatives – knowing that kind of thing about Janet. How would it make him look? No, perhaps it'd be better to keep from an all-out accusation until he found the heat too much to bear. But he would put them into the police's picture. That should get them both visited 'in the course of enquiries' and keep them on their toes. The police had asked yesterday night whether Janet would've let anyone in late in the evening. He'd just kept it general – yes, if she knew who they were – but he didn't name anyone. Because the police had found no signs of a break-in they'd have to concentrate on the alternative. The killer must have been someone she knew. They'd expect him to tell them who Janet knew and would have opened the door to. They'd ask for a list. If they poked around at Farsight they'd soon find out Davies had been a frequent visitor to the house and stood-in for him two years before. If he didn't volunteer his name as someone known to Janet they'd find it strange. They wouldn't unearth Jordan there, no one at Farsight' knew about him covering at the same time as Davies. But once they talked to Davies – and they'd be bound to – he'd certainly tell them Jordan had been to the house as well, and again they'd wonder why he wasn't on the list.

He made up his mind. Tomorrow he'd give the police a list of names with just enough reference to Davies and Jordan to suggest that each had the inside information, and possibly the incentive, to steal any collection money. And to indicate that Janet would have let either of them in if they'd called to see him, and would let them wait if he was out. They'd both better have done as he'd told them – have strong and supported evidence they were nowhere near Swindon Street on the Tuesday evening – so if the police did interview them they'd quite quickly lose interest in them as suspects and wouldn't bother them again. That should send the detectives off looking for others who might have had motive, opportunity and no alibi.

As Bruce saw it, the way they should be thinking was that

someone who knew he was an insurance agent knew there could be cash in the house and had tempted him out for the evening. That someone knocked on the door of Number 29, gave Janet a name she recognised, and, as she opened the front door with a mackintosh over her shoulders because it was chilly, bundled her inside, pulled the raincoat over her head, dragged her into the front room and knocked her senseless. Then discovering there was hardly anything in the cash box, he went back into the room and took his disappointment out on her by beating her to death.

This sounded such a likely sequence of events that Bruce even imagined for a second that was how it had been, until he reminded himself of what really happened.

10

Important Information

Thursday, January 22nd

Accumulated weariness and confidence that his account of his activities on the evening of the murder would stand up to any further questioning allowed him to fall asleep at about three-thirty. When this second night exchanged its wearisome shadow for an anaemic daylight punctuated by the steady drip, drip of rain from the roof onto the bedroom window sill, he got up and immediately was confronted with the fact that he would not be making his wife a cup of tea that morning, or ever again.

His morning ritual was further altered. He could not use the upstairs bathroom, the entire lavatory bowl had been removed, leaving a gaping hole in the floor at the back. So he had to use the outside privy, a bit arduous in the morning cold. He then set about heating water on the gas stove for a shave, which he managed in front of an old mirror at the back kitchen sink.

He wondered how long it would be before he was able to spend another night in his home. If Frances stayed until Janet's funeral, and he knew that depended on the body being released from the mortuary, where else could he find a bed? He might have to ask if the Collinsons could put him up.

Because of what lay on the other side of that closed door into the parlour he felt sufficiently ill at ease to leave the house earlier than he usually did. He would go to a café in the city for breakfast. He went quietly out of the back yard into the entries, and from there into Richmond Park. That way he would avoid walking down Swindon Street past the curtains that were sure to be twitching as nosy and sensation-seeking neighbours observed his departure from what they no doubt regarded as the most notorious house in Liverpool.

At about quarter to eleven he presented himself at the CID offices in Dale Street and was shown into an empty room.

'I'd like to speak to Inspector Bright. I think I have some important information for him.'

He wasn't surprised when that officer was with him in a matter of minutes.

'I understand you have something you want to tell me, Mr Bruce.'

'Yes Inspector. You asked me on Tuesday night if my wife would have let anyone in while I was out.'

Bright took out a notebook. 'I did. You merely told me she would only open the door to someone she knew personally.'

'Since it happened I've been thinking a lot about who she might have opened the door to. People connected with my work, friends of ours, that sort of thing. Of course she would have asked who was there and got a satisfactory answer before she opened it. It's possible, I suppose, someone might have said he was somebody she knew but really wasn't and when she opened it, forced his way in. She wasn't a strong woman. Or in good health.'

The policeman looked up from his writing. 'Go on.'

'The point I'm trying to make Inspector is that the person you're looking for could be someone who knew I collected insurance premiums, thought there'd be a fair bit of cash in the house and knew enough to give my poor wife a name she'd recognise. When he found there was hardly any money there at all he flew into a furious rage and…'

Bright interrupted his flow. 'Mr Bruce, why don't we drop the speculation and get on with the list? Leave the investigation and the theorising to us. Let's do this formally shall we? You talk me through the list of people and at the end I'll have it typed up as a voluntary statement – your second one – and you can read and sign it.'

Bruce nodded his acquiescence and began to give a picture of Glyn Davies as one his late wife would have opened the door to because they had known him over three years and he had been to their home, particularly when Bruce had been ill at the end of 1928, when he had made several visits. He elaborated on Davies' tendency to be remiss with collection money, both at the time he'd doubled for him and later, when Willesden, their joint supervisor, had told him Davies' father had made up shortfalls. During the visits Davies made, he would, Bruce went on, have seen for himself how and where the cash and cheques from premiums were kept between collection and pay-in at Head Office. As he gave this information he was acutely aware he was walking a very narrow ledge, on the one side of which was the need to reassure the police he was hiding nothing and on the other the need to imply he had not seen much of Davies in the past two years. Any future suggestion of a collaboration between the two of them in the commission of the crime could therefore be put away as laughable. To bolster the first need, he volunteered he believed Davies had the use of or owned a car and was engaged to Iris Thomas, whose address he provided; to support the second he gave Davies' home address incorrectly and said he did not know who he worked for.

Even though he was aware of the tricky balancing act he'd engaged in he realised that once or twice he had compromised it. He'd at first claimed not to have seen Davies for at least a couple of months and then only in passing at the café where he played chess and Davies' amateur dramatic society met, yet a few minutes later he found himself telling Bright he'd seen him about Christmas time and had been given a business calendar. He wondered why Bright had not appeared to notice this discrepancy but was relieved not to be picked up on it.

He also inserted into his statements about Davies the existence of another man called Jordan, a friend of Davies', who had also done some of his work when he'd been ill and had visited the house. Janet would have opened the door to him, too. About Jordan he was far less forthcoming than about Davies, other than that he would also know of Bruce's procedures in handling collection money, and that like his friend he had a reputation for financial irregularities. Bruce told

Bright he didn't know where Jordan lived, what he was doing at the moment, nor anything else about him. He ended the list of those who would have been let in by Janet with his work supervisor, Willesden and his deputy, and friends including the Collinsons. He deliberately left another door open by saying, 'my wife had no friends unknown to me *as far as I am aware*.

Having discharged this part of his important information, Bruce went over the 'McQuillian' message at the chess club on the Monday evening and on to describe those he had spoken to in the Menlove Gardens area and Allerton Road on the Tuesday.

When he fell silent, Bright looked up from his note-taking. 'Is that it, Mr Bruce?'

Bruce wondered if he had heard disappointment in the Inspector's voice. Had he perhaps been hoping for a confession?

'Yes. If any of those had called when I was out, my wife would have let them in and invited them into the parlour. Of course, I don't mean to infer that whoever killed her is among the names I've given you. As I suggested, someone could have said he was one of those people just to get in through the front door.'

Bright did not follow up this offering. Instead he sat and looked at Bruce eye to eye for a moment. Bruce didn't like it but knew he mustn't show it disturbed him.

Then Bright said, 'I'll get this typed up as a voluntary statement further to the first one you gave us and you can read through it and sign it.'

He left the room but was back about twenty minutes later. 'The Superintendent wants you to go with me to your house to check on a few things. We'll have a car around in a minute. Oh, and there's a message for you. Your wife's sister has gone back to Brighton. You can stay at Ullet Road tonight.' The news that Frances had not even stayed twenty-four hours certainly surprised him, although he was pleased not to have to ask others to put him up. Having come all that way, surely she'd have wanted to stay for the funeral? Bruce put on his coat and followed him out into the street where they were joined by Sergeant Bowler who Bruce recognised from the evening of the murder. Shortly after, a police car pulled up to the kerb beside them.

When they got into Number 29 Bright told him, 'There'll

be people in and out for a few days, collecting bits and pieces and dismantling some of the plumbing upstairs, so take charge of any valuables, we can't guarantee they'll be secure.'

Bruce went upstairs and took the few bits of jewellery Janet had possessed, together with her Post Office savings book and an insurance policy.

'Are there any other policies?' Bright asked him.

'No, only this one.' And again the little sidestep, '*as far as I know.*'

'Now,' the detective informed him, 'we brought Mrs Clothier, your wife's cleaner, here yesterday afternoon. She told us a small poker was missing from the range in the kitchen.'

Bruce smiled. 'She could have thrown it away with the ashes. It'd be easily done.'

'And', the Inspector went on, 'she said there was an iron bar that was always in the hearth in the front room. It's not there now.'

In a calm voice and with an impassive face, Bruce said, 'I know nothing about an iron bar.' In his head he told himself he was pretty sure it wasn't still in the house. They were supposed to have thrown it away far from there, somewhere where no one would come across it and make any connections.

'She said it was used for dragging out spent matches and cigarette ends that got under the fire.'

'All I can tell you, Inspector, is that I don't recall ever seeing an iron bar.'

A silence fell between them. Bruce thought that would be the end of it but Bright then said, almost as if in passing, though Bruce knew perfectly well there was nothing casual about it, ' We gave Mrs Clothier's description of it to Professor McLintock. He thinks the blows to your wife's head could have been inflicted by a piece of iron like that. Anyway, we're conducting a thorough search for it. The killer might well have disposed of it shortly after leaving the house.'

'Good. I hope they find it and it leads them to whoever did it.'

Bright's response was, 'Mm!' and then, 'can you please give me the suit you wore last Tuesday?'

'What for?'

'We need to do some tests on it. To eliminate it from our enquiries. Now, if you please, show me where it is and I'll take it away. We'll let you have it back when we've finished with it.'

Bruce took him to the wardrobe in the middle bedroom. Bright produced a large carrier bag, holding it open for Bruce to drop the jacket, waistcoat and trousers into it.

As they returned mid-afternoon to Dale Street in the police car, which had been outside Number 29 all the while and attracted the attention of a number of the residents, Bruce stared out of the window.

To him it was now blindingly obvious. They were not treating him as a victim, a bereaved husband; in fact they hadn't done really from the first. If they were they wouldn't demand he attend daily at Police Headquarters and have to ask permission to leave. Taking his clothing, presumably to test it for traces of Janet's blood, just put the finishing touches to it. They must think he killed her. At least that was the impression Bright gave him. He wasn't too concerned with what Connor thought. It hadn't taken him long to work out he was a plodder of limited intelligence, the archetypal Mick. Left to himself Connor would never solve this case and provided Bruce didn't trip up, the man simply hadn't got the intellectual ability to challenge his alibi, apparent lack of motive and the considered way he responded to questions. Bright was a different matter; he worried Bruce. He'd got the intelligence his superior lacked and what made it more unsettling he gave the impression he'd already made up his mind. Bruce felt Bright *knew*. He mightn't yet have worked out the detail but must feel sure he would in the end. And the policeman's manner suggested both dislike for Bruce and that it would be a pleasure to charge him with the crime. It was that personal animosity Bruce found both distasteful – being unscientific and illogical – and dangerous.

Once back at CID Headquarters Bruce found himself taking part in an identity parade. The police had, in short order, pulled in a number of those he had claimed to speak to during his search for McQuillian in Mossley Hill. There were the tram conductors and inspectors, the young man he'd accosted, the occupant of Number 25 Menlove Gardens West, the police constable and the manageress from the newsagents. With two exceptions they all picked him out and the two who couldn't, the young man and the lady from Number 25, he offered and was permitted, to identify them instead.

When it was over, he felt it ought to be a positive step. Surely this meant the police accepted his alibi? If all these people had seen and spoken to him between half-past seven and eight how could he possibly have been at home murdering his wife? Surely they'd have to let him go, allow him to get on with his life?

But no, things followed the by now routine course. The senior detectives held meetings; Bruce was directed to sit in one or another of their vacated offices. From time to time Bright came in and asked a question, then went out again, presumably to settle some point that had been raised during these deliberations. Nothing changed until around half-past eight when a man in plain clothes Bruce had never seen before came into the room.

'Mr Bruce, I'm Detective Superintendent Turner. We've traced the telephone call to your chess club. It was made from a public call box somewhere in the Anfield district around seven last Monday evening. Thought you'd like to know.' Bruce nodded his acknowledgement of this piece of information and Turner left the room as suddenly as he had entered it.

Bruce took out and lit another cigarette and noticed his fingers trembled as he did so. Turner's appearance and statement had come out of a clear sky.

He was inclined to think this was a trap. Why hadn't Bright been sent to tell him this rather than someone he hadn't seen before? In the meeting they were having they'd have told Turner to tell him that; thinking that maybe by introducing a new and very senior face he'd be put off his guard. They were probably lying. How on earth could they have managed to trace a local call? And the timing was just pure guesswork on their part. They'd hoped to get some word or gesture from him they could add to the presumption of guilt.

He suspected them of playing some kind of a cat and mouse game with him. He had a rock-solid alibi for the critical presumed time of death and this had just been confirmed in the most definite way. Someone had made a telephone call to get him out of the house on the following evening and there were other witnesses who could confirm what time that call had been taken at the club and what message it had conveyed. Yet the police were constraining his freedom, getting him to go over and again a narrative of Monday and Tuesday evening which did not vary one iota every time he gave it, instead of coming out with an accusation he could repudiate and challenge them to substantiate or look elsewhere.

A feeling of urgency got him to his feet.

There are two things I must do. Get in touch with Davies and tell him the police might be calling on him very soon and that when he tells them of his movements last Monday evening to have them believe he was nowhere near Anfield so he couldn't have made the telephone call from anywhere in the Anfield area. How do I get hold of Davies? Didn't he say he spent most evenings at Iris's and that there was a phone there? Iris...Iris, what was her surname? Oh, yes, Thomas. I know the address, I can look up the number in the phone directory.

Oh, and I need to speak to Mr Knight too, and hear him say the call had been taken considerably later than Turner told me it was. Then I'll know the police are trailing a false scent across my path. If they've come up with the idea I could've made that call to leave a message for myself, how could I have? When it was made and received I was already on the tram on my way to the club? If I hadn't been I couldn't have arrived in time to start a game.

He noticed a telephone book on a shelf behind the desk in the office. Running the risk that someone might come in while he was doing it, he quickly found the Thomas' number, pencilling it into his pocket book. Then he remembered the chess club met on a Thursday evening as well as a Monday. If he could catch Mr Knight as he was leaving he could ask him to verify the time he had taken the message on the Monday.

The next time Bright appeared Bruce asked him if he could go. 'I really mustn't be too late at my sister-in-law's. They like to get to bed early. And I need to be back at work tomorrow, there's a lot to catch up on. Oh, I also need to know whether my wife's body has gone to the undertaker. I'd like to arrange for her to be buried on Saturday.' He realised that sounded a bit too matter of fact but reflected that the Police Headquarters was not the place to become sentimental.

'I'll need to discuss that with Superintendent Connor. You must also read and sign the statement from the notes I took this morning. Wait here.'

Bright returned with the typewritten sheets, 'Sign each page and put the date in as well. Then sign again at the end.' Bruce read them through, signed where required, then took off his glasses and looked enquiringly at Bright.

'Superintendent says you can go now. The body has been released from the morgue. Here's the Coroner's Order and we need to know which undertaker you want to collect it. You can return to work tomorrow but we'd like you to report in here after work.'

Bruce gave him the name of an undertaker, got up to put on his coat and hat and at twenty to ten hurried out of the room and the building into the chill and dank evening.

He made his call from a public telephone next to Lime Street Station. A woman's voice answered. He asked if Davies was there. 'Yes, I'll fetch him. Who shall I say wants him?'

'Tell him it's the Mersey Amateur Dramatic Society. Just a quick word.' A few seconds later he heard, 'Glyn here.'

'Glyn,' Bruce kept his voice low. 'It's Mr Bruce.' He heard an intake of breath at the other end. 'Go on,' Davies said.

'I've been all day with the police. Don't worry. I've not said anything to them. But look, they may interview you!' There was another intake of breath. 'No, it's routine. They demanded a list of all those my wife would have let into the house if I was out. Obviously I had to mention you – it'd have looked funny if I hadn't.'

'What'll they want?'

'All you have to do is have a story about where you were and what you were doing for both Monday and Tuesday evenings that puts you nowhere near Anfield on either day. Can you do that? Quickly.'

'Yes I can do that,' said as though he were agreeing to take a part in a play. 'Thanks for asking me'. Then, 'Do you want Phillip to be in it as well?'

'If you can reach him, let him know. He was on my list too. But I really don't think they'll bother with either of you much if you have strong stories and people who can back them up. It's me they're after. They seem to be convinced I did it. Only they have no evidence and they're running round in circles. They told me today they've traced the telephone call but only from 'somewhere in the Anfield district.' And they said it was made at seven. It wasn't was it?'

'No, twenty past.'

'Anyway, how could they trace where a local call was made from?'

'They can't. Unless...'

'Unless what?'

Davies lowered his voice. 'When I made the call there was a problem getting through. I had to call the operator. They might have logged the complaint.'

Bruce winced internally but kept his tone calm. 'Well if that happened the more you need to be able to show you were somewhere else at quarter past seven.'

Silence at the other end. 'Are you still there, Glyn?'

'Yes. Thanks for the call. I'll see you at the next meeting.' And he rang off.

Leaving the phone box Bruce walked towards his next objective, to meet, as if by chance, the chess club captain, Knight, at the end of the evening's club meeting. He walked slowly, digesting and evaluating the call to Davies.

Perhaps the vague description Turner had given of where last Monday's call had been made from *was* a trap rather than a lie. If the call was logged because of some problem in passing it through the exchange then the police might have found the record and now know exactly the number and therefore the call box used. That they pretended not to know could only mean they thought he'd made the call himself and wouldn't realise how close on his trail they were now. And they'd given the time of the call wrongly too. Was that part of the same trap? If they knew where the call had come from they must also know when it had been put through to the café. Were they trying to make him think they knew less than they did to encourage him to have a sense of false security? He needed to be reassured that the call was taken about twenty past seven and the only person who could confirm that was Mr Knight. If the man who took the message agreed he did so about seven-twenty then when the police asked him questions he could tell them they'd got the time wrong – so what else had they got wrong? Call their bluff.

He hung around on the corner of Lord and North John Streets until about ten past ten when he saw Knight, together with Collinson and another man, leave the entrance to the café and walk towards the nearest tram stop. As they got there, he hurried up to them. Collinson said, 'Good evening,' but Bruce spoke directly to Knight.

'Can you remember exactly when you took that telephone message for me last Monday night? It could be very important.'

'Around seven o'clock or thereabouts'

'I'd like to get nearer than that if you can remember.'

'I'm afraid I can't.'

'You see, I've been with the police until just now. There are a lot of things that don't add up about this case. So it's important to me and if you can be a bit more specific than about seven...'

'I've just said I'm afraid I can't.'

'...anyway, I'm on my way to my sister-in-law's. The police have cleared me.'

'Oh, have they? I'm pleased to hear it.'

'Yes, they've cleared me. I just hope they lay their hands on whoever did it. There are some questions I'd like to ask him.'

Knight raised an admonitory finger. 'Bruce, the police have been in touch with me over this business. I strongly advise you for your own sake not to discuss it with anyone other than the police as any simple thing you say may be misconstrued.' And he turned his back on Bruce, who in an instant was transported back to his time in the East where he had frequently been made to feel as lowly almost as the natives. He felt the sting of this rebuke from one who had no doubt at all about their respective positions in the social order. The embarrassment was palpable. It was broken by Collinson who asked him when Janet's funeral would be.

'I'm not sure. I'll make the arrangements tomorrow and hope for Saturday. There mustn't be any fuss. She wouldn't have wanted it.'

His tram arrived and he left the others at the stop to wait for theirs.

When he got to Violet's he found a bed made up for him in the sitting room. Frances had left an envelope for him. The message struck him, unemotional as he had trained himself to be, as strangely detached and cold, suggestive of a distance between the sisters only he could guess the reason for.

> Dear Mr Bruce
> I would ask for nothing that belonged to my late sister apart from her fur coat as a keepsake in memory of her. When this trouble is over I would be grateful if you could despatch the coat to me by registered post.
> Yours
> Frances Morris

11

The Shadows

Friday, January 23rd

For the first time since the previous Tuesday afternoon, Bruce's unmistakeable figure was seen in the streets of Clubmoor. In the intervening two days the Anfield murder had taken a prominent position in the local newspapers and any resident along Bruce's collection route who did not know the circumstances and some of the speculation that went with them would have had to be both blind and a hermit. Still, most of those he called on were sympathetic. To the public, if not to the police, he presented a figure of tragedy, not least because that was what he was metamorphosing into in his own way of thinking. He looked convincingly bereaved. Nor was this entirely subterfuge, he felt bereft. It came quite naturally to speak of his loss. His hearers could not have known that the loss he mourned, the *real* Janet, had happened many years before.

A few of the clients gave him odd looks. In a couple of cases when he called he sensed rather than actually saw the window curtain move a fraction and, being identified, there was no response to his knock.

He took his dinner in a local café then the tram back to the lower end of Priory Road from where he walked up to the cemetery. The brisk walk did him good. After hours spent sitting cooped up in CID offices, he appreciated the chance to stretch his legs and circulate the blood.

At the office he handed over the Coroner's permission for the body to be buried, gave the details of the undertakers, paid the burial fee and completed a form sanctioning the service to be conducted outside the rites of the Established Church. He had decided he owed Janet a religious burial but not so much so he would suffer it to be administered by the Church he disliked and despised. The service was arranged for early the following morning.

That task out of the way, he returned to work, catching up on delayed collections. All passed without incident. Shortly before six he caught a tram that would take him to the CID office where he arrived about six-thirty. Almost as soon as he set foot in the door he was collected and taken to Connor's office. The Superintendent and Inspector Bright were waiting for him. He was not asked to take a seat and found himself standing in front of Connor's desk, the chief seated, his number two standing at the right side of it, as though by design they were placing him in a position of one who has questions to answer. Before anything at all was said he began to feel distinctly uneasy. What could they have come up with now? Connor smoothed a sheet of paper in front of him with something typewritten on it. He studied it for a few seconds, then turned it over blank side up and leant forward.

'You saw Mr Knight of the Chess Club last evening.' Not a question, a statement.

He blinked and swallowed. How could the police possibly know that? He responded as calmly and cooperatively as he could.

'Yes. It was on the pavement in Lord Street. We – he, I and a couple of others – were waiting for trams to take us home.'

'You asked him about the telephone message and the time he had taken it.'

Again, a feeling as though he'd taken hold of an electric wire. How could they know that? To know what was said, either they had a shadow, someone unobtrusively watching his movements from close to... or... Knight had reported the whole of their conversation.

'Yes, I did.'

Connor fixed him with a stare that held nothing but hostility. 'You told him the time he took the call was important.'

'Yes, I did.'

Be careful. Think before you speak. Better to sound stupid than give them the idea you've been second-guessing them.

Bruce saw Connor's face change from the hostile impassive to a smile of triumph which said, 'Got you.'

'What did you mean? In what way was the time of the message important?'

Bruce was silent. Connor looked up at him. 'Well.'

'I had an idea. We all have ideas. It was indiscreet of me.'

Connor opened the trap door. 'Perhaps you'd share your idea with us. It might help with the enquiry.'

Bruce stepped over the trap door. 'I can't say why I thought to ask him. I admit it was indiscreet of me. I can't say any more than that.'

Connor's face betrayed his frustration and annoyance, so did his tone of voice. The brogue became thicker. 'Very well, Mr Bruce. Have it your way. But do not discuss any aspect of this case with anyone other than Inspector Bright or myself. Is that clear?'

'Yes, of course.'

'You can go now. I want you to call here every evening after work until further notice. Is that clear too?'

'Yes.'

Bruce walked down to the tram stop, his head reeling.

Am I being shadowed by the police? If I am, by the very nature of it I wouldn't be able to tell. Certainly I wouldn't be able to identify anyone as following me everywhere. There were others waiting at the tram stop last night besides me and the club people but I didn't take any notice of them; they all looked normal. But then, I suppose, a plainclothes police officer trained to do surveillance work would fit in with everyone else, wouldn't he? That's what the job's about. If I'm being shadowed then they're watching to see if I do anything suspicious. But then if they were watching me wouldn't they have asked me who I was phoning before I went to the tram stop and why I hung about in that corner when I'd told the Inspector I had to get back to Ullet Road and could have taken two or three trams out there in the time it took to wait for Mr Knight?

Perhaps it was Knight who told the police I'd been insistent. Perhaps he saw that as some kind of disrespect, me badgering him to say exactly when he'd taken McQuillian's call. All I got out of Knight was confirmation of the time the police said the call was made and I know that was wrong. Why would Knight do that? You know, it wouldn't surprise me if this was the upper levels of the City Police and some comfortably-off senior businessman doing the Old Boy network thing. They'd both be quite happy to cooperate to queer the pitch of someone they saw as lower class than them. Nothing ever changes, does it?

All the way back to Ullet Road he worried about this. Yet at the end of it all he told himself, as he had often done since all this started, the police could not possibly have a case against him. As he got off the tram and made his way to Violet's, he put a positive cast on it.

Monday evening's call had been made around seven-twenty. If the police had traced the call they must know that. At that time he'd been on the way to the Club and couldn't have got there when he had if he'd been the one who made the call. Janet had been killed around eight or a bit after on Tuesday. He'd been miles away then. She'd been alive at just before a quarter to seven and spoken to someone at the front door – probably the milk boy. He'd gone out almost immediately after; to have been talking to the conductor on the tram at Smithdown Road he couldn't have left any later. He accepted he'd just got to go along with the suspicion. After all, if he looked at it dispassionately, it simply meant the police had no idea who'd done it. In pursuing him they were heading up a blind alley from which they'd eventually have to retreat and go somewhere else. But at least if the police were so fixated on his having done it they wouldn't be putting pressure on Davies – he wouldn't be able to handle it – or on Jordan if they ever managed to find him. They could bang their heads against the wall of his innocence until they got tired of it. He'd see them off and then reward himself with the peace, comfort and contentment he'd never had before.

12

RIP

Saturday, January 24th – Sunday, January 25th

Bruce buried Janet at Anfield cemetery early Saturday morning after a short service in a nearby Congregational Church. By now his mourning was genuine. In spite of natural as well as cultivated reserve he wept at different parts of the service and at the graveside. He did not have to simulate grief, he was burying what might and should have been. No amount of self-control could have overcome the poignancy of that or kept back the tears. The only other mourners were Violet and Alfred and Bruce felt the depth of their sympathy for his desolation; he was drawn into the folds of family closeness and he appreciated it.

When they returned to Ullet Road he had to deal with the inevitable question from Violet as to why Frances had come all the way from Brighton but not stayed for her sister's funeral. She could not understand it and felt resentful. 'I said to her, surely you're going to stay for the funeral? Walter's expecting it to be on Saturday. But no, she had to get back to her boarding house. Why would she come all the way up here for not even one whole day? What do you think she wanted?' Bruce, who knew the probable state of relations within the Morris family, had to sound equally ignorant.

'I don't know any more than you do. When I heard she was coming I thought it seemed a long journey to make. It's not as though Janet and she were close. Well, if they ever were it must have been well before we were married.'

'She told me there were two other sisters and a brother. I suppose you knew that.'

Bruce had been polishing his glasses but he stopped, leaving them raised in one hand, clean handkerchief in the other. 'No, I didn't. I'd actually no idea. As I told you, she only mentioned Frances maybe once or twice in sixteen years. If you hadn't found that letter I probably wouldn't even have remembered she existed. Janet never said she had any other relations.'

Violet looked up from setting the table for their belated midday meal. 'What was in the envelope she left you?'

Bruce shrugged and shook his head. In the light of the conversation they were having Frances's note seemed even more abnormal. 'She asked me to let her have Janet's fur coat, that's all.'

Violet straightened up from the table. 'Well, I call that a cheek. What a strange family.'

Bruce thought she didn't know just how strange. There'd been an awful lot about that family he never knew until a short time ago.

He told his sister-in-law, 'No one from her family came to our wedding in 'fourteen. Of course, at the time I didn't think anything of it. She'd told me her parents were dead. Never mentioned any brothers or sisters. I got the impression she was an only child. It was years later it came out she had a sister.'

'How on earth did she know Janet had a fur coat if she hasn't seen her since before her marriage? And in the short time she was here she never went to your house.'

'I really don't know, Violet. It's as much a mystery to me as it is to you. Perhaps they were more in touch by letter than I knew of. Though come to think of it, I remember Janet had that coat when I first knew her. Frances must have seen it and wanted it. It's a beautiful coat and she's looked after it all these years.'

Later that afternoon Bruce asked himself the same question. Why did Frances, who, like Janet, was older than she looked, make a long train journey twice within forty-eight hours? Could it have been because the Morrises knew Janet had an illegitimate son abandoned at birth? Could they have delegated Frances to find out whether this son was involved in Janet's violent death? That might account for her having arrived on a train from Leeds rather than one direct from London, which was what he'd have expected if someone travelled straight from Brighton to Liverpool. Perhaps the brother or one of the sisters lived in the North of England somewhere. That would certainly fit in with where he now knew Janet had been born. He supposed Frances had satisfied herself that Janet's death was probably the work of a violent housebreaker, and reported back to the others that at least there was no vengeful blood relation who might be a threat to the rest of them. That really did seem to be the only explanation – though not one he could offer to Violet.

The following day, looking down from the windows at Ullet Road, in its Sunday state of very little passing traffic and few people, Bruce saw a man walk past on the other side of the road. What attracted his attention was that this man seemed, unusually, to be strolling rather than going purposefully on his way somewhere. Within a few minutes he was back, this time on the same side as Number 83. Bruce looked down at him with growing concern. A little while later the man returned and loitered virtually opposite the building before walking off again. This exercise was repeated several times in the quarter hour Bruce stayed at the window.

He turned away, a by now familiar wave of unease reaching into his stomach and gripping his bowels. The police *had* set a watch on him. Who else could that man be but an officer assigned to note, follow and report back on any movement he might make outside the door of Number 83? Such a use, and expense, of manpower would only be justified if they had him under suspicion.

What did they know, or think they knew, that pointed in his direction other than the general probability, which of course he was as aware of as they, that in the majority of cases where a spouse was murdered the culprit was the other, husband or wife? But there was absolutely nothing to link him with his wife's death. There was no obvious motive. Her life insurance cover was tiny, and no one was able to say their relationship was other than good. The cold, unsympathetic reality had been kept well concealed from prying eyes as was also, he had to assume, her carrying on with Davies and Jordan. The things he knew about her past and her duplicity over her age no one else could possibly know. Physically he might be in a pretty parlous state but there was nothing wrong with him mentally. No one who knew him would say he was given to violent rage, far from it. If Jordan had just done his work to plan, by now the police would be pulling in and questioning all suspected housebreakers, and he'd probably be back in his own house getting ready to start the new life he'd dreamt of for so long.

13

In Limbo

Monday, January 26th – Sunday, February 1st

When, as instructed, he presented himself at the CID office after work on Monday a detective said to him, 'They've been in a meeting all day. It's probably not going to break up until later this evening so you may as well go on home.'

He had wanted to ask if he could return to his house to collect some clean clothes. By Tuesday he was feeling seriously embarrassed. That he was going about in shirt, collar and underwear in need of laundry played on his mind. It had never been his way. Old-fashioned his dress may have been but it was invariably clean and respectable. Frustration over what he saw as a spiteful and unreasonable restriction on his freedom to come and go, even to change his clothes in his accustomed way, goaded him into forgetting Connor's warning not to discuss the case with anybody. He told a sympathetic client, 'Some friend of hers must have killed her. She'd never have let a stranger into the house.'

'A friend of you both, do you mean?'

'No, a friend of my wife's.'

He realised he'd said too much. What if his client, perhaps thinking it helpful, passed on what he'd said? It would get back to Connor and Bright and there'd be more questions. Who were these friends his wife had and he hadn't? He couldn't afford for them to start looking seriously into matters so close to home. He took a hold of himself and muttered, 'Perhaps someone she thought she knew, that's why she opened the door. But it wasn't.' And changed the subject.

After work he called at Dale Street with the intention of getting permission to fetch clean clothes from Swindon Street. This time he was met on arrival as though they had been waiting, and taken straight in to Connor. His request to go home was passed on the nod, then he was asked, 'By the way, did you speak to anyone on your way home from the tram stop that Tuesday night, the night of the murder?'

'No. I think I've already told Inspector Bright I hurried straight home. I was a bit anxious you see. I'd started to think perhaps I'd been lured out of the house on a wild goose chase. That some ruse had been practiced on me.'

Once again the police were suggesting they knew something he didn't. It was their game. They waited for him to look and sound nervous. Of course he'd spoken to someone. Jordan. But the street had been empty. Then it struck him. There'd been that young woman who'd passed by on the other side. But why would two men standing in the light of a street lamp have aroused the suspicions of a passer-by? Still, he knew what he had to do. He must lie freely and easily.

Connor leant back in his chair. 'You're quite sure you spoke to no one?'

'Yes I am.'

'You've said you were in a hurry to get home. You'd remember if you were stopped or addressed by someone you knew before you got there?'

'Well, I wasn't so worried I wouldn't have raised my hat or said "Good evening" to someone I knew. But I didn't.'

'Someone who says she knows you by sight told us you were talking to another man in Richmond Park near the Parish Hall around twenty-five to nine on that Tuesday evening.'

'No. Positively. I didn't.'

To Bruce's relief Connor didn't pursue the questioning any further and told him he could go. On his roundabout journey to Anfield to collect his clean clothes and then to Violet's in Princes Park he had plenty of time to reflect on the impact of chance on best-laid plans. If that blessed girl hadn't come along just then. The last thing he'd expected.

He'd dealt with the question in the only way open to

him. If he'd said he'd spoken to someone he knew, Connor would immediately have asked for the name and, presumably, address. If he'd said he'd been accosted by a stranger – asked the time or for directions – Connor would have demanded a full description. So he had to stick resolutely to his story. He had no contact with anyone between getting off the tram at St Margaret's Church and meeting the Springers outside his yard door. If that young woman had told the police she'd seen him she was wrong. It wasn't him she saw if she saw anyone at all. Her word against his.

The rest of the week and the weekend passed without further incident. As he did his familiar round in Clubmoor, Bruce became aware of police shadows – indeed he began to recognise each one when shifts changed and he took to nodding to them to make it clear he knew who they were. They, on their part, did not interfere with his activities and remained discreetly out of sight when he called at a client's door. Just like earlier in the week he found that with most of those he called on it was 'business as usual', although he was now careful not to raise the subject of the murder of his wife and to discourage them if they showed an inclination to bring it up. Of course he knew the case still preoccupied the main Liverpool newspapers where his clients, and he of course, could read hints that the police anticipated making an arrest within a very short time and were now in contact with the Home Office. But whatever was in the papers he did not see how the police could be any closer to having a suspect they could arrest than they had been the morning after the murder.

On the Wednesday evening, reporting-in to Police Headquarters as he was supposed to do, a young detective buttonholed him as he was going up the stairs.

'Oh, Mr Bruce, that Mr Davies you told us about; we've checked on him. He's talked to us and we won't need to bother him anymore.'

'Oh, good', Bruce was relieved. 'I only mentioned his name to Inspector Bright because he asked me for a list of people my wife would have opened the door to. I never thought he had anything to do with her murder.' His warning to Glyn the previous Thursday had evidently been acted on. He assumed that as the detective hadn't mentioned Jordan, either they hadn't found him or hadn't interviewed him.

For the rest of the week, although he called in each day at Dale Street, he saw no one and went home to Ullet Road as soon as he could tell he was not wanted. By the weekend he was experiencing a feeling of confidence that the worst was over. The police were far up their blind alley, no one was asking him questions anymore and clearly Davies hadn't given them anything new to go on. Perhaps next week he could go back to live at Swindon Street and make a start on pulling together arrangements for his comfortable and cared-for next few years.

14

A Surprise

Monday, February 2nd

Bruce spent the day in Clubmoor. A day that started just like any other. He had read notices in the Liverpool papers on the previous Friday and Saturday that said the police wished to speak to the man seen speaking to another in Richmond Park around eight thirty-five on Tuesday 20th and would he please contact them. Bruce knew there was absolutely no likelihood of anyone answering the police request. This must surely be the last resort. If no one came forward then they could not challenge the accuracy of a single one of the statements he had given them. Once there was no one against whom they could bring a charge they were faced, as he had believed right from the start, with a case that would eventually have to be filed as unsolved.

He finished early and went back to Ullet Road, where after tea he sat down to paperwork at a table in the sitting room. Violet went out to do some evening shopping; Alfred was studying in his room. The place was quiet.

At seven there was a knock on the outer door. Bruce heard Alfred come out and go to answer it, then men's voices.

The door to the sitting room opened and Alfred stood in the doorway. 'There are three gentlemen to see you, Uncle.'

The men had already pushed past Alfred. Bruce greeted them. 'Good evening, gentlemen. Won't you take a seat?'

The three remained standing, their hats firmly on their heads. One of them motioned Alfred to leave the room and then shut the door behind him.

'You know who I am?'

Bruce did indeed know who Inspector Bright was. And who Superintendents Connor and Turner were.

'Walter Henry Bruce, it is my duty to arrest you on the charge of having wilfully murdered your wife, Janet Bruce, and I have to caution you that anything you say in reply to the charge will be taken down in writing and may be used in evidence against you.'

For a moment Bruce was speechless. Though he had subconsciously understood from the moment the three had come into the room that they were not there to ask him questions but for something more serious, his intellect had denied it. It could not be. They had absolutely no evidence and no grounds whatever for doing what they had just done. They were desperate, even bigger fools than he had taken them for and each one of them would regret this to the day they left their posts. He looked from Bright to the others, aware that the Inspector had already produced a notepad and a pencil.

'What can I say to a charge of which I am absolutely innocent?' Into that reply went every instinct, every belief, every feeling. He had not killed his wife and no police force on earth could prove he had.

He was surrounded. The officers collected together all the papers he had been working on at the table and Turner stuffed them into his raincoat pocket. Connor took him by the arm and propelled him from the room. He was handed his coat and hat from the rack in the hallway. There was one last act to perform. Bruce knocked on Alfred's door. The young man opened it, his eyes wide, face pale.

'Alfred, they have come to take me away.'

'I'm awfully sorry, Uncle. Is there anything you want me to do?'

'No. Tell your mother it will be all right. I shall be back again.'

And he was marched down the stairs, out into the chill evening air and into the waiting police car.

Part 4

Accusation

15

Due Process

February 3rd - March 4th

During his time in India and the East Bruce had suffered humiliations and indignities but they turned out to be nothing compared to what he experienced in the hours after his arrest. On the journey to the city lock-up he was squashed between the two superintendents, Bright sitting in front with the driver. No one spoke. The car pulled up outside the main Bridewell in Cheapside. Bruce was hauled out of the back seat and while Connor came round the car, he had time to look up at the forbidding bulk in front of him. He made out a double row of windows in the face of the building. They looked like narrowed and unforgiving eyes watching who was being delivered to the front door. The police officers, one on each side and one behind, marched him beneath a massive stone arch and rang the doorbell. A small aperture opened in the much larger solid door and a disembodied eye observed the party. He heard a good deal of noise from bolts being withdrawn and keys turned.

The door opened onto a vast hall, its size and gloomy lighting clearly intended to overawe and depress any but the hardest and most frequently apprehended malefactor. Lacking experience of trouble with the law, Bruce was duly appalled. Like any common criminal he stood before the custody sergeant who wrote his details into a large ledger. Even in his misery he couldn't help but notice a clumsy attempt at gallows humour framed on the wall behind the officer's desk. 'Please do not ask for bail as a refusal often offends.' The sergeant read him again the charge of having murdered his wife and administered the caution. This time Bruce made no comment to the charge; the whole process and the atmosphere that surrounded it filled him with such misery he could not find any words. He was searched and everything he possessed other than the clothes he stood in were taken from him, itemised, docketed and removed. They even took his glasses. It seemed to him, and he also felt this was the intent and purpose of the procedure, that he was now merely a number on a record and because the charge was murder he was being made to feel the full weight of the law's displeasure, somehow more of a criminal than if he had been, say, a common-or-garden housebreaker.

A constable approached to lead him away. As the man took his upper arm Bruce looked across at those who had brought him there, who had now handed over their responsibility and were about to leave, going out into the freedom that had been so abruptly withdrawn from him. Connor was in particularly good spirits, exchanging banter with the lock-up staff. As he saw Bruce looking at him, he smirked.

There was further humiliation in the conditions of his cell. Seven feet by seven and stark white, the stone floor made the place feel like a cold shelf in someone's pantry. For a lavatory there was a bucket which, although empty, still managed to leave a strong smell of urine that mixed with the other predominant one of stale sweat. He was given a container to drink from that would have been more appropriate for watering a horse. After a delay someone brought him a thin paillasse and two blankets and dumped them on the hard shelf that provided a place to lie down. They smelt strongly of a number of previous users.

There was no provision to have a wash and none was offered him. Exhausted and emotional, he lay down fully dressed on the shelf. The cell remained dimly lit all night and noise from outside his door as well as the frequent patrols of those supervising his custody would have kept him awake even if he had felt able to sleep.

Worse than the chill was the sheer injustice of it all. They'd dragged him from the comfort of Violet's flat and thrown him into this place. Stopped him from doing his work and cut him off from any income. What would his employers think of his being arrested on a charge of murder? And what would his clients, everyone who knew or dealt with him, think? How much damage would this do to his reputation? He knew only too well what people were like; they'd say there's no smoke without fire.

His anger overcame his doubts. He got up off the shelf and paced about the cell. He wasn't going to be there, under arrest, for long. Whatever reasons the police had put together to justify arresting him, he couldn't see how they'd survive a hearing before a magistrate. Once they had to admit there was no hard evidence on which to charge him, only supposition, he cheered himself with being able to see the look on Connor's face when the case was thrown out.

Then the doubts came creeping back.

What was it Jordan had said about how the police worked? That once they'd decided someone might have done a crime they'd make sure there was sufficient evidence to get a conviction. What were the words he used? 'Make it stick.' That was it. Perhaps that's what the police are going to do to me.

He slumped back down on the shelf and sat for the rest of the night wrapped in the blankets, craving the cigarettes taken away from him and gnawing his knuckles.

It was still dark on Tuesday morning when a constable brought him a tin mug of tea and some bread, its staleness not masked by the scraping of margarine on it.

Just before ten he was taken from the cell to the nearby Magistrates' Court for the preliminary hearing.

As soon as he stepped into the dock he realised the extent of local interest in his case. The public gallery was jam-packed and although the buzz of talk grew less it did not stop entirely as the court officials called his name. From within the court he could hear noise outside, suggesting that even more hoped to see the proceedings and were being turned away.

He wondered whether this degree of public interest was good or bad for his case. On balance, he thought, probably bad. The masses were generally ignorant, believing in and guided by whatever sensational rubbish they read in the papers. He was a spectacle provided for them like those who'd appeared in the

Roman Coliseum and the spectators would as soon turn the thumb down as up.

The courtroom was large and well-lit by tall windows. A bespectacled man in a short wig sat alone on a raised platform. He had a pleasant, well-rounded face and looked as though he was very much at home there. To one side he recognised Connor and another police officer, probably senior to him judging by the obsequious way the Superintendent reacted to something the other was saying. Both were in uniform. With them was a third figure, gowned, his face made owlish with large horn-rimmed glasses below a barrister's grey wig.

Bruce stood while the charge was read out again, then saw the gowned man rise and address the Bench.

As Bruce listened to what this man said he became increasingly aware that the fear he had experienced in the small hours and had tried to dismiss was not misplaced. The police *were* out to get him by any means they could. In spite of the sleepless night he was fully alert and concentrated on what the prosecutor, named as Mr Prior, told the court. Prior first described Bruce's arrest and then laid out the case leading to it.

'After the accused, the last person to see the unfortunate woman alive was a milk boy, at six thirty-one, and it is the suggestion of the prosecution that after this boy had called the accused murdered his wife and left the house at about five minutes to seven.'

As this all came out, Bruce was both astonished and enraged. He knew he'd already been coming downstairs just before a quarter to seven when he heard Janet shut the front door on the milk boy. He now grasped why Bright had asked him if he remembered the milk being delivered. They'd got the boy to say he delivered the milk earlier than he did. How had they done that and why?

Worse was to come. Prior said, 'it is a fact he was seen at a short distance away at about ten past seven. To get to that spot he may have left the house at any time from five to four minutes to seven.'

Bruce knew this was a travesty. That 'short distance' had been more than two miles. He'd climbed on to the Number 4 tram at the junction of Lodge Lane and Smithdown Road at six minutes past seven. He'd checked the time by his watch. Was the prosecutor saying he killed his wife between six thirty-one and five to seven? Surely he couldn't be. Their own medical expert had said she was killed around eight o'clock. He'd heard the man tell Connor.

It became clear the police and prosecution were going to allege exactly that.

Prior also suggested that the Monday evening telephone call had been made by Bruce himself. 'It will be proved the message emanated from a call box two or three hundred yards from the house.' And he then confidently asserted, 'it would have taken him just as long to travel from that call box to the café where he received the message, as the time elapsed between the message being received and the accused arriving at the café.'

Bruce knew exactly when the call was made and he was sure Prior did as well. It would have been impossible for him to have made the call at the actual time and then arrived at the club when he did. The police had suppressed the correct time of the call so they could implicate him in the making of it.

Bruce's worry, indeed fright, deepened with every statement Prior made. He presented everything that happened on the Tuesday evening as though it had been an element in an elaborate plot to cover up the fact that Bruce had killed Janet before he had set off for the Mossley Hill area. The only statement Prior made which Bruce actually knew to be true was, 'he says he hurried home, but as a matter of fact he was seen in conversation with some man within a very few yards of his home, apparently standing and talking.' When Prior stated there were four pound notes in the cash box, Bruce, now as it were on his home ground, could contain himself no longer. 'No, sir, that is inaccurate.' He was immediately silenced by court officials; his voice was not to be allowed any function at all in that hearing. It was then he realised he should have had someone to represent him. The police, through their prosecutor, had been able to present a skewed case to the magistrate and no one had challenged it. They had made certain the case would not be thrown out.

Prior applied for a remand in custody for eight days. The magistrate looked over at Bruce.

'Now, if you have anything to say, you may do so.'

Bruce looked across at Connor and the prosecutor and said, 'Nothing, sir, except that I am absolutely innocent of this charge.'

Which was, of course, correct.

The remand was granted.

Returned to his cell, he was offered more tea and bread. But what he had experienced that morning had taken away any appetite. All he could think about now was getting himself a solicitor, one sharp and energetic enough to help him take the police on at their own game and to rebalance the case away from the deliberate attempt to manufacture evidence where there was none.

He recalled a conversation he'd had with Collinson a couple of years before at the chess club. Collinson had pointed out a youngish man playing at a board high up in the order of ability within the club and had said they had there a county-standard player in their midst. As a co-founder of the club, Collinson had been particularly proud of it. He'd then added that this chap, Peter Lovatt he'd called him, was a partner in one of the city's leading firms of solicitors and that if his command of a legal brief was anything like his mastery of the chess board then if it ever came to it Lovatt would be someone Collinson would want on his side.

Bruce made a decision there and then. He would have Lovatt on his side. He needed him.

Before he could ask to make that telephone call a constable unlocked his cell door, poked his head round it and shouted, 'Bruce, get your coat and hat on, we're going for a little walk.'

'Where to?' he asked as he dressed for outdoors, but got no reply.

He was escorted outside into a small courtyard and made to stand in line with nine other men dressed similarly to him and of roughly the same age and physical appearance. The procedure was similar to the one he had gone through a week or so back when he had been identified by the tram conductors and people he had accosted in his search for Menlove Gardens

East, though this time he had a feeling the police were going to spring yet another surprise on him. A sergeant came through a side door into the courtyard accompanied by a young woman who walked down the line, looking at each man, then touched Bruce on the shoulder as a sign of identification and returned the way she had come.

He remembered the young woman tripping so lightly and so fleetingly past on that Tuesday evening as he tried to get sense out of Jordan. Through the perspective of time he also recalled she had looked back at them before turning up into Letchworth Street. She had picked him out as the man seen talking to another in Richmond Park and the police definitely saw her as a critical element in the case against him.

Connor had said she knew him by sight, so a good counsel would suggest she might have been coached to give the police a positive identification though she had not actually seen him where and at the time she claimed to have done. What he did know for absolute certain was the police would never have the satisfaction of the 'other' man coming forward to prove him a liar. He'd go on maintaining the only people he'd spoken to that evening were the Springers.

He was taken back to his cell.

After a few minutes an inspector came in and said, 'Bruce, you are now a prisoner on remand. As such you will be transferred to Walton Gaol and the transfer will be immediate.'

'I believe I have the right to legal representation. I need to speak to my solicitor. On the telephone, as soon as maybe.'

The inspector summoned a constable, saying, 'Escort the remand prisoner, Bruce, to the telephone. He will make a call to his legal representative. Stand beside him while he does so and then escort him back to this cell.'

The journey to the prison was uncomfortable. The van taking him held several other probable felons. One, ugly and brutal-looking, was cuffed to a prison officer and Bruce could see the heavily tattooed forearm that formed the link to his escort. The insignia even ran across the man's knuckles. To Bruce he looked Neanderthal, surely what a real murderer looked like. In the flesh how Dickens might have described one.

He noted with distaste another who was almost equally villainous-looking, but the man saw and interpreted his appraisal. Rattling the chain of his cuff, he turned to face Bruce, squinting at him and hissing from the corner of a mouth covered with cold sores, 'What you staring at, you fucking weed? Think you're some kind of gent do yer, just 'cos you'se wearing a suit?' A warder shouted 'Quiet!' Bruce sat in acute discomfort under the other's concentrated stare which he could feel even though he forced himself to avert his eyes from the malice. What kind of people had he been thrust among? People? This was more like a zoo than a collection of humans. It had the smell of a badly-kept animal cage.

On arrival, to his disgust, he was subjected to the same procedures as all the others in the van. Designed partly to make remand prisoners realise they were now under discipline of an especially strict kind, these activities were also meant to ensure that any fleas, bugs, lice or plain old dirt that prisoners brought in on their clothes and persons were removed.

A prison officer in a smart uniform with medal ribbons and a cap with a peak at such an angle he seemed to peer under it – all bristling moustache, sharp angles and strutting aggression – barked at Bruce to march to the ablutions. This was a chilly, high-ceilinged room with a stone-flagged floor in the middle of which stood a badly-chipped claw-foot bath. The walls, of a pale green made even more institutional by poor lighting, shone with condensed steam. He was ordered to strip and get into the hot bath (mercifully the first, so avoiding the indignity of climbing into water already fouled), dry himself on a rough and well-used towel and then stand about naked waiting for a doctor to examine him. For a final indignity, he was marched into the adjacent room where the prison officer pointed him to a pile of blue uniforms on a table. 'Remand Prisoner Bruce. Take a uniform from the pile.' Bruce turned over several, hoping to detect one that would fit him. 'I said take one. Take the first. This isn't a hotel', barked the warder. Miserably Bruce pulled on a set that could only have fitted a man shorter by a foot or more than he.

In this ludicrous garb he had to have his first consultation with Lovatt in a room set aside for visitors. He knew what a contrast they must offer. Him, tall, thin, unshaven – almost emaciated – embarrassed by his badly-fitting and rough garb and his solicitor, much smaller, neatly-outfitted with a boyish face, slightly protuberant eyes and a full, rather fleshy mouth. But he looked and sounded energetic and that gave Bruce reassurance that he had made the right decision. The two men exchanged polite formalities. In a spirit of no nonsense the contract between accused and solicitor consisted of Lovatt writing out a request for his services in pencil on a spare bit of paper and Bruce signing it.

'I asked for you, Mr Lovatt,' Bruce told him, 'because you're a member of the same chess club as me – in fact Michael Collinson and I started it back in 1922. I'm confident you can help me through this difficulty and you'll want to see justice done on an innocent man.'

'Since you telephoned me, I've already managed to get and read the full account of the prosecution's submission to the preliminary hearing this morning.'

'It was full of lies and half-truths. They're hanging everything on my wife being killed between half-past six and seven and so therefore it could have been me. I'm pretty sure Janet spoke to someone at the front door as I came downstairs to go off to Mossley Hill at just before a quarter to seven. If I hadn't left then I'd never have been getting on a tram at Lodge Lane and Smithdown Road at six minutes past seven, would I?'

Lovatt looked at him thoughtfully and Bruce had the sense of being summed-up. This was the moment when a solicitor either believed wholeheartedly his client was innocent or was prepared to go through the professional motions to defend, and if possible get an acquittal, for someone whose guilt or innocence he could not be sure of.

'Well, from what I read earlier, Mr Bruce, the police don't seem to have any hard proof of opportunity or the slightest evidence of motive. My first thought is they'll have to come up with a great deal more than they've got to make any kind of case. I'll get on to things straightaway. Establishing the time milk was delivered to your house seems to be essential. Do you know who it would have been? Have they delivered your milk for a long time now?'

Bruce thought. 'I don't know precisely the name of the dairy; that was my wife's area. But I think the place was in Sedley Street. Oh, and I'm fairly sure my wife would have taken the can into the kitchen, emptied it into a jug and then gone to the door to hand the can back. I think she'd just done that when I came downstairs.'

'I'll visit the area around where you live tomorrow. Ask a few questions. Find out who delivered the milk and when.'

Bruce was left with the feeling he'd put his trust in the right man and that the prosecution would be unable to repeat the misstatements put forward at the first hearing. It helped him cope with the final awful blow to his pride and sensitivities. For as soon as Lovatt had gone, the prisoner was escorted to the hospital wing of the prison. This was, they told him, standard practice for those on remand for a capital offence. It would allow the medical authorities to watch his condition; he suspected that was another term for observing any signs of mental instability which could be brought up as evidence in court. He heard this with the feeling that at least a hospital bed seemed preferable to a cell, but when they deposited him there he realised how cruel his self-deception had been. Instead of a cell to himself in the main prison he shared a dormitory with eleven others: a dirty, pale green, long room with a wooden floor and rows of beds separated by cupboards where the 'patients' kept their uniforms overnight. There were windows but these were barred and had not been cleaned on the outside for years. By late afternoon the ward was lit only by two rows of low-powered electric lights that enhanced the greenish aspect of the walls. The other inmates had mental problems ranging from near idiocy to full-blown delusions and epileptic fits. How much lower than this could he sink, a contemplative man who treasured his own privacy, to have to spend the hours of his confinement in the close company of lunatics? As he began his first night in a proper prison he contemplated bitterly that he was in this position because of the incompetence of one he had relied on to carry out tasks he had so carefully planned. And because of the sheer blind prejudice of the police who thought he was too clever for them. And because he had no powerful friends.

Before the weekend Lovatt was back at the prison.

When they sat down together in the visitor's room, Bruce showed the strain he had been under. Leaning forward across the table that divided them, even before they had exchanged greetings, 'Did you speak to the milk boy?'

Lovatt leant forward so their heads were nearly touching. His tone was quiet. 'I've not been able to. It seems the police have told him not to talk to anyone and whenever I tried, his father just said he wasn't there.'

Bruce took that news badly. He gripped the edges of the small table with his fingers, 'But the time…' he began.

Lovatt broke in, still quiet and confidential. 'I spoke to others, though, who gave me strong evidence that your wife was alive and taking in the milk at around quarter to seven.'

Bruce knew he sounded urgent, probably irritatingly so, but he had to know more. 'And…'

'There are four youngsters, one of them a girl who shares the deliveries with the dairy owner's son, Billy. They all say, independently, that Billy told them the day after the murder he'd delivered to your house at a quarter to seven. They all told him to go and tell the policeman at your house because it would be important information. And then...' he sat back further from Bruce and directed a forefinger toward his client, '...and this is very important, there was a young chap who delivered the evening paper next door to you at about twenty to seven and saw the milk boy standing on your doorstep waiting. Your front door was open. When the lad moved on, the boy was still there.' He leant forward again. 'And there's more. Your paper was delivered by a different chap, an older one, about five minutes before that. He told me he'd already given the police a statement about it. It all seems to me if the prosecutor says your wife was murdered before you went out then it must have been between a quarter to seven and the time you'd have had to have left home to be able to get a Number

4 tram at six minutes past. It's just not credible. Of course, they're saying the milk was delivered at half-past six. I don't know what the milk boy actually did tell them.'

'I don't know why they're making out she died before seven', Bruce said. 'That night I distinctly heard the professor who came to do the examination on Janet tell the Superintendent she'd died about two hours before he got there. That would've made it well after eight.'

Lovatt pursed his lips and took his nose between finger and thumb. 'Mm, there's something odd about that too. But we'll get to the bottom of it.' He looked Bruce in the eye. 'I've definitely a feeling the police think it must have been you and they've made what information they do have support their theory. They don't seem to be after anyone else. I don't know why. Now,' he went on, 'next Wednesday you appear before the stipendiary again. This time you'll be represented. I'll be there. The prosecutor will probably ask for a further remand. I'll agree. We need more time. If the other side doesn't ask for one, I will. So I'm afraid you'll have to twiddle your thumbs for a further week. Then we'll go back for the Committal. That's when a magistrate decides whether or not there's a case for sending you for trial. He's almost bound to do so but what it should do is let me see the cards the prosecutor's got in his hand. Oh, and at the Committal I'll have a barrister to represent you. I know the very man. He's young and he fights. He won't let the police have it all their own way.'

Bruce looked at his solicitor and liked what he saw. Compact, energetic, softly spoken but already clearly on top of his brief; the right man to get him out of the hole which at the time of his arrest he had felt was bottomless.

Except for a brief period of exercise each day, Bruce, who had by now been given a prison uniform roughly approximating to his height and unusually long limbs, filled the drawn-out hours between meals reading and observing the behaviour of his fellow inmates, some of which he found mildly amusing. There was the one who appeared to think he had been a vicar and who, draped in a bed sheet, standing on a chair, preached about hell fire and sin to a congregation who largely ignored him, apart from frequent injunctions to shut his cakehole. One believed he had an inexhaustible stock of jokes but couldn't remember the punch line of any of them. Others, he found repellent, particularly their throwing food at anyone who sat near them at mealtimes.

He made his second appearance at the Magistrate's Court on Wednesday February 11thand was, as Lovatt had predicted, remanded for a further eight days. Lovatt had little more to tell him in that week other than that the Committal proceedings proper would start on February 19th. On the Monday after this second appearance before the magistrate, he brought to meet Bruce, Stanley Keene, the barrister who would try to show at the Committal that there was no case to answer and therefore there should be no trial. Keene, of a similar age to Lovatt and complementing the solicitor's sharpness and energetic delivery, spoke positively and encouragingly. 'Mr Lovatt and I see the police as being highly selective in the case they've brought against you and we also think there's much they haven't disclosed as they should have done. We'll keep them on their toes at the Committal hearing. If they put forward things that ask to be challenged, that's what we'll do. Depend on it.'

Suppressing his natural pessimism he asked, 'Do you think the case against me could be thrown out?' He folded his arms across his chest, an indication that he didn't expect the answer to be the one he wanted.

Keene did not offer false hope. 'To be honest with you, no. Only a handful of cases have been stopped at the Committal stage in the past few years. Most magistrates have an ingrained opinion that if the police have arrested someone that someone has a case to answer. But we'll do our best, and if nothing else we'll be better equipped to know how to counter their case when it comes to trial.'

Although his brain had told him the moment he opened his mouth that the likelihood was 'no', he still felt dashed down. 'Oh', was all he could manage.

When Keene had left them, Lovatt said, 'We have to consider the legal expenses. What resources do you have?'

'About a hundred and fifty of my own. My brother has

pledged a further three hundred. But that's the total of it, I'm afraid.'

Lovatt got a notepad out of his case and scribbled in it. Then he looked up. 'Well, that'll take us where we want to go for the present. I'll give it some thought. I've an idea.'

'What is it?' Bruce asked him.

Lovatt gave a firm shake of the head. 'No, don't ask me yet. I don't want to raise your hopes. Leave it with me to look into it.'

The prisoner was returned to the 'ward' and sat gloomily at the table in the centre of it, the lines in the book he held unscanned. He was preoccupied with this question of the cost of his defence to which he had not given any thought until Lovatt had raised it. If all his savings were spent on defending himself then he would have nothing left to pay for care and to supplement the reduced income from doing less work through his final years. The irony came home to him that he had partly rejected the path of divorcing Janet because of the cost. The alternative he had taken was going to have the same effect.

On the Thursday morning about half-past ten, wearing his suit and a dark overcoat, he was escorted into the number two Magistrates' Court for his Committal hearing. Mr Keene asked and got agreement from the court for his client to leave the dock and sit directly behind him, from where he could have a comprehensive view of the activity in court.

The first thing he was aware of was the continued interest in his case. The public gallery was as full as it had been for his earlier appearances. Not having access to the newspapers in prison he hadn't realised how much the constant and often sensational press coverage of his wife's murder had made it and him notorious. One or two of the spectators captured his attention. There was one enormous woman, a hat with a feather sticking out of it pinned to tightly-rolled curls, accompanied by a tiny, thin man with a peaked face under a flat cap – the perfect representation of Jack Spratt and his wife. Another, quite close to where the accused sat, picked his nose with a long finger then transferred the result to his mouth. The supply seemed to be endless. There were men in overalls who, for whatever reasons, must have had time to attend during the working week and came prepared with food and drink for a full day's entertainment. Watching a man strongly suspected of murder and hearing salacious and, even better, gory details would provide them with the means to impress their families or the clientele of their favourite pub.

The second thing he noticed was that the bench was occupied not by the man who had heard his remand hearings but by another, elderly and very much less impressive figure. He leant forward and asked Keene who it was.

Keene turned round to him and said out of the side of his mouth 'He's a lay magistrate. Mr Unsworth.'

'Would it have been better if we'd had the stipendiary we had before?'

'Probably. I'll just have to see that Prior doesn't pull any fast ones with him.' And Keene turned back to the front, indicating an end to the conversation, leaving Bruce to grasp that any possibility of there being no grounds for his trial had completely disappeared with the introduction of Mr Unsworth.

At the first remand hearing, Prior's tactics had been to exaggerate the importance of the little he had and to create an atmosphere in which the accused's guilt might be assumed. This time, with additions and embellishments, he improved on that performance.

He now put it to the magistrate that Bruce knew perfectly well where the Menlove Gardens area was but had deliberately given the impression to chess club members at the time he had received the McQuillian message that he did not. The accused knew the area, Prior told the court, because he had been a regular visitor to his supervisor's house, only a stone's throw away from Menlove Avenue but on the other side of that main road from the Gardens. Bruce listened carefully to him.

Of course Prior was perfectly right. But the grounds for his assumption were arrant nonsense. He was saying the reason for Bruce's familiarity with his chief's home was because he'd made frequent visits there during Mr Willesden's extended illness. Bruce knew for a fact not only that Mr Willesden had never had a day off sick in his entire life but that he frequently boasted as much. If it came to it he could perfectly well say the only times he'd ever been to the house in Green Lane were for violin lessons in the winter more than two years ago and it was always dark. Anyway, if asked, Mr Willesden would vouch for the fact that Bruce approached his house from the Allerton Road end of Green Lane and so had no reason to have an idea of what lay further up that road.

As Prior continued, Bruce was now sure of what had previously been just a suspicion. Someone in the police, he thought most likely Bright, had been busy making bricks out of various wisps of straw. He knew he was right when Prior suggested why the accused had not worn his raincoat in his evening visit to Menlove Gardens. 'I suggest the reason he was wearing an overcoat that evening is because his mackintosh had played some part in the crime.'

Keene was on his feet. Addressing the bench, he accused the prosecutor of 'suggesting things'. 'He has a duty to present the case fairly, on the facts alone. He is not addressing a jury.'

The magistrate appeared to be unconcerned. Keene took up the wider implication of what the prosecutor was doing. He continued with the same passion as before, 'His speech will be fully reported in the papers tonight. It will be read by a few who can work out for themselves what is fact and what conjecture. But most will not have that facility and from among them, if this case goes to trial, members of the jury will be selected to try my client for his life. Mr Prior is not entitled to use this opportunity to promote what is merely guesswork. All he is entitled to present are the hard facts. If he has any to present.'

Prior adjusted his glasses, Keene gripped his gown with both hands and they both looked up at the Bench, waiting for the magistrate to take charge, to give a firm, clear statement of the purpose of the hearing and the need to present a balanced argument.

Bruce watched the man with some apprehension. The fellow might be all right dealing out fines and bindings-over but he was out of his depth in a hearing like this where the issue was a capital crime. A magistrate needed to be a lawyer to manage the adversarial exchanges between a prosecutor who would stop at nothing to have Bruce tried, preferably before a jury that already believed him guilty, and a defence led by a young and fervent barrister with a name to make.

In the silence which lasted for a couple of minutes at least, Bruce saw Unsworth's face working, eyes blinking, as the magistrate sought for the right thing to say. Then, gathering himself to utter his pronouncement, 'It must be realised there is a prosecution and a defence.' In itself an unobjectionable statement of the situation in a trial, thought Bruce, but a clear and worrying sign that the old fool didn't know the difference between a hearing where he had to decide only whether sufficient of a case had been made out that a man be sent for trial, and a trial itself where an accused's guilt is the issue, prosecution and defence working to get the verdict each of them desires.

Prior took the staff from the telephone exchange through their statements about the night before the murder.

Hearing what they had to say, Bruce knew the police had deliberately not been straight with him about when the call was made. Turner had put it at 'about seven' but the detectives must already have known the call was put through at seven-twenty. Their attempt to mislead him had led directly to that humiliating meeting with Knight at the tram stop. He wouldn't have needed to be so anxious if he'd known the police actually had the full facts and so knew he couldn't possibly have made that call himself.

At the end of the first day, Bruce felt more encouraged than he had done since his arrest. Although his bed of thorns had been unplanned, unexpected and, in his view, undeserved, it would even yet turn into the bed of roses he so fervently wished for. He had believed from the start that the police would be unable to establish any motive for the killing of his wife or any evidence that he had done it. But he now accepted he had underestimated how important it was to them; a matter of professional pride to be able to come up with a credible perpetrator. Paradoxically, the very notoriety of the crime, which they had done much to encourage, meant they could not admit they had no idea who had done it or why. So they had to put forward the only solution available to them – that the husband was the murderer – and hope that a series of possibilities, might-have-beens and what-ifs cunningly strung together might persuade the public in general and jury members in particular that they had charged and arrested the right person. His barrister, to whom he was warming by the minute, would continue to counter any opinion parading as fact, burst any bubble of conjecture and reduce most of Bright's bricks back to the wisps of straw from which they had been tenuously spun.

Early on the second day, Friday, he had yet another warning of how keen the police were to magnify any barely visible bit of information and present it as evidence for their case. A police constable was called who told the Court, at the prosecutor's prompting, that he had seen Bruce on the afternoon of the murder. On his way to report for duty, he had cycled past the pedestrian insurance agent. 'I saw he was dabbing his eye with the end of his sleeve and he appeared to me to be very distressed. His face was pale, haggard and drawn.' The inference for the Bench was unambiguous. A few hours before slaughtering his wife, Bruce had been contemplating with inner horror and torment the deed he intended to perform and such was his emotional reaction he was openly weeping. The passing policeman, who said he knew Bruce by sight, had registered all this.

What it told Bruce was that the police were pulling out all the stops. He remembered getting something in his eye as he was walking to an appointment that afternoon. He'd pulled his eyelid down to create tears to wash it off. The policeman must have passed him just then. So much for it being his weeping in anticipation of what he was about to do later. He thought it also odd and very much in character of the police methods of investigation that the policeman probably hadn't reported this at the time it happened. If he had, Connor or Bright would have jumped on it and asked what he'd been crying about in the street. He was sure the officer, being stationed locally, would have heard all about the murder, mentioned his sighting to his colleagues and eventually been told to give a statement. It was quite likely he did it after they'd coached him in what he was required to say, and then it ended up on Bright's desk.

Prior called the milk delivery boy, Billy Locke, next. The fourteen-year-old schoolboy stated, 'My father is a dairyman.

I take the milk round between five-thirty and six each night. Up to two weeks ago I delivered milk in Swindon Street. I delivered milk between six and six-thirty. The last time Mrs Bruce took the milk in was January 20th.' Now Bruce and his defence knew for a certainty that the lad was lying. Lovatt had already been told by several witnesses that Billy had first said he was there at a quarter to seven and Mrs Bruce was alive then. Now he was saying something different. The police must have either persuaded or bullied him into changing the time.

On the following Monday the proceedings restarted and Prior produced a number of witnesses, none of whom added anything of value to the argument that Bruce was the murderer. Annie Clothier, the Bruces' 'maid', was put up to say she had gone with Inspector Bright to Bruce's house and told him an iron bar 'about a foot long and as thick as a candle' was missing from where she'd last seen it in the fireplace of the front room of Number 29.

The next day, Tuesday, the prosecutor called Professor McLintock. Much of what he had to say about the manner of Janet Bruce's death was straightforward until he described a blood clot he had found on the rim of the lavatory pan which he clearly intended to be interpreted as evidence of the murderer leaving a trace of the blood from his victim, presumably while using the upstairs bathroom to wash it away from his hands or body.

But the revelation that took Bruce's breath away and removed at one sweep his certainty that even for the police the time of death coincided with his physical presence in Allerton Road was when McLintock averred that on the evidence of the progress of rigor mortis and the extent and nature of the clotted blood, death had occurred at six o'clock.

He wanted to shout out, 'How could he stand up on oath and say that when I actually heard the man tell Superintendent Connor he estimated the time of death at eight o'clock?'

McLintock was followed into the witness box by his medical colleague Dr Prescott, who confirmed his and McLintock's estimate of the time of death. Their scientific opinion was somewhat debased by Prescott's admission that neither man had taken any notes during their time at Number 29. Keene took full advantage of that. 'You go there as scientific witnesses forming expert opinions and you do not take notes?'

With this ruthless dismissal of his expert medical witnesses, Prior saw part of his house of straw collapsing before his eyes. The strain showed. He shouted at Keene, 'Ask the witness questions, don't make speeches to them and we'll all get along better.'

Keene ignored him.

Because Keene was appearing in another case he sought and got, after some difficulty, an adjournment until the start of the following week. When the proceedings started again there was a procession of police officers connected with the case through the witness box. One thing that engaged Bruce's attention on the Tuesday was that it became clear the police had done a number of 'tests' to see how long it took to get from Swindon Street to the tram stop in Smithdown Road where his presence had first been noticed and the time span it established. Sergeant Bowler told the hearing, 'At six forty-nine on Monday, January 26, I made a test of the journey from the rear of 29 Swindon Street to the junction of Lodge Lane and Smithdown Road with another officer. We reached there at four minutes past seven.' He then added that on the next evening the journey had taken twenty minutes. Bruce saw that the object of this was to suggest strongly he could possibly have left home at eleven minutes to seven and got to Smithdown Road in time to catch the tram he travelled on, giving eighteen minutes to kill his wife and clean up. He also found it instructive that they'd made no attempt to see how long it took to travel from his house to the chess club on the Monday.

On the final day of the hearing, Wednesday March 4th, Bright gave evidence. In doing so, he produced the small pocket diary in which Bruce had noted the details of the McQuillian telephone message. Keene, who knew the answer perfectly well because Bruce had told him, asked Bright, 'Are the police in possession of other diaries belonging to the accused?'

Bright dug into his jacket pocket and brought out three small diaries. 'There are these business diaries the accused kept.'

Keene and Lovatt had been sure the police, who had been all over the small house in Swindon Street, had removed the private diaries Bruce told them he had kept and had hoped not to have to expose them to the defence or to the Bench because they were irritatingly free of entries that might suggest motive for Bruce killing his wife.

'Are there other diaries? Diaries of events, thoughts and opinions?' Keene asked Bright.

'Yes, and a record of occurrences.' From his pockets he now produced four notebooks and laid them on the ledge in front of him. 'There's an entry on January 17th 1928 about his falling-out with his wife', he added, trying to the last to make the diaries sound as though they held the interpretation of why someone would butcher his wife.

Keene asked to be given the diaries and read to the court Bruce's entry for the day Janet had come back late from Southport.

'On arriving home, found that Janet had not returned. I waited until nearly one, then thinking something surely must have happened, went off to the Anfield Road police station to see if there was any report of any accident. None. So went back home and found her ladyship had just turned up. It was a relief to know she was safe and sound for I was getting apprehensive, feeling she might have been run over... or something.' Written just over a month before the murder the language did not suggest that the writer was already of a mind to kill his wife. Keene then went on to read the entry for the day Bruce had seen the effects of the freezing fog and had asked his wife to go with him to Stanley Park.

'After dinner I persuaded Janet to go into Stanley Park. She was equally charmed.'

These readings produced an emotional tempest within Bruce. By this stage he was already profoundly remorseful. What he had done had not been worth it and in the damage it was causing to his already fragile health he felt an unseen hand punishing him. He would not benefit from his crime. The image he now had of Janet was from the distant past. He would never have wanted that Janet dead and someone else had delivered those awful blows McLintock had described the previous week. No one could say he had done it.

So after seven days in court in which he had demonstrated

nothing but calm interest in the proceedings, now, with shoulders shaking, his face buried in his handkerchief, he wept. Depending on their viewpoint, those observing this saw the weeping of a loving husband reminded of intimate moments with his late wife, or of one frustrated that he had not simply got away with murder.

That was the end of the committal hearing. Bruce was told to return to the dock for the final act. The clerk read out the formal accusation.

'Have you anything to say to the court?' asked Unsworth.

Bruce stood up straight. He felt defiant and wanted Prior and the police to hear the contempt and scorn he felt for their case. He also wanted this defiance to be reported in the press for the world to read. 'I plead not guilty to the charge. I am advised to reserve my defence.'

He went on to describe his relations with Janet as 'of complete confidence in, and affection for, each other.' He meant it. With the Janet he held in his heart this had always been true. He had erased the other Janet from his memory. He went on, 'I could not get one possible advantage from committing such a deed. Nor do the police suggest I gained any advantage.' In all the hours and words of evidence, the parade of witnesses and testifiers, the prosecution had not been able to suggest even a hint of motive. And then the ring of conviction, the truth, 'I am entirely innocent of this terrible crime.'

It was all to no avail. Unsworth, glad to be shot of this complicated and troublesome case with its edgy degree of huge public interest, a case in which he had been in over his head, pronounced, 'You must go for trial at the next Liverpool Assizes.'

16

On Trial

March – April

For the next two months Bruce was obliged to continue, in Lovatt's words, 'to twiddle his thumbs'. The Liverpool Assizes were in the legal calendar at the end of April; between the end of the committal hearing and the trial proper he could only endure his imprisonment. This meant remaining, as far as possible, on agreeable terms with his fellow inmates. While individuals came and went, two things remained roughly constant – their number and the wide range of mental handicaps they suffered from. As he became more familiar with these damaged men he found he gradually accepted them. He was able to teach dominoes and draughts to a few and then to play with them. One or two appreciated being read to – all were more or less illiterate. Only some of the more demented remained beyond the pale. One in particular had a habit of stuffing morsels of his food into every orifice his body could provide, another masturbated openly and mechanically in front of his fellows several times a day.

He occupied most of his days reading – and thinking about the case the police had developed to secure his conviction.

In discussions with Lovatt and Keene, he repeated his certainty that the committal proceedings had shown just how thoroughly the police had manipulated their sources of information to construct a theory of his guilt. They knew that if he was their murderer he had to have killed Janet with enough time to leave his house and been seen boarding a tram at Smithdown Road at about six minutes past seven. To make this scenario plausible, the milk had to have been delivered not later than a minute after six-thirty and he could not have left the house earlier than eleven minutes to seven. The time of death had to be fixed by expert opinion at between six and seven. In each of these cases the facts had been made to fit the theory. They'd got the milk boy to give an earlier time for delivering at Number 29 than he'd told his friends he had, or been seen by others on the doorstep. The medical experts had perhaps been 'encouraged' to estimate a time of death a full two hours earlier than the first of them on the scene had told the senior police officer who was there, and the time they said it took to get from Swindon Street to the tram stop had been achieved by young, presumably fit, policemen, not a prematurely elderly, chronically sick, fifty-two year old.

Being able to afford a defence had preyed on his mind since Lovatt raised it before the committal hearing. Now it became a constant nagging worry that intruded into his waking hours and gave him disturbed nights. There had been just enough from his own savings and from his brother, James, who had returned on compassionate leave from the Malay states, to pay the legal expenses so far. After that, he could not see how to go on.

As the days dragged past and with too much idle time in which to brood, he let himself lose almost all of his small stock of hope and fortitude. Apart from his brother, the few visitors – people he'd known before that night in January – dried up, and visits from the solicitor hardly lifted his growing misery. Lovatt's only cheering news was that Farsight was keeping his job 'on ice' and had appointed someone to make his collections for him. Conversations with Lovatt were mostly one-way, with Bruce harping on about how the police had twisted the elements of the case. His obsession with their methods and intentions increased when Lovatt told him, which perhaps he was ill-advised to do, that he had a strong suspicion the police were withholding critical information from the defence. After his firm badgered them, they provided a list of the names of people they had interviewed or who had volunteered information. It ran to several foolscap pages and Lovatt had neither the time nor the funds to find and then talk to them all. He did tell Bruce that he had taken steps to counter the evidence from the police constable who claimed to have seen him crying openly in the street on the afternoon of the murder by getting statements from clients Bruce had visited that afternoon. No one said they had seen any evidence of distress; he had been his usual self. Bruce got the impression, though, that Lovatt was aware of a widespread belief in his guilt, not only just in the areas where he lived and worked, but among all levels of society and throughout the coverage of the main regional newspapers.

All this pressed heavily on him. He'd never been physically strong at the best of times and needed calm and predictability. Pessimism, or as he called it, realism, was his natural view of things and having no faith or strong belief system he began to give in to feelings of despair.

Up to that point he had been sustained by the strength of his self-deception. He was technically innocent of the charge against him. There was nothing anyone knew about the relationship between himself and his wife that suggested why he might have killed her and certainly no one could have had any evidence of his having a violent temper. As long as the police didn't suspect that others had been involved in Janet's death, that there had been a conspiracy to kill her – and there was absolutely no indication that they did – then to win their case they would need to convince a trial judge and jury that putting together all the possibles, perhapses, nods and winks pointed to their having correctly identified a cunning murderer who thought he'd been clever enough to pull the wool over their eyes. The prosecution's last, desperate resort would have to be to pose the question, 'Who else could possibly have done it?' Given what Bruce had heard about public assumption of his guilt, in the hands of a capable prosecutor those arguments might be enough to get him convicted. This led him back to the underlying problem that had been wearying and wasting him for weeks. If he could not afford counsel strong enough to stand up to the best the Crown employed, he'd probably be convicted. By late March Bruce reached a point where the part he had actually played in the death of his wife finally penetrated the armour he'd worn ever since that night. He felt increasingly uncomfortable maintaining his innocence to others. He thought wryly that while he might have conspired to have someone murdered, he was not one to whom lying and deception came naturally; he experienced shame when he did so with Lovatt and with his brother, James. Once again he could see himself facing disappointment and defeat.

Perhaps he should think seriously about giving up. Why not make a clean breast of everything? Jordan would be arrested as the actual killer and certainly be found guilty and hanged. He'd get nowhere pleading he was the tool of Bruce, the evil genius. And such a fate would serve him right. Jordan had botched the plan, used far and away greater violence than was necessary and because of him Bruce was penned-up in what, in effect, was a lunatic asylum, his savings gone, awaiting a trial that could easily end in his being found guilty and sentenced to death – and for something he hadn't actually done, and in a way he had never wanted, while Jordan feathered his nest with the Brophys and set himself up for a rosy future. Davies too would be charged, tried and found guilty as an accomplice. He'd get life. Bruce felt a surge of satisfaction. Again it would serve him right. One more unpleasant wastrel out of the way. No loss there. Of course he would get the same as Davies but under prison conditions his disease would worsen. He'd only endure a year, or at the most two. He'd gained nothing from what he'd done. Almost certainly it had shortened his own life and destroyed what little hope he'd ever had. Why not bring the whole thing down on them?

He decided. When Lovatt next came to visit he would tell him the whole story and submit to whatever the confession brought.

He went to bed that night and, for the first time in weeks, fell asleep immediately, only waking when the prisoners were roused first thing in the morning.

On Monday, the next to last day of March, Walter Bruce was escorted to the visitors' room where Lovatt was waiting to see him. On his way there he rehearsed how he would break the news to his solicitor. Since he had decided to come clean he had been more at peace with himself, but still dreaded the moment when he had to tell the younger man that his faith had been misplaced and that the case of W H Bruce was indefensible. He looked pale and nervous as he sat down opposite his solicitor. Lovatt peered at him.

'You're not as well as the last time I was here, Mr Bruce. Has the doctor seen you? I know the waiting must be very hard.'

Bruce opened his mouth to begin his confession. Before a word could come out, Lovatt went on, 'Well, I've some news for you that should cheer you up no end. Do you remember I'd said to you before the committal I had ideas about finding some of your legal costs?'

Bruce nodded.

'I've been able to get a guarantee to cover all of them.'

He was sure he'd misheard. 'All of them? Every penny?'

'Every penny.'

'Where on earth from?'

'It's been a lot of work and I've had to be very patient. I didn't dare let you in on it in case it didn't come off and gave you another hammer blow.' He paused, 'and you've had enough of those haven't you? I was worried your health might not stand it.'

Bruce said nothing. He lifted a hand, encouraging Lovatt to go on.

'Your employers and the Staff Union between them have guaranteed all your legal expenses. I was at a meeting on Thursday at head office in Holborn and that meeting – of the Executive Council of the Union – expressed unanimous belief in your innocence and their determination to see you given every assistance to prove it in court. Where they've led, the Company has followed and they've said they'll make up any shortfall between what the Union collects from members and the final bill.' He looked up at Bruce, his eyes alight. 'And on the strength of that I've been able to engage a King's Counsel to defend you, one of the very best. Mr Keene will assist him. Between them they'll tear the prosecution case to shreds. As far as anything in the Law is capable of prediction, you'll walk away a free man.'

It was some while before Walter Bruce could bring himself to speak. How could he now let down not just Lovatt and Keene but the ranks of Farsight who had delivered such a ringing endorsement of him? He could be defended by a top-flight barrister; the whole farrago of the prosecution's supposition could be shown to be what it was. His savings were intact again and he might yet return home, acquitted, free, able to hold his head high and, perhaps just in time, begin to enjoy the regime of care and comfort that had inspired all that had happened. He reached out and took Lovatt's hand, gripping it firmly in both of his own. 'I can't thank you, and them, enough, Mr Lovatt. You can have no idea what this means to me. Please tell them all how grateful I am for their support.' And a smile spread across his hitherto lugubrious face.

There was more than three weeks to go before court. The absence of a clock in the hospital ward and his lack of a watch, taken away by the prison authorities, were especially trying. He had always run life by clock time but now could only mark the progress of each day by the rituals of meals and exercise and by observing the passage of light across the ward. It made him feel particularly powerless and abused. Easter came – and went – the number of hours of daylight became greater as Spring slipped away. Then early on 22nd April he was summoned from the hospital ward to have his formal clothing, watch, ring, cigarette case and fountain pen restored to him for his appearance in court. As he was about to leave the ward, one of the others, with whom he'd built some kind of bond over shared board games, sidled up to him and thrust something small and hairy into his hand, folding his fingers over it. Bruce opened them. A small rabbit's foot, with a much scarred leather pouch covering one end, lay in his palm. 'It's fer good luck'.

This moved Bruce as nothing in his life had ever done. Here was this childlike unfortunate, with cropped hair and misshapen body, repeating petty misdemeanours and felonies in order to have a roof over his head, food on his plate and refuge from the cruelties of society, not only remembering that his friend was going for trial that day but giving him perhaps the only personal possession he had. Blinking back tears Bruce put his hand on the man's shoulder and placed the talisman in his prison uniform pocket, patting it as he did so. 'Thank you', I'll take good care of it.' The other gave a shy smile.

17

In the Dock

The First Day

The tyres of the prison van swished in the steadily falling rain as it took the remand prisoner on to the Crown Court in the city centre. There he was put into a whitewashed, narrow, tunnel-like cell beneath the main floor.

Shortly after ten that morning his escort, hearing the cry, 'Put up Bruce', took him up the steps into the dock and into full view of the packed public gallery and press. He heard the shuffling and muttering of those who had managed to get a seat in the gallery behind him and he could smell damp clothing. In the open space in front of and below him he spotted Keene and they exchanged nods. Lovatt looked up and raised a hand. A tall man with an aloof expression, eyebrows arched as though in a state of disbelief at the commonness and mediocrity he found around him, looked up but gave no sign of acknowledgement. Bruce identified him as Quentin Fisher, his defending counsel, who would sweep his path to freedom.

The courtroom was meant to impress, public and accused alike, with the might, majesty, dominion and power of the mid-Victorian English judicial system. It did not fail to impress Bruce. He felt the weight of the dominant dark wood panelling enclosing the areas where the jury would sit, the witnesses appear. He took in the massive columns with floridly decorated capitals supporting the roof. Right in front of him a great wooden canopy with the royal coat of arms set into the back wall thrust out over the raised desk and chair of the judge, as though pointing to the dock where he sat. Between him and the horseshoe-shaped well of the court, now crowded and busily active with formally dressed lawyers and court officials, were iron railings, giving the impression that the accused was still behind bars even at his public trial.

The jury filed into their places. Ten men, two women. The clerk of the court asked him if he had objections to any of them. He leaned forward over the rail to Lovatt. 'Are they all right?'

'Tell the court you have no objections', was the reply.

Bruce formally said he had none while taking in the twelve who would decide if he were guilty or not. To him they were a typical group of middle-class Merseysiders. He thought the two women looked mousey. Among the men he spotted a couple similar in appearance to Mr Knight of the Chess Club. These spread themselves comfortably in their places, looked self-satisfied, clearly the recipients of years of good dinners. He thought that whatever conclusions these two men came to about the trial they wouldn't be backward in making them clear to the others. None of the jurors looked in his direction, whether deliberately or not he couldn't tell. They would all have read what the papers had to say about his case. He supposed that was inevitable, unless the trial had been held well away from where the crime happened. Even if they all lived outside the city and its suburbs they would still have been exposed to the torrent of newsprint that had boosted press sales over the recent months.

A call of, 'Silence', and then from a door at the back of the structure that surrounded the judge's bench came a formal procession. Bringing up the rear, the trial judge, Mr Justice True.

To Bruce's sceptical eye there was something faintly incongruous about this short man with full-lips and dark bushy eyebrows in ceremonial judicial get-up – full wig, red gown with white fur trimmings – all of it framed within the massive surroundings of his office. He reflected that you could make the building and furnishings of a Court of Law as intimidating to the layman as you liked, but you couldn't always rely on the appearance of the human actors not to diminish that impression.

Then the court was in session. The voyage he had thought about, anticipated in equal measure with fear for the outcome and longing for it to be over, was now irrevocably under way.

'Walter Henry Bruce, you are indicted and the charge against you is murder, in that on the twentieth day of January nineteen hundred and thirty-one, at Liverpool, you murdered Janet Bruce. How say you, Walter Henry Bruce, are you guilty or not guilty?'

Bruce's voice was strong and audible as he stood upright in the dock. 'Not guilty'.

Bruce watched the individual faces intently as the charge was put to the jurors. 'Members of the jury, the prisoner at the Bar, Walter Henry Bruce, is indicted and the charge against him is murder, in that on the twentieth day of January nineteen hundred and thirty-one, at Liverpool, he murdered Janet Bruce. Upon this indictment he has been arraigned. Upon his arraignment he has pleaded that he is not guilty and has put himself upon his country, which country you are, and it is for you to enquire whether he be guilty or not and to hearken to the evidence.'

As he listened to these formal words, hallowed by long usage, offered to a jury who, he thought, betrayed no concern at the weight of the responsibility being put upon them, his attention was drawn away from them to the antics of the one whom he identified as the leader of the Crown's case against him. Moving about in his seat, constantly reaching up to touch his wig, shifting and then readjusting it and pulling on the sleeves of his gown, the image Bruce had was a convincing impression of a zoo lion kept from his rightful feeding time. A handsome man with an intelligent yet fastidious face; a man working himself up to be the leading actor in this four-day drama and impatient with the droning mechanical whose presence prevented him from leaping onto the stage and mesmerising the audience with his lines and his presence. The moment the clerk had finished speaking, even before he had resumed his seat, Lionel Tournay, KC was out of his.

And within minutes everyone in the court, Bruce more than any, was aware of his persuasive power. The man had physical presence – and he was a consummate actor. Those two qualities combined to magnify and also to focus that power which he directed to one purpose only – to have the twelve jurors hanging on to and believing his every word. There was no place in his opening for the painstaking building of a set of hard facts that would lead to a logical and irrefutable conclusion of an accused's guilt – a conclusion a defence could only hope to counter by appeals to emotion. This was entirely the other way round. The case against Bruce was put in wholly emotional terms. For the Crown, nothing had changed from the speculative suggestions supported by completely misleading statements that Prior had employed at the earlier magistrates' court hearings. But in the mouth and physical gestures of Tournay these became signposts in a skilfully woven tale told dramatically and, importantly, with passion. To those watching and listening, Tournay communicated his complete certainty of Bruce's guilt and his belief that the man in the dock should not be allowed by the scarcity of hard fact to be offered even the smallest chance of getting away with it. He told the jurors they '...would be carried almost irresistibly to the conclusion that this woman was murdered by her husband.' The 'almost' was a throw-away word; he was going to sweep these twelve people along from the very start of the trial to the point where a conviction was the only right and proper outcome for them to think of.

He began by suggesting strongly that the telephone call to the Chess Club on the Monday evening had been made by Bruce himself from a telephone box a mere few hundred yards from his home. A technical fault there had caused the call to the café to fail at first and that had been logged at the exchange. Thus the police knew exactly where and when it had been made. The call, and Bruce's subsequent performance in front of the Chess Club members that he neither knew the caller nor the area in which he lived, were all part of a plan to give himself an alibi for the following evening. Tournay's technique was to offer a statement with an underlying tone of worldly disbelief and then appear to allow the jury the good sense to put the correct interpretation on it. 'You may think...' said over and over again.

His next point was that Bruce's behaviour on the evening

of the murder on the way to, and when in, Mossley Hill was completely compatible with having set himself up with an alibi. Bruce, he said, had spent the entire time drawing attention to himself even after, had he been genuine, he had sufficient reason to believe the address he was looking for did not exist. The reason for that, the jury should infer, was Bruce had always known it did not exist. It was his presence away from his house over a defined period of time that he was aiming to establish. Tournay recited the events of that evening in an almost jocular manner – *this is all so far-fetched surely the accused can't think we take him seriously?*

Tournay moved on to Bruce's arrival back home. He can't get into his house until he has attracted the attention of his neighbours and then, when he has it, miraculously he can open the doors. If he was concerned that something might have happened to his wife while he had been out why would he go first to every other part of the house but where she actually is? And when he finds her battered to death how does he take it? Does he cry out? No. He is calm and collected. 'You might think…' he suggested to his audience, 'this to be a sign of callousness'; the deeper implication being that the discovery was no surprise.

The target of all this imputation and mordant humour was finding Tournay's analysis too close for comfort. Whereas Prior had used what was available to him in a pedestrian way, this chap had the gift of the gab and knew how to work a jury. So far his interpretation of events had been spot-on. The only relief was the prosecution did not appear to have considered the possibility that Bruce had not acted alone.

Tournay was moving on, lifting his presentation of the Crown's case to its high point. The presence of the mackintosh tucked in beside the victim's body had been given great significance by the police right from the time they noticed it and discovered who it belonged to. In court, prosecuting counsel turned this commonplace item into a metaphor for evil. Parts of it had been burnt. Who, he asked, would have wanted to destroy that raincoat? The accused had admitted it was his. Why on earth would an intruder want to destroy it? The garment was soaked in the victim's blood yet not one drop of blood was found outside the front room where she died. He offered an explanation. Not in dry, factual tones but with all the fascinating and prurient detail of a sensational report in *News of the World*. Bruce, he suggested, had been naked beneath the mackintosh when he slaughtered his wife and when he had done the deed he had been able slip out of it as one might out of a dressing gown. He had then, still naked, tried to burn the raincoat but as time was running out he had shoved it under the corpse before going upstairs, washing any splashes of blood from himself and then, dressed in his unsullied clothing, setting off to act out his alibi.

In telling the story, Tournay referred indirectly to 'one of the most famous criminal trials... of a man who committed a crime when he was naked.' None of his lay hearers would have had any idea of which case that had been, even less that it was never established above a suspicion that the killer, who had cut his victim's throat, had done so naked so as to be able to wash the blood away easily. But if a picture is worth a thousand words, Tournay had just painted a scene no jury would ever forget; one that would hammer home the impression Bruce was some kind of deviant. Bruce, the chess-playing, cold-blooded mastermind would have known about this case and seized upon the example as a way of ensuring the police found no trace of blood on the clothing he had worn that night. And he had probably got some kind of perverted pleasure out of stripping off to kill a woman. Watching the reaction of the jury, in spite of knowing the whole account to be fiction, alarmed Bruce.

For his next trick Tournay had a tangible prop. Bruce, he averred, killed his wife with a weapon he could easily put his hands on; it lay in the hearth in the front room and had done for some time. Their cleaning woman had told the police that it was there before the murder but had disappeared immediately afterwards. It was, he said, 'an iron poker sort of thing, like that.' And as he said the words he picked up a piece of iron, similar to the one that was missing, swung it round his head, then continuing, 'amply sufficient to have done this deed', he brought it down upon his table with a crash. Some of the jurors jumped, all were animated. No one could have avoided the connection between that piece of theatre and the crushing blows that had smashed life and brains out of the dead woman. Having got their attention, Tournay described the bar as 'one that could be disposed of without trouble. A thing like that would go into the ground anywhere; there is no difficulty at all.'

As he neared the end of his two-hour one-man show, he reprised the main points of his case. The Monday evening telephone call from a suspiciously nearby box; on the Tuesday the persistent and very public search for a non-existent address; the doors that only opened once his neighbours had been drawn in; his own blood-soaked and partially burnt mackintosh beside the body; the iron bar, just right for inflicting the deathblows, that had mysteriously disappeared from the fireplace in the murder room. He took the absence of motive in his stride. The Crown, he told the court, could suggest no evidence of motive. But, he hastened to stress, 'If you saw a murder committed, you'd be unimpressed if someone said to you afterwards, "but there was no motive for doing it." You'd say, "I can't help that – I saw it."'

He wound up his case in the same impassioned and histrionic manner he had conducted it thus far. 'If this man', gesturing towards the dock, 'did what he is charged with doing, it is murder, foul and unpardonable. Few more brutal murders can ever have been committed; this elderly, lonely woman literally hacked to death for apparently no reason at all. Without any apparent enemy in the world, she goes to her account, and if you think that the case is fairly proved against this man, that he brutally and wantonly sent the unfortunate woman to her account, it will be your duty to call him to *his* account.'

He sat down to a few moments of complete silence. Not a cough, not a shuffle, certainly not a spoken word. Then, releasing two hours of pent up emotion, close attention and minimal movement – beginning as a murmur then swelling to hubbub, spectators, jury and lawyers all turned to their nearest neighbours and vented their reactions.

The focus of all that rhetoric stood, tall, thin, slightly bowed, impassive, leaning on the dock rail. Throughout the two hours he'd shown no sign of emotion. That was his habit;

his breakdown toward the end of the committal hearing wasn't to be repeated. He appreciated that his usual self-control had just been cited as one of the factors pointing towards his guilt and that his exercise of it in court would be observed and conclusions drawn. Too bad. There was nothing he could do about that; it was how he was, how he had always been.

His expectation of how things would be conducted in a Court of Law had just been confounded. He'd assumed legal proceedings would be dry, logical, a form of debate at the end of which verdicts were arrived at through weighing up facts and deciding which evidence could be trusted and which set aside as questionable. Not unlike a game of chess really. His assumption, of course, came from the fact that he would have found such an environment entirely comfortable himself. In the weeks leading up to the trial he'd felt reassured that such methodology would guarantee his acquittal. He had not, could not have, committed this murder and in the absence of any trustworthy evidence the court would have to let him go. He'd never asked himself whether such a refined and balanced process was really likely when juries were drawn from across the spectrum of respectable fellow citizens, for whose general level of thought and judgment he had little respect. He had just witnessed a leading barrister, who could offer no hard evidence at all, encourage a jury to put a rope round his neck with the kind of performance that would have earned several curtain calls at the Empire Theatre. Looking across at his counsel, he'd seen expressions of disdain pass fleetingly across that austere face, the eyebrows arched even higher than usual. Clearly not his way of conducting a case. He reflected that the antidote to Tournay's venom might, indeed probably would, reduce the Crown's evidence to tatters and yet not get through to the jury; they could be bored by the process. He shivered inwardly. Fisher would have to be the sharp scalpel that stung the jury to contrast the blunt instrument with which Tournay had just hit them.

A good deal of that first day was taken up with the Crown parading witnesses to show the telephone call had been made from a public call box only a short walk from Bruce's house;

that it had no light in it and would have been in semi-darkness concealing anyone who made that call; that the caller was a man; that it was logged at twenty past seven on Monday, January 19th; that it was answered at the café which hosted the chess club by one of the waitresses who asked a club official, Mr Knight, to take the call. None of this went anywhere near to offering positive proof that Bruce himself had made the call and Knight, when cross-examined by Fisher, pretty well knocked the proposition on the head. He agreed first the message would have led Bruce to believe there was 'a matter of business' for him if he responded to it and that this probably had something to do with the caller's daughter's twenty-first birthday. Tournay, in his opening speech, had derided Bruce's repeatedly telling various people on the way to and in Mossley Hill that he had 'important business' there, asserting that he could not have known this and had made it up. And then Knight described the voice he heard as 'strong and confident'. Fisher leaned towards him and asked in a quiet, silky tone, 'Do you know Mr Bruce's voice well?'

'Yes'

'Did it occur to you it was anything like his voice?'

'Certainly not.'

'Does it occur to you *now* it was anything like his voice?'

'It would be a great stretch of the imagination for me to say it was anything like that.'

Bruce took a deep breath and relaxed a little. That ought to put paid to the idea he had made the call. The prosecution had meant Mr Knight to reinforce the suggestion that Bruce had made the call but the result had been the opposite. Knight's statement was unambiguous. The voice he'd heard on the telephone was not that of the man he knew fairly well. Bruce thought the only other possibility the Crown was left with was that he'd managed somehow to disguise his voice and hoodwink Knight, a challenge they'd find hard to take up.

He was, though, a bit surprised and disappointed that his counsel hadn't flourished this victory over the heads of the jurors. He was certain the other chap would have done.

In spite of that substantial blow to the prosecution, anxiety remained. What worried him was Knight's mention that just two days after the murder there'd been a great deal of public speculation about the case, much of it to the effect that the husband must have done it. That was why Knight had warned him not to discuss the case with other people. If the jury was of that opinion he needed them to see he was a human being; someone not so different from them and to hear him tell his story and profess his innocence rather than hearing it from others. He decided to tell Lovatt he wanted to give evidence in his own defence.

Between the previous important witness and the next the Crown put up the police constable, Helliwell, the one who, cycling to work on the afternoon of January 20th, claimed to have passed Bruce looking distressed and weeping. They knew each other, of course. For a while the officer had been a Farsight policy holder. A large, and as Bruce remembered him, jovial man, his evidence was the same as he had given at the committal hearing where he had not been cross-examined. Fisher offered him a sensible alternative; 'I wonder if it occurred to you that your eyes could water in the cold. Has that ever happened to you?' The witness agreed. 'And you might rub them?' Again the constable agreed. Fisher put it to him, 'I am suggesting to you that you are mistaken in thinking that the signs you saw were signs of distress occasioned by committing a crime?' Helliwell refused to budge. 'No, I do not think so.'

Fisher took up the challenge. 'If I were to call twenty-five people who saw him at or round about that time and they said he was just as usual, would you say you had made a mistake?' 'No,' came back the response, 'I should stick to my opinion.'

In this little exchange Bruce saw a symbol of the whole police case. A blind refusal to accept there could be any other possibility but his guilt and therefore a stubborn determination to make any fact support that belief.

The Crown had made it a central tenet of its case that Bruce could have killed his wife in the twenty or so minutes between Janet last being seen alive and the latest time he would have had to leave to be at the corner of Lodge Lane and Smithdown Road some time just before ten past seven. For this proposition to have any chance of being accepted, Janet could not have been seen alive any later than six-thirty. So it was vital the milk boy, Billy Locke, stuck to the story he had told at the magistrate's court. Asked by the prosecution, he said he knew what time he'd delivered milk to the Bruce house. 'When I passed Holy Trinity Church, it was twenty-five past six and it takes me five minutes to get to the Bruce's.'

Once Fisher got at him very large cracks appeared in this part of the Crown's case. To an extent they had brought the risk upon themselves. Billy was only fourteen, still at school, and had been coached by the police as to what he should say. On at least two occasions they had got him to repeat the movements of January 20th, starting on foot from the Church and ending at the Bruces' house, stopping off at the dairy to drop empty cans, collect fresh supplies and make two other deliveries. Under their tutelage he had done this once in five minutes and once in six. Given the importance of this timetable to the police case Fisher needed to suggest strongly Billy had probably been hurried through the performance at what in normal circumstances would have been an improbably fast pace. 'Let us see what you have done since you passed the clock at six twenty-five. You have covered a distance of five hundred yards and you have been to the shop. Do you put away your empty cans?'

'Yes.'

'Where do you put them?'

'On the counter.'

'Then pick up fresh cans, walk down this street and make the delivery in Swindon Street?'

'Yes.'

'Do you really say you did that in five minutes?'

As Fisher questioned Billy it became clear that given all he had had to do at the time of his deliveries on the evening of the 20th, and that there had been no one making him hurry, he had more likely taken a good deal longer than five or six minutes. At first Billy stuck to his script. He could hardly do otherwise.

'Yes, I have been over the ground with two detectives and it took me five minutes.'

Then Fisher turned on him. Had he met a group of other youngsters on the following evening – the 21st – and did one of them say he should go and tell the police he had delivered milk to Mrs Bruce the evening before? 'Yes', he agreed, one of them had.

'Did he ask you, "What time were you there?"'

'I don't remember.'

Fisher challenged him. 'Did you say, "At a quarter to seven"?'

'No.'

Fisher asked him again. Billy insisted. 'No, between half-past six and a quarter to seven.'

'You said you were there between half-past six and a quarter to seven? That was true, was it?'

'Yes.'

Fisher paused. 'Why have you sworn today you were there at half-past six?'

'Well I was not sure then.'

'Why are you sure now?'

'Because', said the boy, as though parroting some phrase he had been made to learn, 'I've been over the ground and it has taken five minutes to cover that ground – and that, added to twenty-five past six, makes it half-past.'

As Fisher pressed him on what, according to his friends, he had told them on the day after the murder Billy's discomfort became visible to everyone. The silences between Fisher's questions and the boy's responses grew longer. The Judge noticed. 'What do you say about it? Do not shake your head.' The lad became more confused and mumbled as well as looking about him as if for inspiration as he was pulled further away from his prepared account of what happened and who said what.

'Do you not remember,' Fisher asked him, 'the newspapers had said quite wrongly Mr Bruce went out at six-fifteen?'

'No.' He'd never heard it was in the papers that Mr Bruce left his home at six-fifteen; the reason why the others had said he should tell the police what he knew – that he'd seen Mrs Bruce at six-forty-five – and he denied any of his friends had ever said such a thing. 'You were rather reluctant to go to the police?' Fisher posed. 'Well, naturally', said the boy.

The judge intervened. 'You say you were reluctant to go?'

'No', said Billy.

Fisher pointed out to him that he had just said he *was* reluctant to go to the police.

Confusion had clearly taken Billy over. 'No, naturally I was not reluctant.'

Seeing the mess Fisher had made of one of his key witnesses, Tournay re-examined Billy to stitch up some of the holes.

'Did you know it was said in the papers that the prisoner had left at six-fifteen?' he asked.

'Yes', said Billy. Now he *did* know the papers had said the accused had left home at six-fifteen. Tournay went patiently through the process of getting the boy to tell the court how in the test delivery runs he'd done exactly what he'd done on the 20th in first six, then five minutes. Cunningly he was able to suggest to the boy a motive for his speed on the night.

'Were you early or late that evening?'

'Late.'

'What time do you generally finish your work?'

'I should finish about half-past six.'

'How late did you finish that night?'

'About twenty to twenty-five minutes late.'

'So you were anxious about being late?'

'Yes.'

Bruce saw the evidence of this neat, tidy but still callow schoolboy as that on which the case against him stood or fell. If the jury thought Billy was telling the simple, unrehearsed, truth about his delivery times that evening then they might just accept eighteen minutes as enough to carry out a murder and clean up afterwards. If they suspected he had been persuaded by the police, and perhaps his parents, to help them by giving an unreliable and unlikely account then they were presented with a timetable for murder that was just not believable. He hoped the jury had also caught the judge's concern that the boy's evidence was not being freely and spontaneously given.

The prosecution next offered evidence of a fairly technical and straightforward kind from those who had seen Bruce on the night of the murder either travelling to, or while in, Mossley

Hill. None of it provided anything that would have aroused the interest or stimulated the emotions of a juror. If the intention was to show that Bruce could have boarded a tram at the junction of Lodge Lane and Smithdown Road later than he said he had it was not conclusive and none of those who met and spoke to him that evening said they were conscious he was acting a part.

The prosecution next called Bruce's chief, Albert Willesden, to the stand. Bruce was quite pleased to see him. At the committal hearing Willesden had given him a glowing character testimonial. In the witness box now he described him as, 'An absolute gentleman in every respect.' Furthermore, the witness appeared to be a competent and honest man – a professional manager – so Bruce felt anything he said should be on his side and go down well with judge and jury. Tournay made the point that Willesden lived in Green Lane – 'only a short way below Menlove Avenue' on the map Tournay had a court official hand to the jury – and that Bruce had been several times to his house so, by inference, probably knew his way round that area.

Fisher attacked that inference. He got Willesden to agree that Bruce's visits had taken place two years before and all five of them at about seven-thirty in the winter when it would have been dark. He also got Willesden to say the only reason Bruce had ever visited his house had been to have beginner's violin lessons while looking for and engaging a proper teacher. Referring to the way Bruce would have travelled to Willesden's house for his lessons, 'to get to you, would the best way be the ordinary way to take the tram that comes along the Allerton Road and get off at the corner?'

'Get off at Green Lane', was the reply.

'So that tram would take him nearly to your door; it would not take him within sight of Menlove Gardens, would it?'

'No.'

'Did you, as a matter of fact, know whether there was a Menlove Gardens East or not?'

'No.'

So the court got the clear message that Bruce would have had no reason to explore further up Green Lane as far as Menlove Avenue. Only he knew that he had done so on paper, the position and existence of the three existing North, South and West Gardens and the absence of the East he had got from an up-to-date map.

There was then a protracted to and fro between counsel – with the Judge joining in – as to the procedure for paying-in the collection money from an agent's round. What the prosecution wanted was to show that the amounts kept in Bruce's house were never more than £30, so anyone knowing Bruce's business would hardly feel justified in committing a serious crime to get hold of it. Under cross-examination Willesden said the takings varied and could be as much as £100 on a Tuesday night. Under that same cross-examination Fisher got Willesden to give a reference to Bruce's honesty and competence.

'Scrupulously honest?'

'Absolutely.'

'What about his accounts, were they always in order?'

'Always, to a penny.'

And then his view of the exemplary relations between man and wife.

'Did you know his wife?'

'Yes.'

'What do you say about their relations with each other?'

'The best possible.'

'I think the phrase you used was that, "They appeared to be all in all to one another?"'

'That is so.'

Then there was a strange interlude when Davies's name came up in connection with Farsight collections. Fisher read part of the statement Bruce had made to Bright on the Thursday after the murder in which he'd named Davies as 'a friend of my late wife's and myself'; someone his wife would have admitted to the house and that, 'it was known he had collected premiums which he did not pay in and his superintendent, Mr Willesden of Green lane, Allerton, told me he went to Davies's parents who paid about thirty pounds to cover the deficiency.' Fisher asked Willesden if this were true. Willesden agreed it was, though the amount 'is a little exaggerated.' Having brought Davies's name into the proceedings, Fisher asked that the press should not report it. Bruce heard all this with misgivings.

He wondered why Fisher had done this; certainly *he* didn't want attention drawn to Davies. It seemed an odd thing for his counsel to have done because it hadn't proved anything for or against their case. If he'd gone on to suggest that Davies might have had both knowledge and reason to attempt to help himself to the insurance collections at Swindon Street, he'd have opened up a new line of defence but one that could have been positively disastrous for Bruce. Inwardly he said to himself, *Thank goodness he's dropped it.*

The final witness for the Crown that day was potentially the most damaging to Bruce's case. If the court suspected that in spite of his firm denial, he *had* been talking to someone in Richmond Park just before he got home on the Tuesday evening, then the jury would most likely disbelieve everything else he had said in his defence. Fortunately for the defence, Iris Grange was not a convincing witness. Perhaps she was overawed by her surroundings and the occasion, perhaps she was just not very bright, but she managed first to get the day and the date of her sighting wrong so that Tournay had to correct her. Then she got the time wrong, saying she'd seen Bruce at twenty past nine, by which time he was in his house with the Springers and the first policeman. She also created confusion about the entry which the man she identified as Bruce had gone into after he and the other man had parted; from what she said it seemed Bruce had taken the unlikely step of going in the opposite direction from his home.

Fisher took advantage of her confusion to browbeat her. 'You never gave it a thought at the time, did you?'

'No.'

'No. Why should you? Then there was a murder...' He poured scorn on the fact she'd apparently waited a week to make a statement to the police though she lived only yards from the murder house.

'I am only suggesting you made a mistake. What made you wait all that long time before going to the police?'

'I was ill in bed for one thing.'

'That would not have prevented you from sending for them.'

Though Tournay tried to shore up some of the damage to his witness it was ineffective, giving the court the idea that Miss Grange must have made her statement to the police as a result of their initiative rather than her own, leaving the possibility that her recollection was at best flawed, at worst manufactured.

After he was taken down and just before being returned to Walton Gaol, Bruce and Lovatt had a quick word. The solicitor seemed pleased with the way things had gone. 'Their witnesses, every one of them, have actually worked against them. They haven't made one telling point between them. The Crown's case is entirely hypothetical; nothing substantial in any of it. Mr Fisher's doing a first-class demolition job.'

18

In the Dock

The Second Day

The second day began with the prosecution witnesses adding nothing that might have led the jury to a presumption of Walter Bruce's guilt. Mrs Springer, a matronly woman with a firm mouth and no-nonsense voice, even volunteered a view about how the mackintosh might have got where it did that was diametrically opposed to the one so melodramatically suggested by Tournay in his opening speech.

In cross-examination, Fisher asked her, 'With regard to this position of the mackintosh under the body, you say it was under the shoulder? You did say so?'

'Yes I did'.

'Do you think it possible, from the position it was in, that it had been thrown over her shoulders to go to the front door?'

Mrs Springer frowned, unsure of what he meant. 'I could not say as to that.'

But then the Judge freed her from her dilemma. Leaning forward, he asked her, 'You mean she had thrown it on?'

Before she could say anything, Fisher, to whom this alternative to the 'naked man in a raincoat' was manna from heaven, turned towards the jury. 'Yes, to go and open the door. That is my suggestion.'

Mrs Springer, the prosecution's witness, made the point even clearer.

'That was my idea. I thought that was the object. It just flashed across my mind because it was a peculiar thing, a mackintosh.'

'Did you know she had a cold', Fisher asked her.

'Yes', she said.

In re-examination Tournay could not annul one word of it.

Bruce recognised the value of this suggestion coming from someone the Crown should have expected to reinforce their line. He knew the real reason the mackintosh had been under the dead Janet's shoulder was because originally Jordan had thrown it over her back and head and pinioned her in it. If the Jury accepted that the victim had draped it over her shoulder before she was killed, they would have to discount the idea he had been wearing it.

From PC Evans, who had been the first officer at Number 29 on the evening of the murder, Tournay extracted a comment on Bruce's demeanour during the initial examination of the crime scene. It had been 'cool and calm – well, I thought he was extraordinarily calm.' Bruce could see the beginnings of a prosecution plan here to have him portrayed as behaving very differently from the way most people would expect of someone who had just come home to find his wife slaughtered in the front room. But then Mrs Springer, the kind of witness he thought most people would warm to, had only just before described him as seeming to be in shock, 'Twice he showed emotion by putting his hands to his head and he sobbed', she had said. And then, 'if we were left in the kitchen alone he appeared as if he would break down and he seemed to pull himself together when a great many were knocking about.' The words of one who had been with him within a minute or so of his finding Janet's body ought, he felt, to carry more weight with the court than the necessarily more detached observations of a policeman.

As the morning session went on everyone's attention wandered, distracted by the parade of those who had nothing exciting to say. And then, in an instant, interest was rekindled by the Crown calling to the stand its first and most important expert witness. As the call went out Bruce noticed an increase in the hum of voices and the shuffling of bottoms on seats. The jurors came to life – they'd all looked half asleep till then. The reporters slouching in the press gallery passed comments to each other and, turning quickly backwards, Bruce saw something like a surge passing through the public gallery. This was the big one; the expert who would tell them how and when Janet Bruce was killed; whose knowledge and skill as a forensic medical practitioner and illustrious academic would provide the clear-cut certainties that none of the others called by the Crown had remotely managed.

Professor McLintock, for whom the witness box was a natural habitat, did not fail them. A tall and powerfully-built figure, he bounded up the steps and placed his hands on the edge of the box, head and shoulders thrusting out toward the well of the court, giving every indication of one prepared to enjoy the experience of being treated with the respect his calling, erudition and physical presence entitled him to. As an expert witness the rules of evidence permitted him to express opinions about what had happened and about how and by whom. Once he had given his medical findings and what he deduced from them, judge, jury, lawyers and, of course, common people in the public gallery and gentlemen of the press box, would all see the case was quite straightforward and would be grateful for the presence of Professor Ernest James Warrender McLintock.

He had Bruce's full attention too. This expert's testimony at the committal hearing had corroborated the police theory that Janet had been murdered before Bruce left to set up his alibi in Mossley Hill. Bruce had told Lovatt about overhearing the professor estimate an eight o'clock death, but Lovatt had said that because he hadn't been physically present in the room when these words were spoken, it was tantamount to hearsay evidence and therefore inadmissible in court. They would have to rely on damaging the quality of the professor's current assertion that the time of death had been around six-thirty to seven.

Tournay began by boosting McLintock's stock with a list of his academic posts posed as a question, 'You are Professor of Forensic Medicine in the University of Liverpool and Examiner in Medical Jurisprudence in the Universities of Glasgow, Edinburgh, Manchester and Birmingham?' The professor acknowledged this with a firm nod of the large head and the words, 'I am.'

Tournay asked him, 'When you arrived, what did you see in the front parlour?'

Not for the expert witness the monosyllabic response to counsel's questions. He described at length with a measure of dramatic overtone the position and condition of the body he had examined, the extent of the wounds inflicted on the woman's head, the effects of these wounds in terms of clotted blood, brain matter and bone ejected. As a result of this description the jury was by now fully engaged, all twelve sitting up, hanging on the rise and fall of the booming voice. He went on to describe the progress of rigor mortis, 'the stiffening that follows death', and said that by one o'clock in the morning the victim's neck was rigid.

Then Bruce heard him in a curious and unexpected stumble. One in the morning, the professor said, was two hours after he'd arrived. Tournay was on to that in a flash. 'Three hours after?'

The professor hastily corrected himself. 'Yes, three hours afterwards.'

This imprecision about time surprised Bruce, who wondered whether the professor's outwardly confident display might later be exposed as masking his carelessness with detail.

Tournay was to have another unpleasant surprise a moment or two later.

McLintock announced, 'when I noted that the neck was stiff and the upper part of the right arm, my opinion then was that death had taken place quite four hours before ten o'clock.'

Bruce immediately saw the problem this statement raised for the Crown. Four hours before McLintock got there meant before six. No one had disputed that he'd got back from work after six and even the police conceded Janet had been seen alive at half-past. The professor was digging himself and his side a hole with so much self-confidence; it would be hard to get him to fill it in and start again. At the same time Bruce noticed from Tournay's posture and a tightening of the facial muscles that prosecuting counsel had also seen the hole and was keen to have it filled without delay. He invited McLintock, 'Before you go on, you say you formed the view of four hours. Could you give a definite minimum it must have been? A certain time?' Six o'clock was of no use to the Crown and it would, of course, if McLintock stuck to it, make nonsense of his evidence.

McLintock declined the offer. He folded his arms across his chest. 'The opinion I formed then was that it was over four hours since this woman had been dead.'

Tournay could not let that stand. This was his witness. His key witness. If he could not turn this round he would, in chess terms, have no option but to resign. He asked, 'What would you regard as the possible margin of error in that calculation?'

'It could not possibly be, in this case, more than an hour.'

The judge looked down and said quietly, 'One hour's error would bring it to seven o'clock; half an hour's to half-past six.'

Tournay glanced up at the judge. Bruce thought he saw something akin to gratitude cross that handsome face. He had just been tossed a lifeline. Seven o'clock would do fine. Quarter to, even better. Bruce noticed some jury members nudging each other. And then he heard McLintock say, 'Yes, but there is the other way, and I formed the opinion it was four hours or more.'

Tournay moved him on before he could do any more damage.

In spite of his position, Bruce was amused. They couldn't even stick to the same hymn sheet. He knew McLintock was nowhere near the truth; professionally he was derelict. Janet was killed somewhere between eight and twenty past and yet this paragon of Liverpool's forensic medical establishment put it at not much after six.

By now McLintock was reinforcing the Crown case for the time of death by referring to the state of the blood he had seen surrounding the victim's head at ten that evening. 'This clot instead of being the bright red that one sees in blood that has been shed half an hour to an hour, had the dark appearance one sees in a blood clot that has been shed two to three hours. It was getting a darker red.' That went a good way to bring the court back to a seven o'clock killing.

Tournay looked down at his notes, then up at the professor. 'Did you notice any blood splashes?'

The professor beamed, delighted to be asked.

'There were blood splashes.' Then, like a conjuror producing a breath-taking illusion from his clothing, he took from his pocket sketches of the blood splashes away from the body, 'I have here bits of paper I had in my pocket at the time, and these are a very rough sketch of what I have already described.' Fisher was on his feet straightaway. This was new evidence the defence had never been given and ought to have been. McLintock remained unfazed. It was not new evidence. He had told the committal hearing he had made notes and others had seen him do so. At the hearing no one had asked to see them.

His point was that the position of the blood splashes on the walls, some of which he said had hit horizontally and others more at an angle, being characterised by a blob and a drip, rather like a tear drop; what he called 'soda water bottle marks', informed him that the victim had been sitting on a small sofa in the left hand corner of the room along from the fireplace, her head turned to her left as though speaking to someone else in the room. The first blow made her fall forward and she was hit again lying on the floor. All in all he said, there had been eleven and possibly twelve blows to her head.

After the lunch recess, McLintock took the court through the sequence of blows. The first, at the front of the skull, had been the most severe, opening a wound through which blood and tissue were pumped out as subsequent blows to the back of the head landed and deformed the skull beneath. In his opinion the blows were struck very quickly, probably in less than thirty seconds and the first of them had killed her. This all served the Crown's case that Bruce had killed his wife with great speed, between the time she was last seen alive and the time when he would have had to leave home to go to Mossley Hill.

Looking at the jury, Walter Bruce could see from their expressions and the looks and nudges one or two gave each other that this description of a very rapid killing had made an impression.

Tournay now directed McLintock towards the mackintosh, the centrepiece of his portrayal of Bruce as a calculating, forensically aware and perverted killer. He had McLintock examine the garment and explain the nature and relevance of the bloodstains on it. Some of these, the witness suggested, had spurted onto the outside of the coat from the victim's wounds.

Tournay seized on this to ask whether the blood would have got there in that way if someone had been wearing the coat when killing the woman. McLintock agreed it would have. Tournay took the opportunity to discredit Mrs Springer's suggestion that Janet Bruce had thrown the coat over her shoulders to answer the door.

'When I saw it,' McLintock told him, 'there was no suggestion from the appearance that that was the case... no suggestion of it having been on the arms whatever. Nothing whatever.'

McLintock had more. He had discovered a clot of human blood on the edge of the lavatory bowl in the bathroom. This was, he said of very much the same age as the clots on the rug in the front room and he had taken it up and examined it. The inference for the jury was that someone had gone up to the bathroom shortly after the killing and had washed away blood, a tiny drop of which had fallen on the rim of the ceramic bowl. This could not have been menstrual blood, he said, he had performed an autopsy on the victim and had found no indication of menstrual flow. He also said the victim had never been pregnant.

That statement had Bruce scratching his head. If the professor was right where did that leave the illegitimate son? Could the man have been misinformed and Janet not his mother? In that case why did she go to Southport to meet him? And if she wasn't his mother why didn't she tell him so? On the other hand, if the professor hadn't realised when he did the post mortem that Janet was nearly twenty years older than he'd been told she was, perhaps his findings as to the state of her womb might be mistaken too.

Tournay then waved the iron bar with which he had created such an impression on the previous morning.

'Would it want a very heavy instrument to have caused that fracture, the first blow?'

'Fairly heavy, yes.'

'Have you seen this?' He handed it to McLintock.

'Yes, just such a weapon. If a blow was made with this it would produce the appearances I found.'

His examination-in-chief ended with counsel asking him, an expert in forensic medicine, about his opinion of Bruce's demeanour during the time the professor had been in the house that Tuesday evening. The forensic medical man now presented himself as a psychologist.

'I was very much struck with it. It was abnormal.'

'In what way?'

'He was too quiet, too collected, for a person whose wife had been killed in that way. He was not nearly so affected as I was myself.' He then offered a picture of Bruce coming into the front room, smoking and flicking the ash into a bowl on the sideboard, leaning forward so as not to step in the gore on the rug.

Bruce could not remember having done this but he had to admit to himself that in the state of shock he had been in he might well have. He had been smoking cigarette after cigarette during those awful hours.

Tournay took one final opportunity to impress on the Jury his expert witness's depth of knowledge of blood-clotting.

'Have you, Professor, had very great experience on this matter of clots of blood?'

McLintock puffed out his chest. 'I have been doing this sort of examination for over thirty years.'

Bruce saw Fisher rise to cross-examine. 'I want to begin with the last bit of your evidence.' Before he could say any more, McLintock cut across him. This was his parade and he had no intention of having any of it cut short. He had not yet had a chance to tell the court about the kind of attack on a defenceless woman this had been.

'May I put in this before that? You have not had the position of these blows put in and I have a note I made at the post mortem examination which is very important.'

The Judge leaned forward. He looked surprised. 'You have a sketch?'

Clearly relishing his position as pedagogue, McLintock boomed at him, 'This shows the position after the hair was removed and the head shaved. It shows the cuts.' He produced a sketch of the position of the blows to the head and flourished it at the court.

Fisher turned to the judge. 'I don't see how that can indicate who did it.'

Tournay saw his chance to add a little more to the evidence for the Crown, He had, he told the judge, hesitated to ask the professor about this but the witness clearly believed the court should hear it. He was allowed to continue.

'Why is it important?' he asked the witness.

McLintock expatiated. 'I formed an idea of the mental condition of the person who committed this crime. I have seen crimes, many of them of this kind, and know what the mental condition is. I know it was a case of frenzy.'

This was the peak of his performance. Rather like the solution in a celebrated detective game, the crime was committed by a madman, wearing a raincoat, with an iron bar, in the parlour, on an unsuspecting woman sitting on a sofa engaged in conversation. 'Just', Tournay would have said, 'as I told the jury yesterday.'

Another forensic examination was about to begin. One in which the scalpel in the sensitive fingers of defence counsel would cut through the swollen professorial suppositions and grandiose assertions to expose the shrunken reality of the Crown's case.

He began with sweet reasonableness. 'My client has been under medical observation as to his mental condition ever since his arrest.' The witness agreed.

'If there is anything to be said about his mental condition there are people competent to say it who have lived with him.' Again, agreed.

The screw was tightened. 'If this is the work of a maniac and he is a sane man, he did not do it. Is that right?'

The professor was not yet willing to climb down. The accused might be sane now – after the event.

'If he has been sane all his life and is sane now it would be some momentary frenzy?'

McLintock stuck to his self-acquired expertise as a psychologist. 'The mind is very peculiar.'

Fisher remonstrated with him. Surely it was imprudent to make such an unsubstantiated statement in a trial for murder. McLintock refused to budge. 'Not at all. I have seen this sort of thing before, exactly the same thing.'

'The fact that a man has been sane for fifty-two years and

has been sane while in custody for the last three months would rather tend to prove he has always been sane, would it not?'

'Not necessarily. We know very little about the private lives of people and their thoughts.'

Fisher dismissed this line of argument. 'I want to deal with the evidence and not speculation.'

Bruce, on the other hand, had some respect for the professor as amateur psychologist. He was right, of course. The person who killed Janet *was* unhinged when he did it. He still had been when they met in the street. As for himself, he was perfectly sane, always had been, and he didn't do it. The professor was also right about how little outsiders knew about people's lives. Look at me and Janet, he thought. Everyone says what a loving couple we were.

Having dealt with the theory of the madman, Fisher next went after the theories of the victim having been seated and in conversation, and of the killer wearing a raincoat. McLintock did not know the police had found burn marks on the dead woman's skirt consistent with it having come in contact with a lit fire. Fisher put it to McLintock that the position of the victim if she had been lighting the gas fire when the first blow was struck was very much the same, in relation to the killer, as if she had been sitting on the sofa in the corner talking to someone. McLintock was obliged to agree; it could have been. Fisher pressed on. If she had had the mackintosh over her shoulders when the skirt got burnt, wasn't there also the likelihood that the coat was burnt as well, as opposed to the theory that Bruce had tried to burn it after taking it off? Like an actor in a sword-and-buckler film, McLintock retreated while still engaging in energetic fencing with his opponent. 'There is that possibility, yes.' And, Fisher put to him, someone had pulled the victim by her hair tearing some of it out and dislodging the pad that had formed her bun, and that might have been to get her away from the fire? 'Yes'.

The attack was double-pronged. If the killer had worn the mackintosh as he beat the victim to death, wouldn't more blood have spurted onto it than appeared to have been the case? McLintock grudgingly agreed. And even if he had been wearing the coat with nothing on beneath, the killer would have had blood on his face, in his hair, on his hands and on his legs and feet below the coat hem? McLintock concurred with all of this. Fisher went remorselessly on. The heavily blood-stained killer then went up to the bathroom to wash it all away. What evidence was there when the professor examined the bathroom that these ablutions had taken place? None. There wasn't even a damp towel.

Finally, Fisher turned to the time of Janet's death. This lay at the heart of the Crown case. For the husband to have been the killer the crime had to have been committed in a narrow window between just after half-past six and about ten to seven. If there was any doubt about that timing then the man standing charged could not have been the perpetrator.

McLintock had determined the time of death by the progress of rigor mortis in the hours between ten on the Tuesday night and one on the Wednesday morning. Fisher knew from the committal hearing what the answer to his first question would be.

'How many notes did you make with regard to rigor mortis?'

'Practically none, I think.'

'Can you show me one?'

'I do not think I can.'

Fisher closed in on his victim. 'The powerful and muscular body will be affected by rigor mortis much more slowly than a feeble and frail body?'

'Yes.'

'Was this a feeble and frail body?'

The witness quibbled. But eventually, 'Yes.'

'Then she would be likely, would she not, to be more quickly affected by rigor?'

'A little.'

McLintock was pompous but he was no fool. He realised his confident assertion as to the time of death was being challenged on the grounds that rigor mortis was a fallible test, he had no notes of its progress hour by hour and the condition of the woman would suggest a quicker rate of onset of rigor than he had allowed for. He wasn't going to admit publicly he could have been significantly wrong. Four hours dead when he arrived at ten, that was his opinion and he would not change it.

'So,' said Fisher, 'if she was alive at half-past six your opinion is wrong, is it not?'

'Yes.'

'Does that not convince you what a very fallible test rigor mortis is?'

'No, it does not. I am still of the same opinion.'

Fisher moved to dispose of the idea that the blood clot McLintock had found on the lavatory bowl had been the result of the murderer washing himself clean immediately after committing the crime. Given that there were no other signs that a killer, heavily dabbled in blood, had gone up the stairs and into the bathroom, Fisher suggested to the professor that the blood could as well have been carried there by any of those who were in the house after nine that evening. McLintock himself, or any of the policemen on the scene who had had contact with the body, the raincoat and the clots of blood, could inadvertently have taken it upstairs while examining the rest of the house. McLintock could only agree it was a possibility.

Fisher had done with him. Tournay again worked to repair some of the damage, but all he got were McLintock's opinions that the blood on the lavatory pan had been dropped at the time of the murder and that that death had occurred four hours before ten even allowing for the victim's frailty.

Bruce did a quick mental recapitulation of what the court had just heard. The professor had been shown up to be opinionated, careless and confused about the effects of age and frailty on the progress of rigor mortis. Even the Crown had found him something of a liability; a loose cannon.

McLintock was followed by Dr Prescott, the Police Medical Officer. This was a very different performance from the professor's. Prescott was diffident, what he said was vague and he clearly wanted the court to understand he'd merely played second fiddle to McLintock. Even when the prosecution, whose witness he was, asked him 'what conclusion did you come to as to the time of death?' he tried to evade giving a clear answer. He had not arrived at the house until ten minutes to midnight.

Asked the question a second time, he said, 'The fact that the hands and neck were cold proved to me that death had been some few hours before that.'

The Judge intervened with a frown and an ever-so-slightly raised finger, '"some few hours" means nothing. That may be five, six, seven or ten. I do not know what that means.'

Prescott now corroborated his medical colleague's opinion. 'I thought death had taken place about six o'clock, or,' here he reserved an escape route, 'it maybe after.'

Pressed further he would put a two hour limit either side of six. In other words, the woman might have died any time between four and eight that evening. And the progress of rigor mortis would have been 'normal' because although small, the victim was 'not frail'.

When cross-examined, he supported his opinion both by the progress of rigor mortis 'and on the cooling of the body.'

Fisher took him apart. Here he was, a Police Medical Officer, called to examine a murder victim, and he had not used a rectal thermometer to check the rate of cooling even though he admitted it was 'the best test.' Nor had he made any notes on the progress of rigor; he had not even recorded the times when he checked it.

In this case Tournay did not bother to re-examine. Bruce could see why. The Crown had a reluctant witness; there was nothing to be gained from taking him over the ground again and a lot at risk. As far as he could see the two medical experts had not advanced the Crown case by one jot. They had gone far to destroy it.

The Crown's third expert witness, the City Analyst, finally gave some comfort to Tournay and his team. He got away with not just describing the amount and age of the blood on the mackintosh, which was his field of expertise, but when asked, 'Supposing a person was wearing such a raincoat and nothing else, would you expect a great deal of blood to be on that person, if he were the assailant striking the blows?' he began to put forward theories as to how the blood got there.

'I do not think there would be very much blood after the first blow. There would be a spurt then and afterwards the blood would mainly come from the spurt itself.' He said that if the killer had been wearing the coat it did not follow he would have blood splashed all over his legs and feet. He also suggested the killer might have wiped his feet free of blood on the already stained rug and carpet before going upstairs to wash.

Bruce expected Fisher to challenge the witness for expressing opinions on medical matters about which he had no officially recognised knowledge. Only when Tournay re-examined him to emphasise those opinions with the question, 'Would you expect there to be much blood on his calves and shins?' and got the answer he wanted, 'No, not much', did Fisher take it up.

'Surely that is a medical question?' But he did not pursue it and the Analyst's suppositions reached the jury unchallenged.

Looking round him after the short tea break, Bruce could see the atmosphere in court had changed. The excitement that had animated everyone when McLintock was called had by now subsided and in its place was almost a sense of weariness; an afternoon flattening; the level of drama simply could not be sustained. The Jury had sunk back into apparent lethargy. The end of the day beckoned seductively to them.

The prosecution moved on to present its police witnesses, starting at the top of the tree with Detective Superintendent Connor.

His evidence began with an account of his actions and observations on the evening of January 20th. How he had gone over the house with the accused and found no obvious signs of burglary; no disturbance of drawers or cupboards upstairs, downstairs, and only Bruce's word that items were missing from the cash box. He had ordered up powerful lights; using these he had satisfied himself there were no signs of forced entry from outside. He had observed that Bruce seemed 'quiet and collected, smoking cigarettes and talking generally', but that when asked whose mackintosh was tucked in against the body, he seemed reluctant to answer and had to be asked twice.

The interchanges between the prosecuting counsel and the policeman were conducted in a muted, matter-of-fact tone that matched the time of day and although they made the point that in Connor's professional view there was no evidence of burglary or breaking and entering there was little here damaging to Bruce's case and none of it, as far as he could see, awakened much interest, even in those who appeared to be alert enough to listen to it.

But then, prompted by Tournay, Connor began to suggest strongly that having gone into the parlour when he went through the house looking for his wife, Bruce ought to have got blood on his shoes, unless he already knew where to step to avoid it when he crossed the room to put a match to the gas light. Connor said Bruce had told him he'd done that because when he'd gone into the room the blinds had been drawn and the lights unlit. The accused had also told him that when he looked into the room he had struck a match, seen his wife lying there, thought she might have had some sort of fit and lit a gas lamp. Connor said that even with no gas light lit, the light from the kitchen would have made it possible to see generally what was in there. He had tested this himself only the day before giving evidence. In Connor's view Bruce had no need to strike a match before going into the room and having had no reason to think the carpet was wet with blood would have gone quickly and straight in.

'When you came to the door,' Tournay asked him, 'could anybody get across to the gas without stepping into the blood?'

'It was very, very difficult. On the left side there were two large clots of blood.'

'Was there any blood on the right side of the body?'

'There was none on the right.'

'Looking into the room there, you say on the left of the body he could hardly have missed the blood?'

'You would have to be careful and walk almost sideways. If the accused had gone to his left when entering the room he could not have helped stepping in blood.'

Tournay asked him, 'Did you ever see that night, any blood on the accused?'

'No. I examined him pretty well, his boots, hands and the bottoms of his trousers, using powerful lamps.'

Not only were there no signs of blood on Bruce when Connor first saw him, but not a single trace that anyone had trodden blood outside that front room.

Bruce had to agree with him. He was right of course. He'd lied to the Superintendent who had only drawn the correct inference from what he'd been told. Connor then indulged in a couple of clumsy departures from the truth. Bruce suspected that was because he was anxious to present to the court a more professional approach than the police took at the time. Connor said first that they had not allowed Bruce to sleep at Number 29 after the murder, a fact the man in the dock knew to be nonsense. Later Connor amended that to admit the accused had slept there 'only for one night', a reversal that no one in court seemed to pick up. And he told the court Bruce had been taken down to the police station 'sometime after eleven' to make a statement. Bruce knew only too well the actual time had been twenty to twelve.

More importantly, Connor and Tournay did their best to cast doubt on the genuineness of Bruce's statements to the police by emphasising the cryptic response to Connor's question about what had been the importance to Bruce of the time of the telephone call on the Monday, and by resuscitating the suggestion that the accused *had* been seen talking to a man close to his home on the evening of the murder. When Connor had asked if this was the case the accused had denied it and then when told that someone had seen him doing so – someone who knew him well by sight – he had hesitated, then continued to deny it.

Fisher's cross-examination, unlike that to which he had subjected McLintock, was neither dramatic nor particularly destructive. It did reveal a spiteful side to the policeman that Bruce recognised immediately – after all it was the same Connor who had smirked unpleasantly in his direction when he was about to be humiliated at the Central lock-up, but it was an aspect that was probably not as obvious to the jury or the press and the public. As far as possible in his replies to Fisher he tried to promote his belief in Bruce's guilt rather than show any neutrality.

'You make the point that it is quite wrong to strike a match at the door to light the gas.' Fisher said to him.

'I do. There is no necessity for it. A man living for sixteen years in a little room like that – it was not a natural thing.'

When Fisher suggested to him that the Bruces would only use the parlour if visitors were present and that when it was so used, the lights were lit and the fire turned on, Connor's replies were generally grudging or non-committal, such as, 'I suppose so', 'It is suggested', or bluntly antagonistic with, 'It is still a matter of opinion.'

Fisher confronted him with the evidence that at the time of the murder the lights were lit as was the gas fire.

'The gas must have been lit, the murderer could not have hit her on the head in the dark. And the fire was lit was it not?'

Connor did not want to agree. Fisher drew him to the police's own evidence.

'There are burn marks on that skirt... made by the bars in the gas fire.'

'There are no bars in the gas fire', dodged Connor.

'The asbestos rings of that fire, then.'

Towards the end of his cross-examination Fisher more or less accused the police of wilfully ignoring the statement of a witness who claimed to have seen Billy Locke delivering milk to the Bruces well after six-thirty on that Tuesday evening. Connor twisted and turned. First he did not know which boy the defence was talking about. Then the boy *had* made a statement but long after the events of the night in question so it would be of dubious value. Then the statement had been taken by another officer, he wasn't sure who, and that was all he knew of it.

Even on the issue of the murder weapon, which the police had never found, Connor remained optimistically obdurate. It might still be 'hid in the house' or 'in the adjoining fields.' Bruce was impressed with the policeman's vision of a rural Anfield. The only field for miles round Number 29 was the one the Liverpool Football Club played on.

After Fisher, Tournay threw him a life line. He needed it.

'Would it (the weapon) go down one of the street drains?'

'Easily.'

'You would have to search them all to find it?'

'Yes.'

As he was taken down at the end of the second day, Bruce

could have been forgiven for feeling that his ordeal might soon be over and the nightmare that had become his waking life might end suddenly and completely, leaving him in the calm world of semi-retirement.

In the silence of the police van taking him back to Walton Gaol, he summed up his position at the end of that second day.

They've fired their whole arsenal at me and it has either fallen short or bounced off my defences. We made McLintock look a bumbling fool, his 'expert' views on the time of Janet's death shown to be based on a flawed method of calculation and the range of time useless as a guide to when it might have happened. The other chap, Prescott, simply confirmed that the forensic medical work was amateurish and the conclusions from it worthless. Connor came across as uncooperative and failing in his duty to present facts objectively. It was pretty clear, and he wasn't able to counter it, that he ordered evidence to be suppressed that Janet was alive at a time when I couldn't conceivably have carried out such a killing. If the court believes he did get the milk boy to give false evidence and didn't call others who had a different tale to tell, it leaves the police case against me in rags.

I didn't murder my wife, and on the evidence so far I couldn't possibly have done. After all, English law's the best in the world; you can trust it to see fair play. It's got to be proved beyond any reasonable doubt that you're guilty before you can be convicted. Especially when guilty means a death sentence.

But still, I'm worried about the police's attitude. That means Connor. I don't understand why, but he's got it in for me. He seems prepared to lie, conceal and mislead rather than accept he never had enough evidence to charge me in the first place. And whatever he says, he's been after me from the very first hours of that Tuesday night. Yes, I know I'm guilty of a conspiracy to murder but that's not what they charged me with and not what I'm being tried for. If the police had the slightest suspicion someone else was involved they'd surely have brought it up by now. I'll give evidence tomorrow. I can do that with a clear conscience; what they're trying me for I didn't do. I wonder if Jordan and Davies are following this trial closely. They'd better be. When this is all over I want them to know I looked after them. I kept my side of the bargain even though it has cost me my freedom and put me through pain and degradation. They've got what they wanted without any trouble coming their way.

Back in the prison hospital dormitory that evening Bruce's wizened benefactor edged up to him. 'Good day was it?'

'Yes'. Bruce took out the rabbit's paw from his prison uniform and held it up for the other to see. 'It's working for me. We had a good day. Tomorrow should be even better.'

The other gave his usual weak, rather nervous, smile. 'Just as long as it's lookin' after yer. Hold on ter it.' Bruce put the talisman back and patted his pocket. Both men nodded to each other.

I hope it brings me more luck than it's obviously brought him. When I get out of here I mean to see he gets it back. Together with something to help him look after himself.

19

In the Dock

The Third Day

The early morning of the third day was as wet and miserable as the previous two had been, but Bruce was indifferent to the weather. This was the day he'd be called to give evidence – his opportunity to give the court a clear picture of the kind of man he was; to break free of the caricature of the perverted and frenzied murdering husband so assiduously fostered by Tournay and McLintock. He had been portrayed as a cunning, contriving, killer, second-guessing the police, ruthless, violent and swift in action yet cool and calculating both before and after the deed. His performance in the witness box would give the lie to all that. His evidence would be simple and open, with the ring of honesty – not trying to score points or sound clever but giving the court the impression of a puzzled casualty rather than a knowing perpetrator. Someone who found himself in a position that but for the grace of God could have happened to anyone present. The jury would realise he was not at all the monster created by Mr Tournay. Taken together with the Crown's failure to prove anything against him, he should be seen by jury and public alike as the unfortunate victim of the over-eagerness of the police to close a case. When he'd done this he'd be but a step away from walking free without a stain on his character. But first he had to wait patiently while the prosecution presented its final witnesses, the first being Sergeant Bowler. A tall, well-built man with a long face and a nose that seemed to bisect most of that length, he filled the witness box as his chief, Connor, had done. Bruce remembered him as the one who'd pulled out the raincoat from beside Janet's body and who'd accompanied Bright and him to his home when there'd been the awkward question about the iron bar missing from the hearth.

The Crown was anxious to restore some respectability to the tests the police had conducted to see how long it took Billy Locke to get from the church clock to deliver milk to the doorstep of the Bruce's house.

The prosecution asked him, 'On the nineteenth of February you went with the boy, Locke, did you?'

'Yes.'

'On the route he has described, will you say how you walked and what the boy Locke did?'

'We left directly opposite the clock at five past seven and the boy made his own pace. Inspector Bright was at one side of him and I walked behind him. He went through the actions he did on the night in question when he delivered the milk, eventually arriving at Swindon Street at ten past seven.'

Then he was encouraged to tell the court that tests had shown it possible to get from Bruce's house to the Lodge Lane tram stop in fifteen minutes. Taking the two sets of tests together the Crown made a clear inference that the accused could have killed his wife between six-thirty and having to leave to catch his tram at eight minutes to seven.

Cross-examining him, Fisher wielded his scalpel.

'One of the officers said you jumped on a tram as it came along.'

'It stopped at the request stop and we made a run for it and got on it.'

Bruce hoped that it had got through to the jury that the timings between his house and the tram stop had been achieved by fit police officers jumping on and off moving trams and walking very quickly. No one who looked at him could surely think he would have been able to do the same.

Bowler had also said something else. When he'd prepared Janet for post-mortem, he'd found a one pound and a ten shilling note in a small improvised pocket sewn into her corset. That astonished Bruce who couldn't see why she would have secreted such a large amount of cash in that way. It wouldn't have been accessible for paying or buying anything. She could only have got at it in her own home, so why bother to put it there in the first place? Just one more thing that made him realise he'd never known this woman at all. Unless, of course, she'd meant it for Jordan for services rendered. He found it distasteful but it seemed to be the only explanation. When this was all over and he was back home, he'd look at her savings book and see if she'd withdrawn anything earlier that day.

As with many of its witnesses, the prosecution made a point of asking this one his impressions of Bruce at the time of the murder. 'What conclusions did you come to about his demeanour; what was he like?'

'He impressed me as a very cool, collected man – cool under the circumstances.'

Bruce registered this and felt uneasy. This constant portrayal of him as a callous man who had never shown any distress at the killing of his wife was beginning to build up. Repeat something often enough and people will start to accept it as the truth. He would have to counter that perception from the witness box.

Bright followed Bowler. The prosecution got him to cast doubt on the likelihood that a thief had managed to reach the cash box on top of the shelf in Bruce's kitchen. It would have been difficult, he said, to have used the shelves to climb up to get at the box, there wasn't enough room to get a proper foothold and in any case the shelves were unstable. He accepted, however, that an intruder might have used one of the kitchen chairs.

Like his superior, Connor, Bright was at pains to make out that Bruce had not been treated as a suspect from the outset but perfectly correctly, 'like any other ordinary complainant would be treated. Perhaps a bit better.'

Bruce could not help a wry smile. If being taken in the small hours of the night of the murder to give a statement at the police station, the insistence he report to them the following morning, the hours he had spent at Headquarters in the days afterwards, the number of statements he had given, the attitude of Connor and Bright, the examination of his clothes for blood, was being treated a 'bit better', then what would it have been like for the average victim of a crime?

Like Bowler, Bright was also encouraged by the Crown to tell the court that Bruce had appeared 'cool and calm. He did not seem to be in the least upset. I did not see any emotion at all at the death of his wife.'

'Was there anything particular which drew your attention to that?'

'When I first went into the house on the night of the murder he was sitting in the kitchen. He had the cat on his knee and was stroking it. He did not look to me like a man who has just battered his wife to death.'

Bruce could make neither head nor tail of this. Did the man mean he looked very cool for someone who'd just savagely murdered his wife? Or that he didn't look like a murderer? He hoped the jury would think it the second.

In cross-examination, Fisher made a strong suggestion that far from being treated as the victim of a crime, Bruce had been shadowed by the police from two days after the murder. Bright refused to acknowledge this, repeating he did not know anything about any surveillance.

Bruce knew he'd been followed by plain-clothes officers, although he no longer thought he had been when he spoke to Knight at the tram stop. Either Knight had reported their words to the police or someone else standing at the stop had overheard the conversation and gone to them about it.

Tournay intervened to explain the shadowing as a beneficial service to Bruce; the police being concerned he might meet with some act of hostility from the public while doing his insurance round.

That explanation for having tailed someone who was not supposed to be a suspect added to Bruce's scepticism. The likelihood of any of those he called on physically attacking him was more than remote; it was non-existent. The few who thought the worst of him had refused to respond to his ring or knock. All the rest seemed to be perfectly willing to continue doing business with him. The real reason he'd been followed was so that the police would know if he went off somewhere to check the murder weapon was still where they assumed he had disposed of it.

Much to Bruce's relief, Bright's spell in the witness box

did not add anything that had not already been introduced by the prosecution and certainly no significant threads to arouse anxiety or create surprise for him.

He was, however, surprised and concerned to find that Tournay had one last stratagem. His one 'good' witness the day before had been the City Analyst, mainly because he had got away with offering opinions about the absence, presence and distribution of the blood at the murder scene rather than just its kind and age which was the true area of his expertise – and he had not been challenged over it. Tournay re-called him in an attempt to reinforce the claim that the blood spot McLintock had found on the lavatory bowl was dropped there by the murderer from fresh blood immediately after the crime, something Bruce knew to be arrant nonsense. Jordan would never have gone upstairs; he couldn't get out of the house fast enough. That spot was almost certainly, he thought, carried there by one or other of the crowd of police who had been around the blood soaked front room carpet and had probably relieved themselves upstairs in the bathroom.

The City Analyst had done a number of experiments, using his own blood, to simulate the blob and prove that fresh blood, dropped from a certain height, would take on the shape and consistency of the spot the professor had discovered.

'I judged the height between the pan and the basin to be fifteen inches, and it was on that I made my experiment.'

'With what result?' asked Tournay.

'When the blood drops that height it forms a little clot, and when that dries it clots together and makes a little blob.'

Fisher had been forewarned and had had professional advice the blood could not have been fresh. He did his best to tar this witness with the same brush of incompetence as he had done McLintock and Prescott.

'Have you any notes of your experiments?'

'No.'

'None?'

'No.'

Fisher told him, 'I want you to understand that I am absolutely challenging your evidence and am going to call evidence to contradict it.'

Shortly before noon, Fisher began his opening speech for the defence.

Right at the start he told the court he had to make up for two and half days of the trial having passed before he had been allowed any opportunity to put the prisoner's case in a complete form. Up to then they could only have got an idea of it if they had closely followed the way he had cross-examined the Crown's witnesses. Turning in the direction of Tournay he drew attention to the other disadvantages the defence was labouring under. The prosecution had not just had the chance to put its case long before the defence could be heard but its counsel had done it in a particularly dramatic fashion deliberately designed to weaken any presumption of innocence. The newspapers in the region, too, had given the case heavy, continuous and sensational coverage with which every juror must have been familiar – and this also fed into the picture the prosecutor had painted of the man on trial. Then there was the way the police had handled the case. If there was one kind of crime that was an abomination to them, he said, it was a murder they weren't able to solve. 'They are apt to take a biased view of the case and pursue it relentlessly.' They had therefore felt justified in withholding information from the defence and had not called witnesses whose evidence contradicted their view. He saved his greatest condemnation to last. He pointed a long accusatory finger towards the witness box.

'You have had the pleasure of seeing here,' and he repeated the finger gesture, 'Professor McLintock, and he did that which he must have known perfectly well he had no right to do, he forced upon the court – insisted on saying to you – "Ah, this looks to me like frenzy. I have known cases like that." I say he had no right to do what he did.' His point was that Professor McLintock had made a mischievous and unsubstantiated claim about the prisoner's sanity which he had known was outside the scope of his professional knowledge. Nor, Fisher strongly inferred, should the Crown have allowed, never mind encouraged, him to do so. It had been an act of desperation, 'because the police realise that this motiveless crime, committed by this devoted husband, presents problems which are almost insuperable.' He said it had been established at least twenty years before that the Crown should not call evidence of the accused's mental condition. If there were any it had to be fully disclosed to the defence beforehand and the defence alone could decide whether to use it on the accused's behalf.

Bruce thought that anyone who paid attention to this speech of Fisher's should be impressed by the complete contrast with the one his opponent had made on the first day. It was much shorter – just over half an hour. It was delivered without histrionics, the argument was logical and held up each element of the prosecution case to show the flaws, improbabilities and uncertainties. These were then replaced with more reasonable and understandable possibilities. The scalpel, not the bludgeon.

Fisher came to the end with an appeal to the Jury's humanity. 'You know something of Bruce's history now. He is fifty-two and there has never been a thing against him in his life. He is a delicate man. He is a mild man. Everybody who knew him liked him. He is a man of very considerable education, he is a refined man. Those passages read from his diary will show the sort of man he is – he has very considerable gifts of expression. That is the man who is charged with this frightful crime. A man dragged into the emotional whirlpool of a murder trial because of an over-simplified police attitude to the case which could be summed up in the question, "If he didn't do it, who did?"'

Bruce had had no direct meeting with Fisher. The conduit between them was Lovatt, but he felt the approach Fisher was taking fitted exactly the way he wanted to present himself when he gave his evidence. He was understandably nervous at having shortly to do so. Beneath his outward appearance of resignation, even weariness, commented on by the press reporters, he was keenly absorbing and evaluating what his counsel was saying, the better to be able to add to the impression when his time finally came.

As soon as Fisher had sat down, the court took the lunch recess.

At half-past two it reconvened. As the officials and the jurors took their places, visitors craned forward. There was a low buzz as people prepared themselves for the drama soon to come. Everyone knew Fisher was going to put the accused in the witness box; he had said the court would see what kind of man they were trying. As the moment approached, his doctor would have spotted a sign that Bruce was nervous. His mouth made an 'O', as though whistling silently.

He had debated with himself whether to take the Oath or an Affirmation without the religious overtones. In the end, setting aside his doubts and inhibitions about conventional religious beliefs and practices and also careful to give the Jury no ammunition for prejudice against him, he took the Oath although so indistinctly he could not be heard and he was asked to speak up. He realised that days of remaining silent for long periods had left their mark on a voice never strong and penetrating. Like any instrument – like his violin – it needed to be warmed up.

The warming up began with routine questions. The tall, thin, slightly stooped witness giving a suggestion of an elderly heron in his posture and calmness, in the dark panelled witness box; below him in the well of the court, the meatier, sharp-featured and generally imposing figure of his questioner.

For the next hour Fisher took Bruce through the detail of the evidence in a way that made him feel increasingly comfortable, although he did not attempt to stray outside the framework counsel set for him. Even when Fisher touched on the constable who had maintained he'd seen Bruce weeping and looking distraught on the Tuesday afternoon, Bruce simply denied any feelings of distress and affirmed Fisher's suggestion that his eyes had watered. He did not elaborate by recounting the speck of dirt in his eye. Prompted by Fisher, Bruce also gave an account of his time in Mossley Hill on the evening of the murder that did not depart in any respect from the descriptions of it the court had already heard from others, except when he responded to a question about his awareness of being in Green Lane following his unsuccessful search for Menlove Gardens East. 'Finding yourself in Green Lane, did you do anything with regard to Mr Willesden's house?' Bruce said that he had called at Willesden's house and had no response, something he had not previously disclosed to the police or at any of the pre-trial hearings.

Two important planks of the prosecution case were carefully dealt with. Bruce denied quietly and firmly he had spoken to anyone until he met the Springers in the entry behind his house. He had never seen the young woman witness in his life, though he accepted it was possible she knew him by sight. He also insisted he had been nothing like as cool and collected as the police and their co-workers had maintained. He told the court he had been extremely agitated but tried not to show it. On occasions he had broken down and cried. He had chain-smoked to give himself something to do. 'The inaction was more than I could stand.'

As Fisher reached the end of his examination, Bruce was aware that if the sight and sound of him after so long as a mute and, to outward appearances, distant and withdrawn observer of his trial had stimulated the press and public; to judge from the tenseness of their bodies, necks craned to hear, their expectation levels had risen several notches on the prospect of his being handed over to Tournay for cross-examination. The real drama was yet to come for them – and for him. He was sure most of them were inclined to believe he was a peculiar fellow who seemed too damn self-possessed in the face of how brutally his wife had been murdered; they would be hoping Tournay would bait him like a bear until, exhausted and bamboozled, he condemned himself out of his own mouth and they could say, 'told you so.' The very few who could see he'd been wrongly arrested, charged and tried by a police force clutching at straws would want to see frustration from the Crown at being unable to pin a single thing on him that could not be given a perfectly innocent explanation.

He was fully conscious he was about to fight for his life. He knew, as neither his defence nor those attending the day's proceedings did, that much of the Crown case against him came very close to the truth, even if the approach was from the wrong direction. He had deliberately drawn attention to himself on the journey to find Mr McQuillian; he had not checked beforehand, as the meticulous Mr Bruce would have done had the message been genuine, the address he had been given and how to get there; he had indeed spoken to someone just before going to his house and knew he'd been seen doing so. In the house, the gas light had been lit in the front room even though he'd given a statement saying it was not, and that was how he'd avoided stepping in the mess on the carpet. He had known Janet was dead when he'd entered the room although not how violent that death had been. He had known Janet would bend down to light the gas fire before making herself and Jordan comfortable and, too, that Jordan would use the mackintosh left hanging in the hall to blind and muffle her before hitting her. He'd have to be very careful how he dealt with Tournay's questions and to keep telling himself he had not done what he was charged with.

Tournay began with a machine-gun burst of questions, all different, switching direction rather as a gun might be traversed against an advancing enemy. Where was Mr Willesden on the Tuesday evening? How bad was Mrs Bruce's cold? If the Bruces had planned to have a musical evening rather than his going out, wouldn't the fire have been lit and the lights on? In the photographs taken on the evening of the 20th, wasn't the piano open and sheet music on the stands? Here Tournay was subtly suggesting that Bruce had proposed an evening's music to his wife; had not told her he had an appointment and had killed her as she unwittingly prepared the room for their evening. This would account for the open piano, the sheet music, the fire being lit. And, of course, the sudden irruption into the room of the man wearing nothing but a mackintosh.

Then he switched abruptly to reminding Bruce he had said he had counted the notes in the vase or jar in the bedroom. A bloodstain had been found on the notes. Had Bruce had blood on his hands when he counted the notes? If he hadn't how had it got there?

Bruce dealt with the barrage stolidly and straightforwardly. In response to a direct question he said he had told his wife he was going out that evening and they had discussed it when he had come home from work for his tea. To the best of his knowledge he had never had blood on his hand or fingers, so the bloodstain on one of the notes in the jar could not have come from him even though he had counted them.

Tournay now started to develop the pattern which would define his cross-examination. He held up the main elements of the case to the witness and to the court, emphasising the implausibility of each one. Every question and its supplementaries were framed in a tone of slightly exaggerated incredulity: 'Do you really expect us to accept or believe that?' On his part, Bruce had to contend with the fact that while he was not by nature argumentative, he was highly logical in his thinking and must resist the temptation to engage in cerebral jousting with his interrogator.

Tournay began with questions about how well Bruce had known the area in which he had searched for Mr McQuillian before that Tuesday night, and then focused on the fact the witness had said in his examination-in-chief that he had called at the house of his supervisor, Mr Willesden. Tournay accused him of not having mentioned this in the statements he had given – even the one he gave on the night of the murder.

'Do you say you stated somewhere you called on Mr Willesden that night? You never stated it to anyone till you gave it in evidence today.'

Bruce realised he'd put himself in a corner. He'd told Lovatt he'd called at Willesden's which is how Fisher had come to ask him about it earlier. Tournay had quickly picked up the significance of that slip and was trying to skewer him with it. He forced himself to remain calm; his best course was to act and sound as though he genuinely thought he had given that information in a statement to the police.

'Yes, I think I did.'

'In what statement?'

'I cannot tell you but I think I volunteered that information in some statement.'

Tournay put to the court a strong impression the accused was lying and that he had not, in fact, mentioned this in any of the statements he had made; statements the Crown could produce and would read out if necessary. The inference was that Bruce had not mentioned going to his chief's because it raised the question as to why he hadn't done that immediately he couldn't find Menlove Gardens East. It also raised the question of how well he knew the area if he could find Willesden's house from a direction he said he had never approached it before.

All Bruce could do was to repeat that he thought he had said this when giving one or other of his statements, implying but not saying that the police had failed to take it down, and he did this sufficiently consistently for Tournay to go off on another line of questioning.

The first element Tournay examined was the telephone call. To introduce it, he tried to get Bruce to admit the amounts of money he actually held at home before paying them in were small – so small as to make it unlikely that anyone who knew about them would think it worthwhile to hatch an elaborate plan to steal them, especially since even if he got Bruce out of the house on a wild goose chase he would still have to deal with Mrs Bruce.

'At the end of your week's collecting you would seldom be more than a few pounds in hand?'

Bruce had an answer to that. He was on factual ground, where he felt comfortable. 'The point can be proved precisely, what I have paid in per week over a number of years. It might be twenty or twenty-five pounds, it varied and it might be thirty.' The teacher emerged. Hands firmly on the ledge of the box, his head inclined towards his ignorant pupil. 'You do not realise that in addition to what is known as an industrial branch collection, I might pick up varying sums in the ordinary branch.'

Tournay brought him back from the lecture room.

'You know I am dealing at the moment with the industrial branch; the weekly debit. That is the correct expression, is it not?'

Bruce accepted it was.

Tournay then repeated his question about the sum Bruce might have had in his collection box on the night of the murder.

'By the time you met your outgoings, would it not be the fact that on the Tuesday or Wednesday, you would never have more than a few pounds in hand?'

Bruce fought him off. 'I could have twenty or twenty-five pounds.'

Tournay then turned the argument on its head. If McQuillian existed, he knew enough about the insurance company's methods to know that agents kept collection money at home until it was paid in. Bruce had to agree. Well, then, Tournay commented, 'Anyone knowing the nature of your business would know when your monthly collection would be.'

'An outside person would not know, certainly.'

Bruce recognised immediately that he had tried to divert Tournay away from the point he had been making. And had failed.

Tournay persisted.

'And if he was going to make a raid on your house he would naturally choose the time of the monthly collection.'

'He might.'

The inference for the court was obvious. If McQuillian really existed he was well-informed about Bruce and would not have chosen the evening of January 20th to strike. It was therefore far more likely he did not exist. Bruce felt acutely aware of the threat to his defence. A housebreaker would have had no idea how much he'd find. But common-or-garden burglary had long since been discounted. Now his defence position was that whoever killed Janet lured him out of the house. Someone who knew quite a lot about his business and his routines.

Tournay piled the unlikely on the unlikely. If McQuillian existed, how could he have had any assurance that Bruce would get his message? Or, if he got it, that he wouldn't check the address the next day and find there was no such place? Tournay put it to Bruce that using a call box only a short distance away there was 'ample opportunity for him to have gone round to your house.' If he knew Bruce was out of the house on the Monday, why on earth, Tournay suggested, would McQuillian have bothered to make an appointment for the following night? Why not just go straight round and do the business there and then? And if he didn't know whether Bruce had stayed at home, why leave a message for him somewhere else?

Bruce knew perfectly well what Tournay was leading up to. That both Monday's telephone call and Tuesday's journey to and around the Menlove Avenue area were parts of an alibi which Bruce himself had constructed. What he had to do was to respond to each question or statement Tournay bowled at him by holding a straight bat, 'yes', 'no', or some phrase of agreement like, 'I suppose it would.' There was to be no argument, no attempt to explain.

Tournay moved on to emphasise that Bruce's behaviour on the way to Menlove Gardens, when he got there, and after he had failed to find the place, had been out of character. He had been very chatty, telling everyone he met why he was there, what he was looking for and how he did not know the area at all.

'Would you describe yourself as a very talkative and communicative man – rather the contrary are you not?'

Bruce stonewalled. 'I don't know how I would describe myself. I leave others to do that.'

Tourney persisted. 'Would you say you were a person who would never say more than is necessary?'

Bruce tried to stifle the question, depriving Tournay of any follow up. 'I could not say.'

In his next series of questions Tournay posed the essence of the improbability of the accused's case.

'Does not the whole thing strike you as very remarkable that a man who does not know you should ring you up for business in another district and expect you to go there and yet without knowing whether you had gone or not comes and waits outside your house for the chance of murdering your wife?'

'Yes', said Bruce.

'It is a curious thing, is it not?'

Again, 'yes'. Bruce knew the only way to deal with this was to agree, to accept the strangeness, saying, in effect, 'I'm as baffled as you by it.'

'It would have been easier for him, would it not, to have given a genuine address but a bit further off? 'I suppose it would.' Meaning, 'yes, I agree, the whole thing's a puzzle to me too.'

'If you had been given a genuine address, you would not have needed to make a number of enquiries. One would have been enough. Do you follow me?'

Bruce did, only too well. 'Yes', he said.

'The wrong address is essential to the creation of evidence for the alibi. Do you also follow that?'

Bruce thought in chess terms. Decline your opponent's gambit. He wants to draw you into something. Seem flummoxed. For once, don't agree with him. 'No I do not follow you.'

Tournay worried the point like a dog a bone. 'If you had been told 25 Menlove Gardens West, you would have found it immediately and discovered that no one called McQuillian lived there, wouldn't you?'

'Yes.'

'But if you are told of an address which does not exist, you can ask seven or eight people, every one of whom would be a witness to where you were?'

'Yes.'

'So, to a man who was planning to do this, a wrong address would be essential to his alibi?'

'Yes.'

The picture Bruce was giving to those defending him was that of a genuinely innocent man perplexed by what had happened to him – reeling from the blows of fortune. He could do no more than agree with his tormentor that the whole thing seemed beyond belief. He was admitting, however, that that was how it had been. With hindsight he would have done everything differently. His defence team had no idea of how cleverly he was anticipating and avoiding the bear-traps Tournay laid for him.

Try as Tournay might from every angle, he was unable to make the breakthrough he looked for, the damaging admission, the unguarded response upon which he could fasten, the statement that could be shown to be a lie or invention, the loss of composure that he could present as a pointer to guilt. At the end of the cross-examination he had not managed, other than by innuendo, to expose Bruce's version of events as the fabrications of a cunning murderer, and to that extent as Tournay finally sat down Bruce felt he had had the better of the exchange. Not by much, he granted, but surely enough for the defence to assert the Crown had not proved its case.

Fisher closed Bruce's ordeal, wrapping up his brief re-examination with a final sensational question clearly intended to nail the Crown's image of the killer naked beneath his raincoat, 'When you were playing the violin with your wife were you accustomed to do it when you were naked in a mackintosh; was that your habit?'

Bruce didn't think he could have heard him correctly.

'What was that?'

'To play naked in a mackintosh.'

Now the penny dropped. Bruce did not have to feign shock. He was, deeply, shocked. For once he heard his own voice with some real substance and penetration.

'I have never played naked in my life.'

And no one who could see this figure – elderly, dry, distant, dressed as though the past thirty years had never happened – could have found the thought other than bizarre.

Returned to his position in the dock, Bruce observed his defence make its final onslaught on the most critical element of the Crown's case against him, the time of his wife's death.

A professor of pathology gave evidence that in his expert view his fellow professor, McLintock, was wrong in asserting Janet had been killed as early as six-thirty. From what he had heard McLintock say in the witness box, death was more likely to have happened somewhere between seven and eight, although he made the point emphatically that relying solely on observing the progress of rigor mortis made any calculation unreliable. Body temperature should also have been taken regularly and, of course, notes kept of all observations and the times. He also dismissed the City Analyst's hypothesis about the drip on the lavatory bowl being from freshly-shed blood. To have had the shape it took, he said, it would have been an hour or more old when dropped. This was confirmed by a second witness, also an expert in pathology, who had conducted experiments with fresh blood and had not had results anything like those the Analyst claimed.

Next, Fisher called the witnesses the police had tried hard to ignore in compiling their case. They all stated firmly, and could not be shaken by Tournay, that the milk had been delivered to Number 29 and taken in by Mrs Bruce well after six-thirty. One of them had seen Billy Locke still standing on the Bruces' front doorstep at twenty-three minutes to seven. The others all swore that the day after the murder Billy told them he had delivered to the Bruce house at about a quarter to seven.

By the time Fisher closed the case for the defence it was

nearly seven o'clock. Before the court adjourned, the Judge declared the speeches by both counsel and his summing-up would begin the following morning. The courtroom emptied, Bruce was escorted away back to the gaol but not before having had a chance to speak to Lovatt who gave a generally positive take on the day and on the trial so far. Bruce gathered that his time in the witness box had given no hostages to the prosecution and the evidence of the young people stated, unlike Billy Locke's, clearly and without hesitation to the effect that the milk had been delivered substantially later than six-thirty had driven a coach and horses through the idea he could have committed a particularly bloody murder and dealt with the aftermath in very much less than eighteen minutes.

Back in his prison hospital ward, he went to bed quietly confident that by the same time tomorrow he would be a free man. The lucky rabbit's foot was working.

20

In the Dock

The Fourth Day

Preparing to leave Walton Gaol for St George's Hall on the final morning of the trial, Bruce still felt optimistic. Confident in the essential fairness of the English legal system, he could not see how a jury who had heard all the evidence of the past three days could feel there was 'no reasonable doubt' about the identity of Janet's murderer.

It was heavy overcast when he left the prison and by the time he arrived it was raining steadily. The prospect of getting thoroughly wet and then spending all day slowly drying out had had no effect on the number of those determined to be there for this final day. Every available place was taken when he was brought into court and he saw and felt the anticipation as though it were something the crowd exuded along with the vapour from damp clothing and the pungent odour of sweat caused both by exertion and nervous excitement. They were here for the speeches, to hear the judge sum up, and for the drama. There would be a verdict by the end of the day. And if that verdict were against the accused, there would be a sentence. And in this case if there were a sentence they all knew what it would be. So thrilling; the black cap, no less, and the terrible words that went with it.

In their final speeches both counsels concentrated on the two essential factors that could determine the accused's guilt: the telephone call and the time of Janet Bruce's death.

Speaking first, Fisher wasted no time on the issue of who had made the call. He referred the jury to what he had said about it the day before to the effect that the person who took the call had known Bruce a long time and had said the caller's voice was nothing like his. If Bruce did not make that call, then he was innocent. He reminded the jury that the Crown had produced not one shred of evidence that Bruce had made it. As Fisher moved on, Bruce felt he might also have asked the jury if they thought he had made that call at seven-twenty how they explained his being in the City Café at a quarter to eight?

Fisher spent a large part of his speech reiterating the unreliability of the Crown case that Bruce had killed his wife in less than a twenty minute gap between the milk being delivered and leaving home to go to Mossley Hill. The underpinning of that case was the expert medical evidence that death had occurred between six and seven and that the milk boy had been the last to see Mrs Bruce alive at six thirty-one. But the progress of rigor mortis had been shown to be a hopelessly inaccurate way to calculate the time of death and perversely one important element of McLintock's observations argued against his official estimate of around six o'clock because by his own account when he'd first examined the body there had been only a small amount of the clear fluid element of blood, called serum, that separates from the thicker element. If death had occurred as early as six there would have been a lot of it. So on the medical side there was no strong evidence for murder before seven o'clock; in fact things pointed to it being later. But there were also the witnesses who said Mrs Bruce had been seen alive later than six-thirty giving a strong suggestion the police had coached young Billy Locke to say he'd delivered milk earlier than he did and had deliberately ignored anyone throwing doubt on this timing. Surely, he asked the jury, in deciding the accused's innocence or otherwise they had to consider the time available to commit this violent and bloody murder then remove all traces of blood so effectively that six hours later the police could find none.

Fisher closed his speech on the note he had held all along in this trial. The accused had no discernible motive for killing his wife; he had a character against which 'there is not a word to be said' and 'whose affection for his wife cannot be doubted'. Everything the

Crown had put forward as pointing to his guilt had an alternative and innocent explanation. It was not enough for a juror to think it possible the accused had done this; that juror had to be certain. Otherwise his client was entitled to be acquitted.

Tournay took twenty minutes longer than his opponent to appeal to the jury.

He argued for Bruce's guilt on the obverse of the case Fisher had made for his innocence. For someone other than Bruce to have done it, what motive could *he* have had? Certainly not money. Getting Bruce out of the house pursuing an insurance lead suggested knowledge of the agent's business. The small size of the average weekly sum paid in would hardly justify such elaborate planning. Surely it had not been to kill Mrs Bruce. She had no enemies, her husband had said so, and if the object *had* been to kill her why did McQuillian not do it on the Monday night when Bruce had gone to the Chess Club? And what opportunity did the other man have on the Tuesday evening? If Bruce had checked the address he had been given and found it did not exist, he would not have gone out at all. If he had gone out and immediately found the address did not exist he might have returned home quickly and interrupted McQuillian's activities. If, however, it was Bruce and not McQuillian who had planned and executed what happened over the two days, much of what he said and did on the Tuesday strongly suggested his guilt. His behaviour had been uncharacteristic and the business of not being able to get into his house looked and sounded contrived. How could he not know about an iron bar that had lain in the hearth for months if not years and was used to hook out the cigarette ends Bruce himself threw there?

On the critical question of who made the telephone call, he made much of how close the call box was to Bruce's house. He could have got to it in three to four minutes and there was only his word for the time he left the house to go to the City Café. The other witness to that was dead. Knight had said it wasn't Bruce's voice on the other end of the line. Of course, Bruce had disguised his voice. It was not difficult to do.

On the time of death, Tournay offered the jury the idea of a man who had carefully, meticulously even, planned to kill his wife and establish an alibi. Such a calculating killer could have done it in twenty minutes or a little less. 'I say there is ample time for it,' he told them confidently.

In this closing speech he followed the same themes as in his opening; only the playacting was missing. He even managed to resurrect the picture of Bruce naked beneath a raincoat killing the woman who, all unsuspecting, was getting the front room ready for a musical evening while she waited for him to change out of his work clothes upstairs.

As he listened to these attempts, on the one hand to exonerate and on the other to condemn him, Bruce had conflicting emotions. He was the only person in that place who knew what had happened on the Monday and Tuesday evenings and that enabled him to have, as it were, an Olympian view of the arguments. He was affected by the obvious belief in his innocence of those defending him and no longer felt any discomfort about the degree to which he had deceived them. At one point in his speech Fisher had said, 'Bruce is not an ingenious man who is thinking out the best answer he can give.' Yet that was exactly what, when Tournay had cross-examined him, he had been doing. Knowing he was completely innocent of the charge for which he was presently being tried, he had no compunction at all about contributing to the picture his defence had given of him to the court, especially about his feelings for Janet. In the witness box, Fisher had asked him, 'Is there anyone in the world who could take the place of your wife?' He had said, 'no.' He didn't want anyone to replace Janet. He wanted a wholly different kind of person doing what the dead Janet would never have done. Fisher had asked, 'have you anyone to live with now?' Again he'd said 'no.' True, he hadn't. It made him seem bereft, the object of the exercise. 'Or to live for?' added Fisher. 'No', he'd said again. Perfectly true, the only person he had to live for was himself and that, he knew, was only for a limited time. Fisher had meant his questions to emphasise to the court the pointlessness of any suggestion that Bruce had done away with his wife. A husband who planned to kill his wife, rather than doing so in the red mist of anger, surely did it either for her money or because he wanted another woman in her place, officially or otherwise. If neither was the case here then Bruce was a most unlikely wife-killer.

It seemed to him too that those prosecuting him really did believe him guilty and some of the points Tournay made were uncomfortably close to the truth. He had to acknowledge that when he compared the two speeches, his counsel's had been an appeal to the jury's better nature – to accept that nothing had been proved against his client – while Tournay's had been to their baser nature – to be suspicious, sceptical, grudging, to ask if he hadn't done it, who else could have? He had few doubts as to which was more likely to be effective on the twelve people seated to his left.

But, he reflected, juries surely know counsels' closing speeches are always biased one way or the other; he wouldn't, and no one else should, expect an entirely balanced view from either. Each has a case to win. The jury ought to see them for what they were and surely the judge's summing up would carry the most weight. His balanced view of the evidence he and they had heard, and the degree of direction he gave them should be more influential than the partisan appeals of either Fisher or Tournay. Of course, the Judge might sum up in a way that leaned towards the Crown's case, but even before it began Bruce felt that on any fair balance of probabilities the case against him had not been proved. There had to be a high degree of reasonable doubt, far more than enough to acquit him.

As the Judge began to speak, Bruce concentrated his attention, leaning forward on the dock rail, his chin resting on his fist. Everyone in court would be able see that it was quite a change from the arms folded, leant-back position he had taken throughout the earlier part of the day.

Mr Justice True put the issue to the jury. He used no long words, no flights of fancy, did not beat about the bush. He told them they must, consciously, put out of their minds anything they may have read or been told about the case and reach their verdict solely on the evidence they had heard in court. They were to weigh up the facts from this evidence and decide whether these pointed straight to the guilt of the man in the dock.

'The evidence in this case is purely circumstantial. But

circumstantial evidence may vary in value almost infinitely. There is some which is as good and conclusive as the evidence of actual eyewitnesses. In other cases the circumstantial evidence still leaves loopholes and doubts and possibilities of other explanations, of other persons, and makes the charge against the accused little more than a probability; nothing that could be described as reasonably conclusive.' He went on to offer an illustration. 'Supposing you have a room with one door and a closed window and a passage leading from that door. A man goes up the passage, through the door and into that room and finds another man standing with a pistol, and on the floor a dead man: the circumstantial evidence there would be almost, if not absolutely, conclusive. If, on the other hand, hearing the shot, he went in and there was a second, open, door in the room and he found a man holding a pistol it might be perfectly consistent with the actual murderer having gone out of the other door. The other person in the room might also have responded to the sound of the shot.' He went on, 'If you cannot put the evidence against the accused beyond a probability and nothing more; a probability that is not inconsistent with other reasonable possibilities, then it is impossible for you to say, "We are satisfied beyond reasonable doubt the charge is made out against the accused."'

He finished his overview with this clear direction. 'A man cannot be convicted of any crime, least of all murder, merely on probabilities. If you have other possibilities, a jury would not, and I believe ought not, to come to the conclusion the charge is established.'

The judge reiterated that the only conclusive fact in this case was that a woman had been murdered – and brutally – but he emphasised the question was not 'who did this crime, but did the prisoner do it?' Bruce knew already, even if he were to hear no more, that the Judge was subtly persuading the jury to an acquittal. His spirits rose with every word over the next hour. He would walk free. Connor, Bright, Turner and the whole pack of them had done their worst. And failed.

Mr True went through all the critical aspects of the case against Bruce. There seemed, 'as far as the prisoner is concerned, to be no apparent motive.' Not financial: he had more savings than her. Nor emotional: 'all the evidence is the prisoner and his wife were living together in happiness and in amity.'

He told the Jury the telephone conversation evidence was highly circumstantial and had to be treated as such. As for Bruce's importuning of Knight for the actual time he had taken the call, the Judge said, 'it would be very dangerous to draw any inference seriously adverse to the prisoner from that conversation.'

Of the events at Swindon Street on the Tuesday night, he remarked, 'whoever did the crime, the evidence seems conclusive, must have been very heavily splashed with blood. How in the world was it possible that the murderer, whoever he was, left not a trace behind?'

Bruce thought of meeting Jordan immediately after the killing. He had not seen any heavy bloodstaining or soaking on the man. But at night time it would not have been easily visible on dark clothing, especially with Jordan's overcoat extending to his calves. In any case, he thought, the fact was Jordan had used the mackintosh in a way none of the witnesses and evidence had suggested: throwing it over his victim to deflect the splashes away from him. He probably *had* wiped his shoes clean on the hearthrug before leaving, or had used newspaper which he had then thrown into the range fire; and he had worn gloves. With his getaway already planned, he would have been less concerned about some blood on his clothing than if he had had to leave the area by bus or tram where it might have attracted attention.

As for the time of the murder, which was, the Judge said, 'the most vital part of the case', he clearly thought the time improbably short in which the prosecution had claimed the murder had been committed and the perpetrator set off to see Mr McQuillian. 'If you think', he suggested to the Jury, 'on the evidence as to time, that the times are so short as either to make it impossible the prisoner could have done this, or anyhow to make it very improbable, then', he inferred, 'they could not come to a firm conclusion.' As to Billy Locke's sworn witness that he had delivered the milk and seen Mrs Bruce alive no later than six-thirty, his comments were highly revealing. 'On the basis of that evidence, it was obvious the time was clearly what I may call a *reconstructed* time.' He did not have to say who had done the reconstruction. By not calling the two witnesses who placed Locke at the Bruce's well after six-thirty, he said the police were 'guilty of an error of judgment'.

To Bruce's inner delight, the judge next turned to Iris Grange's sighting of the accused at about half-past eight on the Tuesday evening. This witness, on whom the police had placed such value and had made such prodigious efforts to find the man she saw speaking to Bruce, was dismissed thus. 'There is the evidence of Miss Iris Grange, no doubt saying what she thinks she saw. The prisoner says he was not there and it is word against word. Therefore I put that aside and you will give such weight to it as you think right.'

Bruce looked over at the Jury to see what effect this was having on them. Most of them sat looking down at their feet rather than up at the Judge. One of them, he felt almost sure, was indeed slumped with his chin on his chest – if not asleep, then giving a very good impression of it. He was one of the two Bruce had thought to be likely to influence the others.

The summing-up ended with the questions the Jury must consider. 'Can you say... you are satisfied beyond reasonable doubt that it was the hand of the prisoner and no other that murdered this woman? If you are not so satisfied, if it is not proved, whatever your feelings, whatever your surmises or suspicions or prejudices may be, if it is not established to your reasonable satisfaction as a matter of evidence, as a matter of fact, or legal evidence and legal proof, then it is your duty to find the prisoner not guilty.'

It could not have been put any clearer than that. Bruce, his defence, and probably everyone else in the court, had heard the Judge recommend an acquittal.

Bruce looked at the Jury again. The sleeper appeared to have woken, but he could not tell at all from the faces what effect, if any, the Judge's final words had had on them.

It was now twenty past one and the Jury filed out from the box to go away and consider their verdict.

Even while they were going, Bruce, flanked by two warders, went down the steps from the dock into a narrow area between the entrance to the court and the holding cell where he had begun each day. He found the space poorly lit and uncomfortably crowded, filled as it was with him, his guards and very soon, his solicitor. Nonetheless he felt calm; the outcome surely would be the one strongly recommended in the summing-up – that there was not enough hard evidence to convict him – he would be able to go back to Ullet Road for a day or two before moving back to Swindon Street and getting on with arrangements for a comfortable few years before the inevitable.

Lovatt looked tired. There were dark pouches below his eyes and he leaned against the passage wall for support. Bruce was fairly sure he would have been up most of the night helping Fisher with his closing speech. But he smiled. 'We couldn't have asked for a better summing-up. I don't think I've ever heard a more direct recommendation to acquit. Given how little they have to go on, I wouldn't expect them to be out long', nodding his head in the direction the departing Jury had taken. He put a hand on his client's arm and went back up the stairs to join his colleagues in the well of the court.

Unable to follow him, Bruce took out his spectacles and a cleaning cloth. There was no likelihood of his being able to use them in the dim and restricted space but he began to clean the lenses. It gave him something to do, to concentrate his mind on. A breath on the front, followed by a polish. Then a look through the lens, holding it up to what little light there was. Then the same action again on the back. Another look, another polish. Then the same painstaking process on the other lens. Then, finally, after several passes, satisfaction. The glasses went back in the case, the case snapped shut and returned to his jacket pocket.

One of the guards put a hand on his shoulder. 'We don't know how long we'll be waiting. We'll go back to the holding cell and get you a cup of tea.'

The cell door was left open, and the prisoner and his two guards sipped tea at a small table. No one spoke, the silence full of tension. While their prisoner sat outwardly calm, the warders, who he assumed would have been used to this kind of thing, seemed more strained than he was with the waiting. One fiddled with his wedding ring, then with his watch and chain, while his colleague, having finished his tea, got up, took a few steps around the tiny cell and then sat down again, a performance he repeated several times. As for Bruce, he kept thinking of Lovatt's saying they wouldn't be out long. How long was long? If the decision was really cut and dried they ought to be out not much more than a quarter of an hour, twenty minutes at the outside. He looked at his watch. They'd been out two and a half times as long. What could they have found to delay their return? He felt just the beginnings of fear. But surely they couldn't simply ignore what the judge had put to them? Perhaps one or two of the stronger characters could, and had been spending the best part of an hour bringing the weaker brethren into line so they could all go home. This line of thought left him decidedly anxious.

Then there were footsteps outside the cell and someone peered in and beckoned to one of the guards who went out, closing the door. When he returned he said, 'there's something stirring up top. Sounds as if the Jury's about to return. We'd better go back to the foot of the stairs.'

When they reached the opening leading up to the court, he could hear people moving about above his head. The court was reassembling and his guards took their places on either side of him, an additional one behind. Turning to his right, he asked, 'Can you please fetch my coat and hat from the cell so I'm ready to leave as soon as I can?'

'Feeling optimistic, are we?' The warder turned back down the passage, returning a few minutes later holding the hat, the overcoat draped over his arm. 'I'll hold on to these until you're ready for them.'

He took out his watch again. They'd been out an hour and five minutes. In spite of his request he now felt far from optimistic. He felt a hand on his elbow propelling him forward up the stairs. As his head came level with the dock rail the crowd imprinted itself on his vision – a group of both sexes and all social gradations, distinguished by their physical appearance and dress; the coarse-featured, pale, undernourished, shabbily-clothed at one extreme, the smooth, healthy, well-padded advertisements for bespoke tailoring at the other.

Like a busy swarm they buzzed and hissed, the tone rising and falling, although in the few seconds he had been watching them the level of sound had increased.

He could tell the one thing that bound them together was expectation. They were to be present at the last act – the verdict and maybe a sentence – of the biggest, most sensational trial in Liverpool for half a century. Not one of them would have missed this for the world.

His attention switched to the jury box where the twelve sat, an official in a black gown calling their names and they answering in turn. If he had expected to tell from their faces or the way they sat what they had decided, he was disappointed. They each stared in front of them, no sign of animation at all on any face. He looked carefully at the two women. Surely they would betray their verdict in their look and demeanour, but no. They were as wooden as the men.

The official who had called their roll now asked them who would speak for them. One of the two men he had earlier singled out as likely to influence the others, stood up.

'I will.'

The formal address to the Jury was sonorous and solemn, if archaic. The play was almost over.

'Gentlemen of the Jury', the two women apparently made honorary men for the day, 'are you agreed upon your verdict?'

The portly, polished, balding figure responded.

'We are.'

Bruce felt his nails digging into his palms. They were sweaty.

'Do you find Walter Henry Bruce guilty or not guilty?'

The Jury foreman looked up towards the Judge.

'Guilty.'

And then he turned for the first time and looked directly at the man in the dock. And gave just the ghost of a triumphant grin.

Part 5

Condemnation

21

'...To a Place of Lawful Execution...'

'Guilty.' Said firmly and clearly. The word that many of those in court had come for. The word the minority who had listened to the case closely for four days had not expected to hear.

The word was followed by as much as two seconds of absolute silence broken by a whistle of astonishment high up in the public gallery behind Bruce's back. Then a collective expulsion of the breath, from any individual hardly perceptible, from over a hundred or so like the rushing of a wind. A wind Bruce swayed before, in a reflex action gripping the rail of the dock to keep himself upright. The gasp was a roaring in his ears and at that moment he experienced the merciful anaesthesia of shock.

The crowd noise was silenced. Then the voice of the clerk.

'You find Walter Henry Bruce is guilty of murder and that is the verdict of you all?'

'Yes.' The modulated middle-class tone reinforced the idea that there had been no dissention.

Bruce was only faintly conscious of the clerk addressing him. None of it was real. He was dreaming this. He must have dropped off in the holding cell.

'Walter Henry Bruce,' a voice intoned, 'you have been convicted of murder upon the verdict of the Jury. Have you anything to say why sentence of death should not be passed according to law?'

He had to concentrate. It was not a dream. In front, a sea of faces turned toward him; behind, the sound of a restless and expectant crowd all waiting for him to say his last words in this court. He would not grant them any sensation; any sign he had been overwhelmed by the outcome. He uttered what for him had been his pillar and comfort these past three months. He was not guilty as charged.

'I am not guilty. That is all. I cannot say anything more.'

Below the ledge of the dock his knees were trembling; in his mouth not enough saliva to be able to swallow. In spite of the shock, he noticed, quite sharply in fact, the prison officer who had been holding his hat and coat set them down on a chair. He wouldn't need them now. He looked upward to the seat of justice below the massive overhanging canopy; someone was putting a square of black material on top of the Judge's wig. His rational brain informed his shocked emotions that a corner of the material hung down over the front edge of the wig like a widow's peak. Behind, he heard what seemed to him like a universal smacking of the lips. This was what they had travelled miles, spent days in crowded discomfort to hear. The sentence pronounced with the black cap on, those awful words. Bruce knew those three sentences by heart but because the Judge spoke quietly and the roaring in his ears persisted, he heard none of them. He focused on the face, only an hour or so before seeming benign, now beneath its grotesque covering looking like a gargoyle spouting forth the manner of his death and disposal of his corpse.

The Judge rose and went back into his quarters. Bruce felt a tap on his arm. As he turned, he had time to notice his defenders, their bodies and faces frozen in disbelief. Fisher stood slightly apart from the seated Lovatt and Keene, absolutely still, a picture of shock, defeat, utter incomprehension, staring up at where his Lordship had recently been. Then it was down the steps from the dock to where he had waited so hopefully fewer than twenty minutes earlier.

Back in the holding cell his guards put a plate of food in front of him. He turned his head away, even to smell it made him want to throw up. No one around him spoke to him and only to each other by going outside the cell into the corridor. Bruce sat, catatonic, his eyes shut, stupefied by what had happened. Eventually, around a quarter past three, he was brought to his feet, marched between warders out through a back exit from the courts and hustled into a waiting prison van.

Locked in the van, Bruce sat on the side bench, his feet and legs apart, hunched forward, elbows on knees, head in hands. A head that was just beginning to come out of a frozen refusal to contemplate reality, although it was not entirely ready to do that; what lay ahead was too frightening, too dreadful to light upon and his brain shrank from thinking forward. It did, however, skirt round how he came to be in this situation, convicted and on his way back to the grim façade and dismal interior where he had spent the last three months, instead of being back, secure and celebrating with his relations round a table in Ullet Road. He understood the jury had completely ignored the Judge's guidance and overturned what must have been the predictions of his defenders, probably of the press too, and even those of Tournay and the Crown people who must have found Mr True's summing-up uncomfortable and a slap in the face for them.

The expression, somewhere between a sneer and a grin, of the jury foreman looking across at him while saying the word 'guilty' was imprinted on his mind and tormented him. It told him something he had denied to himself throughout the trial; the jury had come there with a view already formed by what the papers – fed by the police – had said about him. They had not weighed one word of what was said on his behalf. He had put up with people like them all his life. Self-satisfied, pompous, more concerned with where you'd been to school than anything you might have learned there, contemptuous of any one cleverer than they and positively vicious if that person had pulled himself up by his bootlaces as he had. And finally such people had decided to have him killed. They had seen him and what he did for a living as things you squashed underfoot before going on your way; an opinion very much the same as the one Janet had made so clear in recent years. For them, what passed for learning was what they were told by newspapers. How could you expect justice if twelve morons like that were empanelled to pass judgment on the facts of a case? He could imagine, too, a similar expression on Connor's face, although the policeman had not been in court when the jury came back. He'd have had a smirk like the one Bruce had caught the night Connor handed him over. He was overwhelmed with frustration, anger and self-pity. His fingers were wet with tears.

The van stopped suddenly with a jerk, pulling him sideways. Someone opened the rear door and the top half of a uniformed body leaned in. 'Right. Out you get.' Bruce was on his feet, stumbling towards the opening from where he was quite roughly pulled down to the roadway. His attendants fell in beside and behind him and the group progressed to the wing that contained both the condemned cell and the instrument he did not want to think about.

In a small room just off the cell they had spread a sheet of white canvas on the floor. 'Stand on there, Bruce, and take your clothes off. Drop them on the sheet.' Although he had had to do this when arrested and every time he had returned from the committal hearing, though not during the four days of his trial, this particular disrobing had a special significance for him. Off came the last evidence of respectability, of normality, and he could not expect ever to put them on again. First the jacket, then waistcoat, tie, collar, braces, shirt and finally the trousers. As each came off and was dropped to the sheet, a prison officer seized them and went through the pockets before throwing them on a table in a heap. He stood there on the canvas, a gaunt and prematurely aged figure in a vest and long underpants. There was more humiliation to come.

'And the underwear. Everything off.'

Naked, ashamed and shivering, he did something he had never done in his adult life before; he began to cry. Copiously, noisily. All hope, all self-esteem, taken from him.

Someone tossed him a bundle of prison underwear and the grey uniform of a prisoner awaiting execution. Silently, except for sniffs and sobs, he put them on while those who had brought him there looked on impassively.

As on previous occasions his small stock of personal possessions were removed from his discarded clothes, docketed and placed in bags. Watch, pen, wedding ring – and a rabbit's foot. One of the officers held that up – a questioning look. Bruce managed to pull himself together enough to say, 'It belongs to Tommy Flaherty. He's in the hospital wing. He gave it me...' and here he broke down again. Shook his head. Took another grip on himself, '...to bring me luck. Please would someone let him have it back? And tell him how much I appreciated his doing that. It's probably the only thing he has of his own.'

The warder turned to the prison doctor who said, 'I'll see he gets it.'

Bruce added, 'when my brother comes to visit, he'll give you some money from me to be kept for when the poor fellow is discharged. At least', he mumbled, 'if it brought me no luck it will have brought him a little.' The doctor nodded. He understood.

They conducted him to the main cell where he flung himself on the bed and continued to weep silently for some time until the pillow was damp.

There was no sleep to be had that night. Even if his mind had allowed it, this was an entirely different regime from that in the hospital, awful though that had seemed when he'd first arrived there. The lights in the cell glared down on him all night and were not dimmed as the ones in the hospital had been. And two warders, working shifts, sat with him. He was no longer just another prisoner. He was a convicted and condemned murderer and his life must be jealously preserved by the law so no other hand, and certainly not his own, could have the satisfaction of ending it.

The image of an animal in a trap dominated his thoughts, twisting this way and that but unable to make the move that delivered escape. All that night he lay face down, his eyes closed but his brain engaged in repetitive circling round all that had happened since that Tuesday evening. He had been let down time and again. Jordan had botched his plan so badly that all the elements to make the crime seem shocking but inexplicable had simply been thrown away. The police had made him their only suspect mainly because they could not understand someone who was able to keep his emotions under tight control. Knight had fuelled their suspicions by reporting the questions he'd been asked at the tram stop; something he hadn't needed to do. The useless lay magistrate, anxious only to pass the poisoned chalice of the Bruce case on to someone else. And finally, twelve jurors who had maliciously convicted him in the face of the facts and in spite of the advice the Judge had given them.

22
A Hearty Breakfast

He was brought his breakfast at seven on the Sunday morning. A full breakfast, a banquet compared with what they had been given in the prison hospital, but it only served to remind him of the commonplace saying, 'the condemned man ate a hearty breakfast'. He was in no mood to do the meal any justice and found it impossible to imagine realistically that any condemned man could have done differently. He picked at it and though he had not eaten properly for twenty-four hours he left almost all of it on the plate. He noticed he had been given neither knife nor fork, his food had been cut up for him and all he would have had to eat it with was a spoon.

Something else impressed on him his special status. In a small cell off the main one was a wash basin, bath and lavatory. Here, before getting dressed, he was shaved by one of the guards. No condemned male prisoner was to be allowed access to a razor.

He dressed, then made his bed and spent several hours lying on it, face to the wall doing his best to isolate himself from his surroundings. His uniform was scratchy and uncomfortably stiff, yet he slept fitfully from sheer exhaustion.

While awake, something like the fire curtain in a theatre dropped down between his conscious thoughts and the vision of what was eventually to happen to him. Once asleep his unconscious thoughts tormented him with newsreel-like images of being escorted to the gallows that in his nightmare was set up just in the next room to his cell. He awoke just as a noose was being placed over his hooded head until he felt the rasp of the rope on his throat; someone was shaking him. 'Get up off the bed now, there's a good chap. Governor's coming.'

A minute or so later, still feeling bruised and confused by his dream, he stood up as the Governor and his retinue entered the cell. He saw a tall, ascetic-looking bespectacled man with a silver grey moustache the same shade as his abundant hair. The two guards stood to attention. The Governor motioned Bruce to sit on one of the chairs at the table. When he spoke it was with the voice and absence of accent of the genuinely-educated class. 'How are you today, Bruce?' Without waiting for a reply, he went on, 'I'm afraid I have to tell you – the subject and the timing are mandated by law – the date for your execution has been fixed for Tuesday, 12th May at eight in the morning.' The party left the cell immediately.

Bruce stayed at the table, his body slumped forward, his head resting on his arms. One of the guards placed a hand on his shoulder but nothing was said and he was left to his thoughts. Following so swiftly on his nightmare the timing of the announcement could not have been worse. He saw it as the legal system having played with him throughout the trial and now appearing indecently eager to have done with him. There would be just two more Sundays before the sentence was carried out. It was only nine months ago that he'd seen his doctor and been given a sentence of death. But even at worst there'd have been another year to prepare, to do some of the things he wanted to do before the end. And at best he had several years. Now, in not quite two and a half weeks a second sentence of death would supersede the first.

That late afternoon represented the deepest pit of his spiritual journey since arriving home on the evening of January 20th. As he had done before, between the committal hearing and the trial, he turned over in his mind confessing to his part in a conspiracy to murder and implicating Jordan and Davies. Let Jordan feel the bite of the rope. Let Davies spend the rest of his life in gaol. As for him, he'd live out his year, maybe less, and quite a lot of that would probably be spent under guard in a proper hospital. Why not?

Because it was too late. Why would the police reopen a case

when they were glorying in the kudos of their suspect having been found guilty and condemned? Nothing could actually be proved against Jordan. The murder weapon had never been found and even if Jordan had left any traces at Swindon Street on the night of the murder, carelessness and incompetence had certainly obliterated them in the hours that followed. Anyway, even the defence experts had not been able to refute conclusively McLintock's sworn statement that death had occurred before seven. Jordan would highly likely have an alibi for that time. He was either still at work in Birkenhead or on his way home. And as for Davies, it was just word against word. No evidence at all existed to link him to any of it.

This process of analysis was a sign to him that his brain was no longer the numb organ it had been since the previous early afternoon. He felt ashamed he had lost control over his emotions so completely and for so long. He had to face what lay ahead with customary detachment. He ought to start doing that now. He raised his head and looked about him.

The guards were each reading. He coughed. They looked up. 'Anything you need?' one of them asked. Almost without thinking he said, 'Yes, I'd like a chess set. And something to read.'

'When we change shifts I'll pass that on to the right people. You know you're allowed ten cigarettes a day while you're in here. Do you want them now?'

Initially he was surprised. In all the time in Walton he had not been allowed to smoke except during his rare outings for exercise and even then he had had to surrender the stub back to the warders before going up to the hospital dormitory. Any prisoner found inside with even a shred of tobacco was punished. And here they were, handing out ten of them to smoke as and when he felt like it. He did not even have to buy these. That led to an even more uncomfortable reflection. His cell was spacious and comfortable. The main area was larger than the front room at Number 29. There were easy chairs, a carpet on the flagged floor. He had a separate bathroom, not communal showers and a slop bucket in the corner. Even though he had not felt like eating it, the food brought to him was both more plentiful and varied than that served up in the hospital ward. It was as though the prison authorities felt shame about what they were intending to do and tried to compensate for it by being extra considerate. Instead they were emphasising for the occupant how little time he would be there. If it weren't all so grimly serious he'd have found it amusing. 'We'll give you a couple of weeks of superior treatment – then we'll feel better when we come to hang you.' There, he'd said it. And suddenly the word had lost its capacity to terrify and unman him.

The following morning, Monday, he found some comfort in allowing the routine to take him over. The night shift guards changed to a new pair for the day. The relationship between him and them was not one of harsh indifference as it had been elsewhere in the prison. If anything, his warders were friendly towards him, conscious of his predicament almost as if, though they never said as much, they thought him innocent. He ate his breakfast this time. A warder shaved him, he dressed and made his bed. Around mid-morning a senior officer came to see if there was anything he wanted and almost simultaneously a chess set arrived together with – a considerate thought – a book of problems from the games of the masters he could try to work through for himself. There were also a couple of popular novels from the prison library, though not really his cup of tea. He was emboldened to ask if someone could fetch his violin from home. 'Don't worry', he told them, 'I won't play it in here but I would like to see it's looked after.' And while they were doing that, could they, he asked, bring over some of his own books? He wrote out a list for them including his copy of the *Meditations* of Marcus Aurelius.

After lunch his brother James came to see him. For the first time since he had been imprisoned, he was separated from his visitor by a physical barrier. Off the main cell there was a small one where he sat before a glass window edged at the sides by a mesh which enabled conversation. No one other than prison staff would be allowed contact with the condemned man. Behind him stood a guard. Another stood behind his visitor.

James had kept up regular visits before Bruce's trial and now took pains to reassure his brother how strongly he believed in his innocence, and that Violet and Alfred sent him their love.

He told Bruce there had been a strong adverse reaction to his conviction in the newspapers. Both editorial comment and letters from the public were highly critical of the result. 'Heaven defend me from a jury of my fellow countrymen and women', someone had written. He had no wish to dampen his brother's belief that public opinion might lead to a review of the sentence or a petition to the Home Secretary. So he did not articulate his contempt for the very same papers that had reported in full the misstatements Prior had made at the Committal hearing and created a climate in which many readers were sure of his guilt. 'This,' he said to himself, 'is the world. Don't be surprised at anything that happens in it.'

Through Lovatt he had appointed James as his executor and given him power of attorney, so he asked him to take five pounds from his bank account and give it to the prison doctor for Tommy Flaherty when he was finally sent back out into the world.

He was entitled to an hour's exercise in a small, enclosed area where he could not be seen by other prisoners. On that first Monday, warm and sunny, he took advantage of it, enjoying the newly budding flowers in the beds beside the paths.

He was called in early. Lovatt was waiting to see him. Even he was subject to the same restrictions as James, meeting his client behind the glass window. That hardly mattered. Lovatt told him Keene was in London discussing the formulation of an appeal against the verdict. They both believed there were grounds for it. 'I can't tell you how I now regret not having entered a writ to have the trial removed from the Liverpool area. But I was assured that none of the jurors would be from Liverpool. Now we know that wasn't so. They were all local enough to have read up the case in the Liverpool papers. And we've discovered that two of them were actually living in the city, though they'd given addresses in Cheshire.'

'I watched them a lot during the trial', Bruce told him. 'They didn't seem to pay much attention to the evidence. The only time I saw them all sitting up was during Mr Tournay's opening speech. I thought early on there were one or two who would influence the rest and they probably thought I was guilty from what they read before I was tried – before they'd even been selected for jury service.'

Behind the glass, Lovatt nodded. 'Well, the evening after the second day, Mr Fisher said to me he didn't think the jury were listening to him. Liverpool's a strange place. Very tribal. You were an outsider; they'd think you capable of anything. It's happened before you know. Forty-two years ago a jury here, against all the evidence, convicted Florence Maybrick of poisoning her husband.' He looked round. 'She'd have been in that very cell.' Then stopped, seeing Bruce's grimace through the glass.

'Go on', he said, 'what happened?'

'There was such a stink about it the sentence was commuted to life imprisonment.'

'She wasn't freed then? Even though from the evidence she was innocent?'

'No. To make it worse she was given life for attempted murder. Though she wasn't charged with or tried for that. There was some evidence she was having an affair. And, of course, like you she was an outsider. Even more than you. She was an American.'

Bruce reflected on this instance of local prejudice. He certainly hadn't been having an affair and he'd lived in Liverpool for eighteen years. He'd never been made to feel he was an outsider. The jury's thinking in both his and the Maybrick cases was much more likely to do with the old adage 'there's no smoke without fire', and minds too lazy to explore beyond that. He wanted to know why Lovatt thought an appeal was possible and how confident he was it would succeed.

The solicitor counted off the reasons on his fingers.

'The verdict was unreasonable given the prosecution failed to prove that you were guilty and no one else could have been. The judge summed-up for an acquittal. The police deliberately didn't supply us with the statements they took from those they never called and they didn't call some because they contradicted the witnesses they did call. Professor McLintock deliberately went outside his area of expertise by volunteering his opinion of the state of the murderer's mind; that made the issue of motive less important to the court. Perhaps most important, the misstatements and errors Mr Prior made at the Committal hearings were reported as fact, in detail and widely by the press, making it highly likely that jurors drawn from the Liverpool area would come to court with a view biased against you. That's the broad picture. When Mr Keene gets back we'll refine it and draw up a formal notice to the court of Criminal Appeal. Back in the days of the Maybrick case', he added, 'that court didn't exist.'

'How does it work, this Court of Criminal Appeal?'

'We put the grounds for overturning the verdict before a panel of three High Court Judges. The Crown puts the case for letting it stand. The judges decide. There's no jury.'

'And the chances of the appeal succeeding?'

'You can never tell, Mr Bruce. Though I believe the grounds I've given you are strong ones for claiming an injustice has been done. Otherwise, we wouldn't pursue it.'

Bruce was struck by something else.

'How am I going to pay for an appeal? I assume you'll want Mr Fisher again. And there'll be a lot of work drawing up the thing, won't there?'

'Give me a few days. I didn't let you down before, did I?'

After Lovatt had gone and in spite of his concerns about funding the appeal, Bruce felt transformed. Despair and resignation had been banished by hope. And the hope was strong. Surely three senior judges would be far better assessors of the evidence than twelve of his so-called peers – bored, prejudiced and inherently stupid? In front of the cream of the law, whoever represented the Crown, probably Tournay, wouldn't get away with the posturing and histrionics he had employed on the jury. He closed his eyes and imagined Connor's face when his brief victory collapsed in ruins at his feet. One of the warders looked up at that moment and caught the prisoner with his eyes shut, a beatific smile on his upturned face.

On Wednesday of that first week Lovatt and Keene brought him details of the grounds for an appeal. There were ten separate items, providing a comprehensive list of the errors and omissions that in the view of the appellant made his conviction unsafe. In addition to the points Lovatt had counted off on his previous visit there was the claim that at the conclusion of the Crown's evidence the judge should have withdrawn the case from the jury, there being no case to answer. The point was also made strongly that the evidence led by the prosecution at the trial as to Bruce's calm demeanour on the night of the murder had not been attested to by the same witnesses when they had appeared in the Magistrate's Court. The only ground that really mattered, though, was the one on which the Appeal Court alone could order the reversal of the verdict – the first of the ten – that the verdict was perverse because it could not be supported by the evidence offered.

On Friday he signed the formal document which after the weekend was lodged with the Registrar of the Criminal Appeal Court. Events were moving. Lovatt came on the Saturday morning to tell him that Farsight had agreed to fund the costs of his appeal. Next he heard from the Governor the date of his execution had been postponed until his appeal had been heard, then that the date for that hearing had been set down for Monday, May 18th. Two days short of a fortnight to wait.

Strangely, for one who had felt such contempt for the dogma of organised religion, he began to see his arrest, trial, condemnation and appeal as a turbulent purgatory out of which he would eventually pass into the warmth and sunlit comfort of his final years. These he would spend doing what *he* wanted to do, studying, thinking, improving his chess-playing, making up for the time he had spent in a wilderness. And at times he experienced sorrow that the real Janet would not be there to share it with him.

His belief that the appeal would see him restored to his home and relations remained unshaken throughout the rest of his time in Walton. He polished the case of his fiddle and tuned, though did not play, it. One of the warders asked him to teach him to play chess. Bruce was delighted to do so and, of course, had an opponent he could always beat.

He felt surprisingly healthy. Better than since the previous summer in spite of the fact he had not taken the medicine since his arrest. Even in the prison hospital he had been better fed than ever he was at home. Here, in the condemned cell, the quality was excellent and the mealtimes regular. He ate well. His time in prison, he couldn't help acknowledging, had been healthier for him than carrying out his job.

He read a great deal, particularly from the *Meditations*, where he found much to reinforce his own view of the world and which gave him comfort in his predicament. Stoicism taught that virtue was the sole good, which is defined as a willingness to live according to whatever life dictates, recognising everything that happens is divine providence; not only accepting this but being happy about it. It is, he read, pointless both to calculate the utility of something over another and to be concerned with the consequences of one's own actions. Since the virtuous man may not sorrow over his own misfortunes, logically he cannot feel sorry for the misfortunes of others. He also found a philosophy with regard to death that further bolstered his ability to face it with equanimity should, in the long run, all else fail. Death, he learned, is a figment of the imagination; if he dreaded it he was, by definition, still alive and death was absent. If death was present, by definition he was no longer conscious of its presence. What made one fear death were the value judgments one made about life.

By midday Saturday, May 16th, reminding himself he should have been four days dead and buried within the prison grounds, he was ready to leave for his appeal. They had arranged for him to be transferred to Pentonville prison in London, there to spend two days before the appeal hearing on Tuesday and the overnight between the two days it would last.

His own clothes and few possessions were restored to him for his journey and, leaving the cell at Walton, he shook hands with the two warders then on duty. 'Thank you', he said to them, 'and to your colleagues for looking after me in here. You have made a terrible experience bearable for me.'

'Good luck,' they said in unison. One added, 'I hope we don't meet again.' Bruce could only nod his agreement.

Then he was escorted to a waiting taxi and driven through the Saturday afternoon streets to Lime Street Station where he and his guards had a reserved compartment on the afternoon train to Euston. The news of his journey had been kept from the press and the public and he was hurried across the station platforms to the train. Anyone curious enough would have seen a closely co-ordinated group of coated and hatted men. Were the observer acute, he or she would have noticed there seemed to be some physical connection between two of them, although prisoner and escort did what they could to conceal these links.

The guards pulled down the blinds on the windows between the compartment and the corridor and he was given a corner seat by the window. One of the two who had charge of him on the train journey was young and new to the prison officer's job; the other, to whom he remained handcuffed, was obviously an 'old sweat'. Although he was beginning to be affected by rising apprehension about the conditions and the outcome of the following few days, for one who had spent the past three-and-a-half months locked-up save for journeys in a blacked-out van to and from court and who, before that, had hardly escaped the blocked-in landscape of Liverpool and its lower middle-class suburbs for the best part of twenty years, the soft, gentle late spring greenery through which the railway ran was a revelation.

He said as much to the younger guard. 'It makes you realise, doesn't it, that most of England is rural?' With his free arm he indicated the fields, hedges, woods, farms, villages stretching as far as the view from the carriage window allowed.

'This is the first time I've been out of Liverpool', the other told him. 'It does seem very empty.'

'I suppose it's the emptiness that most city-dwellers fear', Bruce theorised.

'Don't know about that. But it'd be not having trams or buses, and picture houses just round the corner that'd get to me. Oh, and neighbours to be there when you need 'em.'

Bruce was sharply reminded of the need for neighbours. He wondered what his in Swindon Street had thought, were thinking, about what had happened to him.

Before he could continue, however, the older guard said directly to his colleague, 'We're not supposed to enter into conversation with a prisoner. It's all right if he asks for something, or if we have to tell him something. But that's it.'

All three were silent and Bruce did not want to make

difficulties for the junior of the pair by continuing to chat to him.

In spite of that, what he could see from the window continued to delight him and for the rest of the journey what would happen at the end of it was pushed to the back of his mind. Not until the railway began burrowing its way towards the centre of the country's – and in his view still the world's – capital did he see the acres of brick and busy streets with which he was familiar back home. He accepted that these surroundings were what he was used to; where, if spared, he would spend the rest of his days.

It was late evening when the train reached Euston and the travelling party was taken to a police van for the short trip to the prison.

Here, his day turned distinctly sour. Before being taken to the cell he had to undergo the same procedure that had so humbled and wounded him after his conviction. He was ordered to stand on a canvas sheet and remove every stitch he had travelled in and once more his possessions were taken away. But there was worse. He was subjected to a rough and humiliating search of his hair and body, ending with the searcher holding a torch and peering up between the spread cheeks of his bottom and feeling between his scrotum and anus while the chief prison officer and the deputy governor looked on. No one said a word. Not even on his first arrival back at Walton as a convicted murderer had he suffered that level of intimacy and degradation. In his misery he felt this was being done out of spite because he had appealed – had had the temerity to challenge the decision of the law – that he was a murderer and should be punished accordingly. It could be the only reason. Coming from a secure institution, watched night and day and denied physical contact with visitors, followed by a train journey where he had been chained to a guard even when using the lavatory, what could he possibly have concealed on his person? The purpose was to humiliate him. No other.

A prison uniform was tossed to him from the outer edge of the sheet he stood on. As he was now a prisoner awaiting the result of an appeal, the colour was, as it had been up to his conviction, blue rather than the grey that had marked him out as a condemned man. They did not need to bark at him. He knew the drill. In complete silence he dressed himself in these hated garments and stood waiting to be escorted to the cell.

The condemned cell and the routine that went with it were similar to the one he had left behind in Liverpool but the warders who remained in his cell every minute he was there were less friendly than the Liverpool ones. He was, after all, a visitor and from 'up north'; not 'their' prisoner and they neither knew nor cared anything about his case.

The first night and day he spent worrying about the outcome of his appeal, a reversion to the mood of the days immediately following his conviction. For most of the time in Walton he had been optimistic and calm, one might have said serene, about the future. Lovatt and Keene had volunteered little about their expectations from the Court of Appeal; even when he had tried to draw some idea of his chances from them they had remained non-committal. Here, on the eve of his appeal, doubts and fears came swarming back, contending strongly with the weaker, rational view that the judges would restore the justice that had been thwarted by a jury of morons.

Relief from this depressing circular treadmill finally arrived when they came for him on the Monday morning, shaved him, gave him back his own clothes and escorted him to a waiting van. Handcuffed again, he was driven off to the Courts of Appeal to hear his fate.

23

All – Or Nothing

If the structure and atmosphere of the Liverpool Crown Court awed all who entered it, whether spectator or participant, Bruce reckoned The Lord Chief Justice's Court at the Law Courts in London did so to a factor of two, or even three.

As the appellant, he was taken to a side gallery with an elevated view of the court. Over the bench where the judges would soon sit hung a gargantuan lion and unicorn, rampant over the motto 'Honi soit qui mal y pense' (Shame be to whoever thinks evil of it). Everything was huge, even a clock so large the passage of time in court could never be ignored; it literally stared counsel in the face. From his position Bruce could see the public gallery. It would not be, as it had in Liverpool, a disturbing, omnipresence behind him. Although far larger than the one at St George's Hall in Liverpool, he could see it was already packed to the limit as if everyone who filled the space knew that history might be made that day. He could also tell they were nothing like, either in appearance or manner, the crowd that had attended his trial. They looked to him like professionals, mainly lawyers he suspected, with a sprinkling of the intellectual and literary lights of London attracted by what had clearly been a well-publicised event to be seen at and to tell others about afterwards.

On his arrival he'd gone into a small room for a brief meeting with Lovatt. He'd not been handcuffed, although a stoutly-built court official remained in the room with them.

'Your brother's in court – with us. He sends you his very best. Oh, and you may be pleased to know that yesterday, at all three services in Liverpool Cathedral, prayers were offered for, and I quote,' he'd looked down at a piece of paper in his hand, '"all who await the judgement of their fellow man and commit them to the perfect justice of Almighty God."' He'd smiled at Bruce. 'That's never happened before, I can assure you. It means something.'

Bruce acknowledged this with apparent gratitude though he had no expectations whatever of a God he had not believed in since he was a boy. 'Yes,' he'd said, 'I suppose that must mean not everyone in Liverpool believes I was rightly found guilty.'

The court assembled, the three judges in their fullest finery of gown, fur trim and wig, the Lord Chief Justice flanked by two other senior judges. Bruce was motioned to sit and the stage was set for Fisher to rehearse the argument – the only one that mattered – that there had been a miscarriage of justice. His principle point was that Mr True had himself pointed out to the jury that there was only circumstantial evidence to link the accused with the crime and that it could certainly not be excluded that someone else had murdered Mrs Bruce. 'There was no eyewitness to the murder other than the murderer and the victim. The evidence was, therefore, purely circumstantial. Mr Justice True directed the jury on the value of such evidence – and I wish to adopt that direction.' He then added, 'if the circumstances were such that they did not exclude every reasonable possibility, then the jury ought not to have found...' he paused for effect, '...ought not to have been *allowed* to find the appellant guilty.'

It was a masterstroke. In one short passage Fisher had seized the full attention of the judges' bench. The Lord Chief Justice leaned forward. He was frowning. 'You say the case ought to have been withdrawn from the jury?'

'Yes, I am saying that.'

'But', he seemed more than a little puzzled, almost hesitant, 'no submission of that kind was made to the judge.'

Fisher explained he had had doubts from the start about the impartiality of the jury, so he had been concerned that if he had made a submission to the judge to withdraw the case and it had been turned down, the jurors' prejudices would seem to have been confirmed. He had fully expected the judge to act without prompting. As he did not, the defence hands were tied.

He had made his point. Bruce's spirits rose.

Fisher then turned to the nature of the jury. He pointed out that even though the jury had been selected from towns around Liverpool rather than from the city itself, newspaper coverage reached far beyond the city limits into those very towns on Merseyside and in Cheshire from which the jurors came. It would have been impossible for them not to have been influenced by misreporting in the press. In his view they did not 'decide only on the evidence they heard.'

Bruce's spirits dropped again. He had some idea of the difficult task Fisher had set himself. During a visit to Walton, Keene had unguardedly spoken of the reluctance of the Court of Criminal Appeal to criticise the jury system or do anything that might weaken it. It would be, he had said, 'tantamount to expecting the bench of Bishops to question the sanity of the twelve apostles.' At the time, Bruce had not taken much notice of the comment, it was only later he had thought over its true importance – that Keene, and presumably Lovatt, were not as hopeful of a successful appeal as he, a legal know-nothing. Bruce listened to Fisher telling the judges in so many words that the jury had been fools and scanned the faces of the three judges to see how they were taking it. There might be too much at stake for them if a jury verdict were struck down – it might undermine the whole system. If on this occasion, why not on others? Rather than risk such an upheaval the Court might, he feared, simply sacrifice the life of one probably innocent man, thinking it a price worth paying for judicial integrity.

The faces were inscrutable. He might have to brace himself to face down a rising sense of panic. He shut his eyes.

Fisher busied himself with presenting the case as, from beginning to end, a miscarriage of justice. The next item on his list was Professor McLintock's performance. As the police surgeon he had gone outside his field of expertise to imply that 'the blows which killed this woman were struck by a frenzied man who was insane.' The inference was that he had been encouraged to do this by the police and allowed to get away with it by counsel for the prosecution.

'Suppose', said the Lord Chief Justice quietly, 'the professor was right. His theory would have applied as much to another murderer as it did to the accused.'

A point Bruce knew only too well to be valid.

In his anxiety to suggest that McLintock's evidence had been yet another part of the overall plan by the police to leave no stone unturned in getting Bruce convicted, Fisher had overstepped the mark. He had to acknowledge the correctness of the rejoinder from the Bench but he would not let go of the idea of the police pressing their case in an inappropriate manner. McLintock's intervention was, he said, 'introduced in a spirit of malevolence'. That was a word too far for a bench of judges and a gallery of lawyers. The judges pursed their lips; the gallery gasped. Everyone was looking at Fisher, who was astute – and flexible – enough to backtrack. Malevolence wasn't what he had meant. 'I substitute zeal', he told them.

The tension subsided, though Bruce continued to study the faces and posture of the three judges. They gave nothing away. If the skill of avoiding the slightest indication of preference when listening to the evidence was the hallmark of an excellent High Court Judge, he thought these three had an abundance of it.

As Fisher progressed, Bruce began feeling this was all uncomfortably like what was said on his behalf at the trial. There could be no proof of his guilt but neither had there been in Liverpool, yet a jury had decided there was enough for them. Perhaps he had been expecting too much, had assumed his defence had discovered something to the effect that the jury had not deliberated properly, that some of them had misled the court over their places of residence, that one or two had bullied the rest into submission. Nothing of the sort had been put forward and Fisher seemed to be bent on accusing the Liverpool police of incompetence and malevolent prosecution – a course Bruce felt would be more inclined to get the Judges' backs up than secure their understanding.

As the afternoon went on he became more frightened, more prey to black thoughts, more regretful he had clung to this lifeline rather than letting go as his understanding of the Stoics told him he should have.

When Fisher sat down after almost four hours of pleading, the court immediately adjourned for the day. Bruce had hoped to speak to Lovatt but his solicitor did not ask for him and he was quickly escorted out of the rear entrance, handcuffed to a guard and taken back to Pentonville to ruminate long into the evening, and through a wakeful night, on the next day's outcome.

The following morning he put on his own clothes again – he had been through the same ritual the evening before as on arrival – and he was wretchedly aware his shirt, collar and suit, which had been laundered and cleaned for him before leaving Walton, were now looking soiled and crumpled after the journey down, their handling by the Pentonville people, and a day in a warm courtroom. Together with feeling jaded from lack of sleep and a surfeit of worry, his probable appearance, for he had no access to a mirror to check it, was not of a man likely to make a favourable impression on three of the most influential and powerful men in the law, if not even in the whole land.

Self-conscious, uncomfortable and insecure, he had to begin that second day in court listening to Tournay arguing that the verdict should stand, beginning with an attempt to dismantle the impression Fisher had created that the jury had been subject to undue influence from local and regional newspaper reporting. He insisted that the jurors all came from outside the city of Liverpool. Bruce knew this was untrue.

Like Fisher, Tournay argued for nearly four hours. The difficulty of their respective tasks now seemed, even to the apprehensive Bruce, to have been reversed. Fisher no longer had to contend with a jury that did not listen to him and he had ammunition to reinforce his assault on the trial verdict. Tournay could not rely on a conditioned and impressionable jury and was attempting to defend a threadbare case that even the trial judge had felt did not make its point.

When Tournay sat down at half-past three the judges turned to one another and held a conversation inaudible to everyone else in the room. The Lord Chief Justice told the court they would retire to consider their decision.

Bruce was taken out into the corridor behind the gallery and, under guard, was allowed to pace up and down, unable to concentrate on anything other than the fact he was now at the 'all or nothing' point.

Someone said, 'I've never known them do this before, they usually know what their decision's going to be by the end of the session.'

He tried to see the recess as positive – a confirmation that the law would not decide arbitrarily, that a discussion was taking place that indicated the matter had never been cut-and-dried. And then his brain clicked onto the opposite track. They had retired because, in spite of what they had heard, they could not agree that a jury, finding on the facts, could have its verdict set aside. The silence in that corridor daunted him. Except for his footsteps and the unusually loud beating of his heart there was no sound from anyone after that initial comment. For three quarters of an hour he waited, the gloomy prognosis now heavily outweighing the positive one, until he and his guards heard the call of 'Silence' from the court. Two or three minutes later he was pushed through the curtains into the side gallery. The judges were back in position, he saw the public gallery even more jammed with spectators than before and the well of the court was now populated with barristers from other courts drawn by the unprecedented hiatus. The amazing thing, he noted, was that in spite of the sheer number of people crammed into that courtroom, he could have heard a pin drop. No one coughed, not a leaf of paper was rustled, everyone, including himself, suspended both mental and bodily functions to wait for the words that would mean life or death for him, Walter Henry Bruce. He was unsteady on his feet, although he gripped the gallery rail, and found it hard to focus vision as if extreme exertion had blurred it. He forced himself to look at the judges' faces but could read nothing there. He told himself that if the decision went against him he would show no emotion and absolutely no fear.

For a further full minute no one spoke. Then, with magisterial slowness the Lord Chief Justice began his judgement. His delivery was toneless; no indication of what was to come. There was a technical reason for this Bruce was unaware of. Every word of the judgement had to be recorded by a writer so it had to be delivered slowly and clearly.

And through the fog of panic, of unknowing, into the mind almost paralysed by the fear of failure and of showing it, he heard the Lord Chief Justice say, 'Suffice it to say we are not concerned here with suspicions, however grave, or with theories, however ingenious. Section four of the Criminal Appeal Act of nineteen hundred and seven provides that the Court of Criminal Appeal shall allow the appeal if they think that the verdict of the jury should be set aside on the ground that it cannot be supported having regard to the evidence.' Like a shaft of light slicing through the fog, the words leapt out at him. Why would the judge recite the Act if it were not going to be used in his favour? He gripped the rail even more tightly.

The judge was in no hurry to go on. Then he added, so painfully slowly, 'The conclusion to which we have arrived is that the case against the appellant, which we have carefully and anxiously considered', he paused, '...and discussed...', the intonation remained flat, the delivery monumental, '...was not proved with that certainty which is necessary in order to justify a verdict of guilty.'

There was a roaring, hissing sound in Bruce's ears, exactly as there had been in the final minutes of his trial. But now he knew, oh how sweet the words, what he would hear next.

'The result is that this appeal will be allowed...' Bruce heard a gasp from several hundred lips, and then, '...and this conviction quashed.'

Part 6

Consequences

24
The Rottenest Crowd

Though he had heard the words that announced he was free, he was unable to move. Just as when he'd heard 'guilty' at his trial it had made him immobile and brain-dead, so now the shock of hearing he was free to go had the same effect. He simply stood there, pale and blinking, his hands gripping the gallery rail.

One of his guards gently prised his hands free and, smiling, motioned him to step back out into the corridor he had shuffled along in such emotional agony barely fifteen minutes before. A door opened; those with him no longer wardens but suddenly transformed into attendants escorting him downstairs to the main hall of the building where Lovatt met him with a big grin, a handshake and a pat on the back, and James with a brotherly hug.

He did not feel then like a man who has just been given his life back. The effect of shock continued to dull his brain and his movements were of one under some automatic control. James helped him on with his coat, handed him his bowler hat and took one of his arms while Lovatt took the other. Between them, they guided him from the exit into the courtyard and to the gates in front of the Law Courts and then hailed a cruising taxi in the Strand. James climbed in with him, Lovatt stood back and shut the door and Bruce was driven off to spend his first night in freedom for fifteen weeks.

In a show of optimism, James had reserved rooms for them in a small boarding house in West London, where a reporter from the *Daily Dispatch* arrived to conduct an exclusive interview with the freed man. Not that he had recovered enough to do more than give a halting and fairly incoherent account of his feelings;

the sub-editors however lent poetic wings to his inarticulate phrases and produced the kind of statements the paper's readers would have expected a reprieved man to utter as he walked free.

After the first proper night's sleep he'd had for several days, Bruce woke early. His immediate feelings were of elation. He was free, and, as he saw it, acquitted of any guilt for the crime with which he had been charged. He could return home, to his job, hold his head high and take up life where he had left it that troubled evening in early February. His modest savings were still intact, thanks to the Farsight Staff Union and the Company itself, so he ought to be able to arrange the care he'd gone through this hell of suspicion, arrest, imprisonment, trial, conviction and the shadow of the gallows to get.

In fact, his financial situation was likely to look better as a result of the ordeal he had been through. The 'interview' he had given the *Daily Dispatch* had been rewarded with a fee and he could see there would probably be others anxious to print his story. Lovatt had briefly mentioned the previous day that his firm intended to take action on his behalf against papers that had made assertions during the period of his arrest damaging to his reputation and inviting public hatred and contempt. They would settle, Lovatt had said; the price easily outweighed by the sales they had made to a readership avid for scandal and lurid exposures.

He had the pleasure that morning of shaving himself for the first time since his trial ended. James had thoughtfully bought him new underwear, shirt and collar, so it was with almost a jaunty step that he and his brother went to Holborn to the head office of Farsight to thank the Union and the firm for its support, loyalty and financial commitment to him. After that, they went to Kew where he felt the prison cobwebs disappear in the warmth of a fine May afternoon surrounded by birdsong and the fragrance of trees. In the evening they took in a musical comedy and he discovered for the first time in many years the capacity to laugh from deep inside at something frivolous.

The following day, in the afternoon, they arrived back in Liverpool. It was a brief stop. They would spend the night at Ullet Road and then go away for a couple of weeks so that he could relax and rest. But first there was a meeting with Lovatt, followed by a celebratory gathering at the local Farsight head office at which Bruce would be guest of honour.

Lovatt had something serious to say to him. 'I think you may underestimate how much opinion here is against you. I've been taking soundings, before the appeal and since I've been back. We'll go after anyone who's libelled you, of course. In fact we've started on that and there should be some movement soon, but my advice is to see if Farsight can't find you the same job somewhere else – a long way away.'

He shrugged it off. 'I've been cleared. By the highest court in the land. Surely that has to count for something with people? I'm going away for a couple of weeks with James – back to where we grew up – and I'm sure by the time I get back and pick up where I left off the fuss will all have died down.'

'Well, I hope so for your sake but don't count on it. These people are tribal. I've said it to you before. No matter how long you've lived here, you're not one of them. A jury of their tribe has been held, rightly in my view, to be a bunch of fools whose verdict was worthless. Most people in Liverpool won't see it my way; it's not something they'll just accept. And the High Court quashed the verdict – it didn't and it couldn't say you were "not guilty". It's as near as dammit to the verdict they have in Scotland, "not proven". And that's exactly how people here will see it. Mr Bruce, I'm saying this for your own good and peace of mind. While you're away, please think it over.'

Bruce and his brother set off the next day for the Furness area of Lancashire where they had been born and spent their youth, and where they still had friends. Long walks and river fishing filled the days.

Violet came to stay for a few days, bringing some confirmation of Lovatt's warning. 'There's a lot of nonsense going round. It had quietened down after the trial but since the appeal was allowed it's grown again. What they're saying is that the police were clearly no match for a cunning chess-playing mastermind like you. I've even heard, though not to my face thank goodness, that you and I were having an affair and Janet found out. Things aren't helped by the police making a big point of closing the case. It's like them saying no one else could have done it.'

'I'm not even a good chess player,' was Bruce's puzzled response. 'if these people spoke to those at the club they'd be told I was anything but a master.'

This was followed by a letter from Lovatt enclosing his firm's account for Bruce to pass to Farsight. The letter reiterated his advice not to return to Liverpool; to seek a transfer to another part of the country. Bruce was adamant in his reply. He would return to his old home and job in just over a week's time. He had nothing to hide. If he did not come back his detractors would be entitled to think it because he was guilty. Lovatt wrote back by return. If Bruce insisted on staying in Liverpool he should live somewhere else than Anfield and work an area away from there as well. Animosity against him was growing, not waning; he would be subject to unpleasant if not actually aggressive treatment both where he had lived and worked.

The placid early summer surroundings close to the Lake District encouraged Bruce to discount much of this as well-meaning but exaggerated concern, the result, perhaps, of Lovatt and the family speaking to a few people – and of overblown comment in the newspapers. He could not believe that those who had done business with him for years right up to the day he'd been arrested would turn against him. He persuaded himself that if prayers had been held on his behalf in the cathedral, surely that meant the general atmosphere in Liverpool was in his favour?

He had to say goodbye to his devoted younger brother whose leave of absence was up. Who, at no small expense, had travelled half across the world to be with him, who had never doubted his innocence, and had been prepared to fund the major part of his legal costs before there had been any mention of Farsight paying for his defence. At their parting the morning after they returned to Liverpool, he was not ashamed to have tears in his eyes.

The house he returned to after almost six months was unaired and silent. He made his way through to the kitchen past the closed door to *that* room. In the kitchen, dust everywhere, three empty saucers on the floor, the cat must have long since found another home. Though the rent had been paid all the time he had been away, nothing had been done to prepare for his homecoming. When he went upstairs he saw that the lavatory pan had been put back, but other than that the place was more or less as he had left it. A more sensitive or imaginative man would never have gone back there at all; even he, determined as he was to 'see it out' and get back to what he thought of as normal life, felt uncomfortable walking round. At least it remained light until about ten that evening, making the experience less oppressive than it would have been in winter and he took advantage of that to do what he knew had to be done – go into the front room for the first time since that Tuesday night.

The blinds were still drawn. He decided to leave them so. It would attract outside attention if he raised them and he was not yet ready for that. He lit the gas lights on the chimney breast and looked around. Very little had changed in here either. Everything had a layer of dust. Some attempt had been made, probably by the landlord, to clean the walls but there were still faint but detectable marks of blood. At least the hearthrug had been removed. The room, like the rest of the house, smelt stale. He would need to get someone in to clean the house from top to bottom. Do it tomorrow.

He decided to sleep in the larger front bedroom where he had spent the last night in this house on the Wednesday after it happened. Turning off the gas, he closed the door on the parlour.

He was by now hungry and thirsty. It had not occurred to him to get in any provisions. Something else he'd need to do tomorrow, but for now he had better go and take a tram into the city centre and find somewhere to get supper. He locked up and retraced his earlier journey. He first thought of going to the City Café, where the chess club met – they wouldn't be there on a Tuesday evening of course – but opted for the refreshment room at Lime Street station. He was reluctant to accept that in spite of dismissing the warnings from Lovatt and his sister-in-law, he was indeed concerned about the reception he would get from anyone who knew or recognised him. That was the real reason why he had changed into jacket and trousers with a soft-collar shirt and a trilby hat, and why he was going to eat somewhere people came and went and had other things on their minds than where he might be. No one seemed to be the slightest bit interested in him and he was able to order a pie and chips and a cup of tea in perfect anonymity.

Going home, as he turned into Swindon Street looking down towards his house, he thought he saw movement, as though someone had slipped away from his front window when his footsteps sounded at the top of the street. Perhaps just a trick of the darkening evening. He let himself in and immediately went up and lay on the bed in the front bedroom.

He got up to a fine, bright morning, one to lift the spirits. Needing milk for his tea and breakfast porridge, he took a jug, left the house by the backyard door and went through the alleys to the dairy that had delivered milk to the Bruces for many years. Mr Locke was in the shop at the front. He looked up as Bruce stood in the doorway. He seemed to be in two minds as to whether to disappear into the back or not. However, he remained where he was. Bruce held out the jug and asked politely for it to be filled. Locke poured milk into the jug and took the offered money, all without saying a word.

Bruce said, 'I'd like to place a regular order for a pint every other day. You know the address, 29 Swindon Street. You delivered to us there for years up to last January.' Locke remained standing and mute.

He felt he had to speak if the other would not. 'If it's delivered at six-thirty or after every other evening, that would be fine. I'll be home from work by then.'

Locke cleared his throat. He did not look directly at Bruce. 'I'm afraid we're fully committed for deliveries at the moment. Sorry.' And he turned his back, withdrawing into the dairy area behind the shop.

Clutching his jug, he returned through the entries. Perhaps he ought to have expected it. After all, young Billy had certainly been coached by the police and had then been dragged into court where defending counsel had called him a liar, even a perjurer. No wonder his father was ill-disposed to have the cause of that as a customer. It did not mean that others would take the same approach to him.

Putting the jug on the kitchen table, he went through to the front door and picked up several letters from the mat, or rather two letters and some folded papers. Opening them immediately, he was shocked at the coarseness and violence of the language they contained. In these crudely expressed, badly-spelled notes he was accused of practising evils and perversions he had no idea existed, as well as of having killed his wife. He was told people in the area knew how to deal with a monster like him.

There had been nothing inside the front door when he'd arrived the previous afternoon. These welcoming notes had been put through his letter box while he'd been out. The neighbourhood had been alerted to his return and these were the first fruits of the kind of thing Lovatt had warned him about.

He collected the pieces of paper, screwed them into a ball and dropped them in the range.

He would not be deflected from his plan by the nastiness of what could only be the least intelligent and most small-minded of his neighbours. Once the novelty of his being back among them had worn off all this would stop.

In the meantime he had to call at the Farsight offices to collect the books and reports needed to resume his insurance round, something he'd arranged to do during his brief visit there before going off on holiday. On the way, he thought he'd see whether he could find a cleaner through the notice boards in the local shops near where he caught the tram to the city centre.

Over breakfast he had written a wanted advertisement for someone to clean a small house a couple of days a week, do a little washing and ironing for him, clean and tend to the range, that sort of thing. He took it into one of the shops. There were two or three customers around the counter who turned to look at him as he walked in, then quickly turned away again. He handed the card to the shopkeeper and gave him the fee, saying, 'Can you put it up quickly?' The man nodded. The card lay face up on the counter. The curious craned their necks to see it. Bruce, feeling a sense of unwelcome, returned the nod and walked out. As he did he heard perfectly clearly a woman's voice. 'A cleaner. At his house. Not on your nelly.'

Bruce strode to the tram stop. Taking up where he had left off was obviously going to be more difficult than he had thought.

At the Company offices he had a meeting with Albert Willesden.

'You sure about taking up your old area, Bruce?' The enquiry was meant kindly. 'It's that you're pretty easily identified there. Trouble-makers can pick you out. We can find you another in a different part of Liverpool, you know.'

The response was polite yet firm. 'You know me, Mr Willesden. I'm not one who walks away from a little local difficulty. Clubmoor's my patch. It's been mine for nearly seventeen years. I know it like the back of my hand and I know the people who live there and they know me. They've trusted me all these years, why should they stop now? I've been cleared. My Company never thought I was guilty, my clients won't have either.'

Willesden sighed. 'If that's what you want, Bruce, you have my support. I just hope you're right that's all.' He pulled the files towards him on the table. 'Now let's get you set up again.'

The next day he started work for the first time for five and a half months. When he got off the tram at Maiden Lane he felt, although it was a return to the familiar, quite exhilarated. How often had he doubted whether he would ever be doing this again? The fact that he was there, his bag packed as it used to be was an achievement. The only difference was that before setting out he had made a list of the calls for the day to remind him together with the notes left by the agent who had filled-in for him. It was in his pocket, though he had more or less memorised it. He meant to enjoy his day, to return home in the evening feeling that things really were back to normal.

His first call was in Antrim Street, a family he had looked after for many years. Janet used to disparage his work, and by extension him, but he had a genuine regard for nearly all the clients making up his round and thought of what he did as a social service. He would never have recommended a policy or an action he did not feel was in their interest and met their generally modest needs. If he felt their situation changed, particularly if they had money troubles, he would not hesitate to suggest ways they could get by with a lower premium, though he would carefully explain what they might lose as a result. He was prompt to pay out peoples' small claims, knowing how important it was in hard times that they should not have to wait for what they were due.

His usual double tap on the door knocker went unanswered. Perhaps they were out, although that had never happened with this client before. The call was regular, every other Thursday. He would collect the premium, chat about the family; a ten minute call. He knocked again, a little heavier this time. No one came. He went back on the pavement and, walking away, turned and looked back. Had the curtain in the front window twitched? Perhaps not. Maybe the agent who'd done his work had changed the routine, though there was no indication that he had.

The next call was not far away in Knocklaid Road. This front door had a bell. You twisted a key and it wound up to produce a ring. He heard it ringing inside the house. Eventually someone came to the door; he could see a shadow behind the glass pane.

The door opened on its chain. Through the gap Bruce saw a woman's face, framed in brown curls, further down, a flowered pinafore.

'Oh it's you, Mr Bruce. Just a mo.'

The chain came off, the door opened. Bruce removed his hat.

'Good morning, Mrs Spence.'

'Come in.' He noticed as he did so she edged past him and peered up and down the street. Evidently satisfied she closed the door and put it back on the chain.

'Go through', she said, indicating the front room. The house was quite like his own. 'Sit yourself down. I'll just take off this pinny and get you your money.' Bruce sat in an armchair and when she returned entered up the payment in the book she held out to him.

'It's good to see you again after all this time. The chap who came while you were away was all right. But he wasn't you.'

'I'm glad to be back, Mrs Spence, believe me.'

A pretty tortoiseshell cat came in from the kitchen and jumped up on to Bruce's lap. 'See. She remembers you.'

'I lost the cat we had', he said, rubbing its cheek with the back of his hand and hearing the welcoming purr. 'After that awful night, he disappeared. Never saw him again. I hope he found a good home.'

'I speak as I find, Mr Bruce. I've known you a long time and I never for a moment thought you capable of doing a thing like that. In the end you've had justice. But you had a terrible time first.'

He shook his head. 'I didn't do it.' There was real conviction. 'But I've got to put all that behind me now. It's over. I just want to be back at work again.'

'It must be so hard. You must miss her so much.'

He agreed.

'There's folk round here who should be ashamed of themselves. When they heard the result of the trial down at St George's Hall a lot of them were very down on you. Won't tell you the sort of things they said.'

Bruce managed a weak smile. 'Don't worry. My solicitor told me some of them. All untrue. And the police encouraged it.

He gave the cat a last stroke and got up from the armchair. The call ended. 'I'm grateful to you, Mrs Spence. You've brightened my day. If most of my clients feel as you do I shan't need to worry.'

Of the twenty or so calls he had on his list that day, four were similar to the one he'd made to Mrs Spence. At the others no one answered the door nor did he detect any movement within the house. Late in the day he called on one of those who had given evidence of his normality following the suggestion floated by the police that one of their officers had seen him in a distressed state on the afternoon of the murder.

She did not conceal from him that many in the area had expressed satisfaction, pleasure even, he had been convicted. These same people had been irritated by the news of an appeal, which however, they were confident would fail, and then angry when they had to accept it had been successful. In these close neighbourhoods of densely packed small houses only a practicing hermit would remain unaware of what others were thinking and saying.

Back home that evening he reflected that his first day had been a bit of a curate's egg, mostly disappointing. For so many of his calls to be fruitless could only mean his clients were avoiding him, either because they genuinely believed he was guilty or feared what might happen if they were seen to have a different view from the majority. His familiar knock advised them of his presence. They did not answer the door and would watch from the obscurity of a curtained window until they saw him move on.

On top of that, when he let himself into the house there were even more poison-pen letters on the mat than on the previous day. He forced himself to look at some of them but quickly gave up. The general gist of them was that he was a calculating and callous murderer, a menace to the neighbourhood. No self-respecting woman was safe from – and this at least produced a rather parched mirth – his sexual appetites. He was a pervert – the naked killer in a raincoat. He had better leave the area he had fouled before those with its real interest at heart got together to make him do so.

What was it that made people do this kind of thing? He concluded it must be because in their nondescript lives, lived constantly on the edge of insecurity, manipulated by those with more wealth and influence, they needed someone to vent their frustration on. Someone or some group they could legitimately hate.

It must take a particular type of person, though. After all, when it came to lack of money and having no social importance he was in no better situation than most of his neighbours and a lot worse than some, like Collinson, or the dairyman, Locke, with their own shops. He would not dream of writing the kind of stuff that was being pushed through his letter box. He decided it came down to education. Most of the letter-writers were illiterate. But while they resented those they saw as better-educated and more fortunate than themselves, they swallowed without question what such people told them in the form of newspaper reports and comments.

He heard a knock at the front door and got up from the kitchen table to answer it. There was no one there. He looked around, walked out to the pavement, looked up and down the street. No one. Shaking his head, he went back inside and closed the door.

About a quarter of an hour later it happened again. This time he was upstairs, tidying the front bedroom, so he looked out of the window in time to see a boy and girl running away up the Richmond Park end of the street.

He had got the range working so he had hot water and was able slowly to clean and tidy up the house. But he realised how much he – and it – had changed. Now he was back and living there it no longer felt like his home, more as though he were a temporary resident in a house belonging to someone else. Which it did. In recent years it had been the home of a couple called Walter and Janet Bruce. But neither of these people existed any more. Janet, of course, in an absolute sense. Walter, in that the man who mooched through the house as though looking for something unspecified and unstated was not the one who had lived there up to late December the year before. That Walter had been set in his ways, insulated, one half of a marriage that had shrivelled up but still retained its skeletal form, routine habits and predictable milestones for every day. The Walter who was there now had had his world shattered and the experience had changed him profoundly and permanently. He who had planned the perfect murder to enjoy a few more years of life had watched helplessly, like a novice chess player, as his opponent took piece after piece until he was only on the board in a position of stalemate because of that opponent's incompetence, not his own skill. He was not dead but he could not derive any satisfaction from his position.

Janet was everywhere. The front bedroom was full of her clothes, some going back to when they had first arrived in Liverpool. He could not bring himself to throw them out and in a practical sense he knew at the present time it would be very unwise to be seen to do so. The front parlour was entirely her domain. The furniture in it was originally hers, as were the pictures, some of which were watercolours she had done herself. And of course the piano. And those faint marks on the walls. He had only been in there the once. Then he had shut the door on it and left it to whatever ghosts and memories it contained. All the same he had started to commune with Janet. The earlier one, the one he deeply missed. All the time he had been in prison he had had no mental or emotional contact with her. But now he was back in the house they had both shared he thought of her all the time. He would look up from the kitchen table and remember how years ago she would smile at him across it, talk to him about his teaching, ask questions and encourage him to aim higher, still believing he could do so. He found himself talking to that Janet, telling her of his loneliness and hearing her telling him to be strong, to appreciate his true worth and not allow others to get him down.

The third night in the house his rest was disturbed by further activity at the front door. This time the nuisance was from adults, at one in the morning calling through the letter box:

'*Wally, Wally wore a mac.*
To give his wife the fatal whack.'

And,

'*Walter Bruce,*
Walter Bruce.
You should've felt
The hangman's noose.'

That grown people would come out at this time of night to persecute him by chanting that kind of rubbish through his front door brought home how strong the feeling against him was and how little those who did it cared whether he confronted them or not. Had he gone downstairs and opened the door he was sure he would have been threatened with physical assault, perhaps even subjected to it. He also knew that he would get no protection from the police. Possibly they had egged-on those who were tormenting him. Sometime in the night he also thought he heard noises downstairs but took comfort from the fact that in his long absence the locks on both outer doors had been replaced – the replacement keys given to his solicitors.

The next morning he returned to his round in Clubmoor. Of the twenty or so calls on his list for the day only four clients answered his knock and one of these did so only to tell him to his face he had made 'other arrangements' for his insurance and did not want Bruce calling again. The other three paid their premiums in an atmosphere of tension; he was not offered a cup of tea all day and the calls involved him remaining standing just inside the front door.

This time he returned home with a new feeling, that of

hopelessness. He had absorbed so thoroughly his own belief that he was innocent of Janet's murder that he no longer remembered, at least not consciously, that he had played any part in it. The shock and disturbance of what he had experienced since his arrest had wiped these associations from his mind; anaesthetised him from the truth. Janet was dead, he was trying to get by without her, and what was being done to him by clients and neighbours was, he wrote in the diary he had taken up again, 'a wicked insult' to her. 'How she would have scorned them all.'

The postman had been kept busy too. There were no folded notes this time but ten stamped letters. After his tea he forced himself to open them. Two, oddly the first two he opened, were warmly congratulatory. He noted the senders' addresses were well away from his part of Liverpool. He set them aside for a reply. It cheered him that there were some on his side, a sensation he needed for the other eight were awful. No senders' addresses for these, the text in block capitals, crude and ignorant he thought, and much the same message as all the others.

Through the evening he endured, stoically it felt to him, a barrage of rat-a-tats and then, after he had gone to bed, the calling of adult voices both male and female, as though in some perverted parody of a group of Christmas carollers. After the first woke him, he pushed cotton wool into his ears and slept through whatever others there may have been.

Saturday promised a continuation of the fine weather. It would be warm but not too hot and his workload was just the half day. Over breakfast he decided to give it a try. Perhaps a different part of his area would be more welcoming to his knock.

Leaving the tram, he walked the half mile or so to a block of streets off to the right of Lisburn Lane. As he arrived at the first house on his list, in Heyburn Road, there were children playing outside one of the neighbouring houses. A woman rushed past him from behind, almost pushing him over, and shooed the children into a nearby door. He knocked on his client's door but no one opened it. A window went up above his head and a woman's voice shouted 'Go away.'

'It's me, Mrs Shaughnessy, Mr Bruce.'

'I know who you are. Go away.'

This attracted others, either at opened upstairs windows or at open doors.

'You heard her,' someone yelled at him. 'Go on, be off.'

He turned and saw two men crossing the street behind him. He turned away from the unanswered door. His next call was in Fairburn Road. Perhaps if he could get there the denizens of this one would be satisfied they had driven him away; they would not follow him.

The men came closer. They blocked his route to Fairburn Road. Both wore a blue uniform with brass buttons; their heads close cropped. Bruce thought – seamen. There were lots of them living in the area, many of them his clients.

'You're the one murdered his wife, aren't you?' one of them said.

Bruce was not physically afraid. It was broad daylight and there were plenty of witnesses. 'No, I'm not,' he said, 'someone else killed her. I was wrongly convicted. The law said so.'

The bigger of the two thrust his head and neck towards Bruce.

'You might have pulled the wool over the eyes of them down in London,' the last three words expressed with all the contempt Liverpudlians felt for the soft southerners, 'but up here we know what you did.' He turned to some of the hangers-around while still directing his remarks at Bruce. 'It's a case of no noose is not good noos for you, Mister Bruce.' He chuckled. His hearers shrieked with laughter. 'We're off to sea this afternoon and we don't want to think of you being around here with our wives and daughters unprotected like. So bugger off while you still can.'

Several women close enough to hear, screeched their satisfaction. 'Go on, Harry, tell him not to come here again.'

Harry moved a step closer to Bruce. 'I'm sure you don't want to make me, or these good people here, really angry. Get out of here right now and stay out. If you come back again on another day it'll get around. Everyone'll be watching. They'll take...' he took another pace forward, '...steps. Oh,' and he jabbed a finger at Bruce's chest, 'don't think the police'll help you. They're just as pissed-off with you as we are.' The women screeched their approval again.

The two men stood aside to let him on to the footpath. They more or less frogmarched him to the end of Heyburn Road where it met Lisburn Lane. Pointing towards the distant Townsend Lane, Harry put a large hand on Bruce's neck. 'Off you go now. Get the tram back to where you live. They can put up with you. We don't have to.'

Bruce spent the rest of the day in his beleaguered house thinking over his situation. He accepted he could not return to the Clubmoor round. Everything Lovatt had told him about the reception he would get had been proved correct. If anything, his solicitor had understated it. And he, in his euphoria at having seen the police defeated and belittled, had imagined he would be welcomed as the instrument of their humiliation. Now he no longer had any illusions. If he tried to go on as though nothing had happened he would probably be attacked, quite likely physically. Could he take up the Company's offer of a collection agency in another area? The kind of agent he was, the sort of work he did, the character of the clients he collected from, it could only be in an area similar, even if distantly removed, from the one he had in effect just been run out of. The affluent suburbs were a different world and it was unlikely the Company would consider him for that kind of agency. In the evening, desperately in need of normality, he went over to Ullet Road. Violet listened to his woes and cooked him a supper but had to tell him she was leaving to join James within a few days, and that Alfred, who had found the opprobrium attached to his uncle had rubbed off on him, had decided to continue his studies at another university. His return home deepened his sense of bereavement. There would be no close family he could turn to for support and he was not able to put away the thought that he would probably never see any of them again.

For in the past few days he had begun to experience signs of ill-health, signs familiar from the summer of the previous year that had led to being in hospital. It was as though the beast had lain quiescent through the great upheaval in his life – having paradoxically felt better during the months of imprisonment than he had done for years – but it was stirring again. He wondered why it should be when the period from Janet's death to his release had been one of unremitting stress and enervating fear, and ever since his arrest he had not been taking the medicine prescribed for him. He steeled himself to visit the surgery for a repeat of his prescription. Before it could be made up for him he had to have a brief appointment with Dr Clarke. It seemed to Bruce that the doctor was notably distant with him. Perhaps he was more aware than others of the tensions which had existed between the Bruces and therefore not immune from the suspicions most Anfield residents had about Bruce's role in what had happened on the evening of January 20th. When he got home he recalled what the doctor had said to him almost a year ago, that given his condition his work was a killer. He no longer had a wife to keep. He could accept a lower income and yet meet essential bills. He still had his savings and, as an unlooked-for benefit from his ordeal by trial he could expect additional income from settlements with those who had made false assumptions about his guilt and had printed them.

It also occurred to him there could be income from selling his story. At first he recoiled from the idea. It wouldn't do. It was what real criminals did – rather like the confessions and revelations peddled for cash by notorious convicted highwaymen a couple of centuries before. The income guaranteed them a better class of custody before they were hanged and probably some welcome security for their nearest and dearest. But the more he thought about it the more acceptable it became. If people treated him as notorious, something he had never wished for or expected, he might as well extract a contribution from his notoriety towards the cost of comfort in what time he had left. It could pay for the nursing he would need, if, he thought, he could find anyone willing to run the gauntlet of his neighbours to provide it.

If the Company would give him a clerical job within head office he could begin to implement the plan for the remainder of his time. He would go in on Monday, see Willesden, admit he had underestimated the degree of ill-will and negotiate a change of role within the Company. He gathered together all the papers and books he had so optimistically collected the previous Wednesday and put them ready, together with the small amount to pay in, for Monday morning.

Sunday provided a short relief from dealing with the expressions of hatred, obscene speculation and threat which every post now brought. The house next door where the Springers had lived until a few days before his arrest was still empty. When he went out for a walk in the afternoon the couple in the house on the other side of his watched him ostentatiously from their front window. When he got back to Swindon Street, near neighbours with whom he had invariably passed the time of day if nothing more, turned into the alleyways or crossed the street when they saw him coming, or in one case, spun right round and walked off in the opposite direction rather than pass him. He reflected that his past policy of keeping himself to himself spared him the agony of hostility from someone he had previously thought a good friend. It did not occur to him that his past aloofness might hold the reason why so many believed the worst of him.

That evening, hearing unusual sounds at the back of the house he went to the scullery window and saw a man trying to hack a piece out of the back door, presumably as a souvenir. When the fellow, who must have climbed over the back yard wall from the alley, realised he had been seen he ran off, letting himself out by the yard door. Bruce went out into the summer evening and re-bolted it and was glad to see the damage to his back door was minor.

Mid-morning the following day he called at the Farsight office and asked to see Mr Willesden. He did not have to wait long; almost, he thought, as though he was expected. He tried to keep the bitterness and anger in his voice to the minimum. 'I'm very sorry, Mr Willesden but it's not going to work. I tried, but after three days it was getting more not less unpleasant. I'm sorry to have to admit defeat but if I can't do my job properly, I'd rather not do it at all.' He told his supervisor about the confrontation with the merchant seamen and the implication that the police would offer him no protection if some in Clubmoor took the law into their own hands with regard to him.

He was both pleased yet surprised when Willesden said straightaway, 'I think we must find you something here, inside. If you took another round anywhere in Liverpool I suspect the news of it would spread and the same thing happen there within a week if not days. I'll speak to my section head and he'll do the same with his opposite number on the office clerical side. You go home and wait. We'll go on paying your present salary until you move over. They'll let you know when to start – it shouldn't be more than a few days.'

Bruce expressed his gratitude. 'Thank you so much. The Company has been very good to me these past six months. I'd hoped to repay by getting straight back to work. But whatever I'm given, I'll do it to the best of my endeavour.'

Willesden rose and patted him on the shoulder. 'You've been an excellent servant to this Company for a very long time, Bruce. It's only right it should look after those who've earned its trust and respect.'

Coming as it did after the collapse of eighteen years work within fewer than three days, that endorsement gave Bruce back some of his self-belief.

He then went and called on Lovatt, whose offices were in the same building. He told him what had happened and the outcome.

'I suppose you had to find out for yourself. I'm sorry it was such a painful lesson. There's some good news though. Those publishers we wrote to on your behalf have settled, so I have a cheque for you, less our expenses of course, but it's two hundred pounds net. And I'm pretty sure there'll be another settling out of court in a week or so. I suppose your salary will be lower in the new job so this will come in handy. And', he went on, 'you'll be relieved to know the costs for the appeal have been paid in full by your Company and the Union, so nothing is needed from either you or your brother, who I suppose has gone back to Malaya.' Bruce said he'd gone immediately after their holiday together. 'Ah yes,' said Lovatt, 'I was forgetting. I've something for you here.' He went over to a cupboard and took out Bruce's violin case.

Leaving Lovatt, Bruce went for lunch. One or two of the stalwarts of the chess club ate here. Seeing them, he went towards them. They ignored him, carried on talking; he ate isolated and miserable. Even those he had expected to be on his side, with whom he had often discussed serious matters and had looked to for intellectual nourishment, seemed not to want to know him anymore.

He went home to wait for the advice of his new job. Home to the regular pile of abuse that came through his letter box, sometimes twice a day. Home to the repeated knocking on his door, to voices calling to him in the late evening and increasingly to the curious, the morbid, the sensation-seeking, who appeared outside his house during the long hours of daylight. There were those who made the short step from the pavement across the low wall to his front window in an attempt to see for themselves where it all happened. A fruitless attempt, of course, since he never went in there to raise the blinds. When he went out as he had to sometimes, those living in the street and round the corner from him stood at their windows and watched him; none of them greeted him, one even spat as he went past the man's front door. He wrote in his diary, 'They are the rottenest crowd I ever struck. Mean and paltry brained.'

On Thursday there was a letter from Farsight offering him work in the Dale Street offices as a clerk. The salary was just over two hundred pounds a year, four pounds a week, less than a quarter of what he had been getting, what with commission, but he could live on it. He could start immediately.

Friday morning saw him directed to a small room at the back of the building from where he was to organise the supply of stationery to the collection agents and keep records of the issues. There was a table, a couple of chairs and a window that looked out at the walls of other buildings and was dark even on a summer afternoon. He was given a young chap as a part-time assistant since there was a physical element to the work, the stationery being issued to him from a store in the basement and then carried up several flights of stairs.

At the weekend the number drawn by curiosity to visit the street where the murder had been done increased to the point that on both days they milled about from the early afternoon to late evening, talking, whistling, calling, rapping on the front door and window and climbing up the back wall to look into the yard. Some took photographs. Those living in the street were not best pleased at this invasion by gawkers and especially not at the amount of rubbish they created and threw on the ground and into the small spaces between the footpath and the front of the houses. A torrent of paper came through the letter box as well as the usual Saturday postbag of anonymous abuse, demanding that he leave so the residents could have their peace again. All weekend he found it impossible to go outside during the day, the number and behaviour of those outside frightened him, so he was short of food and especially of milk which he would have had to go and fetch himself.

By Sunday night he had had enough. He would have to move somewhere else. The house was as notorious as he and it might be a long time before the number of visitors declined. In any case, even when it finally did, there would still be the other residents and the atmosphere was so poisonous it would never return to anything like normal. He did not want to go on living like that.

Although he only now grudgingly admitted it to himself, he had made a huge mistake returning, the result of his stubbornness and lack of imagination. He was not comfortable in the house and would never be again; that weekend he allowed himself to emerge from denial and acknowledge it. He was restricted to the kitchen, his 'laboratory' and the front bedroom. He would not, could not, go into the downstairs front room again, certainly not to sit in there. How could he? To do so would be to create instantly the images and smells of the ghastly scene he had returned to on that Tuesday evening. What he had not expected, had naively thought he could deal with, was that the house would feel so unwelcoming – no longer his, not just because violent murder had been committed in it but also that it had been occupied and rooted over by the police and their scientific experts for weeks while he had not been there. And the house resonated with Janet. Not in any disembodied or ghostly way, he was too practical and unspiritual to go in for that malarkey. But all around him there was evidence of her past occupancy in the form of clothes, possessions and household items she had used, all reminders that she had shared the house with him. These made him feel uncomfortable because they reminded him of the Janet for whom he had had no feeling, and the plan she had driven him to. Of the woman who had first come there during the War, one of only two people, the other his mother, he had ever really loved, there was nothing.

Travelling to work the next morning, he thought through the business of moving away from Swindon Street. It was all very well to tell himself he had to move. But where to? And on that he had no idea. The rent he was paying was about three pounds a month. With the additional money he had had from out of court settlements and the probability that he probably didn't have more than half-a-dozen years to live, he could afford at least another pound a month, possibly more. He would need to look through the classified advertisements in the evening paper to see what was available and at what price.

During his break he went to Lovatt's office to seek advice about his new decision. As he was shown into the solicitor's office, Lovatt came towards him smiling and waving a piece of paper. 'Another cheque for you. The last of the libellers settled on Friday.'

Bruce told him about the difficulties he was having continuing to live in Anfield. 'You were right, it's impossible to carry on like this.'

'Well, all you have to do is give the appropriate notice to the landlord. How much do you have to give?'

'A month.' He spread his hands. A gesture of defeat. 'But where would I go? Certainly not somewhere else in Anfield – or anywhere close to it.'

'Certainly not.' Lovatt agreed with him. The two sat, thinking. Then Lovatt snapped his fingers. 'The money you've had from the settlements. There'd be enough to put down a decent deposit on your own house. You've got a steady job with a rock-solid company. You'd be able to get a mortgage for the rest. If you look a bit further out, at some of the newer areas, there's plenty of choice at reasonable prices.'

Bruce's first reaction to this idea was reluctance. He had never been a home owner. Most, if not all, people of his class and occupation were not and renting where you lived from someone else who could afford to own it was how you got a roof over your head. Paying interest and capital on a mortgage would cost more than renting, and in any case he would never reap the advantage of ownership since the length of time he believed he had left would mean most of the debt would still be unpaid. Neither would he have anyone to leave it to when he died.

Over the following week or so he bought the evening paper and started going through the classified advertising for somewhere to rent. His native caution constrained him. Although he was committed to moving away from Anfield and no longer needed to live there since he now worked in the city centre, he wanted somewhere he could afford where he would not be as easily recognised and persecuted, a combination he found surprisingly difficult to hit on.

One evening later that week he glanced, without any conscious intention, at houses for sale. One of them stood out for him. This was a sale on behalf of a dead person's estate so the price had been reduced reflecting the sellers' desire for a quick exchange. A fairly new bungalow across the river in the Wirral. Five miles from Anfield as the crow flew but a different world from the criss-crossing streets, linking narrow alleys and tightly packed terrace houses occupied by nosey neighbours where he had spent the past seventeen years. He decided to go and have a look for himself, without drawing anyone's attention. If he liked what he saw he would ask Lovatt's firm to act for him in any negotiations with the sellers.

Meanwhile the volume of mail arriving through his door, while less than in the days immediately following his return, still amounted to several letters a day. He had taken to picking them up, taking them to the office and asking his young assistant to open them and only pass on those he felt Bruce should see. This meant the few offering support, sympathy and good luck, to which he inevitably replied with warmth and an old-fashioned courtesy.

On the Saturday afternoon Bruce went from the office across the river and down the eastern side of the Wirral to Bromborough. The train journey to and from the centre of Liverpool was straightforward and the house was a little way along a newish road, an easy walk from the station.

He was able to pass by the house several times without anyone appearing to notice, and liked what he saw. A double-fronted bungalow with a small garden in front and a much larger one at the back. Modest though it was, he felt a sense of space and of peace there.

Back at Swindon Street, he worked out whether he could afford to buy this house – The Haven. He hoped it would live up to its name. He did the sums on the basis that he could probably get a further reduction in the price in return for the promise of a quick purchase. He found he could afford to meet half that probable price with the other half coming from a mortgage. His monthly outgoings on the house would go up to about six pounds from four and of course it would cost him more to travel to work than it did now but he accepted that as the price for exchanging what he had come to think of as a hell-hole for some semi-rural tranquillity.

The next day, Monday, he dropped in again to Lovatt's office, gave him the details of the house and asked him to arrange a proper viewing for the following Saturday through the firm acting for the seller, reiterating how important it was that the viewing should be arranged and carried out in strict secrecy.

A week later, his mind made up, he secured in principle a mortgage for half the purchase price. His inspection had proved it was in good order, unoccupied, and one of a number of bungalows separated from each other by garden space that ensured a good deal more privacy than anyone had in his part of Anfield. He was also relieved to see that the gardens could not be overlooked from the houses on either side if bordered by a high hedge or fence.

Lovatt's firm drew up a formal agreement which he signed before the start of the third week in July, with completion and his move to follow a month later. At the end of July he gave his landlord formal notice of an intention to quit at the end of August. Things had moved quickly, as they needed to do since the unpleasantness in Swindon Street continued and only the sure knowledge that it would end on August 11th allowed him to endure the last weeks with something like fortitude.

Having found a new and, he hoped, congenial home he

wanted to carry out his original plan to have regular, if possible, living-in, nursing care. Though he was not suffering as badly as he had the previous spring and summer there were unmistakeable signs of the disease. He was often tired and then he felt he didn't want to do anything whether in the house or out of it. He was losing weight; his appetite for food waning, and when feeling lethargic he often could not be bothered to cook, making the condition worse. Even though he had not eaten much, from time to time he felt sick and occasionally retched on an empty stomach. More often than earlier in the year he felt the familiar ache in his side. He needed someone else to see that he had good, nourishing, food put in front of him and to ensure that he ate it. But he was also anxious not to communicate his illness at work by sign or word for fear the firm might decide to pension him off, and he could not afford that. He went to work even when he should have gone to bed.

Following his original plan, he sent a polite letter to the nurse at the hospital, the one he had mentioned to Dr Clarke, asking her whether she would consider nursing him privately. He did not get a reply. Whether the letter was lost internally within the hospital system, or intercepted by someone who recognised the identity of the writer and redirected to some waste paper basket, or whether Nurse Tyler, as aware as anyone else in Liverpool, did not care to be alone in a house with him, it did not matter much. That objective, to achieve which the whole plan had been set in motion, he could not fulfil.

In the weeks between agreeing to buy The Haven and moving-in he had plenty of time to contemplate how much his world had changed since the previous December and how he might have been more careful of what he had wished for. He withdrew deeper into denial that he had had any part in Janet's death and so began to consider Jordan and Davies wholly responsible for everything he had suffered, including his present loneliness. His perspective on the past six or seven months shifted. He held Davies more responsible than Jordan. This came from a long-standing deep contempt for the man as a cheap crook with a gift of the gab and, although he did not admit this openly to himself, some jealousy that Janet had found the creature attractive. In the hours of thinking over and again the events leading up to and after Janet's murder, Davies assumed the role of the one who had drawn him into actions for which he was now feeling extremely remorseful. Davies it had been who had seduced Janet, encouraged her to feel she was not too old to play with young men and made it easy for her to do so at her husband's expense. It was Davies who had taken advantage of his absence in hospital to reopen the sordid business begun two years previously and to bring back Jordan as his accomplice in vice.

Thinking this way allowed him to erase from his conscious mind that he had used that adultery to justify removing Janet so he could have a few more years to live. In its place came an idea, growing into a belief stronger every time he visited it, that Davies and Jordan had murdered Janet because she threatened them. The Janet they had murdered bore little resemblance to the sharp, critical, egocentric hypochondriac he had wished to be rid of. They, and particularly Davies, had killed the old Janet whose company he missed so much when he was at home alone. Of course he understood that Janet's actual murderer had been Jordan but now in his mind Davies had been the instigator and promoter, pushing Jordan to eliminate the danger to them both because he had been too weak, too cowardly and, of course, too cunning to do it himself. Bruce was sure that after the event Davies would have threatened Jordan with exposure if he ever said anything about it to anyone and that, worryingly, Davies knew he would never be safe as long as he, Bruce, lived. There must always be in the fellow's mind the thought Bruce could implicate him through some overheard comment or even trail the possibility to whoever might listen that he had gone to Number 29 that night to steal the collection money, the amount of which he had overestimated, and had been caught in the act by Mrs Bruce. So he'd need to keep his eyes open and his senses alert to any signs of Davies trying to meet or follow him. He had seen neither man since he had returned to freedom and he did not want to.

The move attracted much attention from those living around Swindon Street. A crowd gathered as the removal men went about their work. It reacted with oohs and aahs of excitement as the furniture came out. Those familiar with the trial were particularly keen to see Janet's piano and the sofa McLintock had said she had been sitting on when the fatal blow was struck. The crowd also expressed delight that at last this monster of depravity was leaving the area, greeting the departure of the van with whistles, cheers and applause. One or two, bolder than the rest, had already got inside the house under the noses of the workmen and had to be hustled out again. Once the van had gone and the house was obviously empty there was a rush to press noses to the front room window from which the curtains and blinds had now finally been removed.

25

The Man They Did Not Hang

As the summer of 1931 passed into autumn, some of the peace Bruce had longed for during those desperate weeks in the old house was restored to him. Not completely though. The arrival of the new occupant of The Haven and his household goods did not go unnoticed in the neighbourhood, nor did it take long for the public to find out who the newcomer was. The flow of unpleasant letters was diverted from Anfield to his new address after only a few days, and the Liverpool grapevine hummed with the same rumours and speculations. One of the first things he did on moving-in was to have a substantial fence put up at the front and sides of his property to make it more difficult for the curious to look in on him and, conversely, for him to see them. Before long he became aware, through the contents of the letters reported to him by his assistant at work, what his persecutors thought of that and the reasons why he had done it. When it was read to him that presumably he had bodies to bury in the garden, being a mass-murderer, or that it was to conceal his practice of satanic rites, both of them were convulsed with laughter. It was perhaps the only way to treat the apparently endless flood of nonsense.

He continued with his efforts to find someone to look after him, even if it fell short of actual nursing. His advertisements produced quite a few respectable widows and spinsters whose interest in the job evaporated as soon as they discovered who their employer would be.

He had been in his new home barely a month when as he was going, head down, towards the City Café for his midday meal – the only proper meal he would have on a working day – he heard someone call, 'Mr Bruce'. Looking up, he found his way blocked by Davies. He stiffened, almost skipped, and backed away seeking with urgency and no little desperation to avoid this encounter. Davies looked smart, wearing a new light coloured gabardine with a mid-brown trilby covering his naturally wavy hair. He extended a hand. 'Good to see you, Mr Bruce. You keeping well? We must have a chat sometime.'

Bruce's reaction was that of a man confronted by a dangerously venomous snake. He shied away, eyes anywhere but on the man who had accosted him. 'I've nothing to say to you', almost under his breath as he pushed past, going along the street past the café entrance, rather than into it where he was sure Davies would follow him. He did not have any lunch that day and made up his mind not to go there again lest the meeting be repeated.

For the rest of the day he was anxious, even fretful. When he reflected on this meeting that evening at home he was still worried and distressed. Davies would have drawn only one conclusion. That his one-time friend was hostile and in fear of him, increasing any suspicion Davies might have that his involvement in murder could be revealed by the vindictive co-conspirator. Living out in a relatively thinly populated area with substantial spaces between the houses made him feel vulnerable. In the darker evenings a man might be attacked on the way home. Living alone, he could also be watched from the darkened garden, a perfect place for an assailant to conceal himself, waiting for the best time to force his way into the bungalow to remove any possibility of future suspicion and exposure.

Over the rest of the month, as his fears fed on one another, he rigged up bright lights to illuminate the garden, operated by a switch inside the house. He also made entries in his diary so that if anything did happen to him those who found him would also see he had had no doubt about who murdered Janet and then silenced the widower who was on his trail.

Writing in his diary some weeks after the event, though dating his entry as the day it had happened, 'Just as I was going to dinner Davies stopped me and said he wanted to talk to me. It was a desperately awkward position. Eventually

I decided not to hear what he had to say. I told him I would talk to him some day and give him something to think about. He must realise that I suspect him of the terrible crime. I fear I let him see clearly what I thought and it may unfortunately put him on his guard.' He knew, even with his rapidly-dissolving grasp of what had actually happened, that he had taken dramatic license with this account of the meeting outside the café. The first two and the last two sentences were true but the middle was designed to put a more active slant on his response and to damn Davies. Anyone who read this entry would not fail to note that the writer, the innocent co-victim of Janet's murder, had the deepest suspicions of Glyn Davies.

At the same time as he wrote that, in an entry he dated October 6th, he made his fears and suspicions clear yet again. 'I am dreadfully nervous about entering the house after dark. Although I am convinced Davies killed her, yet it is difficult to get any proof.'

His efforts to find someone to live-in and look after him had failed. It worried him because he was not getting the regular, nourishing meals he needed to keep his condition stable and although it had not so far happened, if he had to go to bed for anything longer than a day or two his life would become very uncomfortable. And he found it exhausting to keep the place clean and tidy.

And then one Saturday afternoon in mid-October there was a knock at his front door. Checking from his front bay window as he invariably did, he could see a portly woman, fifty or thereabouts, neatly dressed, hand raised to knock again. He went to the door.

'Mr Bruce?' A firm, clear voice.

'Yes, that's me.'

'I believe you've been looking for a housekeeper.'

'Yes, I have. Haven't had much luck so far.'

'No', she was matter-of-fact, 'I expect you would find it hard. Can I come in?'

He was embarrassed. He'd kept her standing on the doorstep on a chilly autumn afternoon. She must wonder where his manners were. He stood aside. 'Of course, please, Mrs…?'

'Cook', she said. 'I mean Mrs Cook. Agnes.' By way of explanation, 'I'm a widow.'

They sat opposite each other in the front room. Bruce thought she looked like a particularly rosy apple. With a good clear skin and a cheerful face. The room felt cold; he didn't use it much. He got up and lit the gas fire.

She explained. 'I've been looking after an old lady until this last week. Not far from here, Bebington. She's had to go into a nursing home and it looks as if that'll be her last port of call. But she did say to me she knew you'd come to live in Bromborough – she knew all about you, don't worry – and that she'd heard you needed someone to look after you. She said to me at the time she always thought you were innocent, you know.'

Bruce warmed to her. 'And you. You're obviously not afraid of my reputation.'

'Good heavens, no. I followed the case, of course. We all did. But it never sounded as if you were a man who'd kill his wife. And you don't look like one.' She put her hand to her mouth in agitation and blushed. The apple got rosier. 'Oh. I'm sorry, what must you think?'

Bruce reflected on the value of appearances and then sighed, 'I assure you I didn't. Though it seems most people in Liverpool, including those I thought were friends, think I did.'

Mrs Cook returned to the business in hand. 'I was in nursing for ten years. Then my husband died five years ago. He was in the merchant marine; something he caught out East. Came home, died within a few days. I cook of course,' she smiled at the little joke, 'and keep the house clean and tidy. I can live-in; I did for the last few months with my dear old Mrs Lloyd, but I keep most of my things at my sister's up in Tranmere and I usually go back to hers for the night.'

He explained his physical situation to her. 'I'm managing quite well at the moment', he told her, 'but I may have spells of being poorly. Since the terrible night', he stopped, took off his glasses, wiped them, put them back on again, 'I haven't eaten properly. In fact', this with a slight smile, 'the only time I was regularly and properly fed was in the condemned cell at Walton. My doctor told me last year my life depended on getting regular and nourishing meals.'

They quickly agreed that Agnes Cook would become his

housekeeper, coming daily in time to get his breakfast and leaving when he had had his tea, unless he were ill, in which case she would move in to the spare bedroom.

He felt well pleased at this turn of events. He was working inside and he now had someone to look after him. That combination should see him able to keep his illness at bay for a few more years. Although his salary was lower and he had the costs of a housekeeper, he also expected to get a couple of significant sources of additional income.

Lovatt had recently shown him an article in a magazine for ardently evangelical Christians that substituted the earthly Court of Criminal Appeal for a celestial one and implied that as he would have had to do before the latter, Bruce should have confessed his guilt and thrown himself on the mercy of his judges, secular and divine. He had been furious. Not only because he shared Lovatt's concern that the premise of the article libelled him but much more because his name had been used to promote a magazine that represented everything he did not believe in. Lovatt issued a writ and was convinced the publishers would settle for a substantial sum. On top of that, he had been approached by a national, high circulation, weekly paper to provide a series of articles under the common umbrella title of 'The Man They Did Not Hang' – in effect, his life story and experiences, which they proposed to issue early in the spring of the next year, 1932. This venture into publicity would also bring him in a substantial fee. The additional income would, he told himself, more than make up for any shortfall in salary and increase in expenses.

There was another reason for his willingness to tell and sell his story. It would be *his* story, *his* truth, his chance to write history the way he wanted it to appear to others and to present himself as one to whom life had been consistently unkind in spite of all his virtues and efforts. He did not take up his pen lightly or impulsively. He understood that by drawing attention to himself in this way he would be giving ammunition to those who believed him guilty. They would say an innocent victim of a miscarriage of justice would wish to fade from public view, to put the whole thing behind him, certainly not allow a mass weekly readership to put him in the spotlight like someone who makes a music hall turn of his physical handicap. But he took the view that those convinced of his guilt would never be persuaded otherwise. He wanted to influence the much larger public that had no firm opinions about who committed the crime. On top of that there was the cathartic value of setting down a version of his life and its events in a form that met his own opinion and value of himself.

Over the following months, although the paper provided a writer, he contributed his life story as he now believed it to be and the journalist simply tidied up and edited what Bruce drafted for him. The taciturn, reserved, even dry, person all who knew him thought was the whole of him, given a piece of paper and a pen, blossomed into a writer of fiction. The series was his autobiography; the theme a long and epic struggle against ill-health, ill-luck and ill-will, the ultimate outcome of which was the loss of his beloved wife and partner in a perfect marriage and his subsequent persecution by a police force unable to catch her killer and settling for the next best thing, her husband – having prepared the ground with a campaign of innuendo and tip-offs to story-seeking newspapers.

As the series came towards its end he presented himself as the shattered victim of a crime jointly committed by the actual murderer and those who had put him in the dock and within an ace of being hanged. He cannot bring himself to play chess any more. The degree of concentration he needs is impossible for him and he now has no one to play against. Chess had been the thread running through his trial and the essence of the public perception of him as a clever planner – far too clever for the police. He deliberately played up to this image. For public consumption he exaggerated his skill as a chess player. 'I', he wrote, 'who have in the past matched my brain against some of the greatest players in the world...' was his representation of his participation, years before, in exhibition games against all comers played by a grand master on a visit to Liverpool and, of course, tackling chess problems in books. He can no longer play the violin; the memories that go with doing so are too poignant and in any case there is no wife to accompany him.

The violin case itself had been a mute witness of the murder and just to see it brings back for him the horror of the scene in that front room.

But even more important was the opportunity the article gave him to lay a trail to Davies far more eloquent and to an infinitely wider readership than any diary entry. He began by telling the paper's readers that he knew who the murderer was and that he lived in fear of this man who would stop at nothing to remove the one person who could put him in the dock and the condemned cell. He expressed concern that the police were not pursuing any other suspects. 'They refuse', he wrote, 'to give my lawyer or myself any information as to whether and how far they have carried on any investigation.' This all fitted-in with his theme of enduring the ill-will of others, and then came the masterpiece.

He drew his readers into an inescapable connection between Davies, who he was careful not to name, and whoever had murdered his wife. The motive had been theft. Theft by someone who knew him well and knew that money collected from clients was kept in his house before being paid in. Theft by someone with a constant need for cash and who had already misappropriated funds. Theft by someone Bruce's wife would have let into the house if he had called and said he would wait until her husband returned from his visit to Mossley Hill, someone who already knew Bruce was not at home having made the telephone call the evening before.

In this way he made sure that readers could put two and two together and he deliberately invited them to make five. Although perhaps hardly any of them would know of Davies, it would only require a few astute ones to probe and enquire for the connection to be made. As he wrote, his desire to destroy Davies provided the fuel for the closing paragraphs that became a representation of what he believed had happened that evening. Only he changed the perpetrator. Jordan became Davies, in Bruce's mind the instigator of all the evils that had befallen him and who had sullied the spotless Janet who now occupied his heart and head. He wrote, 'He followed my wife into the sitting room and, as she bent down and lit the gas fire he struck her, possibly with a spanner.' He knew that the 'iron bar' had almost certainly been the instrument but he also knew he had denied any knowledge of it to the police. He went on, 'He now had to kill her. To strike her again as she lay on the floor would mean the upward spurting of blood. Two strides took him into the lobby where he had observed my mackintosh and he held it as a shield between him and her body while he belaboured her to death.' Janet's skirt and the mackintosh were singed by the gas fire which was on full. 'Throwing the mackintosh down, he must have dragged her away from the fire and on to part of the coat, leaving her in the position I found her.' Finally, he enjoyed describing the spectacle of the murderer discovering he had hugely miscalculated the amount of collection money in the house. 'I can picture his surprise when he broke open the cupboard and cash box and found only £4 on a Tuesday night.'

As he read and approved the final text, noting errors and omissions as any sub-editor would, he felt he had done everything possible to make Davies the target for police enquiries, if only by increasing the number of the public who might press them to solve this case. If Davies tried to implicate him it would be word against word; the word of a scoundrel and petty crook against that of an honest and blameless man who had been unfairly tried for the crime and acquitted by the highest court there was.

26

Confession

For Bruce, the autumn and winter of 1931-1932 passed without event. The stream of poison-pen letters began to dry up though a brackish trickle remained. He felt lonely. James and Violet were thousands of miles away and he understood why Alfred, having left Liverpool to continue his studies in Glasgow, wished to separate himself completely from his uncle. Although Collinson had staunchly remained his friend throughout, he did not see him. He had never been back to the Chess Club since that Monday night. His social circle was reduced to Mrs Cook.

In the spring the potential action against the evangelical magazine was duly settled out of court and he was able to see a great deal more money in his bank account than he had ever had in his life. And when the publishers had paid him for his story he was comfortably off. This relative affluence did not make him happy. His empty home, in which he found himself unable to enjoy reading, music, chess or any other pursuit, he knew perfectly well was a mockery of the semi-retired, busy, fulfilled existence he had originally planned for himself. Mrs Cook fed him sensibly and well, but he asked himself more and more often to what purpose?

Through the summer and the long days it made him miserable to think the neat modern house with its garden and pleasant middle-class neighbourhood would have been a home the idealised Janet would have loved. Increasingly, in the silent evenings, especially when he could find nothing he wanted to listen to on the wireless, and in the wakeful early hours when pain and discomfort made him move restlessly in bed, in his mind and imagination he walked and talked with her.

As he arrived home after work one early evening in late September, Mrs Cook came to meet him at the door. 'Oh, Mr Bruce, there's a gentleman to see you. I put him in the sitting room. He's been there half an hour.'

Bruce froze. Inwardly he cursed himself for not having warned her never to admit visitors without his say-so. But he had hardly expected anyone to call to see him without warning and in the early evening too.

'A gentleman?' he managed to say without, he hoped, revealing the agitation he felt. 'Who did he say he was?'

'A Mr Jordan. He said you knew him. That's why I let him in to wait for you. He said it was important to see you.'

'Of course, Mrs Cook. Of course. You did exactly the right thing. If you would put my tea to keep warm and wait till he's gone, I'd appreciate it.' The housekeeper nodded. He saw she had felt some of his tension. 'I'll be in the kitchen.'

Taking the handle of the sitting room door, he hesitated. What could Jordan want? He had no physical fear of Jordan as he had for Davies although that seemed strange to him. This was the man who had brutally murdered his wife. But if Jordan had come openly to see him, knowing there was someone else in the house, the only thing he had to fear was what the man might have to say. He turned the handle and went in.

The man he had last seen running away up Richmond Park stood to meet him, hand outstretched. Bruce did not take it but sat in the opposite chair. Jordan stood for a moment longer, his arm still extended, but realising he had been rebuffed he lowered it and sat down again.

'Why have you come here?' Bruce kept his voice low but did not attempt to hide the bitterness in his voice. 'I told you we should never meet again. You got what you wanted out of it. I assume you're married to Mrs Brophy's sister. I also assume you're doing well. From what I see of clothes and the man it certainly seems so.'

The other nodded. 'Yes, I'm one of the family. And yes, I'm doing pretty well. None of them know anything. I...' Bruce interrupted him.

'Well, you've come out of it a lot better than I've done. You know what happened to me. Thanks to you not doing what we agreed. All I've had from it is pain, fear, imprisonment, public humiliation and the loss of every friend I used to think I had. I've had hatred poured all over me, Phillip, so strong sometimes I can't believe it myself. It feels like being up to your neck in filth. And have you any idea what it's like to hear and see a judge sentence you to death?' He rested his hands on the arms of his chair and kept his eyes firmly on the other man.

Jordan looked away. He shook his head.

'Why are you here, Phillip?' Bruce asked again. 'I'm sure it's not to say you're sorry.'

'You've had your troubles Mr Bruce, I grant you that, but I've had mine too. And it was your idea and your plan. And the only thing it's done is produce two damaged men. Three, actually. Glyn, I hear, is a petty criminal these days. Does stupid things like taking cars and gets caught doing it.'

'Davies,' Bruce snorted. 'He's always been a little crook. And he always got caught. Let me tell you…'

'I haven't come to talk about him, Mr Bruce. I can't sleep at night. How can I when the images of what I did come to me as soon as I'm asleep? I have dreams so terrible I feel relief at waking up. My wife can't understand why I'm awake, sweating, in the early hours. I live a lie with her and her family. Only my father…' He broke off.

'Only your father, what?' Bruce detected something uneasy, unsaid, disturbing.

'Let me get the whole thing off my chest, Mr Bruce. That's what I came for. Then maybe I'll feel better.' He looked towards the door. 'Does the housekeeper live-in?'

'No, she goes home every evening.'

'Could you send her home now? I don't want any chance another person hears what I say.' Bruce's face was a picture of doubt. 'Please, I promise you you're safe with me. But this could take a while.'

Bruce got up, went to the door and called, 'Mrs Cook'.

She came out into the hall. 'I think Mr Jordan and I will be some time. Leave my tea warm for me and I'll eat it later. You can go off now. Thank you for waiting.'

'Are you quite sure, Mr Bruce?'

'Perfectly sure. I'll see you in the morning.'

The two men sat silent until they heard the front door close.

'Well', said Bruce.

The other took a deep breath. 'When I went to your house I meant to do it exactly as we'd planned. When she was bending to light the fire, I grabbed the mac from the peg and threw it over her head, then hit her with the bar as you said to do. Then something snapped in me. I'd never wanted to do it. All the way over there I'd been telling myself I was going to murder someone. I'd screwed myself up into a real state. I hated myself and even more I hated her for what I'd let her get me into. When I arrived, for the first time I saw her as an old woman and the whole thing disgusted me to the pit of my stomach. Once she was on the ground I just kept on hitting her. I couldn't stop. I don't remember how many times, only lots of blood flying outwards away from me. Then I smelled burning. It was the mac that had caught the bars of the gas fire, her skirt too. I pulled her away and stamped out the burning bits. I was in a panic. I was sure every sound could be heard by the people next door. I remember wiping my shoes on the rug. Looking down. Not much blood on me, the mac had kept it off. I stuck the bar in my coat pocket and went out through the back. Then I had to hang about waiting for you in the dark alley praying no one would come past, see me and ask what I was doing there. I knew I hadn't finished the job but there was no way on God's earth I was going back in there again.'

He stopped and ran his tongue over his lips. Bruce rose and, wordlessly, took the whisky bottle from the sideboard and poured him a generous glassful. When Jordan had taken some, he nodded at him to go on.

'When I left you I ran down a street and met Glyn coming up. We both ran like hell to where his car was, near that cinema. Before we drove off I got the bar out of my pocket and gave it to Glyn who shoved it between the bars of a drain grating. Then he took me to the station. In the gents there I looked and couldn't see any blood marks on me or my clothes that would be obvious to other people. I had a quick clean up and then went over to the Wirral where I was supposed to be helping out preparing Thomas's birthday party for the next day. No one had missed me and no one noticed anything.

He took another pull at his drink.

'Yes, well. You were out of it. I, on the other hand, finding myself anything but. Because, thanks to you, there were no signs of anyone forcing a window or something and the cash box was still up on the shelf, the police never believed it was a robbery, a housebreaking gone wrong. And my solicitor told me that on the way back from the Appeal in London, that clown, "Super – Intendant" Connor, said he'd suspected me because I didn't howl, beat my breast and call on Our Lady and the Saints like his kind of Irish do when there's a death in the house...'

Jordan cut off what was becoming a rant. 'There's something else I need to tell you.'

Bruce was surprised and showed it. 'I thought you already had. Explained to me why you didn't carry out our arrangement the way we agreed you would. And left me to find the horrible mess you'd made. All right, I understand. I asked too much of you. I misjudged your capacity for self-control. The fault is mine.'

Jordan leant forward in his chair, his tension clear from the tautness of his body and the clenching of each hand. 'Yes, I thought that was the end of it all as well. Your wife was dead, which was what you wanted. I'd kept my side of the bargain. The blind rage went almost as soon as I'd struck the last blow and then it was pity, shame and horror. The days after I spent in a fog. I couldn't believe I'd done something like that except I kept seeing me doing it like it had all been photographed on my mind. But I knew too your wife could never get in touch with Thomas and destroy my future.'

Bruce was about to say 'so you got what you wanted too', but the other raised a hand. 'No, let me go on. About a week after, couldn't have been more, and I was still feeling bad, a policeman came to our house. A sergeant. Bowler, I think his name was. He asked me if I'd ever sold insurance to someone called McQuillian. I had to tell him I had, some years before. You remember how we came to use his name for Glyn's telephone call?'

Bruce nodded but said nothing. He was beginning to have an uncomfortable feeling.

'The sergeant said he'd been checking on all the McQuillians in the city and this one had told him I'd been his agent when I was with Farsight. He then said he had a list of people Mrs Bruce would have let into the house if you were out and I was on it. I said to him, "How did you get hold of my name for that list?" And then he said you'd given them a list of names.'

'I had to.' Bruce butted in. 'Once they were sure there'd been no break-in they demanded I tell them of anyone who might have been let in. I had to give it them. You, Glyn, Mr Willesden, people we knew, other people from work. I thought it'd look funny if I left anyone out. I knew they'd probably ask everyone on the list where they were on the evening of the twentieth. I'd warned you to have some kind of story ready about where you were and who'd seen you that night, so I thought they'd not take it any further.' He stopped and shook his head. 'I didn't know they'd gone round looking for McQuillians.'

He could tell Jordan was experiencing again the tension and fear he would have had when the unexpected visit from Bowler had made it clear he had not been erased from the affair as promised. He knew he'd deliberately glossed over the fact he'd gone and offered the police a detailed statement about Davies and Jordan two days after the murder.

'You must understand, Mr Bruce. In the state I was in my first thought was you'd set me up. When the sergeant asked me where I was and what I was doing on the twentieth, I panicked and said the first thing that came into my head. I told him I'd been in bed all day with 'flu. The moment he'd gone I realised how daft I'd been. All they'd have to do was check with my mother and father and they'd find it wasn't completely true. My parents would be bound to say, yes, I'd been feeling rotten most of the day – I did, they just had no idea why – but then I'd gone over to Wirral in the early evening to help with the preparations for the birthday. I went through hell the rest of that day and when my father came home I told him everything.'

'Everything?' Bruce echoed.

'Yes, all of it. A clean breast.'

Bruce was piecing together some of the elements of this puzzle and the further he got the less he liked the picture it made. It was clear that the confession to his father had not resulted in Jordan's being marched straight to the police station and arrested on suspicion of murder. So whatever his father's initial reaction had been, somewhere along the line he had decided either to hold the knowledge to himself or enlist the help of others to keep it secret. It came back to him, not for the first time but now with increased import, the comment Jordan had made in the waiting room at Birkenhead station that he knew how the police worked. Could his father be in the Liverpool police or in some way connected with it? If he were though, then surely Davies would have referred to it when his friend claimed to know so much about how the police "made it stick." But if he hadn't been arrested when the police had his name, knew he'd worked for Farsight with a past client called McQuillian, and they knew where to find him, why not?

Bruce probed. 'What did your father say?'

'First he was furious. Said a lot of bitter things. Then calmed down and thought for a while. He told me to say nothing to my mother and that he would help me as much as he could. You see my aunt, Dad's sister, is married to a Chief Superintendent in the City Police; well, he was, he's been retired a year or two now. Dad said we'd go and talk to him the next day. And we did.

Though the gas fire had been on almost an hour Bruce felt cold and very tired. As yet he saw through a glass, darkly, but could still make out the shape of what had happened. He was sure what he would be told next.

Jordan fiddled with a waistcoat button. He kept his eyes down on it as he finished what he had come to say.

'Uncle Cyril made me tell him the whole story and then he and my father sent me out of the room to wait. I was out for some time and all I could think about was what would happen to me if my uncle felt there was nothing he could do. At one point I remember, my aunt came into the room. She was surprised to see me and started asking questions. I put her off by saying Dad was asking Uncle Cyril's advice because I'd been falsely accused of stealing something at work. After about half an hour, it felt like a lot longer, they called me back in. Uncle

Cyril said he felt I'd been blackmailed into killing Mrs Bruce and that I was a victim as much as she had been.'

He stopped but still did not look directly at Bruce. 'I'm sorry, but I had to tell you what he said.'

Bruce wiped his face with his hand. 'Yes, I can see that. Then what?'

'Uncle Cyril saw the Chief Constable and Superintendent Connor. He called in a few favours and in any case because of who he was they would always have listened to him. They agreed that I would be kept out of the story. No further enquiries to be made. Then it turned out Glyn had had a visit too and had made a statement, only his account of the Monday night when he made the telephone call didn't match the ones his girlfriend and her mother had given the police. We knew if the police questioned Glyn he'd sing like a canary, so the hounds were called off him as well. The police view was that you'd planned it all, blackmailed me and Glyn into helping you and they would bring it home to you. There was to be no mention of anyone else being involved.'

There was silence. Jordan had told his story; there was nothing more to say. Bruce had no words for him, his mind already preoccupied with the unpalatable truths of the whole affair.

Jordan rose to leave, picking up his coat from the chair over which he had draped it. 'I'll see myself out. This is the end of it, Mr Bruce. The police aren't looking for anyone else. And if you should be inclined to reopen the case by trying to put someone else in the picture, and I mean Glyn, forget it. You'll meet with a wall of denial from the authorities and do yourself no good either.' He thrust his arms into the coat and took up his cap.

'Goodnight, Mr Bruce. I hope I never see you again.' And he went out into the hall.

Bruce did not even get up from his chair. Trembling and lost, he heard the front door open then click shut on the Yale lock. He was alone with his thoughts.

27

Endgame

The outcome of Jordan's visit was the loss of every last bit of Bruce's self-respect. He knew he had failed to make a proper assessment, although the warning signs had been there for him to read, of the calibre and temperament of the man he had appointed to execute his plan and on whose motivation, coolness and skill its success completely depended. His chosen instrument, Jordan, had not just botched the killing of Janet and failed to make it look as if it had happened because she had disturbed burglars, he had turned King's evidence, had not had to appear in court and avoided even a reduced or commuted punishment for the crime he alone had committed.

Bruce knew too how foolish had been his half-hearted disclosure to the police that Jordan and Davies had the knowledge and motivation to steal his collection money, that both had a reputation for misappropriating cash they had collected and would have been let into the house. He had confused an almost unconscious desire to implicate them with the need to account for those who could have been admitted by Janet. The result of his cleverness had been to point the police at a couple of potential suspects with consequences he had not imagined. If they had not called on, had simply disregarded, Jordan, their enquiries would have hit the brick wall of his own alibi, and even with Connor's intuition that his behaviour was not what he expected from a suddenly and horrifically bereaved husband, the case would eventually have run into the sand.

But what he found most humiliating was that from a very early stage the police had known, not merely suspected, his involvement and he'd never had an inkling. They'd played with him, possessors of information they'd kept firmly to themselves. With hindsight he now understood why the timing of Janet's death had to be fitted into their case. They knew exactly when it was. The first estimate McLintock had made and given to Connor had been pretty well right. Once the police realised they had to bring it forward by a couple of hours so his alibi no longer protected him, they worked to create the conditions that would suggest he murdered Janet himself before he went out to Mossley Hill. How many at Police Headquarters, he wondered, had been in on this? Connor, certainly, McLintock probably, Bright, possibly, Bowler, maybe. Getting the milk delivery boy to bring forward the time he claimed to have seen Janet was critical to their case and they had schooled him well.

Bruce now recognised that far from being incompetent and stumbling about in a fog as he had often characterised them, the police had been astute in playing a game where they knew all the opponent's moves in advance but could not allow him to think they did. In spite of his having had a top-notch barrister, which they may reasonably have expected he would not be able to afford, they had almost pulled the net over him. It explained a lot about the way they handled their case. They knew Iris Grange had seen him talking to someone. They knew who that someone was. She was a key witness for them and had she been a better performer in the box her story would perhaps have inclined the trial judge to believe her. Quite deliberately they had not called, or told his defence about, witnesses that would have cast doubt on the six-thirty time of death theory. He also understood now why he had never been intensively questioned by the detectives. They had wanted to avoid his breaking down and confessing to his part in the conspiracy while incriminating the other two. So the policy had been to let him think he would probably get away with it, that the police were bumblers he could outwit, and then when they decided the time was right to arrest and charge him they piled up as much circumstantial evidence as they could, including some blatant falsehoods, that would suggest to the magistrates and then to the trial jury they had got the right man.

The way he had been outmanoeuvred filled him with corrosive bitterness. Even the jury, whom he had frequently branded as morons, perhaps had had an idea of his involvement, if not of the details. These despicable people had seen through him too. The man who had embraced the idea of pulling off the perfect murder had done no such thing.

And over everything else, the knowledge that he had gained nothing. The plan he had concocted to give himself five years of a life with comfort and dignity, enjoying the hobbies and interests he put so much store by, had collapsed around him. He had been driven out of his home to an area he did not know, where he knew no one. Although he had someone to look after him, his nerves were in shreds; he was unable to concentrate on his violin or working through chess problems. His notoriety cut him off from the possibility of taking up music lessons again or joining any chess club. Desperately missing an imaginary companion far removed from the reality he had wanted to be rid of, he saw the result of the past two years as a mocking epitaph on a life of struggle rewarded with chronic failure. He could not even enjoy the money he now had in the bank.

Late in the month following Jordan's visit the pain grew much worse. He struggled home in agony at the end of each working day. A lot of November was spent in bed with bouts of fever, Mrs Cook moving in to be on hand on each occasion. The end of the year came and his New Year Resolution amounted to forgoing any medication or further surgical treatment. He had decided he had nothing to live for, now he only wished the end to come quickly. He told Mrs Cook of his resolve. 'But that's the same as committing suicide', she'd said. As one who had committed murder, albeit at arm's length, he was very reluctant to hear the term applied to the taking of his own life. 'Never say "commit" suicide, Mrs Cook. A man's life is his own to do with as he wishes. I have no reason to prolong mine and it's no crime, nor is it a sin, whatever the law and the church may say. As long as I don't ask anyone else to help me do it.' Having given her notice that her employment would probably not last much longer, he added, 'You will be looked after. You have been goodness itself to me.'

He was preoccupied with what came after death. These thoughts filled most of the waking hours of what he knew would be the final weeks of his life. Since a young man he had oscillated between atheism and agnosticism. His scientific bent and learning inclined him to see all life as finite. When one died that was the end of it. Fantasies about an afterlife were just that – wishful thinking. He had to acknowledge the possibility there might be a creator although he was sure it was not an old man with a long beard. As he had grown older the certainties of his views on death weakened and since January two years earlier he had given it a lot of thought. He arrived late at a hypothesis that at the point of death and after it was possible to communicate, how he did not attempt to guess, with those who had died before him and who had shared a relationship with him while each lived. He would meet his mother, whom he had always cherished, and Janet. Each of them would be purged of the dross of earthly existence and would therefore have no concept or memory of the capacity of living people to hurt and damage each other. As he told Mrs Cook on another occasion, 'I'm quite anxious to find out the nature of "that bourn from which no man returns". Death will be a voyage of discovery.'

So, when on February 9th the ambulance called at The Haven, he went willingly, comfortable that he had settled his affairs. Mrs Cook was unable to look after him any longer and when he was admitted the doctors took a decision to operate on the remaining kidney. As the Liverpool hospital had told Dr Clarke over two and a half years earlier, the likelihood of success was remote and in any case the patient had no will to carry on any longer.

His thoughts as he hovered between post-operative life and death a little over a fortnight later were that he had played a final game of chess. His opponents, the law, had acquired a massive superiority in material and he had finally been reduced to his king. Through their misapplied strategy and his defensive tenacity he had achieved a draw through stalemate. They had not been able to finish him off but had left him nowhere to go.

Author's Note

Those readers familiar with it will have recognised from the start the outlines of the celebrated and never-solved Wallace case from 1930s Britain, of which James Agate, a famous critic in his day, wrote, 'Either the murderer was Wallace or it wasn't. If it wasn't, then here at last is the perfect murder.'

Much in the preceding pages follows the details of that case very closely, to the point that some of the dialogue is lifted directly from what was reported as having been said during the events, and, in particular, from the records of the then Liverpool City Police Force, and transcripts of the committal, trial and appeal court proceedings in the real Wallace case.

There have been several non-fiction accounts. The first from Jonathan Goodman in 1969 – he also wrote a detective novel that owed much to the real case. Goodman claimed to know who the real murderer was but for legal reasons could not do more than drop hints. In 1984, as the outcome of a local radio programme on Merseyside, Roger Wilkes claimed he had evidence that the actual murderer was Richard Gordon Parry. In 1987 Goodman revised his account, also identifying the murderer as Parry. In 2001, James Murphy exonerated Parry and put the onus back on to William Herbert Wallace. In 2012, John Gannon, a Liverpool journalist, developed the thesis that Wallace had conspired with Parry and another man to kill his wife – the other man doing the actual execution. The same year, Ronald Bartle, a retired magistrate, put the finger firmly back on Wallace, though as sole perpetrator. There have been others. Richard Waterhouse, eighteen years before

Gannon, floated the idea of a conspiracy between Wallace and 'a hit man' to do away with his wife.

The Wallace case captured the imagination of many fiction writers both at the time and later; among them Raymond Chandler and P D James and a number of lesser novelists who used aspects of it in their different stories – the telephone call to lure someone away from his or her house to enable a crime to be perpetrated being perhaps the most popular.

Fiction seems an appropriate way to present what was, by any measure, an unusually violent and apparently senseless crime, a sensational trial with an unexpected verdict and an equally improbable setting aside of that verdict by a higher court, the president of which had publicly declared his belief in the impeccability of the English jury system. As far as I know mine is the first attempt to follow the characters, events and localities of the actual case and weave them into a story – an analysis of a (then) capital crime and its consequences which would entertain, inform and, I hope, move the reader, even if the Wallace case had never happened.

As this is fiction I have been able to 'invent' three elements which are critical to the working out of the plot since they provide the protagonist with justifications for having his wife killed. One is his discovery of her true age, the second of her having had and abandoned an illegitimate child, the third her having an adulterous affair with two men well known to him. As for the first, the facts are not invented. The real Mrs Wallace was eighteen years older than she gave out and had attested on her marriage certificate, and she had been carrying on this pretence for a number of years before she married. There is no evidence her husband ever discovered this and at the time of the murder it was assumed by all – and by those who gave accounts of it later – she was the same age as her husband. That is, until Murphy's research turned up her birth certificate and Gannon found that early in the twentieth century she had given false statements in census returns about her age, birthplace, and even first name.

The illegitimate son is pure invention but a plausible one. Murphy's research also showed that when young, Mrs Wallace was 'a mystery woman'. She worked as a governess and teacher in private homes and small private schools in Yorkshire and London and moved about far more than would have been usual at that time, even for an unmarried woman. There is also the conundrum of why an attractive, educated and lively woman did not marry until (in fact) into her fifties.[1]

There is no direct evidence that she engaged in sexual activity with Parry, or anyone else, behind Wallace's back, but at least two of the crime novels written in the years after the case and using it as a background, link the murdered female character's fate to an adulterous affair. Since one of these is the novel by Goodman, it suggests strongly that he may have had his suspicions about this, although in his non-fiction account of the case he did not, or felt he could not, bring it up. The 1990 TV film *The Man from the Pru* hinted at some relationship between Julia Wallace and Parry.

John Gannon is 'the onlie begetter' of the plot I have created for this fictional presentation of the Wallace case. He had exclusive access to the archives of Wallace's solicitors and made a thorough study of the case file held by the current Merseyside police, comparing it with the file in the Home Office (DPP). Neither of these records were available to the public until the early years of this century. In his 2012 account of it he put forward the possibility of a conspiracy between the husband and others, which makes sense of aspects that have baffled and confounded all his predecessors. His conclusions aroused a storm of invective from a number of those whose interest in the case fills page after page of internet sites available when you Google 'Wallace Case'. He also provided evidence that Parry's statement to the police about the Monday evening of the telephone call was a lie and emphasised that once the CID compared it with the statements of his girlfriend and her mother, they must have known he had lied to them. Even more intriguing, he provided evidence of a family link between the man he suggested was also a party to the conspiracy, Marsden,

1 But it seems to have run in the family. According to Gannon, Julia's younger sister, Amy (Frances in this story) married at the ripe old age of 70 and died at 92.

and a very senior – and recently retired – police officer.

I too have searched the police 'Wallace' file and was astonished at what is *not* in it. After more than seventy years of being withheld from the public, the file had been, one can only describe it as 'filleted' before what remained in it was laid bare.

I had access to Gannon's draft a couple of years before his book was published and felt immediately here was a story crying out to be told. The novelist is able to do what the recorder of the case cannot – get inside the heads of those involved and bring the whole thing to life. This is not a criticism of the recorders' writing; Goodman, particularly, writes beautifully, but it's only with Capote's *In Cold Blood* that reporting first crosses over into literature.

Finally, the meeting I describe between Bruce (Wallace) and Jordan (Marsden) is entirely imaginary. For the novelist, the scene is irresistible and, who knows, it may well have happened.

Acknowledgements

It's only right that I should acknowledge the sources of inspiration for this story. Above all, John Gannon, not only for his original approach to the obscurities and deliberately concealed aspects of the Wallace case, but too for his friendly help in answering my many questions, for pointing me in the right directions, sharing his sources with me, and walking me round that part of Liverpool where much of the action takes place. Then to the late Jonathan Goodman, to Roger Wilkes and James Murphy, whose research, interpretation and presentation added to the impressions that fuel a creative enterprise like this.

I'm grateful as well for the help given me in presenting my story from Shirley van de Graaff and Amanda Sington-Williams, who read the drafts and made detailed comments, and finally to my copy editor at SilverWood Books, Agnes Davis, who, as Burns wrote, saved me from 'monie a blunder... and foolish notion.'

MORE FROM THIS AUTHOR:

Nobody's Children

You don't know the half of it. I'm not their stepmother; Ian's not their real father either. They're nobody's children.

Back in 1928, in the interests of social propriety Alice Markham keeps this even from her best friend. What she doesn't know is that Dr Ian Markham is sexually abusing his dead lover's teenage daughter. When the truth emerges, Alice manages to conceal that from prying eyes too, but not from her conscience.

Lightning Source UK Ltd.
Milton Keynes UK
UKOW05f0412240617
303961UK00002B/50/P

9 781781 322048